ACCLAIM FOR GAIL BOWEN AND
THE JOANNE KILBOURN MYSTERIES

"Bowen is one of those rare, magical mystery writers readers love not only for her suspense skills but for her stories' elegance, sense of place and true-to-life form. . . . A master of ramping up suspense." — *Ottawa Citizen*

"Bowen can confidently place her series beside any other being produced in North America." — Halifax *Chronicle-Herald*

"Gail Bowen's Joanne Kilbourn mysteries are small works of elegance that assume the reader of suspense is after more than blood and guts, that she is looking for the meaning behind a life lived and a life taken." — *Calgary Herald*

"Bowen has a hard eye for the way human ambition can take advantage of human gullibility." — *Publishers Weekly*

"Gail Bowen got the recipe right with her series on Joanne Kilbourn." — *Vancouver Sun*

"What works so well [is Bowen's] sense of place – Regina comes to life – and her ability to inhabit the everyday life of an interesting family with wit and vigour. . . . Gail Bowen continues to be a fine mystery writer, with a protagonist readers can invest in for the long run." — *National Post*

"Gail Bowen is one of Canada's literary treasures." — *Ottawa Citizen*

OTHER JOANNE KILBOURN MYSTERIES
BY GAIL BOWEN

The Nesting Dolls
The Brutal Heart
The Last Good Day
The Glass Coffin
Burying Ariel
Verdict in Blood
A Killing Spring
A Colder Kind of Death
The Wandering Soul Murders
Murder at the Mendel
Deadly Appearances

THE
ENDLESS
KNOT

A Joanne Kilbourn Mystery

GAIL BOWEN

McClelland & Stewart

Copyright © 2006 by Gail Bowen

First M&S paperback edition published 2007
This edition published 2011

Library and Archives Canada Cataloguing in Publication

Bowen, Gail, 1942-
The endless knot : a Joanne Kilbourn mystery / Gail Bowen.

ISBN 978-0-7710-1347-8

I. Title.

PS8553.O8995E54 2011   C813'.54   C2011-900313-9

We acknowledge the financial support of the Government of Canada
through the Book Publishing Industry Development Program and that
of the Government of Ontario through the Ontario Media Development
Corporation's Ontario Book Initiative. We further acknowledge the
support of the Canada Council for the Arts and the Ontario Arts
Council for our publishing program.

Published simultaneously in the United States of America by
McClelland & Stewart Ltd., P.O. Box 1030, Plattsburgh, New York 12901

Library of Congress Control Number: 2011925598

Cover image © Blair Witch I Dreamstime.com
This book was produced using recycled materials.
Typeset in Trump Mediaeval by M&S, Toronto
Printed and bound in the United States of America

McClelland & Stewart Ltd.
75 Sherbourne Street
Toronto, Ontario
M5A 2P9
www.mcclelland.com

1 2 3 4 5   15 14 13 12 11

To James Henry Cook,
a truly good and generous man,
and to his great-nephews,
Jess Benjamin Bowen-Bell and Peyton Benjamin Bowen

ACKNOWLEDGEMENTS

Thanks to Jan Seibel for her solid legal advice, to Dinah Forbes for her sensitive and perceptive editing, to Joan Baldwin, the model of a family physician, and as always to Ted, who makes everything possible.

THE
ENDLESS
KNOT

CHAPTER

1

As I bent down to cut the last of our marigolds on the Friday before Thanksgiving, I was as happy as I could remember being. The stems of the flowers were cool against my fingers, and their sturdy beauty and acrid scent evoked memories of marigolds hastily picked by my kids and carried off, stems sheathed in wax paper and anchored by elastic bands, to be given to a teacher or abandoned on the playground. It was a morning for remembering, as filled with colour and ancient mystery as a Breugel painting. Above me, skeins of geese zigzagged into alignment against the cobalt sky. The high clear air rang with their cries. A north wind, urgent with change, lifted the branches of our cottonwood tree, shaking the leaves loose and splashing the lawn with gold. Beneath my feet last week's fallen leaves, bronze and fragile as papyrus, crackled into the cold earth.

For the first time in a long time, there was nowhere I had to be. I was on sabbatical, expanding an article I'd written about the emerging values war in Canada into a book. It was an open-ended project that I found easy to pick up and easier to put down. My three grown children were living independent lives marked by the usual hurdles but filled with promise. They were all strong and sensible people, so I crossed my fingers, enjoyed their company, and prayed that the choices they made would bring them joy. Since my son, Angus, had enrolled in the College of Law in Saskatoon the month before, my younger daughter and I had been alone in our house. We missed Angus, but Taylor was just about to turn eleven, and the world was opening up to her. Listening as she spun the gossamer of unexplored possibilities was a delight neither of us ever wearied of.

Freed from the tyranny of a timetable, I read books I'd been meaning to read, gazed at art with an unhurried eye, listened to music I loved, and revelled in the quiet pleasures of the season Keats celebrated for its mist and mellow fruitfulness.

Best of all, there was a new man. His name was Zachary Shreve and he'd brought with him a piercing happiness I'd forgotten existed. But I had just celebrated a birthday. I was fifty-six and as I walked back into the house, my joy was edged with autumn's knowledge that nothing gold can stay.

The kitchen phone was ringing. I dropped the marigolds in the sink and picked up, expecting to hear Zack's voice. For the last eight weeks he'd been putting in twelve-hour days – first on a case involving the death of a homeless man who had the bad luck to seek shelter in a warehouse on the night the warehouse owner set his property on fire, and now on a high-profile case of attempted murder. Zack called often – mostly just to talk but, if we were lucky, to arrange time together. My caller wasn't the man I loved. It was my old friend, Jill Oziowy, who, after a heady New York experience, had decided to return to the relative sanity of Toronto and her old job as producer of NationTV's *Canada Tonight*. As always, Jill didn't waste time on preamble.

"How would you like to go once more into the breach for NationTV?"

I cradled the phone between my shoulder and ear, picked up the vase on the counter and started filling it with water. "Not a chance," I said.

"At least hear me out," Jill said. "The heir apparent to the anchor job here got picked up last night for having sex with some underage admirers."

"And you want me to talk to him about keeping it zipped."

"No, I want you to replace him as *Canada Tonight*'s eye on the Sam Parker trial."

My pulse skipped. Sam Parker was Zack's client in the attempted murder case. "Jill, I'm not a reporter. I teach political science."

"But you're on sabbatical – which means you're free during the day, and when you did the political panel for us you were great, so we know you don't freeze on camera. And hey – are you still working on that book about the values war?"

"Intermittently."

"Well, not so long ago Sam Parker was the great white hope of the political right in this country. He's still a figure to be reckoned with."

"God, I hope not," I said. "I've been reading some of his old speeches on the battleground issues: abortion, same-sex marriage, Charter rights, judicial activism. He makes my blood boil."

"You can turn down the heat," Jill said. "Apparently Sam's done a complete 180 on a lot of the hot-button concerns. Seeing him up-close-and-personal at the trial might get your scholarly juices flowing again. Convinced yet?"

"Nope."

"Okay, this case is going to need a certain *gravitas*, and face it, Jo, you're the Queen of Gravitas."

"I'm also in a relationship with Sam Parker's lawyer. Still interested?"

Jill's intake of breath was audible three thousand miles away. "Mother of God. You're canoodling with Zachary Shreve."

"As often as we can manage," I said. "Want to withdraw your offer?"

"No," she said. "Jo, have you heard the stories that are out there about your boyfriend? He's brilliant, but he plays rough."

"He doesn't play rough with me," I said. "Now, why don't we drop this and talk about the job?"

"Okay, but I reserve the right to discuss your love life."

"The *job*, Jill?"

"Rapti Lustig will call you with the details. She's network producer in Regina now. You worked with her when you were doing the political panel, didn't you?"

"I did," I said. "And I liked her a lot."

"That's one in the plus column," Jill said. "And there's more. The money's not bad. The trial shouldn't last longer than a month and the work's easy – just sit in court all day, then come out and do a two-minute standup giving our eager nation the background on crime and punishment, Saskatchewan style. So what do you say?"

"I appreciate you thinking of me –"

Jill groaned. "At least mull it over."

"All right," I said. "I'll mull, but I hope you have more names on your list because these days I'm just content to be contented."

Jill snorted. "Contentment's for cows. I'm calling back in an hour, and your answer better be yes."

She hung up and I went back to arranging my marigolds and weighing my options. I truly was enjoying my life, but there were compelling reasons for giving Jill's offer serious consideration. Trial law was a huge area of Zack's life, and I'd never seen him in court. And Jill was right about the allure of the Sam Parker case. Professionally and personally, Sam Parker intrigued me. I wanted to know him better. I wanted to understand how, when his son's situation made his political and personal views collide, he chose to alter his beliefs rather than turn against his child. By any journalist's criteria, the Sam Parker case was a plum, and Jill had handed it to me. As I twirled the last bloom into place, the deciding vote was cast. My old friend Hilda McCourt once said that marigolds carry a great life lesson: they're blooming when you put them in and they're blooming when you pull them out. I wanted to be like Hilda, blooming to the end, and so an hour later when Jill called, I said yes.

Jill was elated. "In addition to everything else," she said, "you'll be doing the media world a favour. The Sam Parker case raises some interesting questions about journalistic ethics, and I don't want some himbo or bimbo using this trial as an audition tape for a job with Fox News."

I laughed. "You and Bryn have a good Thanksgiving."

"You too," Jill said. "Wow, Zack Shreve, and I thought the most daring thing you ever did was skip flossing once in a while."

"My turn to hang up," I said, and I did.

Within minutes, Rapti Lustig called. We agreed it was going to be fun working together again. She promised to e-mail the background information on the case immediately, and then she congratulated me on my new boyfriend.

Jill worked fast.

As I entered Rapti's new contact information into my laptop, I knew the ineluctable cycle of the cosmos was pressing on. It seemed only fair to let my boyfriend know that our lives were about to change.

I dialed his private line at Falconer Shreve. He picked up on the first ring. "This is nice," he said. "I'm always the one who does the calling."

"Then it's time I took the initiative. What are you up to?"

"Chasing my tail," Zack said equitably.

"Why don't you let me chase it for a while," I said. "Come over here for lunch. The menu's limited, but nobody will ask how your case is going."

"You just pushed the right button."

"Good. I'll pick you up – give us more time together. Is noon okay?"

"Perfect," he said. "As are you. Do you know I slept here last night? I fell asleep at my desk, woke up this morning, and kept on working. I'm getting as crazy as a shithouse rat."

"I'll watch my back," I said.

"I'm not after your back," he said.

I was smiling when I hung up the phone, but my sense of being at one with the world didn't last. When I turned around, I noticed a boy standing at our back door. He was framed by the screen, and I tensed at the sudden knowledge that I hadn't been alone. I walked to the door, but I didn't open it.

He met my eyes. "I'm looking for Taylor," he said.

"She left for school twenty minutes ago."

The boy didn't move. "I'm sorry if I scared you," he said. "You were on the phone."

"That's all right," I said. I looked at the boy more carefully and felt my pulse slow. With four children of my own, there had been hundreds of kids through my house and there was nothing about this one to alarm. He was young – perhaps thirteen or fourteen, but he was already taller than me – at least five-foot-eight. He was slender, fine-featured, and dark-haired, a good-looking kid, dressed in a black pullover and khakis. Unexceptional except for one detail. Suspended from a hemp cord around his neck was a five-pointed gold star.

I opened the door and peered more closely. "That's a pentangle, isn't it?" I said. "I haven't read *Sir Gawain and the Green Knight* since university, but I remember that."

His eyes met mine. "I've never met anybody who's read *Sir Gawain and the Green Knight*," he said. "It's the most important book in my life." His fingers touched the pentangle. "Five perfect points, wholly distinct, yet part of one whole."

The boy's gaze was unnerving. For an awkward moment, we were silent. Neither of us seemed to know what to say next. Then the boy gave me a small smile. "I'd better go," he said. "If I'm late, I'll get another detention."

He turned and ran across my backyard towards the alley. I watched until he disappeared, then I gave myself a shake, wiped the kitchen counter, and went upstairs to check my e-mail.

As promised, Rapti Lustig had sent files on the background of the Sam Parker case. There were no revelations, but it was grim reading. I'd followed the case closely and I was acquainted with several of the principals. Kathryn Morrissey, the woman Sam Parker was alleged to have shot at, was a faculty member in the school of journalism at the university where I taught. I knew her well enough to greet her when we passed in the hall or to chat with her while waiting for a meeting to begin, but we weren't friends.

Kathryn was intelligent and articulate, but she was unnervingly self-centred. Once, after she'd just begun at the university, we had lunch together at the Common Table in the Faculty Club. Over the asparagus soup, Kathryn gave a nasty account of her evening at the home of a colleague who had invited her to dinner. The colleague and his partner had a Santa Claus collection they enjoyed, and Kathryn dismissed their collection as kitsch and ridiculed them for being bourgeois. Over the years my kids, like the children of many who worked at the university, had enjoyed the Santas and the sweet, milky tea and lacy cookies their hosts had served them. Kathryn's mockery of their hospitality rankled, and in the two years since that lunch I hadn't sought her out.

In my opinion, she was cruel and untrustworthy. When her book *Too Much Hope* was published, I was proven right.

The lepidopterist's preferred technique for killing a butterfly is to pinch its thorax between the thumb and forefinger. The action stuns the specimen immediately and prevents it from damaging itself. In chronicling the troubled lives of the sons and daughters of a baker's dozen of Canada's most prominent families, Kathryn Morrissey did not display the lepidopterist's humanity. Her subjects hungered for redemption, and Kathryn, an interviewer who was as skilled as she was silken, had seduced them with the promise that confession would bring salvation.

Confess they did. By the time Kathryn's subjects realized they were damaging themselves irreparably, it was too late. She had pinned them to her mounting board and there was no escape. While her subjects flailed, Kathryn typed her notes, submitted her manuscript, and banked the advance from her publisher.

Next to her pitiless exposés of children who had become thieves, brawlers, druggies, drunks, or garden-variety creeps, Kathryn's disclosure that Glen Parker, the only son of Samuel Parker, the new messiah of the fundamentalist right, was a transsexual seemed like small potatoes. However, the revelation that Glen, a theatre major at our university, had changed his name to Glenda and was quietly making the transition from male to female devastated his parents.

The morning after Kathryn's chapter about the Parker family was excerpted in one of our national newspapers, Glenda's lacquered mother, Beverly, appeared at the entrance of her Calgary home and confronted the media who had assembled to record her reaction. Beverly's announcement was to the point. "I no longer have a child," she said, and then she turned on her heel, marched back inside, and slammed the door. Reeling from her mother's rejection and her own public humiliation, Glenda called her father and told him she'd found a way out for all of them. She had a gun, and she wasn't afraid of death. Sam Parker convinced his only child to wait until they talked; then he boarded his private plane and flew to Regina. Later that day, Kathryn Morrissey was sitting on the deck behind her condo having a celebratory glass of wine when Sam approached her and pleaded with her to have the publication of her book postponed. When she refused and laughed in his face, he fired a bullet that grazed her left shoulder.

The bullet came from the gun that Glenda Parker had planned to use to kill herself. Whether the firing was deliberate or accidental would be decided by a jury, but for Kathryn, it was the luckiest of shots. The pre-publication drumbeat for *Too Much Hope* had evoked answering drumbeats, and they were not friendly. Most of Kathryn's subjects were in their twenties – old enough to talk without a chaperone present, but young enough to be foolishly voluble when an ostensibly sympathetic listener was salving their wounds and stroking their egos. Some of Kathryn's more principled colleagues had wondered publicly about the moral code of a journalist who would insinuate herself into people's lives then betray them. There had been critical commentaries and columns so relentlessly negative that even the most diligent publicist couldn't mine them for a blurb.

But the bullet that scratched Kathryn's shoulder silenced the naysayers. It turned out that Kathryn had a flair for the dramatic, and she morphed seamlessly into the role of martyr for a higher cause. Eyes moist with unshed tears, Kathryn admitted that she had left a few bodies in her wake, but lower lip trembling, she explained that she had been searching for truth, and truth had a price. Given her obvious suffering, only the most heartless cur would have pressed the point. Suddenly, *Too Much Hope* rocketed to the top of the best-seller list, where it stayed throughout the long and languid summer. The week before Sam Parker's trial on charges of attempted murder began, *Too Much Hope* was still number one – proof positive that there was no slaking the appetite of readers who hungered for reassurance that the children of the powerful were as fallible, flawed, and fucked up as their own.

Rapti's research was both thorough and depressing. As I closed my laptop, I knew I was in need of fresh air and diversion. Luckily, I had a legitimate excuse for heading out. My copy of *Too Much Hope* was in my office at the university. It had been six months since I'd read the book. One of the gifts of late middle age is the ability to forget what you don't choose to remember. I was going to have to revisit *Too Much Hope*. But there was a more pressing reason for driving out to the university. The Faculty Club made the best picnic lunches in town.

By 11:30, I had picked up the book, cleared out my mailbox, and was at the Faculty Club. The dining room was already filling up. Friday was the Thanksgiving buffet. The air was redolent with the smell of roast turkey, and the chef's pumpkin cheesecake was famous. My friend Ed Mariani, who was head of the school of journalism, was sitting in the lounge. When he spotted me, he leapt to his feet. "Perfect timing," he said. "My colleagues and I have reserved a table in the window room and there's a place for you right by me."

"I'd love to, but –"

Ed raised his hand. "Don't let the prospect of breaking bread with Kathryn Morrissey keep you away. She's not speaking to any of us."

"That must make for harmonious department meetings."

Ed winced. "I've made some boneheaded decisions in my life, but hiring Kathryn was the worst."

"Stop beating yourself up. On paper, she was a catch – an

experienced journalist who'd written two successful books and was willing to move to Regina."

Ed smoothed the front of the shirt he had specially made to hide his ample girth. He owned at least two dozen of these shirts in fabrics of varying weights and colours. Today's was cranberry cotton. "I'm supposed to pick up on subtext," he said. "That media mogul who sued Kathryn for libel was such a preening turd that everybody I knew was glad to see him humiliated, but the truth is that what Kathryn did to him was a disgrace. She wormed her way into his trust, promised him one book, and wrote another."

"Exactly what she did with her subjects in *Too Much Hope*."

Ed shuddered. "Unspeakable. Every time I think about Glenda Parker I want to weep. His father, of course, is another matter."

"*Her* father," I corrected. "Glenda came to this university to start afresh as a woman."

"Point taken," Ed said. "But *my* point is that, as much as I empathize with Glenda, it's hard to root for a champion of enlightenment like Samuel Parker, especially when he's also a crack shot."

"Kathryn's a crack shot too," I said. "But when she took aim at her targets, she knew exactly what she was doing."

"You really believe Sam Parker fired that gun accidentally."

"I imagine that will be the defence," I said.

Ed raised an eyebrow. "Pillow talk?"

I shook my head. "Just a guess. Zack and I don't talk about the case."

"You're kidding."

"Nope. Zack puts in punishing hours. These days the only way we can manage time together is if I meet him at the fitness centre in his apartment building."

"That sounds wholesome."

"And necessary," I said. "Zack's in that wheelchair eighteen hours a day. There are times when he's in a lot of pain. Exercise helps, so we work out and afterwards we wipe the sweat off one another and go for ice cream."

"Very domestic."

"We have a lot of fun together. I just wish everyone who draws breath didn't feel compelled to warn me against him."

"They're trying to protect you, Jo. Zachary Shreve is the lawyer of choice for the rich and dodgy, and he's got a sensational track record. Guilty or not, he gets them off. I guess your friends just thought you'd end up with someone a little more like . . ." Ed threw his hands up in frustration.

"A little more like the gent in the Werther's ad," I said. "Sitting in his sweater coat, chatting with his grandson about the tradition of candy?"

Ed chuckled. "Hard to imagine Zack doing that."

"You know him?"

"We've met. He came to my senior journalism seminar once. He was riveting. He talked about criminal law as a prize fight."

"That doesn't surprise me. In his office, he has an autographed photo of Muhammad Ali in his moment of triumph over Sonny Liston."

"May 25, 1965," Ed said.

"Good Lord. How did you know that?"

Ed sniffed theatrically. "Being gay doesn't cut me off from the manly arts. And the parallel Zack drew between the ring and the courtroom made sense. He said that in boxing, for every bout that ends with a knockout punch, there are ninety-nine decided on feints and small, well-placed blows. According to him, it's the same in a courtroom."

" 'Float like a butterfly. Sting like a bee.' "

"Zack's quote from Ali was less poetic. 'It's just a job. Grass grows, birds fly, waves pound the sand. I beat people up.'"

"That's succinct."

"And menacing. Of course, the kids loved your boyfriend."

"But you didn't."

"To be frank, I found him chilling. I had a sense that if he was in the middle of a trial and someone told him he had to swap cases with the Crown, he'd keep arguing without missing a beat."

"That could be seen as the mark of the professional," I said.

"It could," Ed agreed. "It could also be seen as the mark of a hired gun. Jo, your new friend moves in dangerous circles."

It was a rumour I'd heard before, and I didn't attempt to hide the asperity in my voice. "Zack doesn't 'move in dangerous circles,' Ed. He defends people who find themselves in dangerous circumstances. There's a distinction."

Ed sighed heavily. "Now I've hurt your feelings." He placed a plump, perfectly tended hand on mine. "I know I'm like a mother hen with you. It's just that, in my opinion, you deserve the best."

I covered Ed's hand with my own. "I've found it," I said. "Now let's talk about Thanksgiving."

"Still adept at steering the conversation back into safe harbours, I see. So, are you having a houseful?"

"Actually, a couple of houses full," I said. "The granddaughters will be there as will all the kids, except Angus and his girlfriend, Leah. Leah's aunt, the famous Slava, is taking them to New York to see a performance of *Nixon in China*."

Ed's eyes widened. "The only thing more unlikely than Nixon in China is Angus at the opera. Anyway, good for Slava. Angus needs to learn that not all of life's pleasures involve an athletic supporter."

I laughed. "Couldn't agree with you more. But he and Leah will be missed. We're going out to the lake."

"With the new beau?"

"He owns the cottage – or at least one of them. How about you?"

"Barry and I have been invited to dine with friends. For the first time in my adult life, I'm not cooking a turkey."

"Freedom," I said.

"But no leftovers." Ed's moon face registered genuine regret. "Kris Kristofferson was right. Freedom's just another word for nothin' left to lose."

When I went into the Faculty Club kitchen to pick up my order, I asked Terry, the cook, to add two slices of pumpkin cheesecake. Then, bag lunches in hand, I headed off to meet my Prince of Darkness.

The offices of Falconer, Shreve, Altieri, and Wainberg occupied restored twin heritage houses in the city centre. Surrounded by numbingly generic apartment buildings and shops catering to those who yearned to learn the secrets of stained-glass making or Wicca or iridology, the Falconer Shreve offices had the starchy charm of genteel sisters growing old together in a world that had passed them by. Both buildings had well-tended lawns and round iron planters filled with jumbo gold and rust chrysanthemums. Both had discrete brass plates on their front doors bearing the firm's name in letters that were neither too large nor too small, but just right. Both had ramps to accommodate Zack, who had been a paraplegic since a childhood accident.

In the months Zack and I had been seeing each other, I'd occasionally met him at his office. Like all high-powered law firms, Falconer Shreve was driven by the maxim that those who didn't keep up got left behind. There was always a hum in the air, but that Friday afternoon the hum had reached fever pitch. Denise-Dee Kaiswatum, the receptionist, was involved in a heated dispute with a courier, but she came up for air long enough to roll her eyes and point a manicured nail towards the office of Norine MacDonald, Zack's executive assistant, who with Cerberus-like zeal guarded the door to the clients' room. Norine told me she'd let me know when Zack was free and to make myself comfortable.

There are few agreeable reasons to be in a lawyer's office, but Zack's clients' room was designed to reassure the anxious. The walls were painted a comforting forest green and the furnishings were timeless antiques whose burnished sheen suggested that whatever follies humans contrived, there would always be Windsor chairs to receive their sorry asses and glowing coffee tables on which they could leave their mark. Left to my own devices, I settled in with the morning paper. I had ploughed through the news and sports and reached the Review section when Glenda Parker came out of Zack's office. In her ribbed turtleneck, jeans, and hiking boots, she appeared as androgynous as most university kids. Like many female students, Glenda eschewed makeup, and that year the style in which she wore her cornsilk hair – side-parted and cut short except for a long sleek bang, was favoured by half the young men and women on campus. There was nothing noteworthy about Glenda, except for the fact that every Canadian with access to a remote control had seen footage of her in her previous incarnation as an Olympic-calibre swimmer who competed as a male.

The footage had been shot at a swim meet two years before the publication of *Too Much Hope*. Intended only as a record of a few moments in an athlete's life, the close-up was used as an illustration in Kathryn Morrissey's book. After Sam Parker had been charged with attempted murder, the photo of Glenda, unmistakably male with shaved chest bare and genitals outlined by a Speedo brief, had appeared in

every newspaper in Canada. The image was indelible, and as
Norine introduced Glenda, I found myself searching for the
boy in the swimsuit in the gentle young woman extending
her hand to me.

We exchanged the usual pleasantries of people meeting for
the first time. Glenda's voice was an agreeable contralto, but
she spoke with the care of someone learning a new language.
In *Too Much Hope*, she had confided to Kathryn that one of
the early tasks of transitioning genders was acquiring the
voice of the other. Physical change, she explained, was only
one stop on the transsexual road map. As I looked at Glenda,
I was struck by how young she was – just twenty – but the
pink-purple shadows beneath her eyes suggested that, for her,
the path to self-realization had been riddled with land mines.

"When there's something Zack doesn't want me to have
to testify to, he sends me out of the room," she said.

I caught her eye. "Zack knows what he's doing."

Glenda's expression was wry. "Let's hope so," she said.
"Because he's all we've got."

At that moment, the door to Zack's office opened, and
Samuel Parker joined us, upping the wattage in the room as
he had been upping the wattage in rooms for the past forty
years. In the early 1960s, Sam and his wife, Bev, had been a
folk-singing duo who wrote songs celebrating peace, justice,
and the common man. When the *Zeitgeist* shifted from
concern for Mother Earth to real estate lust, the Parkers'
careers faded, but the lyric beauty of their songs continued
to charm. There were cover recordings and a small but
steady flow of royalty payments. Sam and Bev left the business end of things to Bev's brother, then a strange, weedy
youth with a fascination for speculative fiction and the innovative use of technology. He had, as Sam pointed out in later
interviews, invested the Parker money in one half-assed

scheme after another, until 1971 when IBM got interested in a patent Sam had apparently acquired.

The money poured in with the profusion of the tears of the poor, and the Parkers were forced to re-evaluate their priorities and their friends. Luckily, both proved easy to change. For the past thirty-five years, Samuel and Beverly Parker had been pillars of the political right, big donors to conservative causes, and articulate spokespeople for groups that shared their ideology.

Even with charges for attempted murder hanging over his head, Sam Parker moved with the confidence of a man in charge. Tanned and immaculate, he extended his hand to me and introduced himself. When I explained that I was there to take his lawyer to lunch, he smiled.

"Zack's been working too hard. He deserves a good meal with an attractive woman." He turned to Glenda. "We deserve a good meal too. Any suggestions about a restaurant?"

"Sure," Glenda said. "There's this terrific new vegan place. You'll love it, Dad. They don't even use honey because it's a product of the labour of bees."

The Parkers exchanged glances, then they tilted their heads back at identical angles and laughed at their private joke. "Let's go," Samuel said. "Tofu waits for no one."

Focused on his computer screen, Zack didn't notice me, but I noticed him: his broad, high forehead, his heavy brows, his full lips; his power; his self-possession. I walked over and bent to kiss the curve of his forehead. He looked pleased. "What was that for?"

"Couldn't resist such a good-looking guy," I said. He turned his chair towards me, reached out, and drew me to him. "We have an hour and forty-five minutes till my next appointment," he said.

"Not nearly enough," I said. "But these days I take what I can get."

"It's not always going to be like this," Zack said. "After the trial's over, I'm going to cut back."

I squeezed his shoulder. "Maybe. And maybe, as Dorothy Parker said, the Statue of Liberty is in Lake Ontario. Come on. The meter's ticking. Let's take your car, but I want to drive. I've spent my whole life behind the wheel of something sensible. It's a rush knowing I can open up and leave everybody else in the dust."

Zack grinned and tossed me the keys. "Go to town."

For the first few minutes of our drive, the sheer pleasure of being together in a convertible on a dazzling fall day kept us silent, but when I stopped for a light, Zack turned to me. "So what did you think of Sam?"

"He surprised me," I said. "And he impressed me. I was only with Glenda and him for a few minutes, but it's obvious they love each other. More surprising, given Sam's public persona – they seem genuinely to like each other."

"They're in a lousy situation," Zack said, "but they try to keep it light – make each other laugh."

"I noticed that," I said. "And I noticed something else. When Glenda was alone with me, her mannerisms and her voice were decidedly female, but when her father came into the room, there was a subtle shift back: the voice was lower and the stance was more masculine – trying to make the situation easier for her father, I guess."

"And Sam tries to make the situation easier for Glenda," Zack said. "Even in private, he corrects himself if he refers to Glenda in the masculine. They're good people. A lot of my clients are scum-buckets, but Sam Parker isn't. I wish I could get him off."

"But you're not going to."

"No, we're pretty well fucked. Criminal lawyers learn how to make the most of what they have, but I haven't got anything. The Crown, on the other hand, has motive, opportunity, your friend the ex-premier as eyewitness, and the proverbial smoking gun."

"Zack, don't say anything else."

"Sorry," he said. "Too much shop talk?"

"No. It's not that." I pulled up in front of my house. "I was going to wait till lunch to talk about this, but Jill Oziowy called this morning. She wants me to do a nightly commentary on the Sam Parker trial for NationTV."

"Whoa," Zack said. "Do you want to do it?"

"Yes, I think I do. I'm stalled on that book I'm supposed to be writing, and covering Sam Parker might give me the boost I need." I took his hand. "Besides, I'd get to see you every day."

Zack fixed his eyes on me. "That might not be a good idea."

"Too much proximity?"

"No, I could spend every hour of the day with you and it still wouldn't be enough." He raised my hand to his lips. "Selfishly, I wanted you to keep thinking I was a nice guy."

"You are a nice guy."

"Not when I'm in court," he said. "But that's my problem. You want the NationTV job, and that's good enough for me." He squeezed my hand. "Come on. Let's eat outside. This day is too perfect to waste."

The swimming pool in my backyard was an albatross – a '60s knockoff of art deco with ornamental tiles in peculiar shapes that were impossible to replace and an ancient and cranky circulation system. From May till October, it whined for attention, and siphoned money from my bank account. Every year, I threatened to get it filled in; every year, I gave in to my youngest daughter's plea to extend the pool's life for one last year. That afternoon, as Zack and I came around the side path to the backyard, I was glad I had capitulated.

Under the cloudless cerulean sky, the pool was restored to its former glory. Shafts of sunlight pierced the surface of the water, bathing the chipped turquoise paint in a forgiving glow, transforming my elderly pool into a jewel shimmering with promise. Zack wheeled himself to a grassy spot near the pool, then breathed deeply, as if he could gulp the beauty of the moment into his lungs.

"I could stay here forever," he said.

"Me too," I said. "But we don't have forever."

Zack's brow furrowed into a mock scowl. "Sure we do," he said. "Today we're just a little short of time."

I went inside and arranged our lunch on a tray; then, on impulse, I added the vase of marigolds I'd picked that morning.

When I came back out and placed the tray on the table beside Zack's chair, he was appreciative. "Nice," he said. "All of it, but especially the marigolds."

"You gave me an orchid," I said.

"The first time we made love," he said. "Definitely an orchid occasion."

I handed him his sandwich. "I love orchids," I said. "But I like marigolds too. They endure."

"I'll remember that," Zack said. For the next half-hour we sat with the sun on our faces, eating seed rolls filled with slices of Gouda and Granny Smith apples, drinking iced tea, sketching plans for the weekend ahead, and trading the latest about friends and family.

Zack sighed when he heard Angus had elected to go to the opera instead of the lake. "Angus is the only guy I can consistently beat at poker. Besides, I was looking forward to his tales of life at law school."

"I can help you out there," I said. "According to my son, law school is kick-ass."

Zack beamed. "Good for Angus. The law *is* a kick-ass profession." His smile grew rueful. "Well, most of the time. Anything else I should know?"

"A boy came calling for Taylor this morning."

"She won't be eleven till next month."

"I'm hoping this is just a friend who happens to be a boy. He was wearing a pentangle – like Gawain."

"Should I know who Gawain is?"

"As a matter of fact, you should. Gawain was one of King Arthur's knights. The boy with the pentangle told me that *Sir Gawain and the Green Knight* is the most important book in his life."

Zack chuckled. "Well, if Taylor has to have a boyfriend, I guess we're lucky he's into chivalry."

"We're lucky people," I said.

"We are," Zack agreed. He glanced at his watch. "I should be getting back. So what are you going to do this afternoon?"

"Pack up the car and visit Howard Dowhanuik."

"What's Howard like anyway?"

"Let's see. He still calls me 'babe.' Does that tell you anything?"

"Just that he's a braver man than I am."

"He is brave – brave and smart and funny – at least that's the way he used to be. You would have liked him."

"But I wouldn't like him now."

"At this point, not even Howard likes Howard."

"What went wrong there? I mean, one day he's the ex-premier, a respected elder statesman, and the next day he's a lush."

"The meltdown wasn't that quick," I said. "Howard's ego's been taking a beating for a while now. He gave his life to the party, but the party seems to have forgotten his name, his telephone number, and his principles. His daughters e-mail when they think of him – which isn't often – and since Kathryn Morrissey's book, his son won't speak to him."

"You can hardly blame Charlie for that," Zack said.

"Charlie? You're on a first-name basis with Howard's son?"

"Sure. I don't like surprises. Our firm has talked to everybody we think may be important to this case, and that includes Charlie. I know that he's had a tough row to hoe. That birthmark on his face must have been a terrible thing for a kid to deal with, and according to Charlie, his father was never there."

"Except during election time," I said. "During campaigns we always trotted Charlie out so there wouldn't be an awkward gap in the family picture."

"So you're loyal to Howard because you feel guilty?"

"No," I said. "I'm loyal to Howard because he's always been there when the kids and I needed him. Now it's my turn."

"And you can just blow off the fact that he told Kathryn Morrissey the most intimate details about his son's private life. Jo, Charlie's spent years building his career. People across Canada tune into his radio show because they want to hear Charlie D, the cool, smart guy with the insights – the guy who can make them laugh and show them a way out of their problems. So Howard tells Kathryn Morrissey that Charlie D is a fake – that the real Charlie grew up seeing shrinks every week, that he loved his mother obsessively, and that when Charlie was eight years old he met a little girl named Ariel and for the next twenty years he loved her with such a consuming passion that he made her life hell until she died. What kind of man would reveal secrets like that about his son? What was Howard thinking?"

"He wasn't thinking. He was trying to make amends for all the years he ignored Charlie. Howard believed that when people read about how deeply Charlie had been wounded by his absence, they'd realize they should be part of their children's lives."

Zack's raised an eyebrow. "*And* he wanted to jump Kathryn's bones."

"I'm sure he did," I said. "But Howard loves Charlie and this is killing him." I moved closer. "Try not to lose sight of that when you have him in the witness box."

Zack brushed my cheek with the back of his hand. "Try not to lose sight of the fact that my first obligation is to my client."

I took his hand in mine. "Two fathers. Two sons. Give Kathryn her due – the title she chose for her book deserves full marks."

Zack's gaze was steady. "I didn't know the title had any particular significance."

"Well, it does," I said. "It's from a poem called 'On My First Son' that Ben Jonson wrote when his seven-year-old died. The poem's almost four hundred years old, but it still breaks my heart – 'Farewell, thou child of my right hand, and joy; / My sin was too much hope of thee, lov'd boy.'"

Zack winced. "Jesus," he said. "This case just goes from bad to worse."

CHAPTER

2

For as long as I could remember, I'd given Howard Dowhanuik a bottle of Crown Royal for Thanksgiving. He said he liked his bountiful harvest distilled, and until now I'd been happy to comply. This year I was taking him an apple pie – a wholesome if patronizing choice. Substituting pie for rye had seemed like a good idea, but as I stood, with the pie in the crook of one arm, hammering at the front door of Howard's condo with my fist, I cursed my stupidity in coming and I cursed Howard for not answering. I knew he was there. The drapes were drawn, the TV was blaring, and his 1988 Buick was leaking oil onto the driveway.

The condo was in a quiet cul-de-sac five blocks from my house. When Howard had retired, I'd helped him find it. At the time, the location seemed ideal: distant enough from the house of his son, Charlie, to keep Charlie from feeling smothered; close enough to the legislature for Howard to offer our hapless new premier advice as his cabinet ministers, one by one, got caught with their peckers in the pickle barrel.

Perfect – but nothing worked out.

Once elected, the premier threw up a firewall of M.B.A.s and toadies to protect him from the unpalatable political home truths Howard might have offered. Ignored, Howard sulked and fumed. And along came Kathryn Morrissey.

I glanced across at her house. Pricey as they were, Kathryn's and Howard's condos were pretty much cheek by jowl. It was late afternoon when Kathryn was shot, and Howard had been drinking heavily. It was possible that he was mistaken about what he thought he saw and heard. One thing was certain. He would have been truthful. Howard's politics might have been radically different from Sam Parker's, but Howard had never held people's politics against them.

The broad strokes of Kathryn Morrissey's story and Sam Parker's were remarkably similar. Both agreed that on the afternoon in question, Sam entered Kathryn's yard through her side gate, pleaded with her to postpone publication of her book, and, when she refused, fired a pistol. Kathryn and Sam differed on only one particular, but it was critical. Kathryn stated that Sam had threatened her – aiming the pistol carefully and saying, "How does it feel to know that this might be the last day of your life?" Sam said that to emphasize his desperation he held the pistol out to Kathryn and asked, "Can you imagine how it feels to see your child holding this and knowing it might be the last day of her life?" According to Sam, when Kathryn saw the pistol, she panicked, grabbed for it, and in the scuffle the gun went off.

Howard had corroborated Kathryn's account, and on the strength of his confirmation, the Crown charged Sam Parker with attempted murder. Howard was the Crown's fair-haired boy. He was suffering for that too.

But Howard's misery was not paramount in my mind as I banged at his door. When finally he appeared, unshaven and in need of a shower, I was mad enough to spit. He was wearing the kind of plaid flannel shirt his campaign manager had tried, without success, to get him to wear when he ran against a candidate who radiated a down-home charm that was as ersatz as it was potent.

There was no down-home charm in Howard's greeting. "You never give up, do you, Jo? Does the fact that I didn't answer the doorbell suggest anything to you?"

I thrust the pie into his hands. "I brought you something for Thanksgiving."

He sniffed. "What happened to the Crown Royal?"

"I'm being innovative."

He gazed at me through a rheumy eye. "Thank you for the innovative pie," he said. Then he stepped back and attempted to kick the door shut with a slippered foot.

I stopped it with my elbow. "I'm coming in for a visit," I said.

"Suit yourself," he said. Then, pie in hand, he turned and padded down the hall towards the kitchen. Left to my own devices, I wandered into the living room. The gloom was sepulchral. Heavy drapes banished the light of the outside world, but not its concerns. Three televisions tuned to three separate cable channels brayed news of the latest public incidents of malice, malfeasance, and misfortune. The vinyl La-Z-Boy the caucus office bought Howard when he'd retired eleven years earlier was at the ready. A crocheted afghan lay crumpled on its seat and a glass of amber liquid rested in the indented beverage holder in the recliner's arm. I didn't need to sniff the liquid in the glass. The smell of its predecessors lingered in the air. The coffee table was littered with half-filled takeout cartons from Bamboo Garden, leaking plastic sleeves of soy and plum sauce and soiled and balled-up paper napkins. Home, sweet home.

I turned off the televisions and began picking up garbage and carting it out to the kitchen. Howard watched wordlessly as I dropped the detritus of his meal into the trash, but when I washed my hands and returned to the living room, he followed me. I ignored him. I was a woman on a mission. I opened the curtains and sunshine filled the room.

Howard narrowed his eyes and growled like an aged and pissed-off lion. "What the hell do you think you're doing?"

"Improving the feng shui," I said. "Your environment is working against you."

He shook his head. "Jeez, I knew it must be something."

"Say the word and I'm out of here. It's a holiday weekend. I have errands to run."

He glared at his slippers. "Stay," he said.

"My pleasure," I said. I grabbed the afghan to give it a shake and a copy of *Too Much Hope* fell from its folds. The book bristled with Post-it notes. The thought of Howard sitting in this darkened living room poring over Kathryn's book by the flickering light of his three televisions infuriated me.

"Why do you keep this thing around?" I asked, pitching the book at the La-Z-Boy.

His drink threatened, Howard sprang into action. He retrieved his glass from the beverage holder and drained it. "To remind me," he said.

"Of what?"

"Christ, Jo, why do you always have to force the issue? To remind me of how stupid I am. To remind me of what I buggered up."

He poured himself a refill.

"Good move," I said. "How come none of the self-help books suggest liquor and wallowing as tools for recovery?"

Howard's voice was gravel. "Because the bozos who write them lack imagination. Come down to my office." He wandered out of the kitchen and I followed. I didn't need directions. When Howard had moved into the condo, I'd helped him convert his guest room into an office suitable for an éminence grise. It was a pleasant space, with photographs of the old days discreetly placed to remind people that Howard was a person of consequence, and a new notebook computer and printer to suggest he was moving with the times.

I glanced around. "So what did you want to show me? Everything's the same."

Howard's gaze was shrewd. "You always were observant," he said. "That's *exactly* what I wanted you to see. Nothing's going on. There's not a goddamn thing in my life except a bunch of pictures to remind me of a time when I was useful."

"You're still alive," I said. "You have options. You enjoyed teaching. Call our department head. He'd be thrilled to have you teach a class next semester."

"How much respect do you think I'd get from students after what I did?"

"Howard, students don't care about our private lives. We're a means to an end for them. By the time the winter semester starts, Kathryn Morrissey will be old news."

"Not for me," Howard said. "Kathryn Morrissey will be an anchor around my neck forever."

"Well, you put her there," I said. "You knew what Kathryn did for a living when you moved in next door to her. I've heard you warn dozens of people against blabbing to journalists. What made you open up to her?"

"Marnie's death," Howard said simply.

"Not good enough," I said. "Marnie would have killed you for spilling the family secrets to a reporter."

"You're still angry at me for what happened to Marnie, aren't you?" Howard said.

"I was never angry at you," I said. "I was angry at God. There's a difference."

Howard's lip curled. "Thanks for reminding me."

"You're welcome. Anyway, it's a moot point. Marnie's dead, and she died believing she was going to a better place."

"But you don't believe that."

"I just wish she'd had a chance to spend more time here."

"So do I," Howard said.

"Her death was unacceptable," I said, as in fact it had been.

After devoting her life to raising a family, writing speeches, making cabbage rolls, and shaking hands, Marnie Dowhanuik told Howard it was her turn, said goodbye, and enrolled at the Centre for Medieval Studies in Toronto. Challenged and for the first time praised for her brilliance, Marnie had flourished. She read far into the night, argued over coffee with the other students, and rode across campus on her new Schwinn. One soft spring day, when Marnie was on her way to class, her bike was hit by a car carrying a provincial cabinet minister to a meeting in Queen's Park. The class she was headed for was on the literature of the Antichrist.

Marnie had a penchant for black humour. The fact that, in the end, the Antichrist had used a politician to kill her would have called forth her wonderful dirty, raucous laugh. But the punchline of Marnie's story was a long time coming. She didn't die on that day when the air was sweet with the smell of fresh-turned earth and crocuses. Instead, she was picked up by an ambulance and carried to a hospital where good and caring doctors had to face the fact that, try as they might, they couldn't put Marnie together again. Her body healed, but Marnie herself was irrecoverable. She was sent to a nursing home where the nuns did their best: curling her hair, putting blush on her cheeks, and dressing her in velour track suits in the pastel colours that Marnie despised. Finally, her body was assaulted by an aggressive cancer that carried her away in less than six months. Many thought it was a blessing.

At the memory of Marnie, Howard's eyes lost their focus. "I was there when she died, you know. They kept her doped up, but just before she died she came out of the haze. She knew me. She gave me that wicked smile. Then she said, 'Babe, I'd like to stay, but I have a meeting.'" His face crumpled. "The excuse I'd given her a thousand times."

My throat tightened.

"I had it coming," Howard said thickly. "Still it's not the farewell you hope for from your wife of forty years. Anyway, the guilt kicked in, and I wasn't about to unburden myself to some priest, so when Kathryn asked me about myself, I let it rip – told her I was a lousy husband, a lousy father, a lousy friend, a lousy human being. Probably my antennae should have gone up when she started pressing me about Charlie, but hell, out of the multitudes, he was the one I'd failed the most."

"Kathryn never told you she was writing a book?"

Howard grimaced. "Of course, she did. She's a pro. She didn't want a lawsuit. She said her book was about the price politics exacts on families."

"And you bit," I said.

"Hook, line, and sinker," Howard replied. "I thought Kathryn Morrissey was heaven-sent. As far as I was concerned, she was my path to redemption. Isn't there a line in the Bible about pride closing a man's eyes?"

"If there isn't, there should be," I said.

"Anyway, now that I've lost my pride, I can see clearly. Sam Parker did more than make speeches about family values. He protected his family." Howard slugged back his rye. "If I'd pulled that trigger, maybe I'd be able to look my son in the eye."

"Do us both a favour," I said. "Don't ever repeat what you just said to me."

His face softened. "So you haven't written me off."

"I'll never write you off," I said. "Look, why don't you come out to the lake and have Thanksgiving with us. We have plenty of beds, two huge turkeys, and kids of all ages for you to bark at."

"Thanks," Howard said. "Another time. I'm not very good company these days."

"If you change your mind, give me a call." I kissed his cheek. "And treat yourself to a shave. That *Miami Vice* look went out twenty years ago."

I had parked in Howard's driveway. When I stepped outside, Kathryn Morrissey was kneeling beside my Volvo. As I watched, she flattened herself on the asphalt and reached under my car. It was a surreal moment in a day that was shaping up as memorable, but when a long-bodied silvery Siamese shot out and flew past me, all was explained. Instinctively, I grabbed the cat by the scruff of its neck. Just as instinctively, it scratched me. We both yowled. Ears flattened back, brilliantly blue eyes furious, it tilted its head to look at me. It struggled, but I managed to hold on.

Kathryn pushed herself to her feet. She was wearing a red silk jacket shot through with gold tracings of leaves and splotched with dark blotches of fresh oil from Howard's Buick. She took the cat from my arms, lowered her face into its fur, and began to croon its name: Minoo. Kathryn's relief at having Minoo safe in her arms was palpable, but when she spotted the blood on my arm, her focus shifted.

"Are you all right?" she said, and her concern seemed genuine.

"It's just a scratch," I said.

"Still, it *is* an animal scratch. Why don't you come to my place and we can clean it up?" she said. She laughed softly. "Maybe Minoo has done us a favour. It really is time you and I got to know each other better."

Kathryn's tone was beseeching, but the images of Howard's misery were fresh. "I know everything I need to know about you," I said, opening my car door.

"You don't know anything about me," Kathryn said. "And that's regrettable, because we have common interests."

"Such as?"

Her three-pointed smile was feline. "Too late now," she said. "But when you replay this moment in your mind – and you will – remember that you were the one who was uncharitable. You're going to regret this, Joanne."

I was met at the door to my house by my soon to be eleven-year-old daughter and, behind her, close as a shadow, the boy with the pentangle. "Zack's on the phone," Taylor said, "but Ethan and I are doing something in the kitchen, so could you *please* use the phone in the living room." Suddenly, she remembered her manners. "Sorry. Jo, this is Ethan Thorpe. Ethan, this is my mum."

I smiled at the boy. "Hello again."

"Hi," he said. "Talk to you after, I guess."

"I guess," I said. Then I went into the living room and picked up.

"How's tricks?" Zack said.

"Fine," I said, I glancing at my arm. "Kathryn Morrissey's cat scratched me."

"Want to sue?"

"How much do you think I could get?"

"Depends. With a totally unprincipled lawyer, the sky's the limit, but my plate's full at the moment."

"There goes my beach house in Tahiti."

"Mine too," Zack said. "But I didn't call to drum up business. We've had a little incident at the office, so we've all been told to vamoose until the cops finish checking things out."

My chest tightened. "What kind of incident?"

"A bomb went off."

"Oh my God. Was anyone hurt?"

"No, it wasn't much of a bomb, and I was in the can, so no harm done."

"But you're all right?"

"More than all right. The members of what we laughingly refer to as Sam's dream team are holed up in our accountant's boardroom. We're their biggest client, so we are well cared for. At the moment, I'm dipping biscotti into my latte."

"That's reassuring," I said. "But I'm still shaking. Reassure me some more."

"Come on, Jo. Your late husband was in politics. You know that threats are part of the package. Some guy who's a few fries short of a Happy Meal stubs his toe and goes a little nuts. Then his toe stops hurting and the threats stop."

"I know, just be careful, okay?"

"Since I met you, I'm always careful. Now I've got six lawyers and a client waiting for me, so I'd better get a move on."

"Any chance you'll be at the lake in time for dinner?"

"Not a prayer, but I'll get there as soon as I can." He lowered his voice. "You know what I'm looking forward to? Going to bed with you at night and waking up with you in the morning."

"Getting tired of quickies?" I said.

"Never," he said. "I'm just greedy. This is going to be a great Thanksgiving, Jo," and then before I could respond, he hung up.

Obeying the rule that parents can save themselves grief if they make a little noise before they walk in on their children, I rapped on the kitchen door before I walked in on Taylor and her guest. But the scene that greeted me was as innocent as a *Leave It to Beaver* video. Taylor and the boy were sitting at the kitchen table drinking milk and reading comic books.

Taylor's greeting was sunny. "Come look at this, Jo."

"She won't want to see these," the boy said, but the look he gave me was hopeful.

"Sure I'll want to see them," I said.

"Ethan drew them himself," Taylor said. I took the chair beside her and opened the comic she handed me. As soon as I saw the first frame, I understood why Taylor and the boy were friends. Taylor had inherited her birth mother's talent as a visual artist. There weren't many people her age who could understand what Taylor's art meant to her, but this boy would understand. The drawing, lettering, and shading in the black and white opening panels of his book were skilful, but I knew at once that I was looking at something more than a series of well-executed drawings. Ethan had created a world, the world of a lonely, alienated boy whose unremittingly bleak vision is transformed when he discovers a pentangle in the crypt of a burned church. From the moment he fastens the chain holding the pentangle around his neck, the boy and his life are transformed. The pentangle brings with it a name for those who wear it. The name is Soul-fire, and as Soul-fire, the boy is strong and fearless, an adventurer in a land that is suddenly drenched in colour and filled with loathsome enemies that the hero dispatches with grace. Not surprisingly, Soul-fire bore a striking resemblance to Ethan.

I finished reading and closed the book. "This is terrific," I said. "Really, Ethan, it's a privilege to see your work."

Taylor shot him a glance. "I told you she'd like it."

"Well, you were right," I said. I glanced up at the clock. "Look, I hate to change the focus here, but would you two mind if I put on the radio. I want to hear the news. Somebody planted a bomb at Falconer Shreve today."

Taylor's eyes widened. "Nobody got hurt, did they?"

"No," I said, turning on the radio. "Zack seems to think it wasn't anything to worry about."

Ethan had been sliding the last of his comics into a protective plastic envelope. He stopped and turned to me. "Zachary Shreve is a friend of yours?" he asked, his voice rising.

"He's Jo's boyfriend," Taylor said.

Ethan looked hard at Taylor. "Is he a good person?"

"Well, he's nice," Taylor said. The gaze she levelled at me indicated she needed help steering the conversation.

I winked at her. "Maybe Ethan would like to meet Zack some time," I said.

"I would," he said fervently. "All I know is what I've heard."

"Well, keep an open mind," I said.

The news came on. The bombing was the lead item, but the report was short and vague. A bomb had exploded at a downtown office. There were no injuries and the Major Crimes Division of the Regina Police Force was investigating. Falconer Shreve was not identified by name, and there was no reference to the outcome of the police investigations.

I flicked off the radio. "Not much information there," I said. "I guess we'll have to wait till Zack comes tonight to find out what happened."

Ethan's blue eyes met mine. "You're going to see Zachary Shreve tonight?" he said.

Taylor scrunched her nose. "How come you're so interested in Zack?"

Ethan shrugged. "No reason. Just he's famous. That's all."

Taylor twinkled at me. "He's not just famous. He's Jo's big sparkly top banana."

Ethan stood up so suddenly he knocked his chair over. He righted it. "Sorry," he said. "I'd better get going." He started towards the back door, then stopped and came back. I assumed he wanted to talk to Taylor, but he came to me. "Thanks for looking at my book," he said. His fingers touched the pentangle. "A lot of people wouldn't have bothered."

"I'd like to read the others. Could we keep them for a while?"

"Sure," he said. "I mean, that would be great. Keep them as long as you want. Thanks." And then he was gone, leaving my daughter and me waiting to see who would make the first move.

"Wow," I said.

Taylor ran her fingers through the new, very cool haircut that had replaced her braids the week before school started. "Wow, what?" she asked nonchalantly.

"Wow, Ethan," I said. "I've never even heard you mention him."

"He's new this year, and he enrolled late. He just started at Lakeview a couple of weeks ago."

"That's always tough. Any other kids from his family go to your school?"

"No, there's just Ethan. He used to live in Ottawa with his father, but his dad got remarried, and Ethan didn't fit into the new family, so now he's with his mother."

"Is that working out?"

Taylor shook her head. "I don't know. He just told me about his dad and the new wife with the two little kids. It's kind of sad."

"At least he has his drawing," I said. "He really does have talent."

"I think Ethan would rather have friends," Taylor said.

"And he doesn't have any friends except you."

"I'm not even sure about me," Taylor said. "Ethan's kind of different."

"Different how?"

"He reads all the time."

"I'm glad you didn't hold that against him."

Taylor gave me a bleak smile. "You know what I mean."

"Yes," I said. "I do. So how come you invited him over?"

Taylor bit her lower lip. "After school, everybody was talking about what they were doing on the long weekend and Ethan was just kind of standing there."

I went to her and kissed the top of her fashionably chopped and moussed hair. "Come on. Give me a hand with packing the food, and I'll tell you about my career as an artist."

"You never had a career as an artist."

"Oh yes I did. My design for a wedding gown was in *Katy Keene*."

"What's *Katy Keene*?" Taylor asked.

"Bring me down a couple of laundry hampers for the food and I'll tell you."

Inspired, Taylor moved quickly. In a flash she was back with the hampers.

"Put the fruit and vegetables in that one," I said, "and I'll load up the stuff from the freezer."

"Okay, but now you have to tell me about *Katy Keene*."

"It was a comic book when I was a kid," I said. "Katy Keene was a model, and readers could send in designs for outfits Katy might wear. If the designs were good, the illustrator used them in the next comic."

"And they used yours," Taylor said with unnerving reverence.

"Yes," I said. "They did."

"Do you still have the comic?"

"Somewhere, but I'm not going to dig for it right now."

"At least tell me about the dress."

"Oh, Taylor, it was awful."

"How awful?"

"Well it was covered in doves."

"Real doves!"

"No. Fake doves and they had pink ribbons in their beaks."

Taylor rolled her eyes. "Holeeee," she said. "That is bizarre."

"Thank you for vote of confidence," I said.

She was giggling. "You're not mad, are you?"

"No."

"I really want to see the drawing of that dress," she said.

"Enough to help me clean out the basement when we get back from the cottage?"

Taylor grinned. "Let me think about it."

Our car was full for the drive to the lake. On the seat beside me was a hamper of groceries that there was no room for in the trunk. Our Bouvier, Willie, had a window seat in the back; Taylor was beside him and Isobel Wainberg, the twelve-year-old daughter of one of Zack's partners, Delia, was beside Taylor. Both of Isobel's parents had come down with the flu that was making the rounds that fall, so she was spending Thanksgiving with us.

She was a happy addition. Isobel and Taylor were close and I was very fond of her. She was her mother in miniature: small-boned, smart, burdened with worries, but blessed with a quick wit and a smile that was as dazzling as it was rare. That afternoon, as she and Taylor settled into the back seat with Willie, it was clear that Isobel had something on her mind. She waited until we were on the highway to broach the subject.

"We've been wondering about Glenda Parker," she said. "We've seen the pictures on TV when Glenda was still a boy. And he *was* a boy," she said in a tone that it made it clear that particular point was off the table. "In the pictures where Glenda's wearing a bathing suit you can see that."

"Because Glenda had male genitals," I said.

Taylor was triumphant. "I told you Jo would talk about it," she said.

"There's no reason not to," I said. "What do you want to know?"

"We want to know why Glenda's a woman now," Isobel said. "When you're born, you're either a girl or a boy, right?"

"Most of the time, yes." I said. "Sometimes, it's hard to tell. When my elder son, Peter, was born, the woman I shared a room with gave birth to a little boy too, but there were some physical anomalies. Do you know what that means?"

"I do," Isobel said. "It means something abnormal, like a dog that can't bark."

"Right," I said. "Well, when the doctors examined my roommate's baby, they found anomalies. His parents and the doctors had to make a decision about whether the baby should be raised as a girl or a boy."

"What did they decide?" Taylor asked.

"The doctors did some tests and told the parents the baby could be raised successfully as a boy, so that's what they did."

Determined not to miss a word coming from the front seat, Isobel was pushing against her seat belt. "Did it work?" she asked.

"It seemed to," I said. "Peter played football against the boy when they were in high school. According to Pete, he was a great offensive lineman and a nice guy."

"So that boy's parents made the right decision," Isobel said. "But Glenda Parker's parents didn't."

"It wasn't their fault," I said. "I'm sure the Parkers did the best they could with the information they were given."

Like her mother, Isobel was tenacious. "But they made a mistake," she said flatly, "and now Glenda has to have operations to change her body."

"The surgery is just a part of what she needs to do," I said. "Look, I have a copy of *Too Much Hope*. Why don't you two read the interview Glenda gave Kathryn Morrissey? After that, if you have more questions, just ask. Okay?"

"Okay," Taylor said. For a beat she was silent. "When did Glenda know?" she asked.

"That she was a girl?" I said. "She says she always knew."

"But she tried to be what her parents wanted her to be," Taylor said. "She tried and it just didn't work."

"Yes," I said. "That's what happened."

At that point, Willie was stricken with anxiety by the sight of a passing semi and began barking. By the time the girls calmed him, their attention had drifted to other matters. Lulled by their soft whispers and muted laughter, I gave myself over to the pleasures of driving to the cottage at Lawyers' Bay along a road I had driven a dozen times in the hazy heat of the summer just past.

It had been a pivotal summer for us all. As they had every year since law school, the partners of Falconer, Shreve, Altieri, and Wainberg had gathered at the lake for a Canada Day party. I had rented the cottage of a friend who had once been a Falconer Shreve partner, and my plans were simple: I would dedicate July to reading fat novels in a hammock, eating ice cream, and getting in some serious beach and tennis time with Taylor, and with Angus and his girlfriend, Leah Drache, who had found jobs at the lake. In August, my daughter Mieka and her family would join us and my older son, Peter, who had just bought a vet practice in Regina, would come up on weekends. Idyllic, but as Robbie Burns so famously said, "the best laid schemes of mice and men gang aft a-gley," and our plans had been shattered by a tragedy that ripped through the tranquil beauty of Lawyers' Bay with the primal destructive power of a hurricane. On the Canada Day weekend, Christopher Altieri committed suicide, and his death brought revelations that devastated the partners that had known and loved him since law school.

My first impulse had been to pack up and allow Chris's friends to grieve in private, but Zack Shreve urged me to stay, reasoning that his partners and their families needed to attach themselves to what, from now on, would pass as normal life. It was a sensible offer that turned out to benefit us all. During the month of August, the partners worked from the lake, going into the city only when professional demands made trips necessary. Most nights, we ate together; most days, in one combination or another, we came together for a walk, a swim, a bike ride, or a tennis game. Suddenly, there were many holes in the Falconer Shreve family, and my grown kids with their competitiveness, their bruising sibling humour, and their obvious love for one another smoothed over some bad moments. But the real joy had been my granddaughters. Wearing their flip-flops, bright bathing suits, and flowery sun hats, they solemnly dug holes in the sand and when the waves filled the holes with water, they dug again, reminding us all that, like it or not, life goes on.

August was a transforming month for Zack and me too. We had been drawn together by the heady mix of a hot summer night and powerful sexual attraction, but by the time the first leaves turned, we were not just lovers but friends. The deepening of our relationship surprised us both; so did the fact that Zack, who had always been a loner, gravitated towards my family and liked what he found. His relationship with Taylor and my grown sons was easy and uncomplicated; his relationship with Mieka less so, but he won my granddaughters' hearts and they won his. His wheelchair was an impediment to keeping up with an active three-year-old and a ten-month-old who could scurry across the sand like a crab, but Zack had an actor's voice, full timbered, rich, and strong, and he brought genuine feeling to the story of "The Pigeon and the Hot Dog" that was one of Maddy's summer favourites. She never tired of hearing Zack

repeat the Pigeon's description of a hot dog as being "a cele-
bration in a bun." Neither did I.

Zack had been so absorbed by his work that this was the
first time we'd all be at the lake together since Labour Day. It
would, in a very real sense, be a family reunion, and as I drove
past fields brilliant with the palette of a prairie autumn, I felt
my heart skip with anticipation. Zack was right. It was going
to be a great Thanksgiving.

If the first hours were any indication, the weekend was also
going to have its share of surprises. For starters, there was
an unexpected guest. When I approached the gate to the road
into Lawyers' Bay, my son Peter's blue half-ton was parked
by the side of the road. Peter was sitting on the tailgate, and
so was Howard Dowhanuik's son, Charlie.

Charlie was a complex man who evoked complex emo-
tions, but as I saw him lazily swinging his legs and blowing
smoke-rings from his cigarette, I felt a wash of pleasure. Of
all the Dowhanuik children, he was the one who had been
closest to Marnie and the one who, except in one chilling
particular, most resembled her physically. Charlie had his
mother's clear and penetrating hazel eyes, her finely carved
features, and her beautiful wavy hair, but Charlie also had a
birthmark that covered half his face like a bloodstain and
made strangers avert their eyes.

I rolled down my window. "Perfect timing," I said. "I've
got a ton of stuff to unload."

As soon as he heard my voice, Charlie jumped off the tailgate and came over. "I'll do whatever it takes to cadge a free
weekend," he said. "This was a last-minute decision. I didn't
have time to call and ask if I could join the party." His voice,
rich and comforting as dark honey, was Charlie's livelihood.
His national radio show – part music, part advice, part riffs

on life – was wildly popular with the hotly lusted after fifteen to twenty-five demographic.

I grinned at him. "You can stay, and as soon as I park the car, you can get started."

"Bring it on," Charlie said. "I'm thin, but I'm wiry."

Peter had followed Charlie over. My son gave me a peck on the cheek. "Charlie has promised to behave himself."

Charlie ground his cigarette into the dirt, then picked up the dead butt and slipped into his jeans' pocket. "Environmentally responsible," he said. "Am I off to a good start?"

"Dazzling," I said.

After I punched in the numbers that opened the gates to the cottages on Lawyers' Bay, Pete and Charlie hopped into Pete's truck and followed me in. As soon as we pulled up in front of Zack's cottage, Willie and the girls were out of the car. When the girls started off, I called them back. "Not so fast," I said. "The car needs to be unloaded."

"Let them have fun," Charlie said. "I can pick up the slack. Truthfully, Jo, I'm glad to be here." His tone was no longer playful. "I spent most of the afternoon chatting with cops – hard to do a radio show when you've got two orangutans in blue uniforms sitting across from you looking bored."

"What was the problem?" I asked.

"A bomb," Charlie said.

"At Falconer Shreve," I said. "I know about it. Why were the police talking to you?"

"I was the one who got the call from the mad bomber."

I felt a chill. "What did the person who called you say?"

"He or she – I couldn't tell which, quoted Shakespeare. 'If you wrong us, shall we not revenge?'"

"*The Merchant of Venice*," I said.

Charlie raised an eyebrow. "I guess whoever made the call didn't get to the part where Portia talks about the quality of mercy. The cops seem to think the bomb was intended to kill."

"Did they have any ideas about who it was supposed to kill?"

Charlie and my son exchanged a quick glance.

"Mum's going to find out sooner or later," Peter said.

Charlie shrugged. "The bomb exploded in the clients' room outside Zachary Shreve's office. Apparently, Zack wasn't there at the time."

"He was in the bathroom," I said.

"Well, he caught a break there," Charlie said. "Because I guess his office is pretty well toast."

CHAPTER

3

Zack had been right when he'd said that threats were nothing new in my world. When my husband had been Attorney General, an increased volume of mad-dog phone calls and letters written in crayon was always a tipoff that a full moon was rising. As a member of *Canada Tonight*'s political panel for three years, I'd had my share of attention from the marginal and the delusional. Once, after our panel had sparred over the question of the nation's place in the forests of the nation, a caller who asserted that Christ would return when the last tree was felled paintballed our house. But the distance between a paintball and a bomb is a big jump, and as Charlie's words sunk in, I felt the familiar rat-a-tat of fear. The panic was short-lived. My cellphone rang just as I drove through the gate to Lawyers' Bay. It was Zack, and when I heard his large, warm voice, relief washed over me.

"Great timing," I said. "I just learned that you're in the market for a new office."

"Damn," he said. "I was hoping that particular piece of information wouldn't drift your way."

"Think again," I said. "This is Regina. Sooner or later everybody finds out everything."

"And you have already found out that I'm fine."

"Zack, you could have been killed."

"But I wasn't," he said. "So let's talk about something else. What's it like at the lake?"

I tried to match his insouciance. "Gorgeous," I said. "Not a cloud in the sky and there are leaves everywhere. The lawns look like they've been carpeted. The lake's a little choppy, but we'll be able to take the boat out."

"I'll hold on to that thought," Zack said. "It might just keep me from driving myself nuts trying to figure out how to win a case that is probably unwinnable."

"Where's that famous optimism of yours?"

"I'm still optimistic," Zack said. "I'm just not sure my optimism is justified. Anyway, as Gawain said, 'it's time for fate to take its course.'"

"Where did that come from? At lunch you didn't know who Gawain was."

"I looked him up on the Internet. Great story. Loved that Green Knight."

"You amaze me," I said. "Your office has just been bombed, you've got this huge case going on, and you're playing around on the Internet."

"It's a lawyer thing," Zack said. "I can't stand people knowing things I don't know. Anyway, gotta go."

"Okay," I said. "I'll see you at the lake." But it was too late. He was already gone.

During his first hour at Lawyers' Bay, Charlie Dowhanuik was on his best behaviour. Our family was spread out over three of the five cottages: the place that I'd rented the summer before from Kevin Hynd; the house that the late Chris Altieri's partners had bought from his estate to use for guests, and Zack's. That meant that, in addition to unloading the car and getting dinner started, we had to air out three houses, make beds, and distribute more fresh towels than I cared to think about. Charlie's manic energy was a godsend. By the time Mieka, Greg, and the little girls arrived, the cottages were ready; the big table in Zack's sunroom was set for dinner; the casseroles I'd brought from home were in the oven, and the burgundy was breathing.

As always, the first few moments with Mieka, Greg, and the granddaughters were chaotic. As soon as she was liberated from her car seat, Maddy streaked for the lake. Quick as cats, Taylor and Isobel streaked after her. Lena, aware she was missing something, squirmed out of her mother's arms and crawled after her sister. I scooped her up. In her small fist, she was clutching a Cheezie, sodden and half-chewed. I nuzzled her hair. "Who's the luckiest grandma in the whole world?" I asked, and she rewarded me with a dazzling orange smile.

Mieka reached out to hug me. "It's nice to have the luckiest grandma close enough for a handoff. I'm bushed."

"Long week?" I asked.

Mieka sighed. "They're all long," she said. Greg put his arm around her shoulders. They were the same height, five-foot-eight. They had been together since they were eighteen, and in those days they had both been pleasantly rounded, but over the years, Mieka had grown very thin, and when I bought my son-in-law the Tilley shorts he was wearing, I'd been careful to order extra-large. On a good day, they made jokes about their reversal of the fates of Jack Spratt and his wife, but today was clearly not a good day. They both looked careworn.

Greg filled his lungs with pungent lake air and exhaled with a sigh. "It's good to be away from the city," he said.

"Problems with the business?" I asked.

"Nope. It's thriving," Greg said. He'd been a stockbroker, but when Mieka's catering business took off, he'd quit to manage their company. "Your daughter has a knack for knowing what people want to eat. We're getting a lot of corporate work, which is great, but we need to expand."

Mieka shrugged off his embrace. "Can we talk about this later . . . please?" She read the worry on my face. "Sorry, I didn't mean to snap. It's no big deal."

"Anything that affects you is a big deal," I said. "Why don't I take Willie and Lena down to the lake and give you two a chance to settle in?"

"Thanks," Greg said. "We could use a few minutes alone."

"Take all the time you need," I said. "There's wine on the counter, beer in the refrigerator, and fresh sheets on the bed. We'll be eating around six-thirty." I tightened my hold on Lena. "Ready for an adventure, little girl?"

Charlie seemed to appear out of nowhere. "Little girls are always ready for an adventure. Right, Mieka?" He had changed T-shirts. The new one was black, with the words *I Leave Bite Marks* written in spidery script across his thin chest. He took my daughter's hand in his. "You and your husband can have a glass of wine together any night," he said. "I'm a limited-time offer." With that, he dragged my daughter, laughing but not protesting, towards the tip of the bay's northern headland.

Greg shook his head in amazement. "Charlie still sucks up all the oxygen, doesn't he?" He shrugged. "I may not be charismatic, but I am reliable. I'll get us unpacked."

I touched his arm. "Mieka did look as if she could use a little fun," I said.

"Agreed," Greg said. "I just wish she was having fun with me."

Shorelines offer infinite possibilities for discovery and, after Taylor and Isobel left to explore the changes at the lake since Labour Day, my granddaughters and I puttered, oblivious to everything except the fascinating things that happened when we poked our sticks into the sand at the edge of the water. Good times, but we live on the forty-ninth parallel, and dusk comes early in October. When the last rays of the sun stopped reaching us, we wiped the sand from our hands and went back for dinner.

We were eating at Zack's because his kitchen was the best equipped and his sunroom had a spectacular view of the lake. A mahogany partners' table with fourteen matching chairs dominated the room. Outsized, ornate, and out of fashion, the set had gone cheap at a country auction. In its daytime life, the dark expanse of shining mahogany conjured up images of anxious heirs gathered for the reading of a wealthy relative's last will and testament, but at night, set for dinner and warmed by candlelight, the table was welcoming.

I'd made beef bourguignon, a dish that was one of my son-in-law's favourites. As the lid was removed from the yellow enamelled cast-iron casserole Greg and Mieka had given me for my last birthday, the aroma of beef and wine and mushrooms drifted towards us, drawing us together to dip baguette into rich winy sauce, drink a good but not great burgundy, and exchange news of our lives.

Our talk that night was light-hearted and punctuated by laughter. Just as we sat down to eat, Angus called to say he and Leah had arrived safely in New York and that Slava had scored tickets for the Yankee game the next day. The seats Slava got were right over the dugout, and, as she often did, Mieka led the discussion about how Angus had been born with horseshoes up his ass. Pete, who was seldom the centre of attention, had some funny stories about his adventures opening a vet clinic in the inner city, and Isobel Wainberg was rapt.

"I'd like to be a vet too," she said. "Only I'd like to work in East Africa with elephants and water buffalo and lions and leopards and rhinos."

Mieka smiled at Isobel. "When I was your age, I wanted to be a caterer. Boring, huh?"

Charlie swooped. "There's nothing boring about you. I remember when you wanted to be Laurie in the Partridge family, rockin' and rollin' across the country in a Day-Glo bus, thumping a keyboard and singing backup for your brother and me."

"That's what I wanted when I was six," Mieka said.

"Being six is a state of mind," Charlie said. "I'm still rockin' and rollin'. I have groupies. I get fan mail. I just don't have a Laurie Partridge, with braces on her teeth, thumping the keyboard and singing backup." Charlie turned to my daughter with an intensity that suggested the comments were no longer a joke. "The job's open, Mieka. Interested?"

The charge that passed between Charlie to Mieka was too powerful to ignore. It had to be short-circuited or redirected. "I have some news," I said. "I had a call from *Canada Tonight*. They want me to do a nightly report on the Sam Parker trial."

"Cool," Taylor said.

"Better than cool," Charlie said. "We can be co-conspirators, Joanne, subtly convincing the Canadian public that Sam Parker deserves to be a free man."

"I thought journalists were supposed to be objective," Greg said.

Charlie looked at him coldly. "Nobody's objective. Emily Dickinson says, 'Tell all the truth but tell it slant.' In this case, slant is justified. Sam Parker's a hero."

"A hero who shot a woman while she was sitting in her backyard." Greg's tone was caustic.

Charlie's eyes flashed. "The woman in question deserved to be shot."

Her radar vibrating to unfamiliar tensions, Maddy's gaze moved from the noodles and slivers of beef on her plate to her father and Charlie.

Greg gave Charlie a warning look. "Time to change the subject."

Charlie gave him a mock salute. "Right-o," he said. He turned to the rest of us. "You heard the man. Party's over." He began picking up plates.

"I'll give you a hand," Pete said.

"And I'll get dessert," Mieka said.

Greg watched them disappear into the kitchen and sighed. "Sorry, Jo, I didn't mean to ruin the dinner."

"Dinner's not ruined, just temporarily derailed. And I was the one who brought up the Sam Parker trial. No matter what we say or don't say, it's going to be the elephant in the living room this weekend – especially with Charlie here."

Greg ran a hand through his crewcut. "Every time I see Charlie, I'm glad we live in different cities."

"I'll try to run interference for you."

"I appreciate the offer, but I'm a big boy. So is Charlie. Someone should tell him that his act is getting a little stale. 'Look at me. See what I've done. Guess what I'm going to do next?'" Greg shook his head in disgust. "We don't let our girls behave like that."

"Does Mieka share your opinion of Charlie?"

"Are you kidding? She and Pete and Charlie have this primal loyalty thing going. It goes back to when they were kids. There are months when they don't connect at all, then one of them gets a problem and they're joined at the navel."

"Who's the one with the problem now?" I asked.

Greg's face tightened, then he looked past me and the tension disappeared. "Not Lena," he said softly. "She appears to have packed it in for the day." He reached over and removed his sleeping daughter from the high chair.

Mieka came in from the kitchen carrying a tray with apple pie, ice cream, and dessert plates. Charlie was behind her with the coffee. I reached for my granddaughter. "I'll take the baby, Greg," I said. "You stay here with the others and have your dessert."

Mieka glanced at her husband. "You stay," she said. "You love apple pie. I'll go with Mum. Madeleine looks like she's flagging too." She leaned over and picked up her daughter. "Time for bed, short stuff."

I patted Willie's flank. "Better get a move on," I said. "This is a tough crowd. Nobody here is going to let you lick the bowl."

The night was cool, still, and star-lit – and there was a bonus. "Madeleine, look at the sky," I said. "That's a harvest moon."

"Goodnight, moon," she said. Then, unbidden, she began to pipe the words with which three generations of children, including my own, had been lulled to sleep. As Maddy told the story of the small rabbit who prolonged his bedtime by saying goodnight to everything in his great green room, Mieka and I slowed our pace. Even Willie waited without complaint. Maddy didn't miss a word. When she was through, I caught my daughter's gaze.

"This is as good as it gets," I said.

"I know," Mieka said, and there was a catch in her voice. "You don't need to beat me over the head with your motherly subtlety. I know I'm lucky: two healthy kids, a kind husband, a family who loves me. I'm just tired and PMSing and I'm thirty-one years old and I have to figure a few things out."

"And Charlie's helping."

"He's a good listener," Mieka said. "He doesn't jump in to tell me I should be grateful that my cup's full, when I know it's overflowing."

"The way I just did," I said.

"You meant well," Mieka said.

"Don't put that on my gravestone," I said.

I juggled Lena so I could open the door to the cottage. Unlike the rest of the summer homes at Lawyers' Bay, the cottage where Mieka and Greg were staying was a real cottage: shabby, comfortable, and filled with photographs and memorabilia from decades of happy summers. It smelled the way a cottage should – of wood smoke and the fishy-weedy odour that works its way into bathing suits and beach towels and never comes out no matter how much time they spend airing on the line.

Greg had turned down the girls' beds and left their pyjamas on their pillows: Madeleine's were pink fleece with cupcakes and lollipops, and Lena's were mauve with a pattern of hearts. I shoehorned Lena into her pyjamas and Mieka took Madeleine to the bathroom. In a few minutes they were back. "Smell my breath," Madeleine said. "We got princess toothpaste."

I put my nose next to her mouth and inhaled deeply. "You're right," I said. "There's a definite fragrance of princess."

Her face lit up. "A joke," she said. She climbed into bed and was asleep before her head hit the pillow.

Mieka and I exchanged glances. "They're both down for the count," I said. "Why don't you go back and get your dessert?"

Mieka shook her head. "No, I think I'll stay here with my old mother and absorb her wisdom."

We went back to the living room, and Mieka stretched out on one of the tartan-covered mom-and-pop chairs by the fireplace. I sat in the chair next to hers, and Willie flopped down beside me. "So what do you want to talk about?" I asked.

"Charlie," Mieka said.

"I'm afraid I don't have any expert knowledge there."

"I wasn't asking for insight – just advice. Charlie wants to know if he should go back to the city." She picked at her lip – a sign of anxiety from the time she was three. "I hate seeing Greg and Charlie at each other's throats, but Charlie needs to be with people this weekend. That's why I invited him to come to the lake."

"*You* invited him?"

Mieka frowned. "Did you think he just showed up?"

"No. I just assumed Pete ran into him somewhere, and you know how Pete is about strays."

"Well, you were partly right. Charlie is kind of lost at the moment." She hugged her knees to herself. "Mum, did it never occur to Howard that by blabbing about Charlie's childhood, he was destroying the image Charlie worked his whole life to create."

"The publicity didn't hurt Charlie's career," I said. "There was an article in the paper a couple of weeks ago saying the ratings for Charlie's new show have gone through the roof."

Mieka's laugh was bitter. "So this was a good career move for Charlie. Is that what you're saying? Mum, take a giant step back. You had a rotten childhood. Would you like the whole world to know that you're still trying to get over it?"

I shook my head. "No."

"Then don't minimize what Howard did to Charlie. I was there, and I remember. Charlie and Pete and I logged a lot of time in drafty halls when Howard was premier and Daddy was Attorney General."

"Did you hate it?"

Mieka smiled. "No. For Pete and me, it was a lot of fun. No supervision. Awesome food. Remember those peanut butter squares with the coloured marshmallows? And those teeny tiny rolled sandwiches at the teas? I always meant to ask you how you got the bread so flat."

"We ironed it."

Mieka chortled. "Oh God, you didn't."

"Oh God, we did." I took her hand. "We have some good memories."

"Charlie doesn't," Mieka said.

"Because of his birthmark."

"You know how kids are. I was always glad Pete and I were there."

"As allies."

"Yeah, as allies. Charlie never needed anybody to fight his battles, but it mattered to him that Pete and I were on his side."

"Charlie's mother always said that he didn't have friends; he had fans . . ."

"That's because Charlie's a danger freak."

"Look at me. See what I've done. Guess what I'm going to do next."

Mieka raised an eyebrow. "Pretty much," she said. Her face darkened, and she fell silent.

"Something wrong?"

She shuddered. "Just one of those flashbacks. Remember that boy Charlie beat up in Fairlight?"

"No," I said.

Mieka shook her head. "You have to remember that, Mum. The boy was unconscious. They took him away in an ambulance."

"I remember being in Fairlight waiting for an ambulance," I said. "It was winter and the roads were terrible. The boy's parents were frantic. We were all afraid the ambulance wouldn't get through. But, Mieka, that boy fell down a fire escape."

"He didn't fall down a fire escape," Mieka said. "He and Charlie got into a fight. Pete and I thought Charlie was going to kill him. We tried to pull Charlie off, but he was like an animal. We finally managed to get them apart, but by then the other kid was in really bad shape."

"Why didn't you tell us?"

Mieka's eyes widened. "Weren't you ever a kid? I was so scared that boy would die. I kept listening to the news and reading the obituaries. Of course, I only knew his first name. It was Vernon."

"His last name was Harvey. His parents were long-time supporters. And Vernon Harvey didn't die, Mieka. He grew up and ran against us in the last election."

Mieka grinned. "Wow, talk about alienating a supporter."

It was close to 8:30 when the men joined us. Mieka and I had our feet up on the hassocks and were sharing a pot of tea. Pete gave us a withering glance. "Tough life," he said. "Some of us have been scrubbing pots and pans."

"Be grateful," I said. "Good karma."

"We'll return the favour tomorrow," Pete said. He yawned and stretched. "Speaking of which, I'm calling it a day. I'm going fishing at the crack of dawn. Anyone care to join me?"

Charlie shuddered. "Not me. I'm a nocturnal animal."

"I wouldn't mind going fishing," Greg said. He went over and touched Mieka's shoulder. "Okay with you?"

She looked up at him. "Sure, if you'll take me for a walk now. There's a harvest moon, and I have a moon story."

Greg's face lit with the delight of a man receiving an unexpected gift. "I'll get your jacket," he said.

Charlie appeared about to make his move. I caught his eye and indicated the chair Mieka had just vacated. "Why don't you and I get caught up? It's been a while."

Charlie's smile was vulpine. "Very subtle, but I'll play along because I want to talk about the trial."

"Okay with me," I said.

Charlie slouched on the chair, legs stretched in front of him, hands clasped behind his neck. "Your boyfriend has to win this one," he said.

"He's giving it his best shot," I said. "He believes in Sam's case, and he likes him. He likes Glenda too."

"Glenda is a likeable person," Charlie said.

"You two know each other?"

"When *Too Much Hope* came out, I got in touch with all of Katherine Morrissey's subjects. The plan was to get them to come on my show, talk about the book. Counting me, there were thirteen – a baker's dozen of the misbegotten – about half of them were so fucked by drugs or booze that they couldn't even comprehend what I was talking about. But some of the others were impressive. I don't suppose you heard the show the night Olivia Quinn was on."

"No," I said. "Now, of course, I wish I had. At the time, the only interest I had in *Too Much Hope* was what it was doing to you and your father."

"And now you know," Charlie said.

I touched his arm. "I saw your father today. Charlie, he's going through hell."

"A hell of his own making," Charlie said crisply. "Like all our hells. Now let's get back to something relevant. Do you want me to send you the tape of the Olivia Quinn interview."

"Yes," I said. "I'd like to know how she's doing."

"Consider it done," he said. "Actually, I can send you all the tapes. If you're going to be covering the Sam Parker trial, you should know what the book did to Katherine's victims."

"I agree," I said. "Context is always useful."

Charlie raised his arms above his head and looked at his hands thoughtfully. His skin was, in the title of the old song, a whiter shade of pale. "Glenda Parker thought so too," he

said. "She called me the morning after the shooting and vol-
unteered to go on my show that night."

"That surprises me," I said. "I just met Glenda for a few
minutes today, but she seemed like a person who valued
her privacy."

"She is," Charlie said. "But she values her father more."
Charlie sat up and swivelled to face me. "She's an amazing
person. The night she came to the studio must have been
one of the worst nights of her life. Her private life was suddenly public property, and her family was shattered. But
Glenda had a job to do and she did it."

"What was her job?"

"She wanted people to know that her father was a decent
man and a loving father. She talked about the good times she
and Sam had together when she was growing up – how proud
he was of her when she started swimming competitively.
Apparently, he never missed a swim meet." Charlie's face
hardened. "Of course, as the child of a man who was absent
during my entire life, I found that impossible to believe . . ."

"But Glenda convinced you."

"Yes, and I'm not easily convinced. Glenda was as close
to the edge as anyone I've ever interviewed. We had to tape
because the network had legal concerns, but it was still a
dynamite interview. Glenda talked about how scared she
was when she realized that the feeling she was a girl trapped
in a boy's body wasn't going to go away. She was ten years
old. That's when she started competitive swimming. It was
a gutsy act for a kid. Glenda thought that if she was forced to
compete publicly with a body that was demonstrably male,
she might start to feel like a boy."

"But it never happened."

"No. In her words, the knowledge that she was female
engulfed her. When she finally faced the fact that the only

way she could live her life was as a woman, she went straight to her father."

"And he was accepting."

"Yes. It wasn't easy for him. I guess it wouldn't be easy for any parent, but he was Sam Parker, the defender of family values. To his credit, Sam didn't flay Glenda with chapter and verse about moral abominations. According to Glenda, he took her in his arms and he didn't let go."

I felt a lump in my throat. "I'd like to hear that interview."

"My pleasure," Charlie said. "It's unedited except for one sentence."

"Which was?"

"Just before we stopped taping, Glenda said, 'I'd kill for him too, you know.'" Charlie averted his gaze. "Imagine loving your father that much."

For a few moments, we sat in silence. There didn't seem to be much to say. I think we were both relieved when my cellphone rang and it was Zack asking where the hell I was. Within seconds, a car stopped outside the Hynd cottage. Charlie leapt to his feet. "Must be the Big Man," he said.

I went to the window. Zack's Jaguar was in the driveway. "Good call," I said.

Charlie joined me and the two of us watched as Zack unfolded his chair, snapped it into position, and swung his body from the driver's seat onto the seat of his chair. When Zack started up the path to the house, Charlie put his arm around my shoulder. His body was painfully thin. "Mieka told me she was going to ask you if I should leave. What do you think?"

"It's Thanksgiving," I said. "People should be with people they love."

"Thank you," he said. "That means a lot. Now, I'll get the rock out of here, and leave you and Zack alone."

"Stick around long enough to say hello," I said.

Charlie shrugged. "My pleasure," he said.

Zack was still wearing the suit he had on at lunch, and he looked exhausted, but his voice was eager. "Ms. Kilbourn, you are a welcome sight." His gaze shifted to Charlie. "And you're here," he said, extending his hand. "I hope you're staying for the weekend?"

"That's the plan," Charlie said.

"Good," Zack said. "Then we'll have a chance to talk. Incidentally, that's a great T-shirt."

"Glad you approve," Charlie said.

After he left, Zack looked at me questioningly.

"Mieka invited him," I said. "I take it you don't mind."

"Not at all. Charlie Dowhanuik is a useful person to have around." Zack glanced around the cottage. "So where is everybody?"

"Well, let's see. Angus and Leah made it safely to New York. Pete already hit the sack because he wants to go fishing tomorrow. Willie and I are babysitting the little girls till Mieka and Greg get back from their walk in the moonlight. Taylor and Isobel are at our place watching a movie."

He grinned. "Hey, I like the sound of that 'our place.'"

"And you don't mind that the girls are staying with us?"

"We said we wanted a big family Thanksgiving. Taylor is family, and Isobel is part of the closest thing I have to a family. I value this, Ms. Kilbourn. When I was driving out here tonight, I was trying to remember what I did last Thanksgiving, and I drew a blank. Then I tried to think of what I'd done other Thanksgivings – more blanks. I don't care who sleeps where, as long as everybody's content and you're with me."

CHAPTER

4

Zack's paraplegia affected every area of his life. There were the everyday frustrations of living in a world that often was not accessible; there were times when he was assaulted by muscle spasms or by pain in his shoulders that had simply been performing too many functions for too long. There were complications that arose because the body's organs and circulatory system are not designed to be locked in a partially paralyzed body. Despite all this, Zack was neither stoic nor bitter. He accepted his deeply flawed body as unquestioningly as he accepted his thousand-megahertz mind. For him it was all part of the package.

I tried to follow his lead, and most of the time I succeeded. But he was the most exciting man I'd ever known and I was deeply in love with him. I wanted the casual intimacies that I'd always taken for granted: strolling hand in hand through the park, a quick, spontaneous embrace, a passionate and unpremeditated kiss. More than anything, I wanted to spend entire nights with him, but that dream had proved elusive.

The logistical problems that confronted us were easily solved. The bedrooms in my house were on the second floor, but Zack had an apartment, and Taylor was certainly old enough for sleepovers at the houses of friends. However, she was also old enough to be forming ideas about sexual behaviour, and I wanted to set a good example. My younger daughter was surprisingly open on the subject of what her peers called "hooking up," and we had some frank discussions about the mechanics of sex. More importantly, we had talked a lot about the hollowness of sex without mutual respect, affection, and commitment. Given the circumstances, I wanted to make certain that the relationship between Zack and me was serious before we were open about sharing a bed. By Thanksgiving, we knew, and we had arranged the sleeping arrangements accordingly.

The week had been a full one, and Zack and I were both exhausted. As I slid across the cool sheets and embraced him, it was clear that a deep and serious kiss was going to be the extent of our lovemaking. But some time in the small hours I had awakened, aware of Zack's body warmth and his weight beside me, I drew closer to him and touched my fingers to the side of his neck, feeling the pulse, listening to the rhythm of his breathing, inhaling the scent of his skin. It was a comfort to feel his body beside me, and I was suddenly aware of how much I had missed the solace of lying next to another human being in the darkness. It was good not to be alone, but like the poet Ben Jonson, I knew that love made me vulnerable. Any wound to the man beside me would be a wound to me. The knowledge brought a pang of joy and fear. I moved my head onto Zack's chest and watched the pale outline of my fingers rise and fall against his skin. I turned my head and kissed his left nipple.

Zack stirred in his sleep. "Am I about to get lucky?" he murmured.

I shifted my position and felt his erection. "I think we both are," I said.

Our lovemaking was unhurried and incredibly sweet, and after the great headlong rush we luxuriated in the novelty of drifting off, side by side, hands touching, separate but still connected.

I slept deeply, and when Willie nuzzled me awake to take him for his walk, the pattern of light and shadows in the room jolted me with its unfamiliarity. Then I turned my head, saw my beloved, and my pulse slowed. I was exactly where I belonged. Reassured, I slid out of bed, pulled on my sweatshirt and jeans, tied my runners, and Willie and I hit the road.

Lawyers' Bay is a horseshoe, and Willie and I had run along its beach for an entire summer. In July and August the lake had been alive with the sounds of shorebirds squawking, motorboats roaring, and kids shrieking as they leapt off the high board of the diving tower, but that morning we ran in a silent world. By the time we doubled back, the haunting half-light of dawn filled the sky, and the series of Inukshuk that Taylor, Isobel, and their friend, Gracie Falconer, had painstakingly built along the shoreline were emerging: eerily human, ghostly figures pointing our way home in grey morning light.

When I got back to the cottage, I checked on Taylor and Isobel. They were sleeping the sleep of young women who had eaten pizza, watched DVDs, and giggled far into the night. In our room, Zack, who slept five hours a night whether he needed it or not, was propped up in bed, peering through his glasses at the contents of a file folder. When he saw me he placed his file on the nightstand and motioned me over. "Did you two have a good run?"

"We did," I said, bending to kiss him.

He shuddered. "Cold lips."

"Cold everything," I said. "It's chilly out there."

Zack held up the covers. "Then get in here with me." I took off my jeans and slid in close.

"Better?"

"Much," I said.

Zack rubbed my shoulders. "Do you know what I want to do?" he asked.

I groaned. "If it involves a feat of athleticism, you're going to have to give me time to catch my breath."

"No heroics required," Zack said. "I want to keep doing what we just did. I want to go to bed with you at night, fool around with you in the middle of the night, and wake up with you in the morning."

"I want that too," I said.

"Good, because I've started looking for a house for us – an accessible house where I can trail around after you to my heart's content."

"You want us to move in together?"

"I want us to get married."

"We've only known each other three months."

His eyes were searching. "You're not sure about us."

I met his gaze. "I'm sure," I said. "I'm just not ready."

"Fair enough," he said. "So I'll keep looking for a house and when you're ready, we'll get married and move in."

"You make it sound so simple."

"Life is simple. You decide what you want and you go for it."

"Right now, I want to eat."

He chuckled. "Go for it."

I made coffee and porridge, and we took our breakfast into the sunroom so we could watch morning come to the lake. Peter and Greg were down at the dock putting fishing gear into the boat, shrugging on their life jackets.

"Charlie isn't going fishing?" Zack asked.

"No, and it's probably just as well. He sets Greg's teeth on edge."

"Bad chemistry?" Zack said.

"Bad chemistry exacerbated by bad timing," I said. "Mieka's going through a rough patch in her life."

"I wondered about that. There were times this summer when she had that five-mile stare. So what's the problem?"

"Do you remember that Peggy Lee song 'Is That All There Is?'"

"Sure." Zack sang a few bars in the boozy bass of a lounge singer.

I shook my head. "Is there no end to your talents?"

"Give me fifty years and I'll show you."

"In fifty years, I'll be a hundred and six."

"And I'll still be crazy about you. But we were talking about Mieka."

"Right," I said. "Lately I've had the sense she feels the walls are closing in on her. She and Greg have been married since she was twenty-one, and she's been running her business since she was nineteen. Catering's not easy – the hours are unpredictable and customers can be fractious. Mieka loves the girls, but according to Greg the business is really taking off, and the company needs to expand. It would be a major commitment for them, and I think Mieka's wondering if it's a commitment she wants to make."

"And while Mieka's wondering, along comes Charlie." Zack sprinkled brown sugar on his porridge. "Is it a romance?"

"I don't think so, but in a way that would be easier to handle. Mieka's relationship with Charlie goes deeper than sex. When they were kids, she and Pete and Charlie did that blood kin thing – you know, where each kid cuts his finger and they let their blood flow together. I'm sure most children forget all about it, but with those three it seemed to take. They share a history, and last night Charlie was using that history to shut Greg out."

"Do you want me to see if I can get Charlie to open up?" Zack asked.

"How well do you know him, anyway?"

Zack averted his eyes. "Well enough."

"It would be good to know how Charlie sees the situation," I said. "But don't use your brass knuckles. I have a soft spot for Charlie. You should too. Last night he told me about the interview he did with Glenda just after Sam Parker was arrested."

"We have a tape of it at the office," Zack said. "It got Sam a lot of good press at the beginning. Very helpful."

"That's because before the take aired, Charlie did a little editing."

Zack's spoon stopped in mid-air. "He never mentioned that. What did he take out?"

"According to Charlie, at the end of the interview, Glenda said, 'I would have killed for him too.'"

Zack winced. "Jesus. People are full of surprises, aren't they? That line of Glenda's would have made Charlie's show front-page news."

"Maybe Charlie knows there's more to life than ratings," I said.

"You think he identifies with Glenda?"

"I know he does," I said. "They'd both had painful childhoods. They were both in the process of making lives for themselves, and they were both betrayed and publicly humiliated."

Zack sipped his coffee meditatively. "Still, the decision to edit that line could have gone either way. Thank God, Charlie did the right thing."

"Thank Charlie's mother too," I said. "In all the years I knew her, Marnie never knowingly caused another person pain. She had a truly generous spirit – not a moralizing bone in her body."

"Glenda's mother, Beverly, is cut from more rigid cloth," Zack said dryly.

"You've met her, then."

"Sure. She's the one who hired me. I had to go to Calgary so she could check out the cut of my jib."

"She interviewed you?"

Zack frowned at the memory. "Not exactly. She tried to convert me."

"What did you do?"

"I told her my billable rate was $600 an hour, and she was on the clock. It didn't stop her. She's a True Believer."

"She believes in The Rapture," I said. "I read about it when I was doing research for my book. Legions of the Antichrist on the march. A final showdown in Armageddon. The Second Coming. And of course, the grand finale when the True Believers ascend into heaven, sit on God's right hand, and watch their enemies suffer the horrors of the damned."

"Nice précis," Zack said. "Beverly was more discursive. She went on for about an hour and a half."

"And you charged her?"

"You bet I did, and now that I've seen the way she treats Glenda, I wish I'd billed double."

"I still remember the Bev Parker of Sam and Bev," I said. "Her hair was the colour of toffee, and her voice sounded the way good toffee tastes – melting and sweet with a little burn to give it edge."

"Well, now her hair is – what's that really blonde blonde?"

"Platinum," I said.

"Right," Zack said. "And her voice is hard and very angry." Zack fell silent, seemingly engrossed in the efforts of a squirrel trying to break into the squirrel-proof bird feeder the girls had put up during the summer. When the squirrel gave up and moved along, Zack turned to me. "You think he'll find something to eat?" he said.

"Sure. The girls left nine dollars' worth of sunflower seeds on the ground by that tree where he has his nest."

"A lot of stuff goes on around here that I don't know about," Zack said.

"I'll start sending a daily update to your BlackBerry." I picked up the coffee carafe and refilled our cups. "I wonder what happened to turn the Bev I remember into the Beverly you met."

Zack shrugged. "I'm no expert. The only time Sam and I discussed his wife was over a bottle of Scotch late one night. He is absolutely loyal to her. And he either can't or won't talk about what caused her to change. All he told me was that when Judgment Day rolls around, Beverly believes she'll have a front-row seat to watch her enemies suffer."

"And it doesn't trouble her that her only child will be among the sufferers."

"That doesn't seem to be a matter of concern."

He stared at his empty bowl as if seeing it for the first time. "Is there more porridge? This was really good."

I stood up. "I'll get it."

"I can get it," Zack said. He balanced his bowl on his knees and wheeled towards the kitchen. When he took the pot from the stove, he peered at it with interest. "What's in this anyway?"

"Oatmeal, of course, but also poppy seeds and dried cran-berries. There are supposed to be sunflower seeds in there too, but the girls gave them to your pal, the squirrel."

He wheeled back into the sunroom and started eating. "Do you think Charlie will be up yet?"

"You want to talk to him?"

"I need to know who he told about that sentence he edited from the tape."

"My guess is no one, but if you're anxious, give him a few more hours of sack time before you pay him a visit. Charlie isn't a morning person."

"Fair enough," Zack said. "So what are you up to this morning?"

"I promised Madeleine I'd teach her how to make pancakes. After that, Mieka and I are taking all the girls into Fort Qu'Appelle to the farmers' market. It's the last one till next summer."

Zack looked wistful. "Sounds like fun."

"You're welcome to come," I said.

"I've got way too much work." He covered my hand with his. "It's not always going to be like this."

"There's nothing wrong with this," I said.

The kitchen in the Hynd cottage caught the early light, and Lena had found a patch of sunshine on the floor in which to test out the bouncing properties of Tupperware. Madeleine was at the table with a whisk and a bowl and when she saw me she waved her whisk in the air. "I broke four eggs," she said.

"Without getting a single piece of shell in the bowl," Mieka said approvingly.

"Her mother's daughter," I said. "Let me wash my hands, and we'll get started."

When I rolled up my sleeves, Mieka glanced at my fingers. "You're not wearing your wedding ring," she said quietly.

"It was time to put it away," I said.

"You and Alex were together three years, and you always wore your ring. You're with Zack three months and it's gone."

"Does it bother you?"

As she carried the canister of flour to the table, Mieka's lips were a line.

"You still don't like Zack," I said.

"What's not to like? He's smart and he's rich." She shrugged. "Perfect."

"Maybe we should wait and talk about this later," I said. We both glanced at the girls. Madeleine was raising and lowering her whisk from the bowl so she could watch the egg drip; Lena was still absorbed in the miracles of plastic. They seemed oblivious. Mieka lowered her voice to a whisper. "I don't want to wait till later. You're not wearing your wedding ring, and that means it's serious. Mum, the people Zack defends are scum: murderers and bikers and bigots and rapists."

"Everyone's entitled to a defence, Mieka."

"Especially if they've got a whack of cash. From what I hear, Zack charges top dollar." She pointed at my wrist. "That bracelet he gave you for your birthday didn't come from Wal-Mart."

"Wal-Mart didn't have the bracelet I wanted. Nobody around here did. Charm bracelets with real charms are out of style. Zack went to a lot of trouble to find this." I held out my wrist so Mieka could see the chunky link bracelet more closely. "Those little ladybug charms open up," I said.

Her interest piqued, Madeleine turned to us. "Can *I* see?" she asked.

"Sure," I said. I undid the tiny clasp on the red and black enamel ladybug. Inside was a picture of Madeleine.

"That's me," she said.

"Right," I said. "And inside the green ladybug there's a picture of your sister." I knelt beside Lena and showed her "There you are," I said. Lena reached out, snapped the bug shut, and went back to her Tupperware.

I stood and slid an arm around my daughter's shoulders. "There's a lucky guy in Lena's future. Tupperware's cheaper than Tiffany's."

Unexpectedly, Mieka's eyes filled with tears. She fingered the remaining charm, a small gold disc. "What's this?"

"A Frisbee," I said. "The first time Zack and I went out together, we went to one of Angus's Ultimate Flying Disc games."

Mieka's flipped the disc over and read the inscription: "*Amor Fati*," she said.

"It's Latin," I said. "It means 'Love your Fate.'"

"Am I supposed to love your fate too?"

"No," I said, "but you are supposed to live with it." I handed the measuring cup to Madeleine. "See that line at the top. Start spooning flour in. When it gets to that line, you'll have enough to begin the pancakes."

Madeleine got a chance to do a lot of measuring. Just as we'd settled in to eat, Greg and Peter showed up – fishless and hungry. Then Taylor and Isobel drifted in. And so Madeleine cracked eggs and measured; Lena crumpled paper napkins, and Mieka and I stirred, flipped, and dished out.

There were many golden moments that weekend. The Thanksgiving farmers' market was an extravagant display of beauty and bounty: tables overflowing with root vegetables, so recently ripped from the earth that the dirt still clung to them; jars of jams, pickles, and preserves glowing with the brilliance of jewels; boxes of apples, pears, peaches, and plums fragrant from the gentle summer of British Columbia; heavy breads flecked with seeds and dried fruits; pies with pastry so light that even the wrap covering had flaked it; turkey-shaped cookies iced in garish, child-riveting colours; gourds whose curved phallic shapes conjured thoughts of a God with carnal pleasure on Her mind.

And pumpkins – hundreds of them – in every permutation and combination of size, shape, and colour. Halloween was three weeks away, and Taylor, Isobel, and Gracie Falconer were having a party. They had been scouring the Internet for ideas for a week, and their plans were elaborate. The party was going to be at our house, and the girls were going to turn our backyard into a haunted village of glowing jack-o'-lanterns. We needed a lot of pumpkins and so we cruised the stalls for possibilities: perusing, judging, and, finally, choosing. When we'd filled the trunks of both my car and Mieka's, we headed back to the cottage.

As I frequently did, I had left my cell at the house, and there was a message on it from Jill Oziowy. She was at the office, and when she picked up, she was curt. "Why do you bother having a cell if you never answer it?" she said.

"And Happy Thanksgiving to you," I said.

"Sorry. It's crazy around here."

"So go home," I said. "It's a holiday."

"Spoken like a woman in a relationship with a millionaire."

"I don't think Zack's a millionaire."

"Well, you're wrong. I checked him out. Anyway, I didn't call to talk about Daddy Warbucks. I just scored a live interview with Kathryn Morrissey. She's going to be the lead segment on the weekend *Canada Tonight*."

"Does Sam Parker's side get equal time?"

"No, because this isn't about the trial. It's about journalistic ethics."

"So why not interview a person who knows something about journalistic ethics?"

"Jo, you're supposed to remain neutral."

"Neutral as in letting Kathryn Morrissey shred Sam's reputation two nights before his trial begins?"

"Kathryn will be discussing how journalists pursue truth. Period. It has nothing to do with Sam Parker."

"Bullshit," I said. "You know NationTV wouldn't be letting Kathryn Morrissey deliver her Journalism 101 lecture in prime time if Sam Parker wasn't going on trial."

Jill's voice was icy. "The journalist's obligation to truth is at the core of this trial."

"What about the journalist's obligation to be ethical?"

"You are such a fucking moralist, Jo."

"Finished?"

"No. When I talked to Kathryn today, I told her you'd be doing a nightly piece on the trial for us. I also told her you were in a relationship with Sam's lawyer. She said that didn't worry her. She knew you'd be fair."

"And that's supposed to make me feel guilty?"

"It's supposed to make you reflect on the story I hired you to tell."

"Jill, we've been friends for thirty years, and I think we're about thirty seconds away from doing ourselves some serious damage. I'm going to hang up. Have a good Thanksgiving."

"I'll call you tomorrow night after the interview airs," Jill said and she hung up. No holiday wishes for me.

Zack worked through lunch. When he came over afterwards to take the little girls and me for a boat ride around the lake, I handed him a sandwich and told him about the Kathryn Morrissey interview.

"Well, that's shitty news," he said. Then he wolfed down his tuna salad sandwich.

"Good lunch," he said. "Thanks. Are the kids ready to go?"

"Are you really not bothered by this?"

"Sure, but I'm not going to let it wreck our day."

"Can you teach me how to compartmentalize?"

"No problem," he said. "Can you teach me how to make tuna salad?"

The day was windy, clear, and fresh, and Zack, who usually drove his Chris-Craft across the water at speeds that made my adrenalin pump, took it slow, staying within easy distance of the shoreline as he circled the lake. I was grateful. And there was something else. I had snapped Madeleine and Lena into matching life jackets that signalled their commitment to water safety with a cartoon of a whale and the legend "Buoy, oh boy." As always, I was wearing my life jacket. Standard procedure, but until that day Zack had habitually left his life jacket on the seat beside him: within reach if someone challenged him, but useless in an emergency. That afternoon, he slipped it on before we set out.

As I settled in behind him with the girls, I patted his shoulder approvingly. "Getting cautious in your old age?"

"Nope, just increasingly aware of the fact that I've got a lot to lose."

The sun was still warm at 5:00 p.m., so we fired up the barbeque, threw blankets on the leaf-littered lawn, and ate our burgers outside. After dinner, Mieka and Greg and Pete and Charlie took the boat out, and Zack and I sat, hand in hand, watching Madeleine and Lena play in the lengthening shadows of the trees. That night, intoxicated by fresh air and the novelty of spending the night together, we turned in early. By the time I'd finished brushing, flossing, and slathering on the Oil of Olay, Zack was in bed. I turned out the light and crawled in beside him.

He put his arm around me. "Happy?" he said.

"I am. How about you?"

"If you're happy, I'm happy."

I laughed. "You are such a smoothy. Speaking of which, did you and Charlie ever talk?"

"We did. I took your advice and waited till noon, but I still woke him up. I apologized and told him I had one quick question about the Glenda Parker interview. He assured me that he and Glenda were alone during the taping, and he hadn't told a soul about the edit."

"That's good news," I said.

"It is," Zack agreed. "And Charlie welcomed the opportunity to share it. He said it was important for me to know that I could trust him."

"A story with a happy ending," I said.

"The story's not over," Zack said. "Charlie offered to scramble me some eggs."

"And you took him up on his offer."

"Sure. I figured there was something on his mind, and this close to a trial, I don't leave any stone unturned. Besides, I was hungry."

"So what did Charlie want to talk about?"

"Fathers. He asked if I was close to my mine. I think if I had been, Charlie and I would have eaten our eggs and said sayonara. But lucky for me, I saw my old man precisely once and that was for less than an hour."

"That's the first time I've heard you mention your father."

"There's nothing to mention. Until three years ago, I'd never clapped eyes on the man. But the Hampton acquittal got a lot of media coverage, and my father saw me on television. He called the office, identified himself, and said he wanted to see me. I figured what the hell, so I met him for lunch."

"What was he like?"

I felt Zack's muscles tense. "He was a maggot. A piece-of-shit lawyer who ordered a number of very stiff drinks, pushed his food around on his plate, suggested I throw some business his way, and asked for a little something to tide him over."

"Did you give him money?"

"Sure. I wrote him a cheque. Quickest way to get rid of a maggot is to throw it some meat. He couldn't get to the bank quick enough. I guess he was afraid I'd change my mind. Anyway, he left me his business card and told me to stay in touch."

"But you didn't."

"Nope. After he left, I finished my wine, went to the can, ripped up his card, and flushed it down the toilet."

"He never came back for more money?"

"Many times. Norine handles it."

"By . . . ?"

"Giving him what he wants – in an envelope – sent through the mail. No more up-close-and-personal."

"Zack, I'm sorry –"

"Nothing to be sorry about," Zack said quickly, cutting me off. "Your turn now. What about your parents?"

"They're dead. My father was a doctor. My mother was an alcoholic. For most of my life she might as well have been dead."

"Wow. Both of us, eh?" Zack kissed me and for a moment everything else fell away. When he spoke his voice was gentle. "But we turned out all right, didn't we?"

"Yes," I said. "We turned out all right."

I drew closer and we lay side by side watching the play of light and shadows on the ceiling. "So what happened with Charlie?" I said finally.

"As promised, he made me eggs. While he was cooking, he riffed on all the variations of what he called 'the look' – the way people react when they're confronted with what he referred to as 'people like us.'"

"Meaning you and Charlie."

"Right – the crips and the freaks. There's nothing wrong with Charlie's powers of observation. He had all the responses down pat: the people who focus on a point just past your ear; the ones who keep shifting their eyes searching for a safe place to put rest their gaze; the ones who pretend they haven't noticed; the ones who stare openly. It was disarming."

"You really like him, don't you?"

"I don't know. There's a lot of anger there, but he has what my mother called 'hurting eyes.'"

"Charlie has more than his share of demons," I said.

"He keeps them in check," Zack said. "And I respect him for that. It's not easy coming up with a strategy for dealing with a world that doesn't know how to react to you." He drew me close. "And that's enough about Charlie."

Zack's breathing slowed, deepened, and became more rhythmic. He was asleep, but I lay in the dark for a long time, thinking about the man beside me and wondering about the strategies he used to keep his demons at bay.

Working on the premise that a holiday dinner is the responsibility of everybody who will eat it, the next morning we allocated tasks. And so while Mieka and I each stuffed a turkey, Greg, Peter, and Charlie peeled, chopped, sliced, and diced, and Taylor and Isobel set the table. Zack took care of Madeleine and Lena. He seemed an unlikely choice, but during the summer the little girls themselves made the selection. With the unerring instinct children and cats have for gravitating towards the one person in the world who is not particularly partial to them, Madeleine and Lena had designated Zack as their companion of choice.

Zack had been neither delighted nor appalled. He treated the little girls exactly as he treated everyone else: with undivided attention until it was time to move along. That morning, as the rest of us worked in the kitchen, he led Madeleine and Lena to the piano in the living room and thumped out show tunes while they danced.

The rest of the day passed with the usual benevolent blur of a family holiday that's working well. As we sat down for dinner, I had many reasons to give thanks. Isobel and Taylor had made a centrepiece of an old wooden dough box filled with pomegranates and miniature pumpkins and placed candles in brass hurricane lamps at intervals around the table. My granddaughters, fresh from their nap, were rested and happy. Best of all, everyone was getting along. Charlie was the model guest, and Mieka was making a real effort with Zack. In his self-cast role as paterfamilias, he was going to carve the Thanksgiving bird. Mieka was a professional caterer who had sliced a hundred turkeys, but when Zack approached her for advice, she had given it, and as she placed the bird in front of him she made a little speech about how in Renaissance Italy, trained carvers used to hoist the bird on a fork and spin it in the air, dazzling the guests as slices of breast fell in orderly circles on the plate below. Then, as the pièce de résistance, she presented Zack with a duplicate of her favourite Henkel carving knife as a host gift.

Charlie's reaction was sardonic. "Nothin' says lovin' like a twenty-five-centimetre blade," he said, and we all laughed.

It was the best of times, but the spectre of the trial was always there, reminding us that the best of times has an inevitable corollary. All weekend, Zack's ubiquitous BlackBerry brought news of a dark, complicated world where, increasingly, things seemed not to be breaking in Samuel Parker's favour. As the holiday drew to an end, there was a tangible and immediate worry. The hours before Katherine Morrissey's *Canada Tonight* interview were ticking down, and Zack and Charlie were on edge. As Jill had told me, because of legal implications, the discussion would focus solely on Katherine's view of the role of the journalist. But no one was fooled.

As we cleared away the leftovers, scrubbed the pots and pans, and got the kids ready for bed, everyone was preoccupied. We all knew what was coming. *Canada Tonight* was broadcast at 9:00 p.m. When the familiar trumpet blast signalled the opening credits, the little girls were asleep, and Taylor and Isobel, having pored over the guest list for their Halloween party with the discernment and finely tuned sensibilities of Henry James's protagonists, had repaired to their room at Zack's to address invitations. The rest of us had congregated in the Hynds' living room to watch and assess.

Like all good lawyers and actors, Zack had mastered the art of the cool vibe, but as he wheeled his chair into place I could see the tension in the set of his shoulders. I drew a chair up beside him and reached out to massage the back of his neck. He gave me an absent smile and turned back to the television.

Kathryn had invited the *Canada Tonight* crew into her home, and it had been a shrewd decision. The layout of her condominium was the twin of Howard Dowhanuik's, but where his house had the éclat of a biker bar the morning after a party, Kathryn's place was charming. I'd been there once just before Kathryn started teaching at the school of journalism. I was one of a group of women academics who welcomed new female members of faculty, and I'd been charged with welcoming Kathryn. It was Labour Day weekend, and she had just moved in, but her home already had a serene beauty.

The walls throughout were lemon, the perfect complement for the vibrant colours Kathryn favoured, and for the treasures she'd acquired as a serious collector of Chinese antiques. She had worked for a time in Beijing, and during her stint there had picked up some striking pieces of furniture: a nineteenth-century wedding cabinet, an exquisite red lacquered trunk, a camphor wood carving of a fish and a dragon, an ancient rice bucket, and her prize, a pair of carved wooden figures that Kathryn explained to me represented the mythical Chinese creature, the baku. The baku were dream-eaters, voraciously devouring nightmares, ensuring the sweet dreams of the sleeper.

That night, the camera lingered on the baku as if attempting to penetrate the enigma of these creatures with the bodies of horses, faces of lions, trunks and tusks of elephants, and feet of tigers. After viewers had glimpsed Kathryn's treasures, the camera moved in on the lady herself and on the man who had come to probe the depth and breadth and height Kathryn's soul could reach.

The interviewer, a pudgy man with a bow tie and a cherub's smile, was clearly delighted to have been invited in. He and Kathryn were sitting in wingback chairs on either side of a gas fireplace whose flames, like Mr. Bowtie's questions, flickered but never roared or threatened to get out of hand.

Kathryn had never been more appealing. Her silver hair fell smoothly from a centre part to a point just below her cheekbone. She was dressed casually in black slacks, flats, and a simple silk shirt of the same vibrant pink as the lipstick on her elegantly sculpted mouth. Minoo was curled on her lap, and as Kathryn spoke her slender fingers stroked her cat's lithe body.

From the outset, Kathryn was careful to obey the letter if not the spirit of the injunction forbidding direct reference to the trial. She began by talking about the function of the journalist – not a word about the Sam Parker case, but the trial was the subtext of every syllable she uttered. She disarmed her interviewer immediately by quoting Janet Malcolm, another writer who offered no apology for laying her subjects upon the shining autopsy table and sharpening her surgical blade. "Every journalist who is not too stupid or too full of himself to notice what is going on knows that what he does is morally indefensible."

The interviewer, who was old enough to know better, smirked agreement. What's a man to do when an attractive woman draws him into her circle of intimacy by hinting that, unlike his colleagues, he is neither too dull-witted or narcissistic to understand the rules of the game?

Peter, sprawled on the couch, eyes riveted to the screen, snorted as Kathryn articulated her credo, bamboozled Mr. Bowtie, and took control of the interview. "He's letting her roll right over him," he said. "I probably get 90 per cent of my news from television, so I'm used to soft lobs, but isn't this guy going to challenge her on anything?"

"Tough to ask a challenging question when you're creaming your jeans," Charlie said laconically.

And it appeared Charlie was right. The interviewer was clearly smitten. When Kathryn asserted that a journalist was justified in using any means necessary to pin down the truth, he nodded sagely. When Kathryn explained that she had never tricked or misled a subject but had simply allowed people to reveal themselves, Mr. Bowtie did not suggest that a journalist might have a moral obligation to keep a young or unbalanced subject from twisting a knife in his own entrails.

And so it went. Concentrating on the screen, Zack's face hardened. The interviewer referred to Kathryn variously as "incisive, courageous, penetrating, incorruptible, clear-eyed, and fearless," and that was when he was on the attack. The rest of the time, he goggled like a schoolboy. By the time the camera zoomed in on Kathryn's final meditation about the painfully uneasy relationship between a journalist and her subject, Mr. Bowtie was flaccid.

As the final credits rolled, over a shot of the enigmatic baku, Charlie uttered an obscenity, then he turned to Zack. "What are you going to do about that?" he asked.

Zack shrugged. "Swallow hard. Be grateful."

"For what?" Charlie's voice cracked with anger.

"It's always good to know your enemy," Zack said. "Gives you a better chance of beating them."

CHAPTER

5

I awoke Monday morning to an empty bed. I wasn't alarmed. Zack was an early riser too, but as Willie and I walked through the still-dark rooms of the cottage and there was no sign of Zack, my nerves were on high alert. I was relieved when I saw his wheelchair pulled up to the partner's table in the sunroom. His notebook computer was open in front of him and a stack of law books was within easy reach. He was wearing the blue jeans and shirt he'd been wearing the night before; his head was thrown back slightly, his eyes were closed, and he was snoring contentedly.

I went over and put my arms around him. "The bed's still warm," I said. "Why don't you give it a try?"

He was awake immediately. "Damn. What time is it?"

"Five-thirty."

"I missed a whole night with you."

"There'll be other nights. Do you want me to turn on the coffee?"

"Might as well." He put on his eyeglasses and stared at me ruefully. "I'm sorry, Jo. Charlie came over after you went to bed. He wanted to talk about the case, then I began thinking about my opening, and I realized it sucked, so I made a few phone calls, and one thing led to another. At some point, I must have just bagged out."

"Sounds like quite a night."

"Less than ideal," he said. "Oh, and some people from the office are coming out here for a skull session this morning."

"So I should make myself scarce."

He took my hand. "Not at all. I was hoping to get work out of the way so you and I could have some time alone this afternoon."

"I'm for that," I said. Willie had been patient, but as Zack and I continued to talk, he gave us a baleful look and trotted to the door. "Willie and I better go out," I said. "You and I can figure out our day when I get back."

He kissed my fingers. "I'll make the porridge."

"Okay," I said. "The directions are on the bag, but use milk instead of water. And put in the seeds and berries at the last moment. Got it?"

"Got it. I remember everything that's important."

I pivoted. "What colour are my eyes?"

"Same colour as mine – green. And your hair is dark blond and very shiny and your breasts fit perfectly in my hands and your second toe is longer than your big toe."

"That's supposed to mean I dominate the men in my life."

Zack closed his eyes and sighed deeply. "Ah, domination. I'll sign up for that."

"Name your time and place," I said.

He raised an eyebrow. "Isn't that the job of the dominatrix?"

We took our breakfast into the sunroom, so we could eat looking out at the water. The temperature had dipped during the night and when daybreak arrived, the light was weak and the sky was threatening. It was going to be a grey day.

Zack stirred cream into his porridge and peered out the window. "One good thing about weather like this – it makes it easier to leave the lake."

"Not for me," I said. "I love it here."

"It's a forty-five-minute drive to the city. If you want to, we can live here year-round."

I shook my head. "Wrong time for Taylor," I said. "Her school, her friends, and her activities are in the city. Which reminds me about the boy with the pentangle."

Zack frowned. "The knight in shining armour. I'd forgotten about him."

"If you'd met him, you'd remember. Incidentally, he does want to meet you."

"Okay with me," Zack said.

"I'll be interested in your take on Ethan," I said. "Over the years, a lot of kids have wandered through our house, but Ethan's a standout."

"Is that good or bad?"

"I don't know. He's nice-looking. He's very intense, and he draws his own comic books."

"Good money in that," Zack said. "Comic books are the reading material of choice for 80 per cent of my clients."

"I don't think they'd go for Ethan's comics. They're pretty heavily into moral choice: honour versus lust, self-preservation versus cowardice, integrity versus exigency."

Zack furrowed his brow. "And this kid is thirteen?"

"Taylor says he reads a lot."

"That's a point in his favour. Actually, it sounds like there are lots of points in his favour. Taylor's smart. She'll work it out." He snapped open his notebook computer. "Now if you want to worry about something, check the on-line real estate listings. God, there are a lot of ugly houses in Regina."

"Want me to call an agent?"

Zack shook his head. "No. I said I was going to find us the perfect house and I will."

I laughed. "Everything's a quest with you."

"Nothing wrong with keeping your eye on the prize." He yawned. "Unfortunately, this morning, I seem to be having trouble keeping my eyes open."

"What was on Charlie's mind?" I asked.

"Same thing that's on all our minds. The trial. Charlie wants to make sure that justice is done."

"Did he have any concrete suggestions about how to bring that about?"

"Actually, he did. He read over my opening statement and suggested another approach."

I was surprised. "You let him read your opening statement?"

Zack shrugged. "It's not Holy Writ, Jo. It's just a place where we tell our story and lay out our argument. After I saw Kathryn Morrissey on TV, I had second thoughts about how effectively I was telling our story, and according to Charlie, I was right to be concerned."

"What was the matter?"

"If I was teaching first-year criminal law, nothing. It was a textbook opening. It was also boring as hell. Usually I come in with everything I've got, but I was holding back."

"Because Sam Parker's such a lightning rod," I said.

"Right. The number of calls we've been getting at the office is unreal, and they cover the spectrum. Everybody is pissed at us. The Family Values people think if Sam had applied the rod, he wouldn't have ended up with a kid who can't decide if he wants to play with the boys or the girls. The granola-crunchers are sympathetic to Glenda, but they hate Sam."

" 'Hate' is a strong word," I said.

Zack looked amused. "You just don't want to think ill of your fellow granola-crunchers. But I've talked to the cops over the weekend, and they think that bomb came from somebody who wants to blow me up because I'm defending a Jesus-loving millionaire who believes he has the right to own an unregistered gun."

"How can they tell?"

"Same way I can. I've had dozens of threats from folks who believe in an eye for an eye. The spelling is usually bad and the quotations always come from the Good Book."

"And your bomb threat had a quote from *The Merchant of Venice*?"

Zack raised his eyebrows. "How did you know that?"

"Charlie told me."

"What would we do without him?" Zack said mildly. He looked at his watch. "I'd better get a move on. My eager young associates are going to be here in fifteen minutes."

"They're going to be here by 7:30 on a holiday Monday?"

Zack gave me a blank look. "Is that a problem?"

"Not for me," I said. "What's in it for them?"

Zack shrugged. "More work," he said. Then he balanced his empty bowl and spoon on his lap and wheeled off to the kitchen.

I carried in my dishes and went back to our room. If I was going to be neutral about Kathryn Morrissey, I had some research to do. I pulled out my laptop, Googled Kathryn, and steeled myself to read only the most positive articles about her illustrious career.

Zack's guest room was, like the rest of the cottage, a large and uncluttered space with functional, expensive furniture, art objects that were arresting, original, and executed in rust, plum, and silver – colours that coordinated perfectly with the cool monochromatic greys of the walls. The bed was custom-built, extra large but raised from the floor by the smallest of platforms. The bedding in a palette of warm browns was sleekly inviting. The room was, in short, exactly what a single man would get if he gave a decorator a blank cheque and carte blanche.

The space was so perfectly ordered that it seemed guest-proof, but Taylor and Isobel had unpacked their neon backpacks, slung them over the doorknobs, and fulfilling the manifest destiny of pubescent girls, they had unfurled. On a low square table just inside the door, hair products that promised to tame Isobel's wild curls fought for pride of place with the gels and sprays Taylor needed to keep her new 'do spiky. Creams, lotions, and splashes distilled from rare flowers of the rain forest crowded a shelf designed to hold a smoky glass sculpture whose sole function was to delight the eye. Scraps of lacy underwear in shades the catalogue described as yellow sunshine, green tea, and English rose pooled on the mochaccino bedspread, and stuffed animals, relics of a more innocent age, nestled among the rust and taupe pillows at the head of the bed.

In the span of a weekend, Taylor and Isobel had created a world that was as richly turbulent as their lives. The girls themselves were in the middle of the bed, side by side on their stomachs, hair tousled from sleep, faces rosy, feet kicking the air, reading.

"I can't believe you're awake already," I said.

Taylor glanced up. "We wanted to finish this book."

Isobel put her finger in the book to mark their place and turned the cover towards me. "We've been reading *Too Much Hope*," she said.

Taylor scrambled into a cross-legged squat. "We'd already read the chapter about Glenda Parker," she said, "but after we saw that interview with Kathryn Morrissey last night, we decided to read the rest."

I cleared myself a place on the corner of the bed and sat down. "So, what do you think?" I asked.

Isobel put the book face down on the bed and frowned. Isobel's mother, Delia, had argued several cases before the Supreme Court. Delia's approach to the law was painstaking with every phrase scrupulously considered; every argument turned like a cube to reveal its facets. Her punctiliousness drove Zack nuts. That morning, as her mother would, Isobel considered my question gravely before she answered. "Well except for Charlie Dowhanuik's father, we only have the kids' stories about what happened, but so far it seems as if the parents didn't care about their kids at all."

"Olivia Quinn tried to tell her mother that her stepfather was making her have sex with him, but her mother wouldn't listen," Taylor added. "When Olivia started skipping school and doing drugs and sleeping with all those boys, her mother said she was acting out because she was jealous."

"And Olivia's school said she was incorrigible," Isobel said, pushing herself up to a sitting position. "She was only fourteen years old. Not much older than Taylor and me, but everybody blamed *her*."

"All the kids in that book say their parents blamed them for everything that went wrong," Taylor said.

I turned to Taylor. "Did you read the chapter about your Uncle Howard and Charlie? Howard blames himself."

"That's who he *should* blame," Taylor said. "Every time he needed to get elected, he made Charlie go out and meet people, but when Charlie needed him, he was never around."

Isobel ran her fingers through her explosion of black curls. "Glenda Parker's mother was worse. She *was* around, but when Glenda tried to tell her mother what was going on in her body, she told Glenda that unless she prayed to be delivered, she was going to Hell."

"The worst one of all is Kathryn Morrissey," Taylor said. "Isobel's mother says she got people to talk about their problems by promising they'd help other people. Then she just used what they told her to sell books." Taylor's pretty mouth hardened into a condemning line. "Soul-fire says the worst sin of all is betrayal."

Isobel's face relaxed into mischief. "Oh, Soul-fire. I love Soul-fire. He is so wise and so brave and sooooooo cute."

Taylor reached back, grabbed a pillow, and the discussion ended, as many discussions did with Taylor and her friends, in an old-fashioned pillow fight.

For a while I dodged pillows and shared in the giggles. Then, cognizant of the recreation director's axiom that it's best to kill an activity before it dies on you, I called time. "I'll be the bad guy," I said. "Hit the showers. Zack has people coming out from the office, and when they get here you shouldn't be wandering around in your skivvies."

Isobel shook her head. "Work. Work. Work. Work. Work." She said, and her intonation was exactly the same as her mother's.

When I arrived at the cottage where my oldest daughter and her family were staying, the inside door was open. I peered through the screen and saw that Greg was in the living room reading the paper; the little girls were sitting on a blanket in front of him, sharing a bowl of dry Cheerios and watching TV.

I called through the screen, and Greg leapt out of his chair and came to the door. "Caught me," he said. "Come in, make yourself comfortable, and let me convince you that TV is educational."

"No need," I said. "I just came by to score some Cheerios." I walked over and squatted between my granddaughters. "Hey, ladies, are you sharing?"

Eyes still fixed on the screen, Madeleine picked up the bowl and passed it back to me. "Why, thanks," I said. I took a handful of cereal, kissed her head and Lena's, and went back to join my son-in-law.

"So where is everybody?" I asked.

"Mieka and Pete and Charlie decided to squeeze in one last canoe ride," he said. "You just missed them."

I looked towards the dock. My children and Charlie were dressed alike in blue jeans and dark hoodies. Outlined against the stark background of lake and hazy white sky, their resemblance to one another was striking. They had put one canoe in the water and were sliding in a second. "They're a person short," I said to Greg.

He shook his head. "Those three are never a person short, Jo." He lowered himself onto the ottoman that faced my chair.

"In a few hours there'll be 250 kilometres between Charlie and you," I said.

"True, but Charlie will continue to be a presence in our lives. Did you know that Pete's moving in with him?"

"Nobody told me," I said.

"Apparently, they've been considering it for a while. Mieka said Charlie and Pete were concerned that sharing a house might put a strain on their friendship. I can't imagine anything coming between the three of them, but I guess it was a valid concern. Anyway, now that he's got his clinic, Pete's short of money, and Charlie never misses a chance to burrow in." There was a bitterness in Greg's voice that I hadn't heard before.

"Greg, the trial will be over in a month. Why don't you leave the girls with me? You and Mieka could go some place warm and rediscover the magic?"

"What if the magic is gone?"

I smiled at him. "Then you'll have to find something else to get you through the next forty years."

The Big Comfy Couch was coming to a close. As she always did, Loonette, the clown, was discovering that in the course of her adventures, she had made a mess.

"Madeleine, here comes our favourite part," I said.

Madeleine nodded vigorously. "The Ten Second Tidy."

The four of us watched in silence as Loonette, with the jerky moves of a character in an old-time movie, found a place for everything in the commodious contours of the big comfy couch. When she was done, Loonette and Molly Dolly curled up under their purple silk cover. Harmony had returned to Clown Town.

"Think I could find a couch big enough to swallow Charlie?" Greg said. Then he shook his head in disgust. "Sorry, Jo. I'm becoming a self-pitying asshole." He walked over, turned off the TV, and scooped up his daughters. As they squealed, he played Falstaff. "All right, my scullions, my rampallions, my fustilarians. Time to get dressed, and if I hear a word of complaint, I'll tickle your catastrophe."

Greg and I met the canoeists at the dock. I sent Charlie and Pete up to strip the beds; then Mieka and Greg bundled their daughters into their life jackets and took them for a ride in their favourite red canoe.

I was standing on the dock, watching my daughter and her family vanish around the point, when Taylor and Isobel came down and announced they were going to make certain the Inukshuks they had built this summer were winter-worthy. Each of the Inukshuk had a sight hole in the middle. By peering through it, lost travellers could get their bearings and be guided along the route to the next Inukshuk. As a service to those who would be wandering the shore without a global positioning system in the coming winter, Isobel and Taylor planned to verify the accuracy of the sight holes.

I went with them. There was one particular Inukshuk I needed to visit. As we started around the horseshoe, the wind came up, and the girls and I pulled up the hoods of our jackets and jammed our hands in our pockets. All summer the girls had made it clear that Project Inukshuk was theirs, so that morning I stood aside as they went about their work: packing dirt around a rock that rested on unstable ground; adjusting a flat stone that wasn't placed correctly; checking the view from a sight hole. When they'd finished their work on the Inukshuk at the tip of the west arm, I stayed behind. Without question or comment, the girls went ahead. They knew I wanted to be alone.

The sight hole on this particular Inukshuk pointed towards an old cottonwood tree across the water at the edge of Lake View cemetery. A man I had cared about deeply had been buried there the previous summer. Alex Kequahtooway had been born a few kilometres away on Standing Buffalo Reserve. He had lived with honour, and my life and the lives of my children had been enriched by knowing him. As I watched the graceful branches of the cottonwood move in the wind, and breathed in autumn's pungent scent of decay and promise, I remembered him and said a prayer that this good man had found peace.

The electric blue PT Cruiser was still in Zack's driveway when I came back. Sam's dream team was still hard at it, so I went over to Mieka's. Greg had already packed and loaded their car, and he and Pete and Charlie had taken the girls down to the Point store for a final ice cream cone. Unencumbered, Mieka and I set about the bittersweet preparation for our last meal together at the lake.

The menu required no forethought and less effort: turkey leftovers and Mieka's sweet-potato soup, a recipe born of necessity and, in my opinion, fit for the gods. After the soup was simmering and the plates and cutlery were set out for a buffet, I turned to my daughter. "What do you want to do with the rest of the morning?"

Mieka glanced around, spotted a football, and picked it up. "Want to toss around the football?"

"I could stand to burn a few calories," I said. "Let's go."

Outside, Mieka bounced on her toes a few times, then raised her arms towards the sun. "Great day," she said.

"It is a great day," I said. "And it's good to see you smiling."

"Fake it until you make it," she said. "And I'm *going* to make it, Mum. Greg's right. The business has a great future. We have a great future."

"And it's the future you want," I said.

"It's the future I have," she said. "It's just that every so often 'I have immortal longings in me.'"

I squeezed her arm. "You don't often quote Shakespeare."

Mieka's eyes widened. "That is Shakespeare, isn't it? Lately, I've been wishing I'd paid more attention in English class. Ms. Boucher, my Grade 11 teacher, drilled us in those speeches. But I haven't a clue where that line about immortal longings comes from."

"*Antony and Cleopatra*. Cleopatra says it just before she commits suicide."

"Ms. Boucher tried to talk about context, but there were no extra marks, so I dozed." Mieka's tone was wistful, but she shrugged off the memory. "Too late now, I guess. Might as well forget about Shakespeare and just throw the ball around."

And we did. The rest of the family came home and within minutes our mum-and-daughter moment evolved into a game of shirts and skins. Charlie made certain he was on Mieka's team. For sheer mindless pleasure, few things beat throwing a football around in the cool autumn air, and when the door to Zack's cottage opened, I called time and beckoned to Zack and his company to join us.

Zack introduced his associates. The man, tall and muscular with the curly hair and sculpted mouth of a Michelangelo angel, was Sean Barton. The woman, a sprite with blonde hair cut boy-short, a snub nose, and clever assessing eyes, was Arden Korchinski. Both were wearing jeans and College of Law sweatshirts.

Charlie took control of the situation. "Why don't you guys join us."

Sean was clearly eager, but he was also polite. "Are you sure?" he said. "We don't want to wreck your game."

"My game is wrecking me," I said. "I've had enough. Besides, my granddaughters appear to need some supervision. You take over for me. Arden can play on Charlie's team." I glanced at Zack. "In or out?"

"In," he said. "And I'll play on your old team."

"You really think it takes you *and* Sean to replace me," I said.

"No one could replace you," Zack said.

I kissed the top of his head. "Go get 'em, tiger."

As he always did, Zack played hard, giving no quarter and expecting none. Arden and Sean were both natural athletes, lithe, quick, and aggressive. Huddled with my granddaughters in an old Hudson's Bay blanket singing nonsense songs and cheering on whoever happened to have the ball was, in my opinion, the perfect way to end the weekend.

The collision between Sean Barton and Mieka was quick and vicious. She was trying to intercept the pass that he was trying to catch. He leapt in the air, caught the ball, lost his balance, and came down on top of her. Even from halfway across the lawn, I could hear the cartoon sound of the breath being knocked out of her body as she hit the ground with Sean on top of her. It was clearly an accident. By the time I got to my feet, Sean had pushed himself off Mieka and was on his knees with his face close to hers checking to see if she was hurt. Charlie seemed to come out of nowhere. He hurled himself at Sean, wrapping Sean in his arms and legs and screaming at him to get away from Mieka. Sean was at least a head taller than Charlie and fifty pounds heavier, but when he tried to extricate himself from Charlie's grasp, he couldn't. Of the players on the field, Pete was the first to see what was happening, and he reacted immediately. He grabbed at Charlie and told him to back off, but Charlie was beyond hearing. Pete hung in there, pulling at Charlie's arms and speaking to him in the tough, reassuring voice of a football coach dealing with an out-of-control player. "C'mon, buddy, let it go. Let it go. Let it go." Finally, Charlie did, in fact, let it go. His body – all sinew and rage during the attack – went boneless. He released his grip, stumbled, and then drew himself to his feet. When I saw his face, I was filled with horror.

I had been in the delivery room with Marnie when Charlie was born. He had rocketed into the world two weeks early. It was election night, and Howard was busy consoling the losers and celebrating with the winners. As Marnie's doctor lifted the newborn into the air, the delivery room fell silent. He was a long, thin baby with a birthmark that made it appear as if half his face and neck had been dipped in blood. Like everyone in the room except Marnie, I struggled against revulsion. Over the years, Marnie had taken him to a dozen doctors, but Charlie's blood mask stubbornly resisted treatment. We had all grown accustomed to it. The disfigurement – like his wit, his charisma, and his need – had simply been part of the person Charlie was. So that day, as I tried to catch Charlie's attention, it wasn't the splash of blood on his skin that shocked me, it was the wildness in his eyes. In that moment, he was a fierce stranger who was capable of anything. The moment passed. He shrugged, apologized to us all, and then extended his hand to Sean.

"Sorry," he said. "That'll teach me to skip my meds."

Sean was gracious. "Hey, with that kind of pit-bull spirit, next time I want you on our team."

Zack had wheeled over to join us. "Let's eat," he said. He turned to Sean and Arden. "I dragged you out here on a holiday weekend, the least we can do is feed you."

When the others started up to the house, Zack motioned me to stay behind. "Do you think I should tell Sean to get a rabies shot?"

I began folding the blanket the little girls and I had been sitting on. "No. Charlie and my kids have always been very protective of one another," I said. "Still, that was really stupid."

"And predictable," Zack said.

"What do you mean?"

"Have you ever heard of hypermnesia?"

"No."

"It's the opposite of amnesia. People who suffer from it can't forget anything – no matter how painful."

"It sounds like one of those curses the Greek gods used to hurl around."

"It is a curse," Zack said. "I've seen it in about a half-dozen clients, and it makes them do crazy things."

"And you think that's what was behind Charlie's outburst."

Zack shrugged. "It seems a distinct possibility. When he talks about his relationship with his father, he remembers every slight. And his loyalty to your kids – and to you, incidentally – is primal."

"Primal can be dangerous," I said.

"And expensive," Zack said. "That Jaguar you're so fond of driving was paid for by fees from a man who caught his wife cheating and opted for what my American colleagues call a Colt .45 divorce."

At lunch, there were two topics of conversation: the trial and Halloween costumes. Madeleine and Lena were dressing up as crayons: Madeleine was purple and Lena was orange. And so in the midst of the tense, revved-up talk of witness lists and opening statements, there were wistful reminiscences about Halloweens past and about going out as ghosts or pirates or witches. When lunch was cleaned away, Zack, Sean, and Arden went back to his cottage to work and the rest of us started loading the cars.

After the last stuffed toy had found a home in Greg and Mieka's car, Greg went inside to get the girls.

Alone with my daughter, there were a hundred questions I wanted to ask, but I fell back on the host's question. "All things considered, did you have a good weekend?"

Mieka smiled. "All things considered, it had its moments." She reached up and, in her invariable nervous gesture, began to pick at her lip. I pulled her hand away.

"I'm thirty-one," she said. "I should be allowed to disfigure myself."

Our eyes met. "But you have such a beautiful mouth," we said in unison, and the tension between us broke.

Her eyes met mine. "You're not the only one who worries, you know. I worry about you too. Mum, how much do you really know about Zack?"

"Enough to know that I love him," I said.

"People say things . . ."

"People used to say things about your father. If you live a public life, people talk. It comes with the territory."

"But with Dad, you knew that the rumours weren't true. He had integrity, and you two had this perfect marriage. How can you settle for less?"

"Because what I have with Zack isn't less. In many ways, it's more. For one thing, we're equals – that wasn't true with your Dad and me."

Mieka put up her hands. "I don't want to hear this."

"Okay," I said. "Just remember that no marriage is perfect. I loved your father, and I'm glad we stayed together, but it wasn't always easy."

"Thus endeth the lesson," Mieka said, and her voice was heavy with scorn. She shook her head. "Forget I said that. In fact, let's forget everything we both just said."

"Good call," I said. "Come on, let's go over and say goodbye to everybody."

Zack, Sean, and Arden were sitting at the partners' table, wholly engrossed in their talk.

"Sorry to break your concentration," I said. "But we're heading out."

Zack frowned. "You're not leaving too?"

"I have to get back to the city," I said. "Taylor has school tomorrow, and I should review a few things with Rapti."

Zack ran his hand over his head. "Shit, Jo. I blew it, didn't I?"

"You didn't blow it. We had a great weekend."

"But we should have been together more." He wheeled his chair towards me. "Is there any way you can hang around for a couple of hours?"

Arden and Sean were closing their laptops. "I think we're going to take off," Sean said quietly.

Zack nodded approval. "See you at four – we'll meet in the boardroom. My office . . ." He read the concern on my face and cut his sentence short.

"Your office looks like a bomb went off in it," I said.

Zack looked sheepish. "Set myself up for that one, didn't I? I've been trying to steer clear of the subject all weekend."

I met his gaze. "So have I. Are there any developments there?"

Zack shook his head. "Nope, I talked to the cops this morning. No progress. Norine's getting together a list of clients who have Looney Tunes potential, and she's got workers coming in today to start the cleanup. Everything's taken care of. Time to move along."

Arden checked her watch. "So, the boardroom in two hours, right?"

"Right," Zack said, but he wasn't looking at Arden when he spoke.

I turned to Pete. "Could you drive the girls home in my car, and let Charlie take your truck?"

"Sure," he said. He grinned at me. "You're blushing, Mum."

"So are you," I said. "Now give me a hug and get out of here."

After everyone left Zack turned to me. "It's a forty-five-minute drive back to the city and that gives us an hour and fifteen minutes – ample time for a heavy-duty love sesh."

"What are you talking about?"

We moved into the bedroom. "Something a client of mine told me about," Zack said, unbuttoning his shirt. "My client's theory was that a heavy-duty love sesh cleared the toxins from the body and made a favourable impression on the jury."

"That's insane," I said.

"Maybe, but I leave no stone unturned." He shifted his body from the chair to the bed and patted the place beside him. "Come on. We're wasting Sam Parker's money."

Sam got his money's worth that afternoon. When we left Lawyers' Bay, Zack and I were both relaxed and content. We drove home listening to a Beach Boys CD. Zack kept hitting number twelve – "Wouldn't It Be Nice" – a plangent anthem to the joys of being married because it meant spending the night together and having kisses that were never-ending. When we pulled up in front of my house, Zack leaned over and kissed me. "So did the Beach Boys convince you?"

"That we should be married?" I said.

"Yeah," he said. "So we could be happy."

"We're already happy," I said.

"Agreed," he said. "But if you'd been listening harder, you would have learned that if we were married, we wouldn't have to go to school."

I could hear Taylor's music pounding from halfway up my front walk. No need to fumble for my keys; my daughter was in residence. Before I opened the door, I checked the mailbox. For once I was rewarded with more than flyers and the community newspaper. There was a padded envelope inside – obviously hand-delivered. It was addressed to Taylor. I tucked it under my arm, opened the door, and followed the beat of the drums.

Taylor was curled up on the couch with her cats, doing homework. I turned down the decibels and glanced at the notebook in front of her. "Math," I said. "Well, better late than never, I guess."

She gave me a corner-of-the-mouth grin. "So have you done all your homework for the trial tomorrow?"

"Not a scrap," I said. "What do you say we order a pizza and get caught up together."

"Sounds like a plan," she said. She scrunched her face. "What's in the envelope?"

I handed it to her. "Something for you," I said.

She glanced at the address but didn't open it.

Clearly, she wanted some privacy. "I'll go check our messages," I said. "Let me know when you're hungry."

There were ten new messages – a surprisingly high number considering that I'd had my cell with me all weekend and that Taylor's friends knew how to reach her at the cottage. The mystery was soon solved. There was a curt message from Jill, saying she'd hoped I'd watched the Kathryn Morrissey interview and she'd call me after I'd done my report the next day. The rest of the messages were from Howard Dowhanuik, who had apparently forgotten the adage

"Never drink and dial." He had started phoning me Sunday night just as Kathryn's interview aired. From his slightly off-centre articulation at the outset, it was obvious he'd fortified himself against the ordeal of watching Kathryn turn on the charm coast to coast. Judging from his speedy descent from toasty to drunk, Howard's bottle of Canadian Club had never been far from his side. By the time he made his last phone call Sunday night, he had moved from belligerence to lachrymose affection. I was, he assured me tearfully, his last goddamn friend in the world. Given the fact that he had spent the evening berating me for failing to protect him from himself, the fact that he was friendless didn't come as news.

Howard's final phone call had come at 7:05 Monday morning. He didn't waste time apologizing for his behaviour the night before. It was clear that with the drunk's breathtaking efficiency, he had simply wiped away the memory of his previous calls and moved along. He was now strategizing. His new plan was to track Kathryn Morrissey. From now on, he assured me, she wouldn't take a goddamn step without him knowing what she was doing and who she was seeing. I would be getting regular reports. I could count on that.

As I erased his final message, I was optimistic. In his previous life, Howard had been a lawyer. It was plausible that he had retained some knowledge of the laws governing stalking. Whatever the case, if he was hanging around the bushes eyeballing Kathryn Morrissey, he would be away from the rye bottle. Besides, the fresh air would do him good.

CHAPTER

6

The first day of the trial our city was hit by a freak snow-storm. As I stood at my bedroom window watching the wind whip the branches of the evergreens in our yard and the snow pelt the window, I felt my nerves twang. Anything could happen. From his place beside me, Willie stared at the blizzard, unperturbed.

I scratched his head. "'Winter is iccumen in,'" I said. "'Lhude sing Goddamm.'" Literary allusions were lost on Willie; nonetheless, he cocked his head thoughtfully and followed as I went to the basement to unearth the storage bin that held our boots and the larger one in which we stowed winter jackets, mitts, and toques. I found our parkas, Taylor's new boots, and my old Sorels, went back upstairs, and started layering up. Finally, equipped to battle the elements, I opened the front door and stepped into a suddenly wintry world. The streetlights were still on, and snow was swirling through the halos of light they cast. It was a familiar sight, but one I wasn't ready for.

Nor, as it turned out, was I ready for the sidewalks. Before we reached the Albert Street Bridge, I'd slipped twice. I gave

Willie's leash a tug. "We're cutting our run short, bud." We covered half our route, doubled back, and came home to a silent house. I filled Willie's dog dish, poured myself a cup of coffee, and went back up to my bedroom to check my e-mail. There was a note from Charlie, thanking me for my hospitality and wishing Zack luck. I scrolled down to the quotation Charlie had chosen for his e-mail signature: *Life is Painless for the Brainless.*

As he'd promised, Charlie had attached an MP3 file of excerpts from his interviews with the *Too Much Hope* kids. I clicked it on and went over to the chair by the window to watch the snow and listen.

What I heard shouldn't have shocked me. I had read Kathryn Morrissey's book. I knew the histories of her subjects: the ones who had been discarded like toys their parents had acquired on eBay and had tired of; the ones who had been caught in the crossfire of toxic marriages; the ones who had been freighted with their parents' baggage or whose lives had been appropriated by their parents to fulfill their own needs. And I had read Kathryn's meticulous accounts of her subjects' confused, raging, blighted lives. What I wasn't prepared for was the agony in their young voices. Clearly whatever their failings, Kathryn's subjects weren't brainless.

I was so absorbed in the voices on the tape that I didn't hear Taylor come in.

She was still in her pyjamas, and she was exuberant. "It's snowing," she said. She ran to the window seat and knelt among the cushions so she could peer out the window. "Sweet, eh?" she said.

"Sweet," I agreed.

For a few moments she knelt with her back to me watching the snow, then the voices on the computer entered her consciousness and she turned to face me. "What's that you're listening to?"

"An MP3 file that Charlie sent me of his interviews with the people in *Too Much Hope*."

Taylor settled with her back against the window, her legs crossed in front of her. When a female voice began to describe how, within weeks, she had gone from model child to truant, sexual predator, and druggie, Taylor wedged her hands between her thighs and leaned towards me. "That's Olivia Quinn, the one who got raped." Taylor's lips were tight. "She tried to tell her mother, but her mother didn't believe her."

I walked over to my computer and turned off the interview. "Taylor, you know you can tell me anything, don't you?"

Her eyes filled with tears. "I know."

I sat beside her on the window seat. "Is something wrong?"

She was still for a moment, tense with indecision. Then she leapt to her feet. "There's something I need to show you." She came back with the padded envelope I'd taken from our mailbox. It had been opened. I reached inside and took out *Soul-fire: A Hero's Life, Part IV*. Like its predecessors, Part IV opened in the grey world of alienation and nihilism. Finally, shunned and miserable, the hero takes the pentangle from its secret place in the crypt, drapes the emblem around his neck, and is transported into the brilliantly coloured world of Soul-fire. The enemies Soul-fire encountered were familiar to me from his earlier exploits, but this time, he was not alone. On this quest, he was joined by Chloe, a light-boned young girl with huge brown eyes and fashionably hacked dark hair. The comic ended with Soul-fire and Chloe hand in hand on a verdant sanctuary called the Island of Celestial Light. Behind them, the city was burning.

Taylor was watching my face. "What do you think?"

"Ethan's very talented," I said carefully.

"What do you think about Chloe?"

"I think Chloe's you."

Taylor's voice was small. "That's what I think too," she said.

"If this is too much for you, I could talk to Ethan – or maybe to his mother."

"No! That would just make things worse. I can handle it."

"Okay," I said. I slid my arm around her. "When I saw it was snowing, I brought up the new boots we bought you last spring at Aldo."

In one of those quicksilver mood shifts that signal the onset of adolescence, Taylor was suddenly ecstatic. "The orange ones? Sweeeet. I *love* those boots. This is going to be the best day."

I wasn't so confident. *Soul-fire: A Hero's Life* might have moved off Taylor's personal screen, but Ethan's disturbing portrait of the artist as a young man had stayed on mine. I was reading through *A Hero's Life* seeking reassurance when Zack called.

"Finally," he said. "I've tried this number about forty times. I thought you were stuck in a snowbank somewhere."

"Sorry. I forgot to turn my cell on. Did you try our land line?"

"Yep, and it was busy forty times."

"Taylor must have left it off the hook," I said.

"As long as you're safe," Zack said.

"I am – I'm sitting here reading a comic."

"The Adventures of Pentangle Boy?"

"Right," I said. "How are you doing?"

"Lousy. It's snowing like a son of a bitch, which means my chair is probably going to get stuck and my car is going to get stuck and I'm going to get stuck."

" 'Sing goddamm, damm, sing Goddamm / Sing goddamm, sing goddamm, DAMM.' "

Zack chuckled. "What the hell was that?"

"The last stanza of Ezra Pound's 'Ancient Music.' Anyway, it made you laugh. Anything wrong apart from the weather?"

"I'm facing a jury trial – that always makes my stomach churn."

"After all these years?"

"After all these years. Jo, every lawyer is edgy before a jury trial. People are unpredictable – hammering out a settlement with the other side is a lot easier than taking a case to a jury. Of course, it's also less fun. Actually, I was explaining all this to your younger son five minutes ago."

"You were talking to Angus?"

"He phoned to wish me luck."

"Lawyer to lawyer," I said.

Zack chuckled. "Something like that. I haven't heard so much legal lingo since I was in my first year at law school."

"Did he make any sense?"

"Not a bit, but it was fun listening to him. He loves what he's doing, Jo."

"That's what he tells me, but Angus has a way of channelling only good news my way."

"Well, relax, because he's happy in his work. As am I. I love my work, and I love my woman," Zack said. "I'm a lucky guy. But it's time to make tracks."

"In that case," I said, "I will see you in court. Good luck."

"Thanks," he said. "And, Jo, try to keep things in perspective. I'm going to do everything I can to get Sam off, but whatever happens, when the trial's over, I'll be coming home."

"So I should relax."

"You've got it," he said. "Just relax and enjoy the show."

On the courthouse stairs, I ran into Ed Mariani. The collar of his winter jacket was up, the ear-flaps on his Irish walking cap were down, and his cheeks were pink. He beamed when he saw me.

"Come to see your boyfriend in action?"

"No, actually, I'm *Canada Tonight*'s eye on the Sam Parker trial."

Ed's smile faded. "Nice gig," he said, stamping the snow off his feet. "I wouldn't have minded getting it."

"At this moment, I imagine Jill is wishing she'd offered you the job."

Ed removed his hat and brushed away the snow. "Why?"

"Jill is concerned about my bias."

"Because of the boyfriend."

"No, because I find what Kathryn Morrissey did in her book morally repugnant."

"That *could* be a problem."

"Maybe I'll just stick with safe topics. Maybe tonight I should lead with the inside info on that mural over there."

"Look out, Peter Mansbridge."

"Peter Mansbridge was never a parent-helper on four separate tours of this courthouse. Did you know that the mural is a mosaic of 125,000 pieces of Florentine glass? Did you know that the gent holding aloft the arms of the balance of right and wrong is a symbolic God of Laws? Did you know that the females flanking him represent Truth and Justice? Do you want me to continue?"

"God, yes. If you're that boring tonight, your job is mine." The mirth disappeared from Ed's face. "Talking about truth and justice won't be easy in this one, Jo."

The Sam Parker trial was taking place in Courtroom C, the largest of the building's courtrooms. Those of us with media passes were directed to two rows that had been reserved for us. As we filed into our places, there was only one topic of conversation: the weather. No one had arrived in Regina

prepared for winter. Smart fall suits and expensive foot-
wear had been wrecked by the snow, and journalists were
not amused.

I was wedged between a slender, trendily dressed young
woman whose increasingly frequent bylines on increasingly
more important stories suggested she was on her way up in
the world of print journalism, and a square-jawed, deeply
tanned, ex-anchor who was clearly on his way down. The
young woman's name was Brette Sinclair; the ex-anchor,
who was a foot shorter than I'd imagined him to be in his
anchor-desk days, was Kevin Powers. As soon as he was
seated, he leaned across me to confide in Brette. "This suit is
pure worsted wool, and it's totally fucking ruined. I had it
made in Hong Kong – cost me the equivalent of $785 U.S."

Brette smoothed her silky black hair. "You should have
bought Canadian," she said sweetly. When Kevin straightened
and turned his back to her, Brette silently mouthed the word
asshole, then removed a notebook and a pen from her tiny
fabric handbag, settled in, and waited for the curtain to rise.

On the school tour, I had learned that the judge, the jurors,
the lawyers, and the defendants all came into the courtroom
through separate entrances. It was an arrangement that
made for good theatre, and as the lawyers entered, the buzz
of anticipation subsided.

The Crown prosecutor was a tall, slim redhead named
Linda Fritz. Zack said she was a formidable opponent: smart,
quick, and fearless. She took her place at the counsel table,
opened her briefcase, and began arranging her files without
fuss. Within seconds, Zack and Sam Parker entered and went
to the defence table, but before Sam took his chair he gazed
around the courtroom. He wasn't looking for his wife. Beverly
Parker had decided against attending her husband's trial.
Officially, she was overwrought; in truth, she had refused
to be in the same room as Glenda. But if Beverly had chosen to

shun her child, Sam was drawing strength from her. When Sam's eyes found Glenda, the connection between them was electric. Clearly, they were counting on each other to get through the ordeal ahead. Finally, Glenda gave her dad the thumbs-up sign, and he smiled and sat down. It was all very low-key. He and Zack chatted until court was called to order with Mr. Justice Arthur Harney presiding.

Like many other facets of the trial, the selection of a jury was a grindingly mundane process. The jury panel was brought into the courtroom. There were perhaps fifty people on the panel and they were asked two questions: were they related in any way to the accused or the witnesses? Had they read the transcript of the preliminary hearing? When no one responded in the affirmative, each member of the jury panel came forward and was either accepted or rejected. The Crown had four peremptory challenges, plus forty-eight "stand asides"; the defence had twelve peremptory challenges.

From my perspective, Linda Fritz and Zack seemed to accept or challenge the jury candidates pretty much on the basis of instinct. I didn't know how much digging the Crown had done into the background of the members of the jury panel, but I knew Falconer Shreve's investigations had been casual. Zack's firm had possessed the panel list since Labour Day. It included the ages and occupations of each potential juror. The obvious bad fits had been culled, but Zack believed in common sense and gut reaction, and it seemed Linda Fritz did too. In a little under three hours, the jurors who would try Samuel Parker on the charge of attempted murder were selected.

Zack had rolled his eyes about the impossibility of finding a jury of peers for a right-wing fundamentalist millionaire who made no bones about the fact that he would do anything to protect his transgendering child. As I watched the jury members take their places in the box, I wondered how Sam Parker would fare with the six men and six women who were solemnly assuming their new and unfamiliar roles as "judges of the facts" of his case. They were as typical as any random group you might find searching for videos at Blockbuster on Friday at 5:00 p.m. There was a dapper little man with a scowl and an aggressive combover; two pleasant-faced women with gently permed white hair and seasonally patterned cardigans; a tall, imposing woman with a pale oval face Modigliani would have lusted to paint; two men in three-piece suits; a woman with a Lucille Ball explosion of red curls and a smile that looked slightly demented; two young people, one male, one female – both of whom squirmed and looked distinctly unhappy; a silver-haired gent who turned out to be a serious notetaker; a cocky, meaty man who sprawled in his chair, seemingly defying all comers to explain why they weren't wasting his time; and a woman about my age, wearing a vintage granny gown, lace-up shoes, and the last rose of summer in her glorious salt-and-pepper mane.

Despite Zack's somewhat lackadaisical approach to jury selection, once he had a jury, they were his focus. From the moment they were sworn in, the members of the jury became players in the legal drama, joining the judge, the defendant, the lawyers, and the witnesses on the other side of the fourth wall, that invisible curtain that, in theatre, divides actors from their audience. On that first day, Zack's eyes wandered towards me, but he never established eye contact. Later he told me that only inexperienced, showboating lawyers play to the back of the room. Experienced lawyers remember who makes the decisions, and they keep their focus on the judge and the jury.

When the jurors were seated, Arthur Harney read the jury some elementary points of law and announced that we would recess so the jury could select a foreperson and we could all have lunch.

Brette Sinclair slid her notebook and pen into her vintage bag. Kevin Powers, obviously over his snit, leaned across me again and addressed her. "Do you think there's a decent place to eat around here?"

"I'm sure there is," Brette said. She gave my media identification tag a sidelong glance. "*Joanne* and I arranged to have lunch. I'll give you a report on the restaurant when we get back."

Kevin glared at her. "You do that," he said, and he got up and stomped off.

When he was out of earshot, Brette picked up her bag. "Sorry," she said. "Super-stud and I have some history I'm not anxious to repeat."

I knew Zack would be eating with his client. "I don't have any plans for lunch if you'd like to join me."

She squinted. "Seriously?"

"Why not? What do you like?"

Her eyes sparked mischief. "Cake."

I slipped the strap of my purse over my shoulder. "I know just the restaurant for you," I said. "Follow me."

In its previous incarnation, Danbry's had been the Assiniboine Club, a gents-only place where men with deep pockets could sit in leather chairs, sip Scotch, read their papers, and escape women. Sense and shifting sensibilities had been the death knell for clubs like the Assiniboine, but an enterprising developer had seen the potential in the graceful old downtown building, and that wintry day, Brette and I walked into a restaurant of real charm. We arrived without reservations, but we were in luck – not only were places available, they were prime – in front of the fireplace in the high-vaulted dining room. Brette shrugged out of her trench coat. She was wearing nicely fitted blue jeans, a white shirt, a black cardigan, and a long string of pearls. Her outfit was a theme that would appear with variations throughout the trial.

The server came, took our drink orders, and handed us menus. "What's good?" Brette asked.

"Everything," I said. "But the lamb burgers with gorgonzola are amazing."

She snapped her menu shut. "I accept your recommendation," she said. We ordered and she leaned forward. "So what's your take on this case?"

"Too soon to have a take," I said.

"You're right," she said. "We'll know after the opening statements."

"That soon?" I asked.

She wrapped her pearls around her forefinger. "How many trials have you covered?"

"This is the first," I said.

"Everybody has to start somewhere," she said equitably. "Anyway, the conventional wisdom is that 75 per cent of cases are won or lost in the opening statement."

"Because you never get a second chance to make a first impression?" I said.

She smiled. "My mother used to say that. Anyway, I've never seen Linda Fritz, but I have seen Zachary Shreve, and he's a trip. I covered a trial where he was defending a Hells Angel named Lil Joe. Even slicked up for his court date, Lil Joe was a gorilla, but in his opening statement, Shreve wove this touching story about Joe's kindness to widows and orphans. Of course, he failed to point out that Joe was responsible for a lot of those widows and orphans becoming widows and orphans, but no matter. Shreve got the jury on Lil Joe's side."

"That must have been a killer opening statement," I said.

"It did the job," Brette said dryly. "More importantly, Shreve managed to keep the jury on side. It must have been tough sledding for him. One of the Crown's witnesses – hostile, needless to say – quoted the defendant as saying, 'If you mess with the best, you die like the rest.'"

"Scary stuff," I said.

"Yes indeed, but Shreve got the jury to buy his theory about the facts in the case, so Lil Joe got off. Afterwards when we were doing the post-trial scrum on the courthouse stairs, a contingent of Angels roared past on their bikes. They were carrying a banner: 'Ride Hard. Die Free.'"

I shuddered. "Sounds like a great moment in Canadian justice."

"From what I hear, Shreve is responsible for a lot of those," Brette said.

The server arrived with our drinks and Brette raised her glass. "Thanks for rescuing me from Kevin. I grew up watching him read the nightly news. Doing him was on my life list."

"Like hiking the West Coast Trail," I said.

"Exactly," Brette agreed. "Except they give you a certificate for that. Anyway, onward and upward. What do you know about the judge in this case?"

"Arthur Harney? He's a farm boy. I heard him give a speech once, and he said he became a lawyer because shovelling shit was shovelling shit, and the law paid better than farming. The lawyers I know like him. He's fair. He's not a showboater. He trusts the lawyers to do their jobs. When he quit smoking, he took up origami to keep his hands busy."

"The origami's a nice touch. Mind if I copy?"

"Not at all," I said.

"I'll trade you," Brette said. "I'll bet you tomorrow's lunch bill that at some point this afternoon, Zack Shreve will give Sam Parker a LifeSaver."

"A LifeSaver?"

"Yep. Shreve and Lil Jo must have gone through a dozen packages during his trial. The intent is to show the jurors that the defendant is just an ordinary guy."

"I have a lot to learn," I said.

"Stick with me," Brette said. "I'm young, but I'm savvy."

When court reconvened, the jury announced that they had chosen a foreperson. I'd put my money on one of the three-piece-suit men, but the jurors picked the earth mother. Given the many complexities of Samuel Parker's case, an aging hippie with flowers in her hair was probably as good a choice as any.

Linda Fritz's opening address to the jury was admirably economical: no theatrics, no emotionally loaded language. Her summary of the facts of the case was concise and concrete. Samuel Parker's only child was a transsexual, making the transition from male to female. Glenda Parker had given an interview explaining the process to Kathryn Morrissey. The interview had been intense, and its appearance in Kathryn Morrissey's book *Too Much Hope* had repercussions. Publicly humiliated and hounded by the media, Beverly Parker had been hospitalized for exhaustion; Glenda herself had considered suicide. Samuel Parker had attempted to have publication of the book stopped, but when his lawyers told him he had no legal recourse, he had taken matters into his own hands. The Crown would prove that Samuel Parker had, with forethought and intent to kill, fired a pistol at Kathryn Morrissey. Linda Fritz then gave a quick sketch of the evidence the Crown would bring forth, including that of a witness who heard Samuel Parker utter threats against Kathryn Morrissey and who saw Samuel Parker take aim and pull the trigger.

I noticed that Linda Fritz stood very close to the jury box during her opening statement. In her barrister's robes with her smoothly coiffed red hair, she was a striking figure, and the jury was attentive. Only once did she change position, but once was enough. Towards the end of her opening, she began to sneeze. When she went back to the counsel table to get a tissue, her connection with the jurors was broken. Zack, who had been watching Linda Fritz carefully, noticed that the jury's attention had wandered momentarily towards the defence, and he pounced. More accurately, he reached into his pocket and pulled out a package of LifeSavers. The jury's eyes were on him now. When, very slowly, he unwrapped the package and offered a candy to Sam Parker, everyone was watching. Sam took the LifeSaver and smiled his thanks. It was a small moment, but a nice one.

Beside me, Brette Sinclair whispered, "Bingo."

Linda Fritz finished her opening statement with the assertion that the job of the Crown is to see that justice is done. It was a powerful statement, but the jury's attention had been diluted. They listened respectfully, but Linda knew she had lost momentum, and as she resumed her place behind the Crown prosecutor's table, her shoulders were tense.

Zack's opening was quiet. He wheeled over to the jurors and in a voice so soft it was almost a whisper, he introduced himself. "My name is Zachary Shreve," he said, "and I'm Sam Parker's lawyer. My task is to show you the kind of man Sam is and to show you what was in his mind and heart on the afternoon of May 16. It's a duty I'm proud to undertake, because Sam Parker is a decent man.

"My learned friend, the Crown prosecutor, has done a commendable job of laying out the facts in this case, but you and I know that facts without context are like paving stones before they're set in sand. Until they're anchored, you can make paving stones point in pretty much any direction you choose. With all due respect, I think my learned friend is pointing the stones in the wrong direction. So I'm going to put the facts into context – anchor them down. I'm trusting that you, as 'judges of the facts,' will make certain that we come out in the right place.

"You have a serious responsibility ahead of you. Serious responsibility is something that Sam Parker understands. Sam is a father who loves his child. That's why he's in this courtroom today. When Glenda Parker confided a matter of the utmost privacy to a journalist, and she betrayed him, Glenda's father acted. That's what parents do for their children. That's what a father does for his son."

Before that moment, Zack had always been careful to refer to Glenda in the feminine. The reference to Sam and Glenda as "father and son" had been a slip, but the jury, which to this point had been dutifully attentive, was now alert. Zack picked up on the change in the emotional temperature immediately. He shook his head and a little half-smile played on his lips. "There's a primal bond between a man and his son," he said, and his emphasis on the word *son* was unmistakable.

Beside me, Brette breathed the words "son of a bitch."

As he continued, Zack's voice was sonorous, pitch perfect for the tale he was telling about a decent man thrust into unthinkable circumstances who was guilty of a grievous error in judgment but not of attempted murder.

I glanced across at Glenda Parker. Her outfit for court was smart and androgynous: grey slacks, a black turtleneck, and an unstructured black jacket. Her only jewellery was the heavy gold band she wore on her ring finger. When Zack first used the phrase *father and son*, Glenda flinched, but from that moment on, she was stoic. All of the horror – the pictures of her competing as a male swimmer, the unpacking of her private life – everything she feared most was coming to pass, but it was in aid of a good cause. Her father's trusted barrister had found a note that resonated, and so Glenda swallowed hard.

Zack wheeled close to the jury. "Sam Parker loved his son," he said. "That was his crime. That was his 'sin.' Four hundred years ago, a poet lost his first-born son. He wrote about a father's anguish. 'Farewell, thou child of my right hand, and joy; / My sin was too much hope of thee, lov'd boy.'"

The meaty man rubbed his eyes with the back of his hand.

Zack went to him. "The poem makes me weep too. But those lines didn't make Kathryn Morrissey weep. For her, they were just material. She needed a title for her book, so she took what she wanted from a father's heartbreak. She needed a best-seller, so she took what she wanted from the broken lives of young people who trusted her. All Sam Parker did was love his son. He did not attempt to murder Kathryn Morrissey."

The courtroom was silent. Linda Fritz stared studiously at her files.

"Bull's eye," Brette said admiringly. "Also bullshit."

When Zack wheeled back to his place behind the counsel table, he touched his client's arm and said a few words. Glenda Parker was sitting directly behind them. She stood, squeezed Zack's shoulder, then bent to kiss her father's head. The gesture delivered a message more powerful than words. "Whatever it takes," the kiss said. "Whatever it takes."

Later, as I stood on the courthouse steps with Rapti Lustig running through the points I was going to cover in my report of the trial for *Canada Tonight*, I didn't mention the kiss. But as the snow swirled around me, and Rapti dabbed at my imperfections with Max Factor, the memory of Glenda's pain was sharp. So was the memory of the gusto with which

Zack had played his trump card. But when he came through the glass doors of the courthouse, his focus had shifted from the trial to me, and I remembered why I loved him.

He glowered at my bare neck. "Where's your scarf?"

"I couldn't find it this morning."

"How long do you have to stand out here?"

"I don't know," I said. "Probably another ten minutes."

He reached up, flicked off his own scarf, and handed it to me. "Take this."

I knotted his scarf around my neck.

"Better?" he said.

"Much," I said. "It's still warm from you."

"Anytime you need a little body heat."

Rapti scowled. "Hey, you two – get a room."

Zack raised an eyebrow. "Don't I wish?" At that moment, Linda Fritz came through the courthouse doors, and Zack called her over. Without her barrister's robes, Linda looked surprisingly vulnerable. It was clear from the hectic glitter in her eyes and the rasp in her voice that the volley of sneezes in court had just been a prelude: Linda was well on her way to the miseries of a cold.

She took in the scene. "What's up?" she said.

"I wanted Joanne to meet you. Although since she's already seen you in action, I guess we can skip the formalities."

"You were terrific in there," I said.

"Not terrific enough," Linda said glumly. "But tomorrow is another day – speaking of which, I have a ton of reading to do."

Zack's tone was matey. "If you'd accept our invitation to join Falconer Shreve, eager associates would simplify your life."

Linda blew her nose loudly and turned to me. "This man can't get it through his head that I actually like my work. He believes that when Falconer Shreve calls, I should just put on my lipstick and hightail it over to the dark side." She coughed. "Zack, for the record, I don't get my thrills from pulling the hair out of other people's drains. I'm happy where I am. Je ne regrette rien."

"The offer's always open," Zack said. He took my hand. "Gotta go. I'm going to meet my guy back at the office. I'll call you tonight." He pulled me towards him and kissed me. "I love you," he said.

Linda Fritz pounded her ear the way a swimmer does to get the water out. "Did I hear what I thought I heard?"

Zack frowned. "I told you Joanne and I were seeing each other."

Linda blew her nose. "I thought it was like all your other relationships. Slam bam, thank you, ma'am. You're always a pal afterwards, but love . . . hey, who knew?"

Zack grinned. "I wasn't counting on it either, Linda, but I got lucky. Take care of that cough."

My first report on the Sam Parker trial was complicated by a wind that was either keening into my lapel mike or lashing my hair in front of my eyes. But I stuck with it, and my report live to the East Coast was on time and on target. We all agreed the spot had gone well and as I removed my microphone, I felt a wash of relief. One show down, probably twenty more to go.

On the way to my car, I spotted Ethan Thorpe. He was walking through the parking lot behind the courthouse. He was wearing a full-length black coat with the collar pulled up against the weather – a figure of Gothic romance. I called to him. "Hey, Ethan."

He whirled around and recognized me. "Ms. Kilbourn – hi!" Turtle style, he pulled his head even farther down inside his collar.

"What are you doing down here?" I said.

"A project," he mumbled. "For social studies."

"Well, court's over for the day." I said, "Can I give you a lift home?"

"No!" His voice cracked with adolescence and emotion. Clearly, he didn't want me invading his private space. He tried to smooth the rough edge of his response. "Thanks, but it's okay. I like walking in storms." Then he turned on his heel and, in an exit worthy of Soul-fire, vanished in the swirl of snow.

Taylor and I watched my debut on *Canada Tonight* together in the family room. When the host gave a rundown of the stories the show would be covering that night, an image of me flashed on the screen. Taylor's new fashion radar was on full alert. "Hey, that scarf you're wearing would look really great with my orange boots."

"You'll have to talk to Zack. The scarf belongs to him." Taylor's smile started small and grew. "Zack would give you anything you asked for."

"Of course, he would," I said. "He's passion's slave."

Taylor's eyes widened.

"I picked up the phrase *passion's slave* from Soul-fire," I said. "Which reminds me, I saw Ethan downtown today. He was in the parking lot behind the courthouse."

"What was he doing there?"

"He said something about a social studies project. Anyway, I offered him a ride home, but he wanted to walk in the blizzard."

"He doesn't like being around other people much," Taylor said.

"How come?"

"Because he thinks other people don't like him."

"Is he right?"

By a stratagem I had come to recognize well from my years as a mother, Taylor deflected the question by changing the subject. Luckily for her, she had help. Just as the silence between us was growing awkward, my segment on *Canada Tonight* began. Taylor's relief was palpable. "Hey, your show's starting," she said.

We both watched critically. When it was over, Taylor flopped back on the couch. "Too bad about your hair weirding out in the wind like that, but what you said sounded good."

"Thanks," I said. I stood up. "And since I get to perform again tomorrow, I'd better do my homework."

Taylor ran her fingers through her choppy bob. "Maybe get some hairspray too," she said thoughtfully. "Gracie says Curlz Extra will keep your hair glued down in a monsoon."

Like many best-laid plans, my plan to make a quick run to Shoppers Drug Mart for industrial-strength hairspray and curl up with the background information Rapti had sent went awry. As I was rinsing our dishes, the phone rang.

It was Angus telling me he and Leah had a blast in New York, and that he was available 24/7 if I needed help with any legal points. I thanked him, told him I loved him, and went back to the dishes. I'd just put the last plate in the dishwasher when Howard Dowhanuik called.

His voice was thick. "I fucked up," he said.

"Stop the presses," I said.

"Okay," he said. "I deserved that." His voice was muffled and barely comprehensible.

"Howard, hang up and call me again. There's something the matter with this line."

"It isn't the line. It's the towel I'm holding up to my goddamn face. I fell and cut myself."

"How bad is it?"

"Bad enough. I'm bleeding like a stuck pig. I need to see a doctor."

"Keep the pressure on the wound," I said. "I'll be right there."

Like a gracious host, Howard was at the door waiting. A bloody bath towel was pressed to the left side of his face. Behind him on the tiled entrance floor was a liquor store bag that appeared to be leaking booze and blood. Recreating the sequence of events didn't require much imagination.

"Let me guess," I said. "You tripped coming in the door and fell face forward on your bottle of rye. It broke and cut your cheek."

Howard eyed me malevolently. "You always were a smart broad. Now take me to the emergency ward."

Two of my four children were risk-takers, and I knew from experience that the waiting time in emergency could be hours. I drove Howard to a walk-in clinic near the hospital. Whether it was the basset droop of Howard's good eye or the blood that was dripping from his towel to the clinic floor, we were attended to quickly. Howard had just finished answering the admitting clerk's questions when a nurse appeared and directed him to examining room F. I went with him.

"Are you going to hold my hand?" he asked.

"No, but you might have trouble remembering the doctor's instructions. I'm here for backup." I had just memorized the symptoms of West Nile Fever from a poster on the wall when the doctor came in. He was middle-aged and courtly. He glanced at the admission sheet on his clipboard. "Good evening, Mr. Dowhanuik," he said. "My name is Winston Govender." He removed Howard's bloody towel and peered at the wound. "A nasty one," he said. "What made the cut?"

"Glass," Howard said.

"Was the glass sterile?"

"Bathed in alcohol. As was I," Howard said gloomily.

Dr. Govender's smile was perfunctory. He went to the sink and scrubbed his hands. "I'll stitch you up now. You were fortunate, Mr. Dowhanuik. Just a few millimetres higher and you could have damaged your eye."

"My lucky day."

"It was indeed," Dr. Govender said, and he set to work.

Howard's cut required nine stitches. When the procedure was completed, Dr. Govender washed his hands again and then pulled up a stool next to Howard and scrutinized his handiwork. The flesh around the black line of stitches was already puffing up and blooming purple. Howard was going to look like hell in the morning and for a lot of mornings after.

"You're going to experience some pain tonight," Dr. Govender said. "I can give you something to ease it, but you must answer a question for me first. How much do you drink, Mr. Dowhanuik?"

Howard sighed heavily. "Not enough, Dr. Govender. Not nearly enough."

We left without a prescription, but with written instructions about how to care for the wound. When I pulled up in front of Howard's, he thanked me and beat a path to his door. I wasn't about to let him escape that easily. I followed him in, found the phone book, opened it to the number for Alcoholics Anonymous, and handed it to Howard.

Howard glanced at the page. "What am I supposed to do with this?"

"You're supposed to call the number," I said.

Howard glared and thrust the phone book back at me. "Ian always said that you were a goddamn Sunday-school teacher."

I felt the sting. "What else did my husband say?"

"That you were a moralist – a pain in the ass who never got over being twenty-two and idealistic. That everything was black or white for you. That you never grew up enough to understand that life is lived in shades of grey."

A lump of sadness formed at the back of my throat.

Howard peered at me. "Jesus, now you're crying. I'm sorry, Jo. What can I do?"

I handed him back the phone book. "Call the number," I said. "Call Alcoholics Anonymous."

When I got home, Zack's car was in my driveway, and he was in my living room staring at his BlackBerry. I came into the room and he held out his arms. "At last," he said.

I went to him. "Have you been waiting long?"

"Nope. Just got here." He looked at me closely. "Have you been crying?"

"Yes."

"You want to talk about it?"

I took a tissue from my coat pocket and blew my nose. "Am I a moralist?"

"No," he said, "you're moral. There's a distinction." He leaned back and gave me an appraising glance. "I take it your question didn't just come out of the blue."

"Howard fell and cut his cheek open on a bottle of booze. I spent the last couple of hours at the Medicentre getting him stitched up."

"And after Howard was stitched up he called you a moralist?"

"According to Howard, he was just quoting Ian, who apparently also called me a Sunday-school teacher and a pain in the ass."

"Well, Ian's not here to defend himself," Zack said. "So why don't we find ourselves a place where we can sit down and talk this out?"

As soon as we got into the family room, Zack pushed himself out of his chair onto the couch. I moved close to him, ran my hands over his chest, and breathed in his aftershave.

"Better?" Zack said.

"Yes," I said. "You are always exactly what I need."

"And you're always exactly what I need." Zack squeezed my shoulder. "Try not to let what Howard said get to you.

He made an ass of himself tonight. He was probably just lashing out."

"Maybe. But what he said had the ring of truth. At the end, Ian and I had a lot of flash points."

"I'm sorry."

"So am I."

Zack leaned towards me in his arms. "I love you very much."

"I love you too," I said.

"In my opinion, that means we should be together."

"Unfair," I said. "I'm tired and vulnerable."

"I'm tired and vulnerable too," he said. "But you don't hear me whining."

"That's because you're tough."

"Says who?"

"Brette Sinclair."

"The pretty girl with the silky hair that you were sitting next to in court."

"We had lunch together too," I said. "I'm learning a lot from her."

"For example . . . ?"

"For example, she predicted you'd do that LifeSaver trick with Sam – very clever."

Zack laughed softly. "Just a variation on a theme," he said. "If a female lawyer has a male client who's accused of a violent crime, she touches his arm, gives him a little pat on the shoulder just to show that her client's not all that scary."

"Maybe I should give you a few more touches and pats in public – humanize you."

"Bad idea," Zack said. "It's my job to be scary. As long as I don't scare you . . ."

I didn't respond.

Zack pulled away. "I don't scare you, do I?"

I touched the furrow that ran down his cheek. "You did today," I said. "You've always been so careful not to refer to Glenda as Sam's son. I thought it was a matter of principle."

"The first time was a slip," Zack said. "But the moment it happened, I knew I'd connected with the jury. I'd hit the sweet spot – I could feel the ball fly off the bat and soar over the outfield fence. I was in the game, and I needed that."

"For you or for Sam?" I said.

"I don't know," he said. "All I know is it felt really good." He ran his finger over my lips, then kissed me. "That wasn't the answer you wanted, but I'm not a hero, Jo. I'm just a guy who needs to win. And when I win, my clients win. Can you live with that?"

"I guess I'm going to have to," I said.

Shades of grey. Shades of grey.

CHAPTER

7

Every night during the trial, Rapti Lustig e-mailed me more background information. Early that first week she forwarded an article about criminal lawyer Eddie Greenspan in which the writer riffed on the idea that in a jury trial, everything but the basic script is choreography and improvisation.

During its first week, it seemed the Sam Parker trial was desperately in need of a script doctor. The job of the Crown was to establish the evidence, and for Linda Fritz that apparently meant taking police officers through every line of every note they had made on the case. Her dogged precision exasperated Zack, but since his job was to make sure the police and the Crown had done their jobs, she gave him a good base from which to work. And so we listened as the Crown called witness after witness to buttress its case and the defence picked away endlessly at the testimony of officers who were accustomed to testifying and were unlikely to risk their careers to falsify a detail like the angle of the sun on a late afternoon in May.

Throughout the period Brette Sinclair referred to as "the parade of the essential but boring as hell witnesses," I found my attention drawn to the jurors. Like the members of any ensemble cast, they were beginning to declare themselves as individuals. The angry man with the aggressive combover turned out to have an odd mannerism. He responded to everything the lawyers or the witnesses said with a vigorous negative shake of the head. Until Zack figured out the shake was a tic not a comment, he was distinctly uneasy. The foreperson with the shoulder-length salt-and-pepper hair had arranged her features in a mask of serenity that suggested she had withdrawn from the courtroom's swirl of bad karma and negative thoughts. The young people made no attempt to disguise their boredom at the lacklustre performance they were forced to endure. Their faces were blank, as if they had detached themselves and were listening to invisible iPods. The Modigliani woman and the meaty man had become Zack's partisans, smiling encouragement when he did well with a line of questioning and dropping their gaze when the judge (as he frequently did) chastised Zack for pushing too hard (as he frequently did). The notetaker grew more note-takey, barely glanced up at the proceedings, so intent was he on recording everything. The Lucille Ball wannabe seemed pathetically eager to lighten it up. On the trial's third morning, an earnest young constable described in precise detail the size of a bullet hole; when he was through, she rewarded him with a rubbery grin. The men in the three-piece suits were clearly impatient, like senior managers forced to listen to the concerns of underlings. The ladies with the gentle perms drifted off from time to time as ladies with gentle perms will when the topic of conversation turns to the trajectory of a bullet.

The one real source of drama that week was Linda Fritz, who, it became increasingly clear, was suffering from the mother of all colds. On the first day it had attacked her voice, roughening it and reducing it to a painful croak. By the second day, Linda could barely whisper, and the judge gave her permission to use a lapel mike to question her witnesses. The cough that was plaguing Linda when we met had grown noticeably worse. To my ears, it sounded like bronchitis.

The ladies with the seasonal sweaters watched Linda with anxious eyes. From the outset, they had been sympathetic to her; now they looked as if they'd like to take her home and get her under a croup tent. The beefy guy was clearly pissed off that he was in the room with a walking petri dish of viral stew, and he and the Modigliani woman ostentatiously flattened themselves against the back of their chairs whenever Linda approached the jury box. The three-piece-suiters contented themselves with raising a handkerchief to cover their nose and mouth as if they were walking through the city of the plague. The *I Love Lucy* juror produced a bottle of hand sanitizer and passed it around. Interest in the testimony of "the essential but boring as hell witnesses" waned.

Zack was uneasy too, but his concern wasn't hygiene. He was genuinely fond of Linda and he respected her as an adversary. When she failed to pick up on inconsistencies or points that she normally would have hammered home, he was at first baffled then concerned. She seemed to be having trouble hearing, and on the morning of the fourth day, she didn't even bother trying to put on her game face. She soldiered on until the luncheon recess, but when court reconvened, she was not in her place and when the clerk announced that the Crown had asked for a continuance, and that court was adjourned until Monday morning, the relief in the courtroom was palpable.

I did my standup for NationTV and headed home to a long nap and some prophylactic echinacea and vitamin C. Zack was giving a speech at a dinner in Saskatoon on Monday night. We were planning to stay over and savour the pleasures of a first-class hotel, and I didn't want to miss the pampering.

Saturday morning Zack came over for pancakes before he went back to the office. He had news of Linda Fritz, and it wasn't promising. The virus that had begun as laryngitis moved to bronchitis and then an ear infection had turned her right ear deaf. Her eardrum was bulging due to the pressure of fluid behind it. She was on massive doses of antibiotics, but it would take up to three weeks for the fluid behind her eardrum to be absorbed. She was off the case.

"She must be disappointed," I said.

"She's furious," Zack said. "I went over to her apartment this morning. She still feels like shit, but not being able to prosecute this case is making it a hundred times worse. She put in a lot of hours on this one, and she thought she could win." He picked up the maple syrup and flooded his plate. "Can you think of anything we can send to cheer her up?"

"What does she like?"

Zack furrowed his brow in concentration. "Practising law. Beating me."

"How about a dartboard and a picture of you."

"Perfect," he said. "So what are you up to this morning?"

"It's moving day. Pete's moving in with Charlie."

"Big job?"

"No. Pete's got his truck and he travels light. Charlie's coming over to help. If you stick around, you can see him."

Zack checked his watch. "I have a few minutes. Hey, I got our reservations for the Bessborough – the lieutenant-governor's suite."

"I'm impressed."

"I was hoping you would be."

"It'll be fun to get away to Saskatoon for a night."

"Even if it means spending the evening with a bunch of lawyers."

"As long as I end up with the lawyer of my choice." I kissed him on the head. "Now, I'd better find Taylor and get her to her art lesson. If you're not here when I get back, give me a call."

Zack *was* there when I got back, so was Charlie Dowhanuik. When I walked into the kitchen, they fell silent.

I joined them at the kitchen table. "So what were you guys talking about?"

Charlie's eyes met mine. "My father."

"When was the last time you saw him?"

"I don't remember," Charlie said tightly. "And, Jo, I don't want to talk about him with you."

"Fair enough," I said. "So how's the big move progressing?"

"Haven't done a thing, but I figure it should take us twenty minutes to load the truck. You know Pete – fourteen boxes of books, some sports equipment, and two garbage bags of clothes."

"Don't forget his collection of baseball cards. I've been trying to get them out of here since he went to vet school."

Zack leaned forward in his chair. "I've got a foul ball from the sixth game of the Toronto/Atlanta World Series in 1993. I caught it myself."

Pete came in. "The game where Joe Carter hit the series-winning home run. I watched that on TV – it was great."

"It was a lot of fun. Anyway, if you want the ball, say the word."

"I want the ball."

"My pleasure," Zack said.

Charlie stood up. "Now that everybody's happy, let's get this move underway. The faster we get this over, the faster I can get back to bed." He walked over to Zack. "I'll be in touch."

They left and I turned to Zack. "So what's Charlie going to be in touch about?"

Zack's green eyes were thoughtful. "Things you don't want to know about. Can we leave it at that?"

"Do I have an option?"

His cell rang, and Zack flashed me a mischievous smile. "Saved by the bell," he said. As he talked, I put some eggs on to boil for lunch. After Zack ended the call, he came over and grabbed me from behind. "My lucky day," he said. "Garth Severight is replacing Linda."

"Garth Severight isn't formidable?"

"He has his strengths," Zack said. "He's quite the orator, and he looks like Mr. Big, from *Sex and the City*."

"However . . . ?"

"However . . . he's got this monster ego. He doesn't listen, and he always knows best. Linda's ten times the lawyer he'll ever be, but he'll torch her case and go in with his guns blazing."

"He sounds like an idiot."

"Pretty close," Zack said equitably. "And best of all, I know how to push Garth's buttons. Nothing I do ever fazes Linda, but Garth reacts to me. I had a professor who said that if the only tool you use is a hammer, every problem begins to look like a nail."

"And Garth Severight's only tool is a hammer?"

"Yep, and he uses it indiscriminately. No finesse, no reflection, just bang, bang, bang, bang. It makes juries edgy and it drives judges nuts. A couple of years ago, we were in front of a judge with a notoriously short fuse. I honestly thought she was going to spontaneously combust. Garth saw it too, but every time I hove into view, Garth would start in. Rat-a-tat-tat. Rat-a-tat-tat. He couldn't seem to stop himself." Zack shook his head, remembering. "Even I felt sorry for the poor fuck."

"So you stayed out of his way?"

Zack was incredulous. "Are you kidding? I made sure I was in his face every single second."

"You're licking your chops," I said.

"Sorry," he said. "But with this case, it's been a while. Anyway, I gotta go. Tell Pete I'll drop the ball by. Hey, maybe you and I could go over later on today and check out his new digs."

"And you and Charlie could get together and talk about the things I don't want to know about."

Zack nodded his head approvingly. "No flies on you, Ms. Kilbourn. No flies on you."

On Monday morning, when Howard Dowhanuik took his place in the witness box, it was clear there were no flies on my beloved either. All weekend, I had fought the urge to get in touch with Howard. I had hoped that, left to his own devices, he might pick up the phone and call AA. On Sunday night, he had phoned me. He sounded sober, but he was good at that.

"Meet me for breakfast tomorrow?" he said. "I'll buy."

"Sure," I said. "What's up?"

"Nothing. I need to be distracted."

"Hard to turn down such a gracious invitation," I said. "Where do you want to go?"

"Humpty's. They make a great Meatlovers Pan-Scrambler: eggs, hash browns, ground beef, bacon, and ham. The whole thing is covered in cheese sauce."

"Does it come with a fibrillator?"

"Yes or no?"

"Yes. I'll meet you there."

I continued packing for the trip to Saskatoon. Zack and I were flying there as soon as court was over that day. As I zipped my best dress into a garment bag and added strappy pumps, an evening bag, and the long black slip appliquéd in lilies that Zack liked, I tried to focus on the romance of staying in the lieutenant-governor's suite with the man I loved. But all I could think of was Howard and the ordeal ahead.

Taylor was sleeping over at the Wainbergs Monday night, so I dropped her bag off at their place on the way to the restaurant. Delia Wainberg, already dressed for the office, met me at the door. She was full of questions about how I thought the trial was going, so I was late getting to Humpty's.

Howard was sitting at a booth in the corner. He had done what he could about shaving, but the railroad track of stitches on his cheekbone had clearly defeated him. His bruise had mutated to a purplish green and it bristled with a three-day growth of hair. He looked like hell, and as he picked up his mug, it was clear he was suffering from a killer hangover. His hands were shaking so badly that the coffee slopped onto the Formica tabletop.

I pulled some napkins from the dispenser and mopped up. "You've got a tough morning ahead," I said. "Herbal tea might be a better choice."

"Strychnine would be a better choice," he said. "But this is what I ordered. You're not my mother."

"And I thank God for that every day of my life," I said. "But you've been a good friend, Howard. You stayed with me the night Ian died, and you were there all those months when I crawled into a hole and didn't want to crawl back out. You drove me to the hospital the time Pete got that concussion playing football –"

Howard raised his hand in a halt gesture. "I don't need the Life and Times crap, Jo."

The server came to take my order and to deliver Howard's Meatlovers' Pan-Scrambler. After she left, Howard rested his jaw in his palm and stared at his plate.

"Come on," I said briskly. "You're hungover. You need to eat. Shovel in some of that health-food special in front of you."

Howard picked up his fork obediently and took a bite. He could barely swallow.

"Okay," I said. "Save the manly meal for another time. Just try to get a piece of toast down."

It was a silent and miserable breakfast. When I was finished eating, I left some bills on the table. Howard, who was normally the most generous of men, didn't fight me for the cheque. "I'll see you at the courthouse," I said. "Do me a favour. Don't have anything to drink before you take the stand."

As I was going up the courthouse stairs, Zack was coming up the ramp. There had been a warming trend over the weekend. The snow had melted; the sidewalks were dry; the sun was bright and the air was mellow. Zack was wearing a lightweight mochaccino suit and a red tie.

"I like your tie," I said.

"I like everything about you," he said.

We stopped in the lobby under the mural celebrating our majestic legal heritage.

"How bad is it going to be?" I asked.

Zack shrugged. "It depends on how prepared Howard is. Have you seen him?"

"We had breakfast together – at Humpty's."

Zack's smile was faint. "How's he doing?"

"He's a little under the weather. He'll be all right. Howard is a good man, Zack."

"That may be true," Zack said. "But he's not my client."

"Still . . ."

"There is no 'still,'" Zack said. "Howard is the Crown's chief witness against my client. His testimony can send Sam Parker to jail."

"So you're going to tear Howard apart."

"I'm going to do what I have to do for my client."

"No matter what," I said.

Zack's gaze didn't waver. "No matter what. There's a saying among criminal lawyers: 'If you don't have blood on your hands, you're not doing your job.'" He turned his chair. "I do my job," he said, then he wheeled over to the doors, hit the accessibility button, and disappeared inside.

After Zack left, I went to the courtroom in search of Howard. He wasn't there. It was entirely possible Garth Severight and the Crown were keeping Howard hydrated and calmed, but somehow I doubted it, and when I went back to the lobby and saw a young lawyer from the Crown's office frantically scrutinizing the lobby and the street, I knew I'd been right to worry. So far, Howard was a no-show.

I took a place on the bench beneath the mural and waited. I knew that, as he always had, Howard would come. The lobby emptied of press, interested parties, and spectators, and I was suddenly alone with that hollow-pit-in-the-stomach feeling I'd had as a child when I was late coming over from the dorms and I'd arrived to find the school halls empty and silent.

I had just about given up hope when Howard appeared. He no longer looked defeated or hungover. He just looked drunk. He was fumbling with a small metal tin of breath-mints, and he'd obviously given himself a fresh shellacking of Crown Royal. I took the tin from him, popped the corner, and handed it back to him. He threw a handful of mints into his mouth.

"Feeling better?" I asked.

"Like the bottom of a latrine," he said. "But I'll get through."

I sniffed his breath. "You do realize that those things aren't working," I said.

Howard studied the label on the tin with a drunk's care. "Freshens the breath," he read. His eyes were sorrowful. "Seems like you can't believe in anything any more, doesn't it?"

His words were prescient. The first witness that morning was not Howard Dowhanuik, but his son, Charlie. When the court clerk called Charlie's name, my heart lurched, but I wasn't surprised. As promised, Zack had dropped by Charlie's house with the baseball on Saturday afternoon. When I'd gone upstairs to help Pete unpack, Charlie had stayed behind with Zack. Now Charlie was in the witness box.

I stared at Zack, but he didn't return my gaze. As Garth Severight took Charlie through his testimony, Zack never once looked my way. Charlie's story was simple. He had approached Garth over the weekend and offered to substantiate Howard's story. Garth had jumped at the offer.

Severight's eagerness made sense. Howard was not an ideal witness. According to Zack, Linda Fritz knew Howard had a drinking problem and that he was hostile. She would willingly have left him off the Crown's witness list except for one fact. Howard was prepared to testify that he had heard Sam Parker threaten Kathryn Morrissey and that he had seen Sam raise and aim the gun. Without Howard's testimony, there would be a gaping hole in the Crown's case. Howard might have been a compromised witness, but the Crown needed him. Charlie's testimony could plug up the holes.

When Charlie took the stand, Brette Sinclair put her mouth to my ear. "Finally – something interesting."

Hair neatly brushed back, shoes shined, suit pressed, Charlie was the epitome of the responsible citizen. He was also a very effective witness who told his story well. According to Charlie, his father had called him the evening of the shooting and asked him to come to the condominium. Although he and his father were estranged, Charlie had agreed. His father had been agitated on the telephone, and Charlie had been concerned that something had happened to a family member. As soon as Charlie arrived, his father described an incident that had happened twenty minutes earlier. According to Howard, he had been out in his yard when he heard a man shouting. In May, the trees between Howard's condo and Kathryn's were leafing, but he had a clear view of what had happened. The man, whom Howard recognized as Sam Parker, raised a gun, pointed it at Kathryn Morrissey, and pulled the trigger.

Howard told his son he had dialed 911 and reported the shooting. He had not left his name. Charlie suggested that 911 probably logged all incoming phone calls, and that Howard should prepare to be interviewed. He then made a pot of coffee for his father and stayed with him until a police constable arrived.

Zack's eyes were hooded as Charlie testified. There were no interruptions to mar the silken flow of Charlie's performance. When Garth Severight returned to his place at the Crown's table, he was purring with satisfaction.

As Zack approached the witness box, Garth was still preening. Zack's voice was warm. "Hello, Charlie. It was good of you to come forward the way you did."

Charlie shrugged. "I try to do the right thing."

"Still, a lot of people – especially young, successful people – might not have bothered." I gazed at the jury box. For the first time since the trial started, the young jurors had dropped their masks of ironic detachment.

Charlie D was famous. Suddenly, they were into the trial big time.

"Your testimony was very helpful in giving us a picture of exactly what happened that afternoon," Zack said. "For example, you said that after you explained to your father that his call to 911 would have been logged and the police would be coming to his house, you made him a pot of coffee. Considering that you and your father were estranged, that was a friendly thing to do."

"It was a necessary thing to do," Charlie said firmly. "My father was drunk. He was in no condition . . ."

Severight was on his feet. "This is hardly relevant."

Mr. Justice Harney overruled him. "It speaks to the competency of the case's only eyewitness. I'll allow it." He turned to Charlie. "You may continue."

"As I said, my father was drunk. I thought the coffee might sober him up so he could give a coherent explanation of what he'd seen."

Zack was cool. "So your father wasn't in a state where his words could be trusted?"

Severight was on his feet again. "The witness is not an expert on degrees of drunkenness, m'Lord."

Zack smiled at Severight. "I'll rephrase that. Charlie, could you describe your father's state when you arrived at his condominium that evening."

"He was slurring his words. His gait was unsteady. At one point, he tried to pour himself a drink and he missed the glass. He was very emotional – maudlin even."

"Can you elaborate on that?"

"As I said, my father and I were estranged, and he was crying about that."

"Anything in particular trigger this show of remorse?"

"He said that what Sam Parker did made him ashamed of himself."

Zack narrowed his eyes. "Why would your father be ashamed of himself?"

Charlie turned towards the jury. "Because when Sam Parker's child was betrayed, Sam did everything in his power to protect her."

"And your father didn't protect you?"

"How could he?" Charlie said. "He was the one who betrayed me."

CHAPTER

8

After Charlie left the stand, there was silence in the court-room. His revelation about Howard's state on the night of the shooting was the stuff of prime-time drama, but it was Charlie's anguish that stilled our tongues. A glance at the jury box was enough to see that the jurors had been deeply affected by Charlie's pain. The notetaking man with the angry com-bover had capped his pen. Apparently, Charlie's testimony had convinced him that human beings were a waste of ink.

I didn't know whether it was a blessing or a curse that someone from the office of the Crown had decided to sequester Howard until it was time for him to testify, but as he climbed into the witness box, the question was irrelevant. Sam Parker's freedom depended on what happened next.

Garth Severight greeted his star witness with the gush of a high school debater meeting a political idol. His game plan was built around Howard's status as a former premier and a man of integrity; come hell or high water, he was going to stick with it. At first, it seemed Garth had made a good call. The hostility in the courtroom was palpable, but drunk or sober, Howard was a pro who had spent a lifetime gauging audiences. Our ex-premier delivered his testimony with enough self-deprecating references to his own bad judgment, pride, and stupidity to disarm all but the meanest of his foes.

It was a credible performance and, again, one that was not interrupted by the defence. Throughout Howard's testimony, Zack peered over his glasses, faintly amused at Howard's rueful admissions of fallibility, stone-faced as Howard acknowledged that he had been disloyal to his son. If Garth Severight sensed a storm brewing, he didn't show it. When he finished his examination, the Chief prosecutor strode back to the Crown's table and resumed his seat with the satisfied air of a man who once again could feel the wind beneath his wings.

As Zack manoeuvred his chair towards the witness box, my pulse spiked. He had told me once that if he'd had the lousy luck to be born in Spain, he would have been up shit creek because the continental European legal system didn't permit cross-examination. That day, Zack wasn't the one with the lousy luck. From the moment Zack gave Howard a sympathetic half-smile and bade him good morning, Howard was doomed.

"How tall are you, Mr. Dowhanuik?"

The question came out of left field, and Howard looked confused. "A little over six feet," he said finally.

"You just told us that you happened to be gazing over your fence when you saw Mr. Parker enter Ms. Morrissey's yard. Is that correct?"

"Yes."

"But in his testimony, Constable Gerein said that the fence that separates your property from Ms. Morrissey's is six and a half feet tall. To see what you described in your testimony, you must have been standing on tippytoe, Mr. Dowhanuik."

There was a burst of nervous laughter in the courtroom. When Howard remained mute, Zack wheeled closer. "Were you standing on your tippytoes, Mr. Dowhanuik? That's a question."

"No," Howard said.

Zack's face wrinkled in exasperation. "Then how did you see what was going on?"

"I . . . there was a little stepladder against the fence."

"A little stepladder – that's right. Constable Gerein noted that too. So you heard a man's voice, picked up your little stepladder, and moved it to the fence so you could see what was going on. Is that correct?"

Howard flushed crimson. "No, I was standing there."

"On your little stepladder?"

"Yes."

Zack made a moue of disgust. "Why ever would you be doing that?"

"I was watching."

"You were watching Ms. Morrissey?"

Howard nodded.

"The court clerk needs your answer in words, Mr. Dowhanuik."

"Yes," Howard said. "I was watching Ms. Morrissey."

"Was this the first time you spied on Ms. Morrissey when she was in the privacy of her yard?"

Howard's face was an unhealthy crimson. "Not the first time, no. I'd been watching her for a week. Since the book was excerpted in the paper."

"What are you, some kind of peeping Tom?"

Garth exploded from his seat. "Objection. Objection, m'Lord. Objection." Rat-a-tat-tat.

Arthur Harney winced at Garth's volley, but he sustained the objection.

"I'll try again," Zack said agreeably. "Mr. Dowhanuik, tell me why you were standing on a stepladder spying on your neighbour."

Howard's fire might have been dampened, but there was still a spark. "I wanted her to know that I was watching her."

"Were you attempting to intimidate her?"

"I wanted to remind her that I was there."

"You wanted to remind her that you were there?" Zack repeated the explanation mockingly. "After you moved next door to her, you and she spent many intimate hours in each other's company. Ms. Morrissey's a well-known journalist. Did she need you standing on your little stepladder peering in on her to remind her that you were her neighbour?"

"She needed to know how it felt to have her privacy violated," Howard said defiantly. "She needed to know what it had been like for Charlie and me."

"So you were angry at her for what she'd written about your family in her book."

"Yes."

"Is that why you didn't go to her aid after she was shot?"

Howard's head dropped. "I called 911," he muttered.

"But after you called 911, you didn't go to Ms. Morrissey to ascertain how badly she'd been wounded or to reassure her, did you?"

"No."

"You weren't in any danger, Mr. Dowhanuik. The assailant had fled the scene. You've testified to that. But instead of doing what 99 per cent of the people in this courtroom would have done, you left Ms. Morrissey out there bleeding and alone and you . . . What *did* you do after you called 911?"

Howard seemed confused. "I called my son," he mumbled.

Zack sighed. "Now again, that doesn't strike me as the course of action 99 per cent of us in this room would have followed. Why did you call Charlie?"

The casual use of Charlie's name hit a nerve. For the first time, Howard seemed to realize that the defence knew more about his actions that afternoon than Garth Severight had led him to believe.

Zack withheld his next blow, but he made certain Howard knew it was coming. "I asked you a question, Mr. Dowhanuik," he said. "The jury has heard your son's version of what happened after he arrived at your condominium. What's your version?"

"Charlie advised me."

"Really. Now that is interesting. You hadn't committed a crime. Unless we count the peeping Tom incident." Zack waved his hand towards the Crown's table. "I know. I know. I withdraw the characterization of the witness. But, Mr. Dowhanuik, this is where I'm having a problem following your thought processes. I know you were angry at Ms. Morrissey, but she'd been shot and you had witnessed the shooting. Why would you just hop off your ladder and leave Ms. Morrissey out in her yard alone and bleeding while you called your son for advice?"

"Because I was drunk," Howard said.

"Ah," Zack said with a Cheshire smile. "Finally, we've arrived at the crux of the matter. You were drunk. Were you so drunk, you couldn't navigate the distance between your house and Ms. Morrissey's? Officer Gerein paced off the path between where you were standing on your little ladder and the spot where Ms. Morrissey was enjoying her wine. He testified it was less than ten metres. That's not much of a walk. It was still early – 4:30 in the afternoon. How many drinks had you had?"

"I don't know," Howard said. "It had been a difficult time."

"You mean the time since you became aware of what Ms. Morrissey had written about Charlie in your book."

"Yes."

"The fact that you'd played the role of Deep Throat for her must have made the situation even more depressing." Zack wheeled closer to the witness box. "And you were already depressed, weren't you? You were using the prescription drug Paxil?"

"Yes."

"And . . ." Zack looked at his notes. "Your drug regimen also includes prescriptions for high blood pressure, high cholesterol, and something else . . ." Zack squeezed his eyes shut in concentration. "Chronic back pain – Charlie said you were also being treated for chronic back pain."

Garth Severight rose to protest Charlie's information as hearsay, and Mr. Justice Harney upheld his objection. It didn't matter. The knockout punch had been delivered. Howard knew that his son had revealed everything to the defence. Bruised, battered, and desperate, Howard was a fighter on the ropes, but Zack kept pummelling. "That's quite the chemical stew, Mr. Dowhanuik. I'm certain your doctor didn't suggest that you add alcohol to the mix."

"No, my doctor told me not to drink."

"And still you drank."

"I did."

"How many drinks have you had today, Mr. Dowhanuik?"

"I don't know."

"More than three?"

"Yes."

"Five? Six?"

"I don't measure."

"Do you have a flask of liquor with you right now?"

"Yes."

"And you've taken all your medications?"

"Yes." Zack turned his chair so that his back was to Howard. "We've been pretty close to each other for the past twenty minutes. Do I wear eyeglasses?"

"I didn't notice."

Zack turned, faced Howard, and adjusted the black wire-framed glasses he'd worn throughout the cross-examination. "Let's try again, Mr. Dowhanuik. What colour was the dress Ms. Morrissey was wearing on May 16?"

"I don't remember."

"Blue. Ms. Morrissey was wearing a blue dress. Attention to detail doesn't seem to be your strong suit, Mr. Dowhanuik. But we'll persevere. On the afternoon of the incident, was Ms. Morrissey sitting or standing."

"Sitting at a kind of little table."

"Was she reading or staring off into space, or what?"

"I think she was reading."

"Just to let you know, there was no reading material found at the scene, Mr. Dowhanuik, so wrong again." Zack glanced over at Garth Severight. "Usually, the Crown does a better job of coaching its witnesses."

Severight popped out of his chair. "I object."

"Sustained," Arthur Harney barked. "Cheap shot, Mr. Shreve."

"I apologize, m'Lord. So, Mr. Dowhanuik, Ms. Morrissey was sitting at her little table. Then, according to your version of events, my client entered her yard through the side gate and said what?"

"I don't remember his exact words."

"You remembered them an hour ago."

Howard pinched the bridge of his nose and stared at his knees.

Zack was unrelenting. "Do we need ask the court clerk to read you the words that you swore were true an hour ago.

I'm confused, Mr. Dowhanuik. An hour ago, you swore under oath that you remembered exactly what my client said to Ms. Morrissey. Word for word. And now you don't remember. Could you give us a paraphrase?"

"I don't think so."

"But you *testified*. You swore on the Bible that what you were about to say was the truth, the whole truth, and nothing but the truth, so help you God. You were so confident of your memory then that you swore that you could relate exactly what was said on May 16. That was five months ago, Mr. Dowhanuik. All I'm asking is that you paraphrase what you said an hour ago. Surely you can remember what you told us an hour ago?"

Howard stared fixedly at the knees of his pants, as if he hoped that somehow the answer would appear there. It didn't. After an agonizing wait, he finally responded, "No, I can't."

Zack was looking intently at the jury. Aristotle understood the mix of pity and terror an audience feels at the fall of a good man. Zack might or might not have read Aristotle, but he could read a jury and he knew this one had had enough. When he spoke again, his voice was kind.

"Mr. Dowhanuik, no one here today wants to humiliate you. As my friend pointed out repeatedly, you are an ex-premier. Why don't I just take a stab at relating what was said, and if anything I say differs substantially from what you swore to an hour ago, you sing out. Fair enough?"

"Yes," Howard said.

"Good," Zack said. "Now, I'm an ordinary guy. I don't have total recall. A lot of time, I have problems remembering where I parked my car, but I think I can convey the gist of your testimony about the conversation between Ms. Morrissey and my client. According to you, when Ms. Morrissey spotted my client, she said 'What are you doing here?' He replied, 'This is destroying my family. I thought perhaps if we talked . . .' At that point, Ms. Morrissey cut him off, saying, 'Your lawyer has already been in touch with my publishers. You have no grounds for a lawsuit. The book is in the stores. It's too late . . .' Am I in the ballpark so far, Mr. Dowhanuik?"

"Yes," Howard whispered.

"You told us that, at that point, Mr. Parker took out a pistol, aimed it at Ms. Morrissey, and said, 'How does it feel to know this might be the last day of your life?' And then you remember a gunshot. Surely, you can fill us in on the circumstances of *that* moment. A man's freedom depends on your answer. What happened in the seconds before the shot was fired, Mr. Dowhanuik?"

"I don't remember. It was all so fast. One minute she was sitting in her chair drinking wine, the next she was on the ground bleeding."

Zack exhaled as if relieved at the completion of a distasteful task. "Thank you, Mr. Dowhanuik, the people appreciate your co-operation."

Like a felon, Howard bolted from the witness box. Zack wheeled into his exit path, blocking him. "You were a lawyer, Mr. Dowhanuik. You must remember that you're supposed to wait for Mr. Justice Harney to tell you that you may step down."

For a brief and heartbreaking moment, the two men at the centre of my life faced each other. Whether it was the booze or the disgrace, Howard was unsteady on his feet; in his wheelchair, Zack was a coiled spring. "You didn't let me finish," he said. "Ms. Morrissey was not found bleeding on the ground. She had gone inside her home, and was putting pressure on her wound. She, too, called 911. When the EMS arrived, she opened her front door and admitted them herself.

"Mr. Dowhanuik, I hope you know that our encounter today has brought me no pleasure. My friend is right in saying that most of us know you as a fine, upstanding citizen, the clear-eyed leader of our province, but liquor and drugs have a way of distorting vision, of making a person see things, not as they are but as he wishes they might have been." Zack wheeled over to the jury box. "Members of the jury, judges of facts, when you deliberate over Mr. Dowhanuik's testimony, remember what you saw today – a man stitched and bruised from a drunken fall, his eyes bloodshot, his hands trembling, who, despite what I'm certain was diligent coaching from the Crown, was unable to get his story straight. Ask yourself if you would want your fate determined by the testimony of this man. Ask yourself if the testimony he delivered and then couldn't remember an hour later was the truth or some drunken, drug-addled fantasy he spun out of his desperation and guilt." Zack wheeled back to the defence table. As if as an afterthought, he threw Howard the sentence that liberated him. "Oh, no more questions."

As he left the courtroom, Howard was a broken man. I remembered Zack's hesitancy about having me cover the trial for NationTV. He'd said he wanted me to keep believing he was a nice guy. He hadn't been a nice guy with Howard. He'd been mocking, diminishing, intimidating, and menacing. On our first date, Zack and I had eaten at a restaurant that looked over the Qu'Appelle Valley. It had been a spectacular summer night and after we ate, we gazed across the hills and Zack said that the still waters and green pastures beneath us made him understand the Twenty-third Psalm. In that instant, I felt a sense of communion with him that had never left me. Now it was gone. I was dazed. What Zack did to Howard was primal: bone hitting bone until the weakest of the combatants was destroyed.

Brette had been crouched over, writing frantically; when Howard finally left the witness box, she slumped back in her chair and exhaled theatrically. "Wow. At J school, they told us that cross-examination is the greatest legal engine ever invented for the discovery of truth, but that was brutal. And how about Charlie D's dramatic last-minute appearance on the witness list? I kept waiting for Shreve to object, but why would he? Charlie D turned out to be a great witness for the defence."

"Too great?" I said.

Brette rubbed her hands together. "You mean his obvious rapport with Zack Shreve? Are you suggesting collusion? It's a possibility, but Shreve's too smart for that. He's playing it close to the line though – 'cusp collusion' – almost illegal but not quite. That's Shreve's specialty – the whiff of sharp practice but nothing blatant enough for the Law Society." Brette twirled her pearls. "So far, Shreve's doing a good job of salvaging his case. In my opinion, the verdict in this trial is now officially up for grabs."

More unanswered questions, but despite everything, when court was adjourned for the day, the tension I'd been holding in my body drained. Howard had been chewed up and spit out, but he was alive and as the old adage has it, "while there's life, there's hope." I'd told Rapti that Zack and I were flying to Saskatoon, so when I stepped out of the courthouse she and the cameraman were already set up and waiting. She shuddered when she examined my face. "You have definitely lost your glow," she said.

"You have a kit full of blush and bronzer," I said. "Work a miracle." Rapti dabbed away dutifully, then stepped back to examine her handiwork. "Not great," she said. "But definitely better." I snapped on my microphone. Just as I was about to start, Zack came out of the courtroom.

He came over to me. "Mind if I watch?"

"No."

Rapti raised her hand. "I'm counting down, Jo." I watched her fingers. "Five, four, three, two . . ."

The last finger fell and I began, "It was a good day for the defence in the Sam Parker case . . ."

When I was through, Zack said, "Let's get out of here. Sean's bringing the car around."

"My overnight bag's still in my car. Do you think Sean would mind driving the Volvo back to my place?"

"Sean's an associate," Zack said. "He'd eat ground glass if he thought it would improve his chances of getting a promotion." He glanced down the street. "Here's our car. Do you want to drive?"

"Yes," I said. "It'll be good to feel I'm in control of something."

The glance Zack shot me was questioning, but he stayed silent. When we were away from the courthouse, he reached over and massaged the back of my neck.

"You're pretty tight there," he said. "Are you mad?"

"I'm not mad, just shaken. I could hardly recognize you today. You were –"

"A ruthless son of a bitch?"

"Pretty much."

"I had a job to do."

"And Charlie helped you do it."

"Charlie was more than willing to co-operate."

"At what point does rapport with a Crown witness become collusion."

Zack's gaze was probing. "When someone can prove it," he said.

"So you're okay with all these private arrangements you and Charlie made."

"Why wouldn't I be?"

"Because they're illegal."

"Not illegal – just close to the line. I have to win this case, Jo."

"Even if winning means bending the rules."

"Rules are made to be bent. I never go too far."

"You went too far with Howard today."

"That's a different issue," Zack said.

"No, it isn't. You used Charlie to get to him, and then you gutted him. What happened to the quality of mercy?"

"With luck, the jury will extend it to my client."

"And you don't care about what you did to Howard?"

"Jo, I didn't force the booze down Howard's throat this morning. He made a choice, and he has to live with it. If Howard had chosen to stay sober this morning, he could have cleaned our clock, but he didn't, so I went after him."

"But you had him, Zack. You showed that his memory of what happened that afternoon couldn't be trusted. That was all you needed to do. You didn't have to keep pummelling him."

"Are you sure of that? Are you absolutely certain that at that point in Howard's testimony, I'd won my case? Because I didn't know that. I still don't. What if I'd got squeamish and pulled back and a juror who was wavering went against me. Nice lawyers lose cases they shouldn't lose. I don't, because I don't leave anything to chance."

He continued rubbing my neck. "Better?"

"I wish this day was over. I hate flying."

"I know you do. Jo, you don't have to come if you don't want to."

"But you have to be there," I said.

"That doesn't mean you do."

I saw the exhaustion in his face. "I think it does," I said. I touched his hand. "Besides I'm not about to miss my chance to sleep in the lieutenant-governor's bed."

The logistics of getting a wheelchair onto a small plane were humiliating for a man who didn't take kindly to being dependent on the kindness of strangers. As Zack was being shunted aboard, I tried Howard's home number. No one picked up. I dropped my cell in my bag and mounted the steps into the plane.

When the propellers revved, my body grew tense. Zack, who knew I was a nervous flyer, squeezed my hand and leaned towards me. "You okay?"

My teeth were gritted, but I was reassuring. His mind at rest, Zack closed his eyes, and before we'd left the runway, he was sleeping the sleep of the just. He would, I knew, sleep deeply during the thirty-five minutes we were in the air, and he would awaken refreshed. I envied him. Alone with my thoughts, I examined the face of the man who had become so central to my existence.

There is a vulnerability in the faces of most sleepers – a relaxation of the facial muscles, a slackening of the jaw, but asleep or awake, Zack never seemed to lose control. In the grey afternoon light, his face was as familiar to me as my own, and that was the problem. I was deeply in love with him, and yet that day in court he had been a stranger. The man I knew was warm, compassionate, loving, humane; none of that had been in evidence as he destroyed Howard Dowhanuik. I wasn't naive. I understood that Zack had a job to do, but like the pain in a troubling tooth, the question Mieka had whispered in my ear before she left at Thanksgiving stabbed me: How much did I really know about this man?

As the plane started its descent, I leaned close. "Time to wake up," I said. He turned towards me and grinned lazily. "And I wake up to you, Ms. Kilbourn. I am blessed."

Built in the dirty thirties on land that slopes towards the South Saskatchewan River, the Bessborough Hotel has the rococo extravagance of a chateau in a children's fairy tale. When times are tough people dream of champagne, and the

Bessborough has always been a champagne hotel: liveried doormen, polished brass, deep and welcoming chairs in the lobby, rooms of understated luxury that promise discretion. The clerk who checked us in wore a suitably conservative hotel uniform, but she had dyed the tips of her braids aqua marine. According to her discrete identification badge, her name was "Heaven Olsen." We live in a time of flux.

Our suite on the sixth floor was spacious and quietly grand with champagne on ice and a sinfully inviting bed. It was a place for romance, and as I straightened Zack's tie and felt the warmth of his breath of my forehead I wanted him, and I knew he wanted me. But as Mick Jagger memorably sang, what we want is not necessarily what we need. That night I needed time to think and so, for the only time since I'd met him, I was relieved there was no time for Zack and me to make love.

We arrived at the reception in time for a glass of Veuve Cliquot before we went into the dinner. Zack was delighted when he realized that we'd been seated with Linda Fritz. Ignoring her warning that she was a walking corpse, he reached over and embraced her warmly. "God, you're a welcome sight. How are you doing?"

Linda's pleasure in seeing Zack matched his. "I'm a little dented, but definitely better. I seem to sleep all the time, and I'm taking these massive doses of antibiotics so I can't drink. Anyway, I'll live. But what's really killing me is watching my case blow up."

"You heard about what happened today?"

"Are you kidding? Howard Dowhanuik's meltdown was topic A during the champagne reception. I still can't believe Garth let it happen. Are you slipping stupid pills into his water jug?"

"No need," Zack replied. "Garth self-medicates."

Linda laughed. "You're telling me. The day I finally packed it in, Garth came over to my apartment. I told him to get an adjournment. He could have had three weeks to get up to speed on this case. It's hard on a jury to wait, but it's better than going in there unprepared. Garth refused to listen. I tried to brief him on what was coming up, but he just gave me his big fat stupid smile and told me that it was his case now and I shouldn't worry."

Zack chuckled. "I have to admit, I'm grateful. If you'd been sitting in that chair, I would have been in a lot more trouble."

"You think I don't know that," Linda said.

"Would you believe me if I said I wish you'd been able to finish the case?"

Linda glared at him. "I had a virus, not a lobotomy. Anyway, enough shop talk. We're boring Joanne."

"Not at all," I said. "Just prepare to hear your thoughts about Mr. Severight on NationTV tomorrow night."

The waiter set down our salads: arugula and watercress served with smoked whitefish and roasted peppers. Zack and I dug in, but Linda just gazed at her plate.

"Aren't you going to eat that?" Zack asked.

"No," Linda said. "It looks tasty, but my malaise makes everything taste like cardboard."

"Give it to Jo, then," Zack said. "She loves smoked white-fish."

Linda pushed her plate towards me. "Be my guest," she said. "Consider it a thank you for the dartboard and the lovely photograph of our friend here. It's brought me hours of pleasure."

Zack put his arm around me. "I told you she'd like it."

Linda observed us with interest. "How long have you two been a couple?"

"Not long enough," Zack said.

"Three and a half months," I said.

Linda gave Zack the thumbs-up sign. "Way to go. That's three months, thirteen and a half days, and about eleven hours longer than most of your relationships."

There were eight of us at table, and for the rest of the meal we chatted about the inconsequential and pleasant topics that people talk about when the food and wine are excellent and the mood is mellow. After the chocolate mousse had been served and the coffee poured, a string quartet began to play "The Lark." I drank in the beauty of the music and of the small white tulips in our centrepiece and felt the pieces of myself knitting together again. Zack leaned close and whispered, "You look happy again."

"I am happy again," I said.

"Then so am I," he said, and we sat hand in hand and listened to Haydn, and all was right with our world.

Before the speeches started, I excused myself and went to the ladies' room. As I was freshening my makeup, a blonde wearing a very short emerald dress caught my eye in the mirror. Her mascara was smudged and she was having trouble focusing. She had, it appeared, drunk well if not wisely.

"So you're Zack's latest," she said.

I met her mirror gaze. "I am," I said, reaching for my lip liner.

The blonde reached into a sequined evening bag and found her lipstick. "He's a son of a bitch," she said. "And he'll dump you." She began outlining her lips, overshooting the mark in more than a few places. I didn't bring the matter to her attention. "He'll be classy about it," she said. "There'll be some serious flowers and a handwritten note, but he'll never call again."

"I'll take my chances," I said.

"*Caveat emptor*. Don't say you weren't warned. One way or another, Zack has fucked 90 per cent of the people at this dinner tonight."

I turned to her. "Are you through?" I asked. "Because the man I love is about to give a speech and I'd like to be there."

"The man you love," she repeated. "I *am* impressed. Is the man you love still into threesomes?"

"He doesn't need a threesome," I said. "He has me."

As exit lines went, it wasn't bad, but my heart was pounding, and the walk back to the ballroom seemed agonizingly long. I slid into my place at the table just as Zack was about to speak. When he saw that I was seated, he gave me a conspiratorial grin and began. He opened with Mel Brooks's trenchant observation about retirement: " 'Never retire! Do what you do and keep doing it. But don't do it on Friday. Take Friday off. Friday, Saturday, and Sunday, do fishing, do sexual activities, watch Fred Astaire movies . . . My point is: Live fully and don't retreat.' " It was a good opening and it got a laugh. When Zack moved to a more measured assessment of the accomplishments of the retiring dean, his comments were gracious and touching.

When my life had centred on politics, I'd written more than my share of speeches, and I knew Zack's speech had been effective, yet the applause when he was through was oddly grudging. I glanced around the room and I noticed that the faces of the guests were closed. They had enjoyed the speech, but they didn't like the speaker. For the first time it occurred to me that Marnie Dowhanuik's assessment of her son might also be true of Zack – that like Charlie, Zack was a man who had fans, not friends. Both were men who needed to win and that meant they would always be surrounded by people they'd beaten. Remembering the blonde's cutting appraisal of Zack, I felt a chill.

We were silent as the elevator took us to our suite. Once we were inside, Zack turned to me. "So what happened?" he said. "You were happy again, and now you're not."

"Let's get some sleep," I said. "We can talk about it tomorrow."

"Uh-uh," Zack said. "Not if it means you sleep on one side of the bed and I sleep on the other. Why don't I make us some tea and we'll talk about what's bugging you?"

There was a table and chairs in front of the window that overlooked the hotel's formal gardens. In gentle weather, brides and grooms would exchange vows in those gardens and sip champagne under the cherry trees. Now, in mid-October, the lawns were leaf-strewn and the trees were spectral. Symbols everywhere.

Zack wheeled over, picked up the basket of teas the hotel supplied, and brought it to me. "A cornucopia of possibilities," he said. "What's your pleasure?"

"Camomile," I said.

Zack started the tea and came back to me. "Your turn for a good deed now. Can you untie this damn tie?" I untied it and handed it to him. "Thanks. Now, why don't you tell me what's wrong."

"When I went to the powder room tonight, I had an unpleasant encounter with an old girlfriend of yours."

"Who was it?"

"I didn't catch her name. She's blonde. She was wearing a very short green dress, and she has amazing legs."

"Margot Wright," Zack said. "She's with Ireland Leontowich."

"Another lawyer."

"They're everywhere," Zack said. "And I like your legs. Anyway, Margot and I saw each other for a while and then we broke it off. End of story."

"It wasn't the end of the story for Margot. She's still steaming."

"So what did she say?"

"She said you were a son of a bitch. I let that slide. Then she said that one way or another, you'd fucked 90 per cent of the people who were at the dinner tonight. And I let that slide. Then she asked if you were still into threesomes."

"And you didn't let that slide."

"No, I said you didn't need threesomes because you had me."

"Sounds like you handled the situation." He stroked my cheek. "But you're not happy, so what Margot said must have got to you."

"Yes, I guess it did."

"Which part?"

"All of it."

"You want people to like me."

"It sounds stupid when you say it, but yes, I do."

"Jo, with a couple of exceptions, the people in that room weren't my friends, they were competitors or adversaries. It doesn't matter if they like me. What does matter is that they respect me because that means that, a lot of the time, they'll settle rather than face me in court. And, believe it or not, that's good news for everybody."

"I understand that. What I don't understand is why you have to play so hard to win."

"Because that's the way I am. I'm like that guy in *Candide*. 'I'm neither pure nor wise nor good, but I do the best I can' – for my clients, for my friends, and, if you'll let me, for you. I've never lied to you, Jo, and I'm not going to lie about what Margot said. There were threesomes. You may have noticed that the mechanics of sex don't always work for me. Three-ways with interesting partners helped for a while. But what you told Margot was true. As long as I have you, I don't need anybody else. I've loved you since the night we had dinner at The Stone House. You reached over and took my hand, and for me, that was it. If what Margot said has screwed us up, I won't know what to do next."

"It's not just Margot, it's everything. I just wonder if we're moving too fast."

"You think that hasn't occurred to me. Jo, ask anybody – ask Margot, for crissake – I've never been known to rush into commitments. There was never any reason. I had everything I needed: my job and my law partners, and then last summer when Chris drove his car into the lake and everything at Falconer Shreve turned to shit, I felt like somebody had dropped a piano on me. When I was finally able to focus, there you were. And despite everything, even losing Chris, I knew that the best part of my life had just begun."

Zack had been sitting across from me at the table. He moved his chair so he was beside me. "And now it seems you're finished with me," he said. He was pale and the shadows of exhaustion under his eyes were deep.

But it wasn't pity that drew me to him. The words formed themselves. "Whatever happens, I'll never be finished with you," I said.

He slumped with relief. "And I'll never be finished with you," he said. "Not ever. Come here. Let me unzip you." I stood and turned so he could undo my dress. I let it fall to the floor. I was still wearing my bra and the black slip with the lilies Zack liked.

He kissed the small of my back. "I think we're ready to get married," Zack said.

I turned to face him. "So do I," I said.

He drew me to him. "Thank God for that," he said. "Thank God for that."

CHAPTER

9

My first thought when I awoke the next morning was that Zack and I were, in the parlance of a gentler time, betrothed. My second thought was that we had forty-five minutes to shower, dress, and get to the airport if we were going to catch the 6:00 a.m. flight that would get us back to Regina in time for the trial.

It was going to be a big day. Kathryn Morrissey was testifying. The filmmaker Jean Renoir once said that the trouble with life is that everyone has his reasons, and Kathryn, articulate, attractive, and intelligent, would be a force to be reckoned with as she explained hers. Even Garth Severight wouldn't be able to blunt her effectiveness on the stand. Since *Too Much Hope* had been published, Kathryn had given a hundred interviews placing her actions in a context that suggested she was acting in the finest traditions of the third estate. She was going to be a thorny problem for the defence, but as the propellers revved for the flight home and Zack snapped open his computer, his focus was not on the Crown prosecutor's appealing victim but on real estate.

"I found us a house," he said. "I must have looked at fifty listings, and I knew you wouldn't like any of them, but this one is different."

"Can I see it?"

Zack slid his laptop over to me. I glanced at the screen. "I know that house," I said. "I've walked by it a thousand, thousand times."

The statement was not hyperbole. I had lived in my house for more than thirty years, and this house was on my route when I ran in the morning. In a neighbourhood of two- and three-storey houses where people tended to visit, it was an oddity – a sprawling, well-tended, one-storey ranch house that never showed signs that human beings lived inside. No toys, bikes, basketball hoops, seasonal wreaths, or holiday lights – just stone gargoyles on either side of the front door and discrete but tasteful landscaping that did not draw attention to itself. It was a quiet house that looked over the same creek my house backed onto.

"Ever been inside?" Zack said.

"No."

"Well, click onto the virtual tour. That'll give you an idea. Incidentally, if you don't like it, I'm going to suck gas."

"But I shouldn't feel any pressure," I said.

"Nah, of course not." His tone was light, but as I gazed at the pictures his eyes never left my face.

Zack had no cause for concern. The house was a winner. The rooms were spacious, the windows were large, and the hardwood floors seemed splashed with sun. The kitchen was strictly 1960s, but it had generous counter space, hickory cupboards, and a walk-in pantry. The bedroom Zack and I would use opened onto a deck that looked out on the creek. There was also, *mirabile dictu*, an indoor swimming pool. "I think we just got Taylor's vote," I said.

"How about your vote?" Zack said.

I took his hand. "It's a great house," I said. "But this is a big step for me. I've lived in my place since Mieka was born."

"If you don't want to move, we can get your house retrofitted."

"It's a two-storey house. Zack. We'd have to put one of those gizmos on the stairs so you could get up to the second floor. You'd hate that."

"I could live with it. I want to be with you, Jo. I can put up with whatever it takes. I'm not going to fuck around about something as insignificant as having to use a gizmo."

I met his gaze. "You'd really put up with that just to please me?"

"Sure. We're not kids. We don't know how much time we have." His look was searching. "So what do you think?"

I rubbed his hand. "I think we should make an offer on the new house," I said.

Zack was meeting Sam at the office before court, so on the way back from the airport he dropped me at my house. Whether I'd been absent for ten minutes or ten days, Willie was ecstatic to see me. Like Zack, he believed in going for what he wanted. In Willie's case, it was his leash. I snapped it on, changed into my runners, and headed for the door. When I opened it, Ethan Thorpe was facing me.

We both jumped. Ethan blushed and stared at his feet. "You must think I'm a stalker or something. I just didn't want to miss Taylor."

"But you did miss her," I said. "I was in Saskatoon last night, so Taylor stayed with a friend."

"A friend," he repeated miserably.

"You can see her at school," I said.

"I wasn't planning to go to school," he said.

"Why not?"

"Because it's going to be a bad day," he said. He fingered the pentangle that hung from the piece of hemp around his neck. "Sometimes, it's just easier to stay away."

"Ethan, why do you wear that pentangle?"

"The same reason Gawain did – to remind me that I should have courage and seek the truth." He flushed. "I get the message," he said. "I should be more like Gawain."

"You could give it a try."

When Ethan left, he was headed in the direction of school, but he was a boy who could change direction easily. He wasn't mine, but I felt the kinship an adult who has been solitary as a child feels for the lonely, and I found myself hoping that wherever he was going, he would make it.

I checked my watch and realized that if *I* was going to make it to court by nine o'clock, Willie and I would have to truncate our run. Instead of setting out for the lake, I led Willie through the backyard towards the levee that the city had built on both sides of the creek to protect us from floods during spring runoff. Indigenous bushes had been planted on the banks and now, after an early snow, the few leaves that clung to the branches had a spare Japanese beauty. Willie and I crossed the bridge that linked my neighbourhood, Old Lakeview, with the Crescents, the neighbourhood of the house where Zack and my daughter and I might now live.

I walked along the levee until I came to the spot where it met the yard of my new house. The levee's uneven turf was not favoured by joggers, so Willie and I were able to sit on a rock in the pale morning sunshine and reflect in peace on the changes that were about to overtake our lives.

I had told Zack that the indoor swimming pool would win Taylor's vote, but it was the new house's proximity to the creek that won mine. My life and the lives of my husband and children had been inextricably linked to it. When Ian had come back from a rancorous night in the legislature – too much emotion and too much Scotch, we had walked along the bank of the creek until his head was clear enough for sleep. In the year after he died, I'd walked the creek alone – remembering, and trying not to remember.

In winter, the creek froze over and the kids skated on it and tobogganed down the bank behind our backyard and partway up the bank that led to the house Zack and I might live in together. My future had been there all along. Seemingly, the Turks were right about kismet: the course of events is predestined. All we can do is keep a firm grip on the toboggan.

I was watching Willie decide whether his fate was linked with that of a duck floating on the glassy water when my cell rang. It was Zack. "Sam and Glenda send their best wishes," he said. "They're happy we're getting married."

"I'm happy we're getting married too," I said. "Willie and I are on the levee, scoping out the new house."

"We can get the keys and check out the inside when court's over. Hey – shouldn't you be getting down here?"

"I have another half-hour," I said.

"You might want to speed that up," Zack said. "Big doings today."

"Kathryn Morrissey is testifying," I said. "I know that."

"There's an added attraction," Zack said.

"Care to elaborate?"

"No, but when you come into court, take a gander at who's sitting in the front row of the seats reserved for the public."

The added attraction was worth more than a gander. Six of the thirteen subjects Kathryn had written about in her book had found seats that put them right in her sightline when she testified. If Charlie hadn't been sitting with them, I might not have made the connection immediately. The photos Kathryn had chosen for her book had shown the *Too*

Much Hope kids at the worst moments of their lives. With the exceptions of Charlie and Glenda Parker, whose only crime was a private burden they were forced to bear in public, Kathryn's subjects had been whirling black holes of self-destruction. They had been photographed drunk, stoned, beaten up, or under arrest.

Without exception, the young people in front of me were well groomed, self-possessed, and clearly struck by the gravity of the situation. As survivors of tragedies that had been played out in full public view, the *Too Much Hope* kids were also the subject of intense and feverish scrutiny from the press.

When I slid into my accustomed place next to Brette, she was gleeful. "This is going to be *so* good. The word is that Charlie Dowhanuik arranged for Kathryn's victims to be here today. She's a cool one, but this is going to throw her." She looked down at her notebook. "I need your opinion. I think I've identified everybody, but is that really hunky guy on the end Morgan Dafoe – the kid who drove the family speedboat into the dock and killed his friends?"

"It is him," I said. "He's in medical school now. Kathryn promised him she'd write about how he's trying to make up for what he did."

"He was drunk, wasn't he?"

"Yes," I said. "He was also fourteen years old. A friend of his mother's decided Morgan was cute, and it would be fun to get him drunk."

"What happened to the friend?"

"She got a slap on the wrist."

Brette swore softly. "And two kids die and another kid's life is mutilated." She stared over at the row where Morgan was sitting. "Speaking of mutilated lives, wasn't Krissy Treadgold supposed to have her anorexia under control?"

"When Charlie Dowhanuik interviewed her last spring, she said she'd gone to a clinic that specializes in eating disorders and she'd managed to turn things around." I glanced at the young woman sitting next to Charlie. She was dressed fashionably in a vintage black velvet jacket whose generous cut couldn't disguise the fact that the body inside was stick-thin. As she turned to talk to Charlie, Krissy Treadgold's profile was as sharp-edged as a carving. "She doesn't look cured to me," I said. "She looks as if she should be hospitalized."

"The book pushed her over the edge," Brette said flatly. "I did a story on eating disorders, and you're never really cured."

"Kathryn Morrissey is planning to make a victim's impact statement," I said. "Maybe the defence should get impact statements from the victims of the victim."

Brette grimaced. "You know, when I think about Kathryn Morrissey, I wonder if I have what it takes to be a journalist. I've read the texts. I know that truth is elusive and that the journalist's job is to go in with a flaming sword and cut through all the contradictions and self-justifications until she finds out what really happened. But Kathryn knew the truth – we all did. Most of those kids had screwed up big time, but a lot of them were trying to make amends. All Kathryn cared about was selling books." Brette snorted derisively. "I'd rather scrub toilets."

"I'm sure the defence would be pleased to hear that."

"That part maybe, but not the rest. Kathryn may be opportunistic, but she didn't deserve to be shot."

"So if you were on the jury, you'd vote to convict Sam Parker?" I said.

Brette chewed on her pearls. "If I were on the jury, I'd be feeling like Solomon about to cut the baby in half."

If Howard Dowhanuik's testimony had been a slug-fest, Kathryn Morrissey's was a soap opera. In retrospect, even the unpredictable was predictable. Dressed in a suit of soft grey, with hose and shoes in complementary grey, her silver hair smoothed back to set off her untroubled brow and brilliant blue eyes, Kathryn was a casting director's ideal of the brave but suffering victim. When the court clerk called her name, Kathryn approached the bench, glancing at the jury box long enough to fix her image in their minds, then she stepped in front of the judge's bench and waited to be sworn in. A flawless performance until she stood to take the oath and her eyes met those of the six men and women whose lives she had ripped apart by her blithe disregard for their trust and their need.

Kathryn was a professional, but the appearance of the *Too Much Hope* kids was a distraction, and before she placed her hand on the Bible, she shot an angry glance at Garth Severight. He should have spared or at least prepared her for this, but he hadn't, and now she would have to tread carefully. As Garth approached the bench to take her evidence, she was not happy. Kathryn was knowledgeable enough to realize that the Crown prosecutor was not her lawyer, but she knew she was his main witness, and she should have been told what was up. It was a variant of the old legal truism: false in one thing, false in all things. Garth had let her down and now Kathryn was on edge, wondering what other traps awaited her.

That said, she acquitted herself well. Garth led her through her testimony with the courtly attentiveness of a gentleman at a cotillion. There were no surprises in her testimony. She had been enjoying a glass of wine on her deck. Sam Parker had appeared through her side gate. She recognized him from his appearances in the media. He was very emotional. He asked her to postpone the publication of her book. She explained that was impossible. He asked her if she realized what she was doing to his family. Kathryn told him people must accept responsibility for their own actions. According to Kathryn, her statement infuriated Sam Parker. He became, in her words, "a madman." He pulled out his gun, aimed it at her, and said, "How does it feel to know this could be the last day of your life?" Certain he was about to kill her, Kathryn lunged at him. Sam pulled the trigger. At this point in her account, Kathryn grew teary, and Garth produced a snowy linen handkerchief and handed it to her with a flourish. Lazy as a lizard sunning himself on a rock, Zack watched the testimony with hooded eyes and a small smile playing on his lips.

As Garth ceded his place to the defence, the energy level in the courtroom rose. The cage match between Zack and Kathryn had been hotly anticipated. The consensus was that he was good, but she was no slouch. She had been interviewed many times, often by questioners who were hostile, and she had learned to spin an awkward question, turning it back on the interviewer, making it seem that he, not she, was the character assassin. But as Zack wheeled towards the witness box, Katherine seemed surprisingly nervous. Her eyes darted towards the row in which the *Too Much Hope* kids were sitting and she asked for a glass of water.

Zack waited as the water was brought and Katherine sipped and composed herself. "Set your mind at ease, Ms. Morrissey," he said. "There'll be no pyrotechnics here. The Crown and the defence are in agreement on the basics of what happened on the late afternoon of May 16. We differ only in our interpretation. You say Mr. Parker's actions were intentional; Mr. Parker says what happened was an accident. Disregarding Mr. Dowhanuik's testimony, which I believe we can safely do . . ." Garth leapt to his feet and fired off a machine-gun round of objections. Zack heard him out, withdrew his statement, and turned back to Kathryn. "At any rate, Ms. Morrissey, it seems this case boils down to a matter of she said/he said, so what we're working towards is getting a clear picture of exactly what happened in your encounter with Mr. Parker."

Garth was on his feet again. "Is there a question in all this?"

Zack nodded. "Actually, I have a number of questions." He moved his chair closer to Kathryn. "Ms. Morrissey, you said that after you refused to postpone publication of your book, Sam Parker became 'a madman.' Exactly how did this madness manifest itself?"

Kathryn's lip curled in disdain. "He became red in the face. He gesticulated wildly. He was out of control."

"Did Mr. Parker mention where he had been in the hour before he arrived in your backyard?"

"He said he'd been with his daughter."

"Did he elaborate?"

"He said something about his daughter being in a state of anguish."

"Did he explain why?"

Kathryn raised her chin defiantly. "He said Glenda was upset about my book. He said she had a gun and she had threatened to kill herself."

Zack smiled. "Thank you. A very complete answer. So the gun Mr. Parker used was not his own. It was his daughter's."

Kathryn shifted position. "Yes."

"Then we can conclude that Mr. Parker didn't come from Calgary to Regina with the intention of killing you."

"He obviously decided that later," Kathryn said. "Otherwise, why would he arrive in my backyard, gun in hand?"

Zack frowned. "I'm confused," he said. "I thought the weapon was concealed. Mr. Parker came to plead with you, Ms. Morrissey. He wanted to save his daughter's life. Why would he be waving a gun around?"

"The phrase *gun in hand* is just a figure of speech," Kathryn said dismissively.

Zack nodded. "Of course. Still, this is a court of law. Sam Parker's future will be determined by the accuracy with which you recall his words. With all due respect, Ms. Morrissey, you should attempt to be precise. Now, at what point did Mr. Parker tell you that his daughter was contemplating suicide?"

"When he asked me to postpone the publication of my book."

"So when you heard that Glenda was suicidal, your response was that she had to accept responsibility for her own actions. That's a little heartless, isn't it?"

Kathryn furrowed her brow. "It might have been later."

Zack cocked his head. "I'm sorry. What might have been later?"

"Mr. Parker might have told me about his daughter's state of mind later, when he took out the gun."

Zack made no attempt to hide his pleasure. "Then you and Mr. Parker are in agreement on that point," he said. "Good. And you've already testified that after he came through your gate, Sam pleaded with you to postpone publication of your book, and you refused and made your speech about people being responsible for their own actions. So you've corroborated that part of Sam's version of events. And now you agree that when he took out the gun, he didn't threaten you, he told you that the gun he was holding had been in his daughter's hands that same day. Sam didn't want to kill you. He wanted you to know that he was desperate."

Kathryn flushed with anger. "That's not the way it happened. Sam Parker tried to kill me. That's the truth."

Zack sighed. "So, we're back to she said/he said."

Indeed, it did seem the combatants had reached an impasse, but then, in true soap-opera fashion, there was a shocking development. Krissy Treadgold, the wispy blonde whose eating disorders had been explored with such clinical zeal in *Too Much Hope*, stood up and braced herself against the railing that separated the gallery from the business end of the courtroom. She was directly in front of Kathryn, and for a beat, I thought she was about to shout out an accusation. But the drama took another turn. Krissy crumpled against the railing and then fell to the floor. In the confusion that followed, one image was indelible. Glenda Parker had been sitting next to Krissy, and when Krissy fell, Glenda dropped to her knees and raised Krissy's head so that it rested in her lap. Then, very quietly, she asked someone to call for a doctor. Obeying some kind of herd wisdom, the rest of us gave the two young people their space, watching but not intruding on the small circle of intimacy that enclosed them. When the EMS team arrived, Krissy had regained consciousness, but she was deadly pale and clearly in medical trouble. As the gurney that she'd been placed upon was wheeled out of the court-room, there was silence. Her illness had made her unnaturally small. With her thin blonde hair loose about her shoulders and her vintage velvet coat, she looked oddly like Alice in Wonderland. To add to the Through the Looking Glass quality of the moment, when I turned towards the back of the court-room, I spotted a couple of unlikely spectators: Howard Dowhanuik was sitting in the back row and Ethan Thorpe was standing out in the hall, watching.

Zack, who had turned his chair to watch the dramatic events in the gallery, wheeled towards the jury box. One look at their stricken faces told him all he needed to know. "I only have one more question for the witness," he said. "Would you do it again, Ms. Morrissey?"

Kathryn was clearly irritated. "What?"

Zack moved back to face her. "Given what you know about the impact your book has had on the lives of its subjects, would you write it again?"

Kathryn didn't hesitate. "My obligation was to the text. People's feelings are secondary."

"No matter how much they suffer," Zack said.

"Their suffering is not my concern," Kathryn said, and her voice was flinty. "And to answer your question, yes I would write the book again."

"Thank you," Zack said. "No more questions."

And, as it turned out, no more witnesses for the day. Sam had been scheduled to testify, but Zack had asked for an adjournment, citing the fact that his client was obviously under the weather. During Kathryn's testimony, Sam had suffered a chill, and he was now feeling dizzy and unwell. Mr. Justice Harney took one look at him and adjourned court until the next morning.

The decision was humane. Glenda had tried to keep up Sam's strength and spirits through a regimen of morning laps in the hotel pool and nightly games of cribbage, but the vigour I had noticed when I met Sam was gone. The energy seemed to have been sapped from him. It seemed he had been easy prey for the bug that was making its rounds in the courthouse.

When Zack went back to change out of his barrister's robes, I walked outside to do my five-minute standup on the day's events. I had just unclipped my microphone when Zack came out of the courthouse. He was in high spirits. "What are your plans for the next hour?" he asked.

"Nothing that can't wait," I said. "What did you have in mind?"

"How would you like to check out the new house?"

"I'd love to," I said.

"Good," Zack said. "The agent for the seller is going to meet us there in ten minutes. I told him we wanted to see the place on our own, so he's going to unlock the door and meet us afterwards to answer our questions."

"Boy, you're good," I said.

"Highly motivated," he said. "Ready to go?"

"Absolutely."

As promised, the agent was waiting for us at the house. He let us in and agreed to come back in an hour. After the man left, Zack held up his cellphone. "Ms. Kilbourn, you will note that I am now turning this off. I hope you appreciate the symbolism."

"I do, but couldn't they disbar you for that?"

Zack gave me a wide smile. "Probably, but you still have a job."

We took our time walking through the silent rooms. The only sound was the swoosh of Zack's wheelchair on the hardwood. It was, as the virtual tour had shown, a solid house of big rooms filled with light, outdated fixtures, and endless possibilities. The indoor pool that was the house's only noteworthy feature had been installed because the previous owner's physician had prescribed swimming as therapy. Both the pool and the room that housed it were new and bleakly functional. Zack made a face when he saw them. "Looks like a high school gym," he said.

"Taylor's going to see those bare walls as a gift," I said. "She's been talking about doing a mural, and if a room ever called out for a mural it's this one."

"You think she'll be happy here?" Zack asked.

"I think we'll all be happy here," I said.

"In that case, let's check out the bedroom. Because the real estate agent says it's neat."

The real estate agent was right. Filled with the saffron light of afternoon, the bedroom was immensely inviting. I threw open the double doors and walked out onto the deck. "In good weather, we'll be able to sit out here and watch the sun rise over the creek," I said.

"So what do you think?" Zack asked. "Is this the one?"

I gazed across the water. "Hey, look over there – on the bank by that wolf willow – a beaver."

"Is a beaver a good omen?" Zack said.

I rested my hand on the back of his chair. "No. A beaver is a beaver. But think how much fun it'll be to have him for a neighbour."

There was intriguing news from the realtor. If we were interested, we could purchase the lot next door. The current owners had bought it, intending to build a greenhouse there, but their plan had never materialized. As I paced the lot, I could see Taylor's new studio taking shape. By the time Zack dropped me off at my place, the wheels had been set in motion.

"What are you going to do with the rest of the afternoon?" Zack said.

"Errands," I said. "And there is no shortage of them. I'm going to pick up some photographs that I had framed for Pete's new clinic and take them over to him, then I'm going to make a chip, dip, and pop run for Taylor's party. After that I'm going to curl up with the background material on closing statements that Rapti sent me. It appears that the trial is winding down and I want to be ready. How about you?"

"I want to be ready too," Zack said. "I'm going back to the office to ponder, yet again, the best line of questioning for Sam."

I kissed him goodbye. "It's going to be so good when all this is over," I said.

"Yeah," Zack agreed. "Especially if we win."

Pete's clinic on Winnipeg Street had been a pawn shop in its previous life, but Pete and his friends had given it a coat of paint to erase the lingering stench of desperation. The office now smelled of paint with a musky overlay of animal – very pleasant. The joint was jumping. School was over for the day, and owners of pets with problems were out in force. Pete had his work cut out for him. There were four boys with dogs of intriguingly mixed lineages, a determined-looking girl about Taylor's age with a litter of kittens wrapped in a blanket, and an old man with a parrot in a cage. None of the animals was happy to be there, and they made their displeasure known. Despite the bedlam, Pete's assistant, a university student who was volunteering at the clinic to polish up his resumé for the admissions board of the vet college, was cheerful.

"This isn't as bad as it looks, Ms. Kilbourn," he said. "There's an organizational principle at work here. Believe it or not, everything's under control."

"Glad to hear it," I said. "Any chance I can see Pete for a second? I have a gift for the new office."

"Let me buzz him. He's just nuzzling two hundred pounds of English mastiff."

"I'll keep my distance," I said.

"This one's a sweetie. His name is Pantera – you know, like the heavy-metal group."

"Actually, I didn't know," I said. "But thanks for filling me in."

"No problem. They're in examining room one."

Pantera was splayed on the floor, grooving while Pete rubbed his belly.

I went over and stroked Pantera's flank. "He's a beauty," I said.

Pete raised his eyebrows. "Do you want him?"

"Serious?"

"Very."

"What happened to the owners?"

Pete walked over to the corner sink and began to wash up. "They dropped their mastiff off to be neutered and never came back. When I called, they said they didn't realize how big he'd be, and they hoped I'd find him a good home. I've been calling everybody I know, but so far no luck."

"If he's been mistreated, he might be difficult."

"He wasn't mistreated," Pete said. "He was just inconvenient. It turned out he was too big for his owners' apartment."

"Their apartment? What were they thinking?"

Pete shrugged. "They saw a mastiff on that TV show *American Chopper* and thought it looked cute."

I bent and nuzzled Pantera. "If I didn't have Willie, you'd be a definite possibility," I said. I straightened and turned to my son. "Pete, keep me posted about what's happening with this guy. Now, I'd better let you get back to work." I handed him the package. "Here's a present – some old photos of you with our dogs. I had them framed for your waiting room."

"I'll look at them on my break. Thanks, Mum, and don't worry about Pantera. I'll take him home with me until I figure out what to do." Pete dried his hands. "Might be good for Charlie to have him around too. He's obsessed with this trial. If Sam Parker's convicted, I think Charlie will implode."

"Maybe you should remind him that no matter what happens to Sam, he still has a life to live. That's what Zack keeps telling me."

"I'll give it a shot, but I think the words would have more weight coming from Zack."

"He'll be at the house tomorrow night," I said. "He promised Taylor he'd help with the decorations for her party. Why don't you and Charlie come over and give us a hand?"

"Sounds like a plan," Pete said. "Charlie's not a big partisan of the human race, but he admires Zack."

"Zack's going to be anxious about the verdict too. He and Charlie can form a support group."

Pete laughed. "I can't imagine either of them in a support group."

"Neither can I." I gave Pantera a rub. "See you tomorrow night. Bring our friend here. Let's see what Willie makes of him."

Zack and his colleagues had spent long hours deciding on the witness list for the defence. To convict Sam Parker of attempted murder, the Crown had to prove, in the ponderous language of the law, that Sam intended "to cause the requisite degree of bodily harm coupled with the necessary recklessness as to its effect." In lay terms, that meant the Crown had to prove that Sam was both cold-blooded and irresponsible. His temperament was key, so there were solid reasons for producing witnesses who would testify that Sam was a good and responsible man who, placed in untenable circumstances, had committed an act that was utterly uncharacteristic.

Sam provided a long list of friends and associates who were prepared to attest to his moral fibre, but when Zack and his colleagues interviewed Sam's friends, they discovered a troubling common denominator: all were rich, powerful, and short-fused when it came to being challenged. The consensus was that Sam's friends would not fare well in cross-examination, so Zack thanked them for their co-operation and went back to exploring his options.

Glenda was anxious to testify for her father. More than anyone except Sam, she could have given insight into his state of mind on the afternoon of May 16. She would have been a compelling and sympathetic witness, but Sam refused outright to allow her to testify. His daughter had suffered enough, he said, and that closed the matter.

So, as Sam Parker was sworn in on that cold October morning, he was the sole witness for the defence. He was impressive. When he'd come into court with Zack and Glenda, he had appeared depleted, but as he settled into the witness box, Sam came to life. He had spent a lifetime in the spotlight and he seemed to draw strength from the fact that he had every eye upon him. It was a phenomenon I'd observed in other public figures, and that day it served Sam Parker well.

Spine ramrod-straight, eyes blazing, Sam was a man to be reckoned with. As he went through the by-now-familiar narrative of events on the day of the shooting, Sam's baritone was melodious and firm. He faltered only once – when he described seeing Glenda in her apartment holding the gun with which she planned to end her life. Sam's agony at that memory was still painful to observe. When he testified he was in a state of shock as he drove to Kathryn Morrissey's condominium, his words had the ring of truth.

Sam did not attempt to use his mental state to excuse his actions, and his refusal to ask for pity gave power to his testimony. Given context, Sam's rationale for carrying a pistol when he turned up in Kathryn's backyard made sense. He said he had simply been afraid to leave Glenda alone with a gun. He had, he admitted, been frightened, stupid, and guilty of execrable judgment, but on one point he was resolute: he had never intended to harm Kathryn Morrissey.

His story was believable, but Kathryn Morrissey's account had been credible too. Sam's defence team had assessed their chances of winning the game of she said/he said at around 50 per cent. The odds weren't good enough, and so Zack decided to go for broke.

His direct examination of Sam had focused on the fact that Sam's actions on the afternoon of May 16 were a response to the unendurable stress Kathryn Morrissey's book had caused the Parker family. The argument was plausible, but there was a worrying footnote. Sam Parker was known to be an expert marksman. As an articulate opponent of gun registration, Sam had built up extensive media files, and every one of them included footage of him brandishing a firearm and stating that he found target-shooting a great tension reliever.

When Zack asked Sam how he typically dealt with stress, there was nervous laughter in the courtroom.

Sam was prepared for the question. "I pray, I swim, and I go to the shooting range," he said.

Zack smiled. "Your abilities at prayer and swimming are none of our business," he said, "but how would you estimate your skill as a marksman?"

"I've been shooting all my life," Sam said. "I hit what I aim at."

"What do you normally aim at?"

"Metal targets," Sam said. "Just the standard recreational shooting setup."

"So when you're shooting for recreation," Zack asked, "how far away are you from your target?"

"When I'm feeling sharp, six hundred yards. When I'm feeling old, five hundred yards."

There was more laughter in the courtroom. Sensing that people were beginning to like Sam Parker, Zack waited until the laughter died down.

"And whether you're feeling sharp or old, you generally hit your target?" he said finally.

"I always hit my target," Sam said. There was no boasting in his voice. He was simply stating a fact.

"If you were aiming at a target a yard away from you," Zack asked, "would you say your chances of hitting it were 100 per cent?"

Sam nodded. "100 per cent."

"How far from Kathryn Morrissey were you standing when the gun you were holding went off?"

"Very close," Sam said. "A couple of feet."

"Yet you only grazed her shoulder," Zack said.

"Yes," Sam said. "The shot only grazed Ms. Morrissey's shoulder."

Kathryn Morrissey was sitting in the front row behind the Crown's desk. Sam's eyes found her. "I am thankful every moment of the day for that, Ms. Morrissey," he said. "I hope you believe that."

It had been a strong finish. To close its case, the Crown had to get Sam to admit that he wanted to kill Kathryn Morrissey. Try as he might, Garth Severight was unable to get that admission. His cross-examination put a couple of dents in Sam's testimony, but it didn't do any serious damage. When Sam stepped down, everyone in the courtroom knew it had been a good day for the defence.

During the trial, Taylor and I had created a comfortable routine for our evenings: an early dinner, homework, some time to goof and gossip while we watched TV, and then bedtime. That night after I read Rapti's notes, Taylor and I watched something as funny as it was forgettable and were in bed by 9:00 p.m. I called Zack to say good night before I turned off the lights. The trial had consumed him. The dark circles of exhaustion under his eyes had become permanent. I had stopped asking him when or if he slept.

"How's it going?" I said.

"Not great," he said. "Did Sam seem okay to you today?"

"Where did that come from?" I asked. "Everybody I talked to this afternoon thought Sam did well."

"I'm not talking about his testimony," Zack said. "I'm talking about his health. When he got off the stand, he looked as if he'd been bled dry."

"It's been a gruelling experience for everybody," I said.

"I guess," Zack said. "And I'm about to make it worse. My closing statement is six times longer than it should be, and it's boring as hell."

"I can help," I said. "Get a pencil."

"Is this a joke?"

"You're beyond jokes," I said. "My cheat sheet from Rapti says a closing statement is where you bring your story to a close and make certain the jury writes the ending you want. She also says you should end with a bang: move from the particular to the universal – convince the jury that your case gives them insight into the mystery of the human condition."

"Not bad," he said. "So where did Rapti go to law school?"

"Actually, she's a proud graduate of the cosmetology program at Kelsey Institute in Saskatoon."

"Well, the cosmetology program does good work. That's sensible advice. Anything else?"

"Be sure to wear your red tie."

"I'll be wearing my robe. The jury won't know what colour my tie is."

"But I will."

The next morning as the jurors filed in, their faces were grave. The tension in the air was thick. I checked the room for familiar faces. Charlie and the other *Too Much Hope* kids were in the first row. Krissy Treadgold was notable by her absence. Howard was sitting at the back.

Garth Severight's closing statement was carefully composed. He commended the jury for the gravity with which they had assumed their burden; he gave a careful précis of the evidence. The facts he cited were the same as the facts that would be cited by the defence, but the story he chose to tell was very different. The Sam Parker of his story was a brash, wealthy oilman who was accustomed to getting his way at all costs. As he spoke I watched his face, and I was struck with the realization that Garth, the clown whom we had dismissed as stupid and egotistical, believed every word he was saying. His case had gone south on him. Linda, a smart lawyer with confidence in her ability, had believed Sam Parker should be charged with attempted murder and that she could prove her case. Had the Crown gone for a lesser charge, the outcome would have been different, but to prove beyond a reasonable doubt that when Sam entered Kathryn Morrissey's backyard he had murder, not rapprochement, on his mind had been a tough sell for Garth Severight.

During the trial we had mocked him, but as Garth delivered his earnest closing statement, I was moved. His address to the jury touched upon truths to which we all paid lip service. No one, not even a millionaire, not even a person with powerful political connections, is above the law. If the justice system that governs our dealings with one another permitted people to take the law into their own hands, none of us would be protected. The words he uttered were aphorisms, but they had power because it was clear that Garth believed what he said.

I glanced over at Zack. He was alert but impassive, and I remembered Ed Mariani saying that Zack could have argued either side of a case with equal fervour because his interest was not in justice but in winning. As Garth made his final plea to the jury to summon the courage to bring in the verdict that the evidence supported, I knew Zack could have uttered Garth's lines brilliantly, but brilliant as he was they would have lacked the fervour I heard in the voice of this limited man who believed every word he said.

At the outset, Zack's closing statement was tight and quietly emphatic. He analyzed the evidence and found it wanting – not because the police hadn't done their job but because they had brought forth no credible witness to establish that the shooting had been anything other than an accident – the result of a terrible, terrible lapse in judgment by a good man who had been under incredible pressure. He underscored Howard's lack of credibility. Zack's point was simple. For a conviction of attempted murder, the Crown must prove forethought and that the defendant's action was deliberate. They had, he said, failed to do this.

Then having dealt with the facts, Zack went to town.

"Once upon a time," he said, "there was a man who loved his child. How many stories do you know that begin like that? Ten? Twenty? Every culture in every time has a story that begins with that one simple sentence. And that's how Sam Parker's story begins – with a father who loved his child so much that when his child was betrayed and despondent, he was prepared to do anything to save her. As a God-fearing, law-abiding man, Sam Parker went to his lawyer to see if the law could help him. It could not. Faced with a shattered family and a child prepared to die rather than cause him further pain, Sam Parker flew to Regina, took the gun from his child's hands, and went to talk to Ms. Morrissey. He was hoping to appeal to her humanity. It was a faint hope, but it was all he had.

"We all heard Ms. Morrissey testify that her obligation is to her text and that the suffering of those who trust her is not her concern. I was chilled by Ms. Morrissey's statements. Judging from your faces, you were too. Can you imagine how a loving father would respond to those words?

"Only two people know for certain what happened in Ms. Morrissey's backyard. You've heard from them both. As importantly, you've seen them both. You've been able to take their measure.

"You heard Sam Parker testify that, unlike Ms. Morrissey, he knows what he did was wrong. He would not repeat the stupid and harmful action he took on the afternoon of

May 16. He's a good man, and good people recognize their mistakes and learn from them. I ask you, as judges of the facts, to see that justice is done here. Don't punish a good man because he loved his child. Humans are fallible. We make mistakes. Sam Parker made a mistake. Love makes us foolish, but it also ennobles us, transforms us into people who put the needs of those we love above our own needs. Please remember that when you determine the future of Sam and his family."

As Zack wheeled back to his table, Brette whispered, "Shreve gets both ears and the tail for that one."

"What are you talking about?" I said.

Brette leaned towards me. "In a bullfight if a matador does a lot of manly cape-swooshing before he kills the bull, the crowd awards him both ears and the tail."

"So you think Zack won his case?"

"I don't know," Brette said. "But he sure swooshed his cape."

Mr. Justice Harney began his charge to the jury by giving what I had learned were standard instructions about the credibility of witnesses, the weight of circumstantial evidence, and the concept of reasonable doubt. His charge on the law centred on proof of intent.

He read the relevant passage from the Criminal Code: "'A conviction for attempted murder requires proof of the specific intent to kill. No lesser *mens rea* will suffice. The key element of the mental element in this offence is the intention to cause the requisite degree of bodily harm, coupled with the necessary recklessness as to its effect.'" He ruled that the jury could find Samuel Parker guilty of attempted murder only if the Crown had established proof of intent; that is that they had proven the accused intended to cause bodily harm to the victim.

"One for the defence," Brette said, and I felt a small blooming of hope.

The judge outlined the evidence presented during the trial; then, without drama, the jury filed out to begin their deliberations. There was the usual hubbub in the courtroom. Brette and I packed up our things, said we'd see each other on the day the verdict was returned, and exchanged good-byes. When Zack left the courtroom with the Parkers, he looked over and mouthed the words "wait for me."

We caught up with each other in the lobby under the mosaic of the God of Laws. Zack rubbed his hands over his face and yawned. "Well, the ship has sailed," he said. "I'm going to back to the office with Sam for a few minutes. After that, we're free. What do you want to do?"

"What I want to do is irrelevant," I said. "What I have to do is paint eyeballs for Taylor's Halloween party. Are you up for that?"

"Hand me my brush," Zack said.

CHAPTER

10

The days before the jury's verdict were a time of limbo, but if this was limbo, I didn't need Paradise. For weeks, Zack's life had centred around Sam's trial and now there was nothing to do but wait. I thought he would be preoccupied and on edge, but with Zack there were always surprises. After the case went to the jury, he spent a few hours at the office catching up, then at 5:30 p.m., he arrived at my house with a bottle of wine, and we made dinner together. We had eaten with Taylor and were clearing up when Delia Wainberg arrived with Isobel and Gracie Falconer. The girls had made a last-minute decision that everybody at the party should carve a pumpkin with prizes awarded to the coolest, the lamest, and the grossest, so Delia was taking them off on a final pumpkin run.

Alone at last, Zack and I settled at the kitchen table with a bowl of white floating candles and brushes and paints to transform the candles into bloodshot eyeballs. Zack set about his task with quiet concentration. A visitor from another planet might have believed he'd never seen the inside of a courtroom.

"This is nice," he said.

"It's called Ordinary Family Life," I said.

Zack smiled. "Well, I like it. It's good to think about something other than the case."

"Then I miscalculated. I assumed you'd want to talk about the trial tonight, so I invited Charlie and Pete over."

Zack applied a stroke of red to an eyeball and held it out to me. "Does this need more anything?"

"Taylor tells me the first rule of art is always take one thing away."

"I notice Taylor chooses not to work in eyeballs," Zack said. "What are these for, anyway?"

"The night of the party we float them in a bowl of slime and light them."

Zack nodded. "As long as I know. And I don't mind seeing Charlie. He's been a reliable ally."

"So I noticed," I said. "Pete's bringing over his new dog."

"A new dog? When did that happen?"

"Today. I saw him this afternoon. He's an English mastiff and he's huge."

"But good-natured?"

"Very. He's just been neutered, but he seems pretty happy."

Zack winced. "I wouldn't be happy."

"Well, Pantera's braver than you – he was still in there smiling and twitching."

Zack stopped painting. "Pantera, huh? That's a nice tribute to a great metal band."

"You know who Pantera is?"

"Everybody knows who Pantera is. The day Dimebag died was the 9/11 of rock."

"Who was Dimebag?"

"Pantera's one-time guitarist. He was shot by a deranged fan."

I shook my head. "How do you know these things?"

Zack finished his eyeball and held it up for my approval.

"Perfect," I said.

"Not bad," he agreed. "Anyway, when I have lunch with my clients during a trial, we talk about what they want to talk about. One of my guys was a serious Pantera fan. After the trial was over, he sent me some CDs."

"To thank you for getting him off."

"No, to console me for not getting him off."

"There's a lot about you that I don't know," I said.

"There's a lot about you that I don't know," he said. "I thought that's why we were getting married – to find out."

"What happens if you don't like what you find?"

Zack shrugged. "I'll live with it," he said. "Speaking of our marriage. When are we going tell your family?"

"Taylor's birthday's on a Friday. I was thinking we could invite Mieka and Greg and Angus and Leah down on the weekend to celebrate her birthday and make the big announcement."

"Let's invite the Falconers and the Wainbergs too. They're as close to family as I have."

"Sounds like a major shindig," I said.

Zack looked at me hard. "You don't look very happy about it – cold feet?"

"Just a twinge. Everything's happened so fast with us."

He reached for my hand. "Too fast?"

"No," I said. "Every time I look at you, I know I don't want a miss a moment of our life together."

It was a nice moment, short-circuited as many nice moments in my home were by the arrival of one of my kids or their friends. This time the friend was Ethan, and he was positioned at what appeared to be his favourite post: the kitchen door.

I walked over and invited him in. He was wearing a black knit watch cap that made him appear older than thirteen. As always, he was jumpy and abrupt. "Is Taylor here?" he asked.

"She and Isobel and Gracie went out to buy more pumpkins for the party."

"I didn't think I'd be invited," Ethan said. "But Taylor asked me today at school." For a beat, the three of us stared at one another, waiting for deliverance. "I should get out of here," Ethan said. "If Taylor sees me, she'll think I'm stalking her."

It was an exit line, but Ethan didn't exit. Finally, accepting the inevitable, Zack threw Ethan a lifeline. "Why don't you stay for a while? I've wanted to talk to you since I noticed you in the courtroom."

"You *saw* me?" Ethan's voice cracked with alarm.

"You were always somewhere around the doors at the back, right? So what's the deal? Are you interested in becoming a lawyer?"

"No," Ethan said. "I'm interested in justice."

Zack's mouth twitched to suppress a smile. "They're not supposed to be mutually exclusive."

Ethan flushed. "Sorry, I didn't mean to sound like a dork."

"Neither did I," Zack said. "So, do you think justice will be done in this trial?"

"I don't even know what justice is in this trial. At first I thought I did; now I'm not so sure. That's why I keep coming back."

"That's why I keep coming back too," Zack said.

"To make sure that the right people are punished."

"And to make sure that the right people go free," Zack said.

"That's a noble aim." Ethan's fingers crept towards the pentangle around his neck. "The poet says that Gawain possessed five virtues that made him a noble knight – love and friendship for other men, freedom from sin, courtesy that never failed, and pity. His five senses were free of sin, his five fingers never failed him." Ethan's eyes were glazed as he quoted the ancient lines. " 'And all these fives met in one man / Joined to each other, each without end / Set in five perfect points / Wholly distinct, yet part of one whole / And closed, wherever it ended or began.' "

For a moment he seemed to exist in a parallel universe; then he vaulted back to ours. He stood up so suddenly that, in what appeared to be his signature move, he knocked against the table. Zack reached and caught his jar of paint just in time.

"Now you really will think that I'm a dork," Ethan said.

"Not at all," Zack said gently. "I enjoyed our talk, Ethan. Maybe we can do it again sometime."

"Okay," Ethan said. "I'd better get home."

"I'll tell Taylor you stopped by," I said.

Ethan looked stricken. "No. Please. Don't. She'll think I'm insane."

And with that, he raced off into the dark.

Zack stared at the door through which Ethan disappeared. "I'd forgotten how much being thirteen can hurt," he said.

"Was it a bad time for you?"

"Apart from being friendless, hornier than hell, and convinced that the only person I'd ever have sex with was myself, it was a blast."

"Well you have me now. All your troubles are over."

"And believe me, I'm grateful. When I was thirteen, I never thought my troubles would be over. I'll bet Ethan doesn't think so either. What's his home situation?"

"His parents are divorced. He was living with his father, but his father's new wife doesn't want Ethan. He's with his mother now. She doesn't seem to want him either."

"So faced with a shitty world, Ethan spends his time with Gawain."

"And longs to spend time with Taylor," I said. "And that is beginning to trouble Taylor, which means it's beginning to trouble me."

As soon as the girls got back with their pumpkins, they began drawing up rules for the contest, an activity that was abandoned the moment Pete's truck pulled up and Pantera unfolded himself from the back seat. Ungainly, enthusiastic, graceless, and boundlessly energetic, he was irresistible. The girls ran him around the backyard, then I brought Willie out and everybody bundled up and came out on the deck to watch Willie and Pantera get acquainted. The night was crisp and starry – perfect weather to sit on the deck and observe the meeting of the titans. But we had miscast our titans. After a few rips around the yard with Willie, Pantera spotted Zack, loped over, dropped his great maw on Zack's lap, and refused to budge. Rejected, Willie slunk over to me. Pete offered wieners and praise in an effort to induce his new dog to play, but Pantera wasn't buying. Finally, we accepted the inevitable. The girls drifted back inside to plan; the rest of us stayed outside and talked.

For Charlie, only one topic mattered: the trial. "So what's going to happen?" he asked Zack.

Zack rubbed Pantera's head. "Serge Kujawa used to say that speculating on what a jury is doing and why was a total waste of time, so he spent all his time speculating."

"So if you're speculating, you must have some idea about the outcome."

"I'd say our chances are fifty-fifty," Zack said. "If Linda Fritz had been there all along, the odds would have been different."

Charlie pounced. "But Linda Fritz wasn't there."

"And the charge she decided on was. That was a break for us. With attempted murder, the Crown has to prove intention to kill and that's difficult to prove. If the Crown had gone for a lesser charge, it would have been a slam-dunk for them – even with Garth."

"Then why didn't they go for the slam-dunk?" Pete asked.

Zack absently wiped Pantera drool off his slacks. "Why do people do anything? But Linda's a person of principle, and I think she genuinely believed that when Sam pulled that gun he intended to kill Kathryn Morrissey. She also knew that Sam had the money to mount a strong defence."

"And that's relevant?" Pete asked.

"There's an old saying, 'The more evenly matched the lawyers, the better the chance of justice.' Linda knew Sam had enough money to get a fair kick at the can. And truthfully, no matter what the jury decides, I think Sam had a good defence. Now, I don't know about you, but I'm going inside. It's getting cold out here."

I stood back to watch how Pantera would react when Zack wheeled away. Pantera watched for a moment, then trotted off behind the chair as if he'd been doing it all his life. I felt the wisps of a challenge developing in our lives.

The girls' Halloween party was Zack's introduction to pre-teen, pre-dating culture, and he was as captivated as Margaret Mead had been when she clapped eyes on Samoa. The ritual of boys and girls trying to impress one another while pretending not to be impressed by one another was intriguing, and the fact that these girls and boys were in costume gave the ceremony an extra fillip. As there had been every year since my kids were little, there was a solid contingent of *Star Wars* characters: Princess Leia with her light sabre; Queen Amidala with her royal pistol, Luke Skywalker and two Darth Vaders. Marge Simpson made an appearance with a swarm of bats and a half-dozen pacifiers nesting in her elaborate cone of hair; Grace, Isobel, and Taylor had dressed as triplets – a clever choice because they were inseparable, and a funny one because they were as physically different as it was possible for three girls to be. Zack had a lot of fun spotting and identifying costumes, but there was one that baffled him. "What's that kid supposed to be?" he whispered, pointing to a boy with a plastic dagger and little boxes of cereal stapled to his track suit.

"I thought you'd get that one," I said.

He frowned. "Well, I don't."

"He's a cereal killer."

Zack beamed. "Clever."

We'd doled out the chili and were just about to slip into the family room with Zack's collection of *The Simpsons'* Halloween episodes when Ethan arrived. He was late, breathless, and without a costume.

"Am I too late?" he asked.

"Of course not," I said. "There's some food left if you're hungry."

"Thanks," he said. "I don't feel like eating. But Taylor mentioned something about carving pumpkins, and I'd kind of like to do that."

"Then you're timing is perfect," I said. "Because they're just about to start." I reached into my utensil drawer and pulled out my favourite paring knife. "Take this," I said. "Good carving tools are in short supply tonight."

"Thanks," Ethan said. "I've got my own knife." He sounded as if he was close to tears. I touched his hand. "Is everything okay?"

"Nothing's ever okay for me," he said bleakly, then he turned and walked into the party.

Zack and I were just nicely into our third episode when my daughter popped in with the ballot boxes for the winning pumpkins. Taylor had shown me sketches of the design she was planning. It was of a phoenix, and as she described how the flames would flicker behind the bird rising in flames, I figured she was a lock for the coolest, but Ethan's mystical heraldic coat of arms with its glowing pentangle surrounded by a ring of flaming hearts won hands down. His prize was three hours of Phantom bowling at the Golden Mile Lanes, and whether it was Taylor's genuine delight at his win or the fact that the other kids had voted for him, Ethan was ecstatic.

"Maybe it'll work out for him, after all," Zack said.

"I hope so," I said. "No kid should think his life is over at thirteen."

"No," Zack said. "C'mon, enough gloom. Mr. Burns is just about to remove Homer's brain."

We looked at each other and recited Mr. Burns's trenchant line. "'Dammit, Smithers. This isn't rocket science. It's brain surgery.'"

Later, as he zipped his jacket and pulled out his car keys, Zack gave the pumpkins glowing in our living room a final glance. "Is it always this much fun around here?" he asked.

"Stick around," I said. "The best is yet to be."

The next morning when I walked into St. Paul's Cathedral for the 10:30 service, Zack was at the back of the church waiting.

"What are you doing here?" I said.

"I thought you'd be pleased."

"I am pleased," I said. "And surprised. You didn't mention anything about this last night."

"It was an impulse," he said. His eyes took in the stained glass, the vaulting arches, and the oak pews. "Nice," he said. "Is this where we're getting married?"

"It's my first choice," I said.

"Then it's my first choice," Zack said.

The accessible area was at the front to the left of the altar. By the time we took our places, many members of the congregation had a chance to see Zack and me together. Zack was oblivious, but I wasn't, and as our dean came forward to give us communion, a lot of necks were craned. The recessional hymn was "Let Streams of Living Justice." Zack had a sonorous bass and a musician's ability to pick up tunes, and as he belted out the line "abolish ancient vengeance: proclaim your people's hour" more than a few heads turned our way. I had spent my entire life going quietly about my business. Being married to a head-turner was going to take some getting used to. When we were leaving, our dean, a generous and open-minded man, seemed startled when Zack offered his hand, and he hesitated for a split second before taking it. I was going to have to get used to that too.

As we walked to our car, Zack gazed towards the park. "Hey, look at that," he said. "You can see my apartment from here. Want to see the view from my balcony?"

"I've seen the view from your balcony," I said.

"I'll throw in lunch. We can order in from Peking House. Think about it – almond prawns, those silky sheets you like, and me. Yes or no?"

"Yes."

It was a fine afternoon. We ate, made love, napped, went down to the fitness centre in Zack's building to work out, came back to the apartment, showered, and crawled back between the silky sheets. We were lying there, discussing how to spend the evening, when Glenda Parker called. In an instant, Zack's mood shifted.

The news was not good. After he'd rung off, Zack rubbed his hand over his eyes. "Glenda's worried about Sam," he said. "The tension's getting to him. No surprise there. I've spent my share of time in hotel rooms when a jury was out. All you do is stare at the wall and imagine the worst."

I put my arms around him. "Anything we can do to help?"

"Have you got a magic wand?"

"No, but I do have a fireplace and a quiet house. Taylor's having supper at Gracie's. Why don't you invite Sam and Glenda to come over for a couple of hours tonight? We could light a fire and have a drink. You said they like to play cribbage – it might be fun to play a few hands."

The Parkers arrived at a little after seven. They brought some very good wine and some very good chocolate. Thoughtful guests, but it wasn't the gifts that made me glad I'd invited them. The trial had clearly taken its toll on them both and their relief at being in a private home was poignant. As strained as he was, Sam was gracious. "This means a great deal to us, Joanne. I know you and Zack don't have much time together."

"We were together all today," I said. "Besides, this is a treat for me. I'm a big Sam and Bev fan. I have all your records."

Sam was incredulous. "Still?"

"You were one of the reasons I never threw out my record player."

"I haven't heard those songs in years."

Glenda put her arm through her father's. "It'd be fun to hear them again, wouldn't it?"

Sam and Glenda exchanged glances. "Yes," Sam said. "It would be fun."

"It's settled then," I said. "Zack, why don't you get everybody a drink, and I'll bring down my record player."

Except for the fact that nobody was smoking dope, the next hour was like many hours I'd spent when I was in university and Sam and Bev were the coolest thing on the Canadian music scene. The Parkers and Zack and I sat around the fire listening – really listening – to Sam and Bev. I had forgotten what a perfect blend their voices were: his was pure and oddly vulnerable; hers, husky and filled with power.

As the artists who'd covered their songs had learned, the music of Sam and Bev resonated powerfully with a wide range of audiences, but for those of us who remembered the passionate certainty of the era that had forged them as artists, there was a special pleasure. Sam and Bev had been a mirror of what we hoped we were: idealistic, smart, world-changing.

Their eyes fixed on the fire, Sam and Glenda's thoughts were their own, but after listening to her mother sing a particularly moving song about a child who gets lost at the fair, Glenda asked her father, "What happened to her?"

Sam shook his head. "I don't know. All I know is that what was best in Beverly and me found a place in you."

After that, there didn't seem to be much to say. We listened to the rest of the record, then we got out the cribbage board. The evening passed companionably – kibitzing about cards, making small talk, and laughing. More Ordinary Family Life, but the four of us were content. When they were leaving, Sam held out his hand to me, then, changing his mind, embraced me and leaned down and embraced Zack.

As I watched their taxi pull away, the tears came.

Zack shot me a worried look. "Hey, what's that about?"

I fished around in my pocket for a tissue. "Weltschmertz," I said. "Sorrow for the sadness of this world."

Zack turned his chair back into the house. "Fair enough," he said.

Given our city's early snowfall, it seemed we were destined for a chilly Halloween, but the benevolent weather that had arrived the second week of the trial was staying with us, and the kids in my neighbourhood were buoyant with hope that this year their costumes wouldn't be hidden by ski-jackets and snow-pants. I was feeling buoyant too. Zack had called that morning to say that the house inspection had been completed. Our new house had passed with flying colours, and the realtor was certain the offer we put in would be accepted. If I was interested, we could go over and start measuring. I didn't have to be asked twice. As soon as Taylor left for school, Willie and I walked across the bridge and along the levee to our new house.

Zack was in the driveway when we got there. He handed me a jeweller's box. Inside were two charms: one was a tiny castle; the other was a key. "The castle is supposed to be the Bessborough Hotel. There's a date on there."

"The date we decided to get married," I said.

"The key is to everything – the house, the car, my heart, the place at the lake, the boat, the whole shebang."

"That's quite a shebang," I said.

"Maybe, but I get you. Now let's go in there and see what we need to do to turn this joint into our dream home."

As Willie scrutinized this potentially challenging environment, his toenails made a clacking sound on the hardwood. The clacking was a good sign. Hardwood made Zack's passage through the house easier. In terms of accessibility, we had been lucky in our choice. The new house was generously proportioned with doorways and hallways already wide enough to accommodate a wheelchair and flush thresholds. But as Zack continued to make notes on his BlackBerry, I became aware of how much we would have to change: there were his and her bathrooms off our bedroom. The bottom cabinet beneath the sink in Zack's bathroom had to be removed to accommodate his chair and the sink traps and pipes had to be padded to keep his legs, which had no feeling, from being burned. A grab-bar and a shower seat with non-skid legs would have to be added to the bathroom. In the kitchen, counters would have to be lowered, doors put on sliding rails, and rollout shelves and lazy-susans added for all the cupboards. The list seemed daunting to me, but Zack shrugged it off. "We'll get a good contractor and it's November – people in the trades are happy to have work. The realtor said we'd be smart to go with a whole new kitchen – what do you think?"

"I've been wanting a whole new kitchen for twenty years."

"That's settled then," Zack said. He held out his arms to me. Our kiss was passionate but awkward, as it often was between a standing person and one bound to a wheelchair. As usual, we both ended up laughing. "You know what we need in here," Zack said. "A bed."

"Let's get one like the bed at the lake," I said. "Lots of room and a good firm mattress. Where did you buy it?"

"Beats me," Zack said, "But Norine will know." He flipped open his phone and dialed Norine's number. His greeting was high-spirited, but within seconds the joy drained from his voice. "Okay," he said. "I'll call Sam. Thanks." I knew without asking that the verdict was in. It was soon – too soon. The consensus had been that there'd be no decision until at least the middle of the week.

Zack was already calling Sam's room at the hotel. "No answer," he said. "They're probably swimming. Jo, I've got to get downtown."

"Okay," I said. I was wearing blue jeans and a T-shirt, but as luck would have it, I'd put on my best jacket, and Zack's cashmere scarf had been in the jacket pocket. The camera would shoot me from the waist up. "Let's drop Willie off, and I'll come with you." I read the anxiety in his face. "Is this necessarily bad news?"

"Honestly, I don't know. I've been through this more times than I want to remember, but it's never easy. You get close to people during a trial, and Sam and Glenda were worth getting close to."

During our time together, I had never seen Zack park his car in the space reserved for the handicapped, but that day at the courthouse, he drove into it without comment. We were rushed, but we weren't the only ones who'd been caught off guard.

As Zack disappeared down the corridor to get ready for court, Garth Severight was right behind him, shrugging into his barrister's robe. Not long afterwards, Sam and Glenda came through the front door. Sam was wearing a three-piece suit; Glenda was in slacks, a shirt, and a jacket. Both had damp hair. Zack had been right about the call catching them during their morning swim.

I slipped into my place in the media section and waited. The air was tense, but the protocol that governed the delivery of the verdict was low-key. The jury filed in. Zack and Garth both turned towards them, then having seen enough, turned away.

The court clerk's voice was mechanical. "Ladies and gentlemen of the jury, have you agreed upon your verdict?"

The jury foreperson stood. There were no flowers in her hair today. Her thick mane was braided and twisted into a neat chignon at her nape, and she had traded her granny gown for a sensible black wool dress. I tried to decide what her newly conservative clothes choice augured for Sam. I didn't have long to ponder. There was no theatrical pause for effect. In a voice as flat as that of the court clerk, the foreperson stated that the jury had agreed upon a verdict.

The court clerk read his lines: "How say you? Do you find the accused guilty or not guilty on the charge of attempted murder?"

Zack and Glenda were stoic, but Sam, surprisingly, had lost his composure. As he stood to hear his fate, he looked grey and unwell. The jury foreperson looked neither to the left nor the right. "We find the accused not guilty," she said.

I found myself almost insanely relieved. Sam and Glenda Parker held each other for a moment, then both leaned over to embrace Zack in his chair. Zack grinned, turned to catch my eye, then moved towards Garth Severight's table. The men exchanged a few words, then Zack headed for the exit with the Parkers. Charlie Dowhanuik and the *Too Much Hope* kids stood to follow them out of the courtroom. Krissy Treadgold was back. Looking more Alice-like than ever, she was dressed in a filmy blouse and her blonde hair was tied back in a large velvet bow. She was still wearing her hospital bracelet. Charlie turned towards me and raised his arms in a sign of victory.

Suddenly exhausted, I threaded my way through the melee. By the time I got to the foyer, Zack had taken off his robe, and Sean, the ever-obliging associate, was at his side. He handed Zack and his clients their coats, then provided a wedge to get them through the crush towards the area on the courthouse steps for the inevitable media scrum.

I put on my jacket, raised my eyes one last time to the mural of justice in the foyer, and left through the double doors. The whole sequence took less than five minutes. By the time I walked onto the portico, Sam and Glenda Parker were accepting congratulations and Zack was fielding questions from the press that had closed in on them. I crossed the courthouse steps and overheard Garth Severight trotting out a maxim that was both ancient and true: "The Crown never wins or loses. The Crown's job is to see that justice is done."

The temperature was a chilly ten degrees, but the atmosphere was warmed by the giddy heat of victory. Against all odds, the defence had triumphed. When Sam Parker appeared to slip and fall into Zack's chair, the moment seemed one more instance of the dizziness that affected us all. Grinning, Zack stretched to catch him, and there was laughter and an impromptu scattering of applause. Glenda reached over to help her father up. She was smiling, but as she saw his face, her smile froze.

"Call 911," she said. "And somebody help me get him inside." A police officer who'd been detailed to prevent any incidents when the verdict was delivered stepped forward, took one look, made a call, and then moved Sam from the snowy steps. Zack pushed his way back into the building. There was a crush to get inside, but whether from respect or some sort of atavistic fear, we all kept our distance from the stricken man lying on a blanket spread on the marble floor of the foyer. Glenda knelt beside her father, holding his hand and murmuring reassurances. Finally, the EMS people arrived, strapped Sam Parker onto a stretcher, and carried him to the waiting ambulance. Above us, in his majestic red robes, the God of Laws held aloft the arms of the balance of right and wrong. I glanced at my watch. It was 11:15.

CHAPTER

11

Sam Parker's collapse set in motion a series of aftershocks that exposed fault lines in many lives, mine included. But in those first moments, all any of us could do was react to this sudden and devastating fracture in the order of things.

Zack was hyper-alert. "Let's get down to the hospital. Glenda shouldn't be alone."

"Give me the keys," I said. "I'll bring the car around." But as I started down the stairs in front of the courthouse, Randy, the cameraman from NationTV, grabbed my arm. "Give us five minutes, Joanne," he said. "You were standing right next to Sam Parker. Rapti will want something."

Zack was close enough to overhear the exchange.

"Do what you have to do," he said.

"I'll be at the hospital as soon as I can," I said.

I walked over to my usual place on the courthouse steps, clipped on my lapel mike, and watched Randy set up. When he signalled me to go ahead, my hands were shaking. I jammed them in my jacket pockets and began to speak. My voice was reassuringly steady and by the time I'd finished my standup, I felt stronger, restored by the experience of doing an accustomed job. Randy offered me a lift in the NationTV van and I took it. He dropped me off at the main entrance to the hospital, and I made my way through the cluster of smokers shivering outside in their blue hospital robes, crossed the lobby, and headed for Emergency.

Zack and Glenda were in the waiting room.

"How's Sam doing?" I asked.

"They're moving him to Intensive Care," Glenda said, her voice small and strained.

"Has anyone called your mother?" I asked.

Zack moved his chair closer to Glenda. "You have enough to deal with," he said. "I'll make the call."

Glenda shook her head. "I should be the one to tell her." She reached for her cell.

"Probably best to use a land line here," I said. "There's a pay phone over there by the door."

Zack and I watched Glenda walk to the pay phone, then steel herself to call her mother. I didn't need to hear Beverly's side of the conversation to know that Glenda was getting a tongue-lashing. When she came back, Glenda was pale. "My mother says it's all my fault."

Zack and I both started to offer reassurance. Glenda waved us off. "Don't worry about it," she said wearily. "My mother has been blaming me for everything since I told her I was a girl."

The physician who approached us was a tall, no-nonsense woman whose hospital badge identified her as Roses Stewart. Certain that the name must be Rose, I checked again, but that whimsical final *s* was no mistake. There was a romantic in Dr. Stewart's past.

"Are you Sam Parker's family?" she asked.

"I'm his daughter," Glenda said.

"It might be best if we sat down," the doctor said.

Television has taught us all to read the signals of tragedy. Glenda closed her eyes, shutting out the messenger. "He's dead," she said quietly.

The sorrow on the doctor's face was real. "I'm sorry," she said. "We did everything that could have been done. It was simply too late."

Glenda nodded numbly. "Can I see him?"

"Of course," the doctor said. "But why not wait till we get some of the tubes and wires out of the way."

"No," Glenda said, tilting her chin. "I want to see him now."

"All right," Dr. Stewart said. "Come with me."

After they disappeared down the corridor, Zack uttered an expletive.

I rubbed the back of his neck. "You should call Beverly," I said. "It would be cruel to let her show up here thinking there's still hope."

"You're right," Zack said. "Although I wish you weren't." He wheeled towards the nursing station. As he talked to Beverly, I could see him fighting anger. When he came back, he was coldly furious. "Grief has not softened Beverly's heart," he said. "She'll be here in an hour, and she wants me to make certain that Glenda is nowhere around. To quote the lady, 'I don't want Sam's death to turn into a freak show.'"

"What did you say?"

"My first impulse was to tell the widow to go fuck herself, but then I thought about Sam. His family life was complicated, but he loved his wife and he loved his daughter. Anyway, I told Beverly I'd get Glenda out of the way."

"Glenda won't object," I said. "When she comes back, she and I can get a cab and go back to my place."

Having deferred the meeting of the Parker women, Zack and I sat back to wait . . . and wait. When Zack checked his watch and realized Glenda had been gone half an hour, he narrowed his eyes. "Maybe somebody should get her out of there," he said. "This is getting a little weird."

As if she'd read his mind, Dr. Roses Stewart strode through the doors from Intensive Care. She seemed surprised to see us in the waiting room. "Glenda left twenty minutes ago," she said. "She only stayed with her father for a few minutes. I apologize. Someone should have told you."

"It's a crazy day," Zack said simply. "But I could use your help. There will be media people downstairs wanting answers. Is there someone who can give them the facts and get them the hell out of here? Mrs. Parker is coming to the hospital straight from the airport. She shouldn't have to deal with the press."

"I'll talk to them," Dr. Stewart said. The three of us were silent as we took the elevator to the main floor. But as the door opened, Dr. Stewart turned towards us.

"I'd just heard the verdict when they brought Mr. Parker in," she said. "All the time I was working on him, I kept thinking how relieved he must have been to know he was a free man."

The press had been shepherded into a boardroom on the main floor. Dr. Stewart's announcement was brief. She gave the time and cause of death, and said there was no point asking questions because she had no answers. Then she walked out of the room. The press spotted Zack and when they redirected their energies to him, he followed the doctor's lead and told everyone he had nothing to say, so they might as well go home. There was grumbling, but with no reason to stay, people left. When the boardroom had emptied, Zack rubbed his forehead. "Jesus, Jo. I'm going through the motions, but I really can't believe any of this."

I could see the sorrow gathering. "Come on," I said. "Let's blow this pop stand. There's a Robin's Donuts down the hall.

We can have a cup of coffee and be back in the waiting room at Intensive Care by the time Beverly arrives."

The hospital's Robin's was called The Heartbeat Café – a questionable choice for a place that pushed caffeine, sugar, carbs, and grease, but in every other way it was identical to its sister stores in the franchise: metal tables and chairs, perky servers in brown and orange uniforms. Zack peered gloomily at the displays that featured every conceivable permutation and combination of fried dough and glaze, then turned to me. "Why don't they serve martinis here?"

"No initiative," I said.

"They're missing a bet. Life's lousiest moments call for something more than coffee, and right now you and I are three for three: Sam's dead, Glenda has vamoosed, and Beverly's on her way."

I picked up our coffee and followed Zack to a table.

"Do you want me to stay when Beverly comes?"

Zack sipped his coffee. "No. You'd probably feel compelled to kill her, and I don't think I can handle any more complexities today."

"Is she that bad?"

"Worse. She talks about Jesus so much you think he'll be dropping by for lunch, but Beverly's Lord wouldn't be a lot of yucks. He's pretty heavily into abominations and transgressions."

"It's hard to believe someone could change so much," I said. "Last night when I heard that funny little twang in her voice, I remembered how much she and Sam meant to me. When I listened to them, I really believed we were the generation that could make a better world."

"Beverly made herself a better world," Zack said. "Can't blame her for the fact that the poor and downtrodden didn't know how to pick their investment counsellors."

We finished our coffee and said our goodbyes. Zack went to the front door with me and waited till I got a taxi.

When I got home, I went straight to our family room. The crib board and cards were still on the table. Sam had given the cards a double shuffle before he slid them back into their case. "Luck for the next player," he explained. Despite everything I felt a rush of gratitude. Out of nowhere, an old Dr. Seuss line came into my mind: "Don't cry because it's over. Smile because it happened." I picked up the jacket of the LP on the turntable. The album was called *Skylarking* and the photo on the cover was poignant: Sam and Bev, young, lithe, and exuberant, were frolicking on the rigging of a sloop. The sail of the sloop was billowing and the sky above was cloudless and impossibly blue. Nothing but good times ahead.

Seconds later, the phone rang again. The voice was familiar, but I couldn't place it. Luckily, she identified herself.

"Joanne, it's Kathryn Morrissey. I wondered if I could come by and talk to you for a few minutes. I need your help."

I was livid. "You really are a piece of work. Sam's body is still at the hospital and you're already lining up interviews."

There was a silence. "I didn't know he died," Kathryn said.

"Well, he did – about an hour ago. He had a massive coronary, and it killed him. Find a radio. You can hear all about it."

"You sound as if you think that somehow Sam Parker's death is my fault."

"Kathryn, do you have any idea of the impact *Too Much Hope* had on Sam's life?"

"Sam Parker died of a heart attack, Joanne. You said so yourself. A heart attack is nobody's fault. It just happens."

"My God, Kathryn. What kind of human being are you?"

"What kind of human being are you, Joanne? I told you I need help. Can't we at least talk?"

"No," I said. "We can't. Smarter people than me have fallen for your line, but I have the advantage of hindsight. I know what you do to people who trust you. I have nothing to say to you, Kathryn. Not now. Not ever. So, do us both a favour – delete my name from your address book."

As I always did after I'd lost my temper, I felt better for thirty seconds and then infinitely worse. But as depleted and ashamed as I felt, I wasn't ready for a rematch with Kathryn. When the phone rang again, I checked call display before I answered. It was Jill Oziowy.

"Quite a day for you, huh?"

"Zack and I were with Glenda when the doctor told her Sam was dead."

"God, that must have been miserable."

"It was. And then to add to the misery, I just had a call from Kathryn Morrissey."

Suddenly Jill was all business. "What did she want?"

"She wanted to talk. She said she needed my help."

"Perfect. We're doing a piece on the life and death of Sam Parker on *Canadian Morning*. Call Kathryn back and ask her to meet you at the studio tonight. I'll get Rafti to set it up. We can add your interview to the piece."

"Jill, Sam Parker died today. If you want to talk to Kathryn, call her yourself. I'm not playing any more, and I told her that."

"Mary, Mother of God, why would you do that?"

"Because, in the words of the sage, 'There is some shit I will not eat.'"

Jill's tone was cutting. "So while you stay lily pure, Kathryn is already on the phone with another network arranging her first live interview about the Sam Parker case. Christ, Jo, how dumb can you be?"

"Apparently very dumb," I said. "I thought you shared my opinion of *Too Much Hope*."

"That's personal. This is professional. Your boyfriend would understand."

"Meaning?"

"Meaning you might to want to take a look at how Zack Shreve operates. He knows that when you've got a job to do, principles get in the way."

"Okay. Time to shut it down. You're talking about the man I'm going to marry. No more slams. Got it?"

"Yes, I've got it," she said. "I assume you'll still do the *Canadian Morning* spot."

"Have Rapti call with a time," I said. "But, Jill, I really liked Sam. Don't expect me to be impartial."

"I'm sure Kathryn Morrissey's interview with the competition will balance things out," Jill said acidly. Then she slammed down the phone. It seemed our friendship was about to become another casualty of Kathryn Morrissey's ambition. I wanted to cry. Instead, I went into the kitchen and made a pitcher of martinis. Zack had taught me his recipe – Citadelle Gin, enough Noilly Prat to round out the sharpness of the gin, and ice. I put the pitcher and two glasses in the fridge, arranged cheese and crackers on a plate, filled a bowl with more olives, then made up the hide-a-bed in the family room. When Zack arrived, I handed him a martini at the door.

He grinned. "Hey, aren't you supposed be naked and wrapped in Saran Wrap when you do that?"

"I'm out of Saran Wrap."

"Naked would have been okay." He sipped his martini. "Oh God, that's good. Come here." He kissed me. "You're good, but the world is an awful place."

"I take it your encounter with Beverly didn't go well."

He handed me his martini and pointed his chair towards the kitchen "All Mrs. P cared about was 'maintaining dignity,' which meant keeping Glenda away from the press, and the size of my bill – which, incidentally, grew every time she opened her yap." Zack cut a piece of Oka and wolfed it.

"This is just what I needed. Thank you. Thank you. Thank you. I'll make it up to you. How are you doing?"

"Not great," I said. "But hanging in. I had a phone call from Kathryn Morrissey."

"Whoa. What was on her mind?"

"She wanted to talk – said she needed my help."

"I'm guessing some publisher has offered her a bundle to write about the Sam Parker trial."

"That was my thought too," I said.

Zack popped an olive in his mouth. "So what did you tell her?"

"I told her I had nothing to say and she could delete my name from her address book."

"That sounds final."

"I hope so. If I never see the woman again it will be too soon."

"Moi aussi. Hey, one piece of good news. Glenda got in touch. She left a message at the office, apologizing for running off. She said she just needed to be alone. I understand the impulse. I feel like someone's peeled the skin off me."

"Is the martini helping?"

"Yes. So is the food. So is being with you."

"I've got the daybed made up. When we're finished our drink, I thought we could unplug the phone and take a nap."

Zack's eyes widened. "That is the best idea. Let's go."

The day of the party the girls had covered the windows in the family room with pale green tissue paper and fixed huge construction paper talons and beaks against them. Taylor had been so taken with the effect that she'd asked if she could leave the decorations up till Halloween. The afternoon light straining to come through the green tissue paper gave the room an unearthly glow. Zack took it in and nodded approvingly. "Sealed off from the world with giant birds to guard us," he said. "Let's stay in here forever." We took off our clothes, fell into each other's arms, and slept.

Two hours in the comforting proximity of a lover was therapeutic. By the time Taylor, Gracie, and Isobel came home to get ready to go trick-or-treating, the daybed was up and we were dealing with life. Zack was back at the office, and I was sitting at the table with my laptop, running through the Sam Parker file.

The girls and I ate dinner early. By the time we rinsed the dishes, the first small trick-or-treaters were at the door. I took my place by the bowl of candy and the girls went upstairs to get ready.

The triplets outfits Isobel, Gracie, and Taylor had worn at their party had been a hit, but everyone had seen them. Tonight the members of the trio were going out as cheerleaders. Taylor and I had had a discussion about the wisdom of girls their age going out at all. The innocence of an early Halloween evening had a way of souring when the hour grew late and only unaccompanied adolescents roamed the streets. But Taylor had pointed out, sensibly enough, that she would be with Gracie and Isobel, and I had asked her to promise to be home by 9:30 p.m. It had been a compromise, and when the three girls came downstairs in their cheerleading outfits, I was glad I'd caved. With their pompoms, pleated skirts, and heavy sweaters, they looked very 1950s and very cute. I got out the camera and shot enough Kodak moments to satisfy even me.

Given everything, it was good to be distracted by the repeated ringing of the doorbell, and the appearance of ghoulies and ghosties and long-leggety beasties and things that go bump in the night. Willie wasn't impressed by our string of visitors, but I was, and when the phone rang, I was feeling mellow enough to try a seasonal greeting. "Happy Halloween."

"Happy Halloween to you too, Jo," my son-in-law said. "How's everything in the Queen City?"

"I guess you heard the news about Sam," I said.

"Yes, I did. I'm sorry. I know you and Zack liked him."

"Yes we did. Very much. Anyway, is everything okay with you?"

"Well, I'm looking at two tired, happy little girls whose Halloween bags are bulging with candy. So that part of our lives is fine. I was just calling to check on Mieka."

"On Mieka?"

"Isn't she there?"

"No. Why would she be here?"

"She said she needed to make a quick trip to Regina. She took off about five o'clock this afternoon."

"Are you sure she was coming to my house?"

Greg sounded distracted, as if he was reconstructing the scene. "I guess I just assumed that's where she was going. After we heard the bulletin on the radio about Parker's death, Mieka got a phone call. She said something like, 'Don't do anything, I'll be right there.' Then she told me the girls' Halloween costumes were laid out on their beds and asked if I'd mind taking them around. I filled in the blanks and assumed you were the person on the other end of the line."

"And you didn't ask Mieka why she was coming to Regina?"

"No, she said she'd be back tomorrow morning." He paused. "Jo, the truth is, Mieka and I are walking on eggshells these days. I didn't want to start anything."

"I'm sorry," I said.

"Why? You weren't the one who called. My guess is it was Charlie, the bottomless pit of unmet needs. Do you happen to have his number?"

I gave my son-in-law the number, hung up, and began to fret. I was so absorbed in my own thoughts that I was surprised when I heard Taylor come in. I looked at my watch. By my reckoning, she still had half an hour to howl. I called out hello and waited for her to do what she did every Halloween:

dump her candy on the kitchen table and give me a blow-by-blow of the evening's events while she sorted her treats into piles on the basis of their desirability. But tonight, my younger daughter just said hi and headed for her room.

"Hey wait," I said. I followed her upstairs to the landing. "How was your evening?"

She sat on the top step and flopped her pompoms listlessly back and forth. "It was good until Ethan caught up with us."

"What happened?"

She sighed. "Nothing *happened*, Ethan was just way too intense. He made everybody so uncomfortable they just went home."

"Leaving you alone with Ethan."

Taylor nodded numbly. "And then things got really weird."

"Weird how?"

"Ethan was just different than he usually is. For one thing, he's stopped wearing his pentangle, and that was, like, the most important thing in his life."

"Did he say why he'd stopped wearing it?"

"Just that he didn't believe in it any more. He said the pentangle was just a piece of junk."

"Something must have happened," I said.

"Ethan wants to run away, and he wants me to go with him." Taylor's voice broke. "All I ever wanted to do was be his friend."

"I know." I put my arm around her and was struck again at the delicacy of her bones. She was still a little girl. "Why don't you give me those pompoms and go up and have a shower. I'll make us some tea."

Beneath their turquoise eyeshadow, my daughter's eyes were troubled. "Maybe you should talk to Ethan's mum."

"I'll call her tomorrow," I said. "Now, jump in the shower. When you get out, I'll have your bed turned down, and the tea will be ready."

I'd just finished warming the pot when Mieka phoned. "Mum, I just got off the phone with Greg. I know I should have called before, but to be honest I was hoping I could get in and out of town without bothering you. I figured you had enough on your plate."

"Thanks for the consideration," I said. "But since I know you're here, you might as well fill me in."

"Charlie had a crisis," Mieka said. "Peter called me this afternoon. Apparently, when he heard that Sam Parker died, Charlie went a little nuts."

"As Zack says, the hits just keep on coming. So what happened with Charlie?"

"He thought Kathryn Morrissey was responsible for Sam's death, and he wanted to punish her."

"You mean physically?"

Mieka's voice was tight. "We're handling it, Mum. Pete and I've always been able to bring Charlie down. It's going to be fine. Anyway, I love you. And for once in your life, don't worry."

"Easier said than done," I said. "But I'm glad you and Pete are there, Mieka. Charlie's always better when you're around."

Mieka laughed softly. "Believe it or not, it goes both ways. I'll call you when I get home."

The morning of All Saints' Day was grey and misty. Taylor came down to breakfast wearing her favourite outfit: a pink shirt, jeans with pink appliquéd hearts on the pockets, and a matching jeans jacket.

"Looking swish," I said.

She poured herself a glass of juice. "I don't feel swish, but I thought I could at least look good."

I smiled at her. "One of the great lessons of life: fake it until you make it."

"I have an early rehearsal for our Remembrance Day program," she said. "Any chance I could get a ride to school?"

"Sure, what time do you have to be there?"

"Eight-thirty," she said.

"No problem," I said. "My spot on *Canadian Morning* is in twenty minutes. Zack's going to drive me. We're planning to go over to the new house after I finish, but we can swing by here and take you to school first." I looked at her carefully. "Taylor, do you want a ride because you're afraid of running into Ethan?"

She lowered her eyes. "Yes."

"This has gone far enough," I said. "I'll call Ethan's mum this morning."

Taylor looked unconvinced. I put my arms around her. "It's not always like this between girls and boys," I said. "Most of the time, it's a lot fun. Look at me. I ended up with the big sparkly top banana."

My big sparkly top banana followed me into makeup when we got to NationTV. It was comforting to have him nearby sipping coffee and making small talk with the young man who was spraying my hair and correcting my lip line as *Canadian Morning* played mutely on the TV in the corner. My cell rang just as I was getting out of the makeup chair.

"Where are you?" Jill said.

"Where I'm supposed to be," I said. "Just getting out of the makeup chair, heading for the set."

Jill sighed. "Jo, I'm sorry."

"For what?"

"For hanging up on you. For second-guessing you. For slagging you. For slagging the man you're going to marry. For being a lousy friend. Is that enough?"

"It's a start," I said.

"I'll call you after the show and continue to abase myself. Oh, one good thing. Kathryn Morrissey was supposed to be on *Canada A.M.* this morning, but she was a no-show. The host was stuck talking to an old lady with a narcoleptic dog."

Rapti did a nice job producing the Sam Parker segment. There was a two-minute reprise of the trial; then Max Chan, the host of *Canadian Morning*, and I talked about Sam Parker. Max was a fine interviewer – quick and sensitive. Our discussion about how Glenda Parker's personal crucible had caused Sam Parker to re-evaluate his stance on cultural issues was good television. Zack was in the studio with me, and when I finished, he gave me the thumbs-up sign.

When Zack and I dropped Taylor off at school, I watched until she waved from the door and disappeared inside; then Zack and I drove towards the new house. We'd just pulled into the driveway when my cell rang. I looked at the caller ID and cursed technology. The number was Howard Dowhanuik's. Guilt made me pick up. I'd left messages at Howard's, but I hadn't seen him since the trial ended.

As always with Howard, there was no preamble. "There's some trouble here," he said.

"What kind of trouble?"

Howard tried his usual tone of sharp command. "Just get over here."

"Not good enough, Howard. I haven't heard from you in days. I have a life of my own. If you want me to come over, I'll need a reason."

"Jo, I need you to come and I need you to bring Zachary Shreve. I need help."

"Howard, what's happened?"

His tone changed. "Please just come to my house. I need a friend and I need a lawyer."

CHAPTER

12

Zack's notoriety and the fact that he was in a wheelchair were useful that morning. By the time we approached the entrance to the cul-de-sac where Howard lived, the police barricades were already up, and people in uniforms were moving purposefully over the careful landscaping, festooning shrubs with yellow crime-scene tape, snapping pictures, dropping samples into plastic bags. Most of the attention was centred on Kathryn Morrissey's condominium. An EMS vehicle was parked in her driveway, but the emergency lights were not flashing. Zack angled his car beside a police cruiser, opened his door, and turned to the back seat to get his chair. My heart was racing. A young officer came over.

"So what's going on?" Zack asked.

A flash of recognition crossed the young cop's face. He knew who Zack was, and he knew what Zack did for a living. Keeping a trial lawyer on the other side of the barricade would be a pleasure.

"Police business," the officer said.

Zack unfolded his chair and manoeuvred himself into it. "Fair enough," he said equitably. He pointed to Howard's house. "I have lawyer business over there, and I'd be grateful if you lifted your barricade for a moment so I can get my chair through."

The officer clenched his jaw, but he moved the barrier and let us pass.

Howard met us at the door. I was relieved to see that he was both clean and sober. The stitches on his face had healed sufficiently to allow a proper shave, and his shirt and slacks were fresh. The living-room curtains were drawn, but the televisions were silent, and there was nary a glass nor a bottle in sight. The place smelled pleasantly of woodsmoke, but when I glanced at the fireplace, I saw that in his frenzy of housekeeping, Howard had even vacuumed up the ashes from his fire.

Howard extended his hand to Zack. "Thanks for coming," he said. Then, surprisingly, he extended his hand to me. "You too. I appreciate it."

"So what's happening?" Zack said.

Howard's narrative style had the finesse of a drill sergeant's. "Somebody died next door."

"Was it Kathryn Morrissey?" I asked.

Howard nodded.

I felt my stomach clutch. Zack and I exchanged glances. "So what's my role here?" Zack said.

"It's no secret that the lady and I didn't get along, and Kathryn Morrissey was murdered."

Zack put his hand up in a halt gesture. "Stop right there. For one thing, Joanne's in the room, and lawyer-client privilege won't extend to her. For another, I don't know what your involvement is, but if you're in deep, there are a number of reasons why you'd get better representation from someone other than me. I can give you a name."

"Let's hear it," Howard said.

"Margot Wright. She's an excellent trial lawyer and given that the victim is female and you're male, Margot's your best option. Do you want me to make the call?"

Howard nodded.

Zack picked up his cell, and within minutes it was settled. Howard asked us to stay until Margot arrived, then, in a gesture that was unprecedented when there was a woman around, he went into the kitchen to make coffee.

I went to Zack and rested my hands on his shoulders. "I'm glad you suggested another lawyer."

He raised an eyebrow. "Even if it was Margot?"

"Even if it was Margot."

"Good, because to be honest, I haven't got the stomach for this one. Usually, I get a real rush when I smell a red-meat case, but not this time. I know too much, and everything I know makes me sad."

"Me too," I said. "So we'll introduce Howard and Margot and go back to our measuring?"

"Let's give it a shot. I'd rather watch our house take shape than spend fourteen hours a day working on a murder case."

"I can't believe those words are coming out of your mouth."

"Neither can I," he said. "I guess the Statue of Liberty is inching towards Lake Ontario, after all."

Howard came back with a pot of coffee – real coffee on a tray, a carton of half-and-half, a bowl of sugar, and four mugs that appeared to be clean. Then he went to the window and threw open the drapes. "Nobody's going to tell us what's happening. We're going to have to find out for ourselves."

Howard's timing was impeccable. Zack had just moved closer to the window when the EMS crew came out with a gurney bearing a body in a body bag. My knees began to shake. Zack reached his arm around my legs to steady me.

Howard spoke for us all. "Such a small bundle to cause so much grief."

The three of us were silent as the gurney was loaded into the ambulance, and the ambulance drove off. It was impossible not to be stunned by the horror of what was unfolding, but the ceremony of dealing with the coffee helped. I poured three mugs full. "Who found the body, Howard?" I asked.

He dumped a heaping soup-spoon full of sugar into his mug and stirred. "I overheard one of the cops say it was her kid."

"Kathryn never mentioned that she had a child," I said.

"And I never saw a kid there," Howard said. "Must have been pretty quiet."

At that moment, a sleek black BMW made its way through the barricades and sidled up to Zack's car.

"Here's Margot," Zack said.

Margot had a few words with the cops outside and then, briefcase in hand, she marched ahead. Her blonde hair was casually tousled, as if by a friendly wind; her lipstick was very red, and her open camel-hair coat revealed a creamy form-fitting dress that clung to a form that deserved to be clung to. Zack performed the introductions. When it came to me, his smile was playful. "I believe you two have met," he said.

Margot's eyes found mine. "Not my finest hour," she said.

"Nor mine," I said, extending my hand.

Margot took my hand. "Congratulations," she said. "I mean that. I hope you and Zack will be very happy. Now if there's nothing else . . . Mr. Dowhanuik and I need to talk."

"Is that all right with you, Howard?" Zack asked.

Howard grunted assent.

Margot reached into her bag and removed a tiny red leather case. She opened it and handed me her business card. "If there's anything I should know about, give me a call. Zack has my unlisted number."

"Sounds like the bases are covered," Zack said. "Ready to go, Joanne?"

"Just a minute." Howard beckoned me over. "Tell Charlie everything will be okay," he growled.

Zack had to steer the Jaguar carefully to get through the onlookers and media trucks that had begun to assemble outside the barricades. I felt a twinge of guilt when I spotted the NationTV van, and an even bigger twinge when I saw Brette Sinclair pushing her way through the crowd. That said, I'd had enough. When we stopped at the corner to let a young mother with a jogging stroller cross, Zack turned to me. "So do you think Howard killed Kathryn Morrissey?"

"No, but I wish I knew what he and Margot were chatting about. What did you make of him asking me to tell Charlie that everything will be okay?"

Zack shrugged. "It's certainly a statement ripe for interpretation. Could mean 'don't worry about me.' Could mean 'don't worry about Kathryn's murder because I've got it covered.'"

"Could mean a lot of things," I said, "but let's not go into the Twilight Zone. There was no reason for Howard to kill Kathryn. Whatever damage she could do to him had already been done. And sodden as his brain has been of late, Howard's too shrewd to confess to murder on the off chance that Charlie might be involved."

Zack's glance was quick but assessing. "So you think Howard must know something?"

"Or *thinks* he knows something," I said. "After the shooting, Howard kept a close eye on Kathryn Morrissey. If he was watching her place last night, it's possible he saw Charlie."

"Howard's a drunk, Jo. It's possible he sees a lot of things. The fact is there was no reason for Charlie to go to Kathryn's house. The trial was over."

"And justice had been served," I said. "But Sam Parker was dead, and Charlie blamed Kathryn."

"You talked to him?"

"No, Mieka and Peter did. Apparently Charlie was livid. He thought Kathryn should be punished for what she'd done. Pete couldn't control him, so he called Mieka."

"And Mieka was able get Charlie to cool it?"

"I don't know," I said. "But we should probably find out before Howard gets himself in any deeper."

I took out my cell and started hitting the speed dial. My daughter didn't answer, neither did my son or Charlie. "No luck," I said. "Would you mind dropping me at NationTV – I might be able to find out something there."

"Your wish is my command," Zack said. He patted my leg. "I've always wanted to say that to a woman, but it's so cheesy."

"And cheesy doesn't matter with me?"

"No, because we're committed. We spent four hours looking at paint chips so we could find a colour we could both live with for our bedroom. You'd never put yourself through that with another guy." He executed a neat U-turn and we were back on Albert Street. Five minutes later we were at NationTV.

"If you need a ride home, give me a call," Zack said.

"Where are you going to be?"

"Back at our house, working on the list for the retro-fitting."

"You're the most focused human being I've ever known," I said.

Zack shrugged. "The sooner those bedroom walls are painted Lavendre de Provence, the sooner we can move the bed in."

I gave my name to the commissionaire at NationTV. He called Rapti and she buzzed me through the door that led to the newsroom. Rapti wasn't in her cubicle. She was by the window, with a telephone cradled between her ear and shoulder, taking notes. When she saw me, she held up a finger indicating one minute. I took a chair and perused the latest photos of Rapti's cat, Zuben. Rapti hated cats, but she loved Zuben, with whom she shared what she characterized as a complicated and deeply textured relationship.

I was trying to decide whether a photo of Zuben in a Santa hat was ironic or deeply textured when Rapti came over. "Where have you *been*?" she said. "Jill's been hollering at me because she couldn't find you."

"I was watching the EMS team bring out Kathryn Morrissey's body," I said.

Rapti sat down on the edge of her desk. "You knew about that already? That must mean your boyfriend has been hired to defend somebody."

"No. It just means I was at the wrong place at the wrong time. However, I am prepared to exchange information. What do you have?"

"Not much yet," she said. "Kathryn Morrissey was killed with . . ." Rapti squinted at her notepad. "I can't make out my own writing, but they were some sort of Chinese carved figures."

"Baku," I said. "She owned a pair of them. They're supposed to capture bad dreams."

"They weren't on the job last night," Rapti said tartly. She stared at me. "Trade you places. I need the computer." We switched and Rapti, an effortless multi-tasker, began typing up her notes and filling me in. "From what we've heard," she said, "Kathryn Morrissey's death was horrific. Her murderer used the baku to bludgeon her to death."

I swallowed hard. "Any idea who did it?"

"Not so far. Kathryn Morrissey's son found her this morning." Rapti checked her notes. "He's thirteen years old."

I shuddered. "Imagine finding your mother like that. He'll never get over it."

"I guess not," Rapti said. "We're trying to track him down, but he seems to have been invisible."

"Try the neighbourhood schools," I said. "If he is thirteen, he has to be enrolled somewhere."

"Good thinking," Rapti said. She tapped into the Regina school listings. "Boy, who knew there were this many schools in Regina?"

"You can eliminate most of them," I said. "Given where Kathryn Morrissey lived, the logical possibilities are Pope Pius XII and Lakeview."

"Eeny, meeny, miny, moe, I choose Pius XII," Rapti said. She aimed a perfectly manicured nail at the keypad of her telephone and tapped in the number on the screen. When her call was answered, she gave me a thumbs-up sign. "This is Rapti Lustig from NationTV," she said "Do you have a student there by the name of Ethan Morrissey. He's thirteen. Thank you, I'll hold."

"Ethan," I repeated, and my chest was heavy with the burden of information I didn't want to carry. "And you say he's thirteen?"

Rapti heard the apprehension in my voice. Her eyes darted from her computer screen to me. "Something you can contribute?" she asked.

"He's not at Pius XII," I said. "He's at Lakeview. The surname isn't Morrissey, it's Thorpe."

Rapti's eyes blazed with interest. "Anything more?"

"He's a friend of Taylor's," I said.

"Let me phone Lakeview," Rapti said. I sat down while she made the inquiry.

Suddenly, it was too much, the covered body on the gurney, the baku, the fragile vulnerable boy finding his mother. "Rapti, I've got to get out of here. I'm feeling sick."

"Hang on, Jo," said Rapti. "The police have found him. They're taking him to his dad's."

Somewhat relieved, I stood up and left while Rapti was thanking someone at Lakeview for their courtesy. I took a cab to the new house. Zack was in the living room hard at work on his notes.

He beamed when I came into the room. "Perfect timing. There are decisions to be made, and I don't want to make them alone."

I didn't respond. Zack moved closer to me. "What's wrong?"

"Everything," I said.

For the next fifteen minutes, I sat on the floor, and Zack stroked my hair and offered comfort as I related what seemed increasingly to be a nightmare. "I don't know what to do next," I said finally.

"Sure you do," he said. "Find out the truth. The only thing worse than knowing is not knowing."

I pushed myself to my feet. "So I guess my move is to go to Charlie's and tell him that, despite the fact that a woman he hated was murdered and he may or may not have been in the neighbourhood at the time, he has nothing to worry about."

Zack raised his eyebrows. "That ought to start the ball rolling," he said.

Charlie's house was in the city's core, nestled between a pawn shop and a building that had once been an adult video store but now sold discount bridal gowns. Only a bride who was a retail addict or suicidal would have ventured into that neighbourhood after dark, but the 1930s bungalow that Charlie tenderly restored for a woman he had loved and lost was an oasis of sweet innocence. With its Devonshire cream clapboard, dark green louvred shutters, and lace curtains, the house evoked a time when people left their doors unlocked and visited with neighbours on soft summer nights. It was a welcoming place, but that afternoon my only greeting was from Pantera, who was body-slamming the door in his eagerness to see who was on the other side.

I'd given up and started back down the walk by the time Charlie finally came to see what was going on. When he called my name, I turned and saw that he wasn't alone. Peter and Mieka were standing behind him in the shadowy hall. Faced with a stranger at the gates, my children and Charlie had obviously decided to present a united front.

Pantera's tail-wagging was manic, but nobody else seemed glad to see me. As the silence grew awkward, I waded in. "So what's going on, Mieka," I said. "I thought you were going back to Saskatoon this morning."

Pete, always the peacemaker, took over. "Mum, this isn't a good time for you to be here."

"It's not a good time for you to be here either," I said. "Shouldn't you be at the clinic?"

His face flushed with embarrassment. Pete and I had always been close; shutting me out was hard for him. "We just have a couple of things to work out," he said miserably.

I stood my ground. "I have something to work out too," I said. "Charlie, this morning your dad called Zack because he needed a lawyer. We were at your father's condo when the EMS workers took out Kathryn Morrissey's body. It wasn't a great way to start the day, and the situation isn't going to get any better. I think we need to sit down and talk about what happened last night."

No one offered me a chair; in fact, no one even budged. The signals were clear: any conversation we had would be brief and tense. For a few moments we faced one another in uneasy silence. "So is Zack Howard's lawyer?" Mieka asked finally. Her hand had been resting on Charlie's upper arm. Now it slid down until her fingers found his.

I tried to ignore the intimacy. "No," I said. "Zack didn't feel he was the best choice, but he did introduce Howard to someone else."

Charlie's voice was cold. "Why does my father need a lawyer?"

"I don't know. But he did ask me to deliver a message to you. He said, 'Tell Charlie that everything will be okay.'"

Mieka and Peter exchanged glances.

"Anybody care to fill me in?"

"Sometimes there are things it's best not to know," Pete said. "There was some confusion last night – can't we let it go at that?"

"Pete, a woman was murdered."

Charlie stepped closer. "We were together all night."

"The three of you? Am I supposed to believe that Mieka left her kids on Halloween so she could stay up with you and her brother eating popcorn and watching horror movies?"

"It wasn't the three of us, Mum," Mieka said quietly. "Pete had an emergency at the clinic. It was just Charlie and me."

"All night?"

"All night," she said.

"But, Mieka, if you were asleep in a different room . . ."

"I wasn't in a different room, Mum. I was with Charlie." She looked away. "I'm sorry, Mum."

"I'm not the one you need to apologize to," I said. I peered into my purse, found Margot's card, and handed it to Charlie. "This is the number of your father's lawyer. Call her or don't call her. Your choice."

When I left, nobody waved goodbye.

Driving home, I made a conscious effort not to think about anything beyond the consolations of a hot shower, warm pyjamas, and a long nap. Half an hour later, clean and in my favourite flannelettes, I thought sleep would be possible, but I was wrong. The photographs of Mieka, Greg, and the girls on my nightstand were impossible to ignore, and I was still staring at the ceiling when I heard Taylor come home from school. I pulled on my jeans and sweater and went down to meet her.

She was sitting on the cobbler's bench in the front hall. Her jacket and backpack were on the floor beside her. She was taking off her boots, and her face was pale.

"I wish I'd known she was Ethan's mother," Taylor said.

I remembered Kathryn's phone call. It was possible she had just wanted to talk about the problem that was developing between our children. More coals heaped upon my head. "I wish I'd known too," I said.

"It must have been hard for Ethan coming here," Taylor said thoughtfully. "Remember how weird he was that day he found out Zack was your boyfriend?"

"Yes," I said. "Sometimes people are a little taken aback when they meet Zack. I thought that's all it was. And then when Ethan started going to the trial, I figured it was a case of hero worship."

Taylor narrowed her eyes. "Why would anybody worship Zack?"

"Well, he's pretty successful."

"A lot of people are successful," Taylor said. "That's no big deal. Besides, Ethan said he was interested in justice."

"Like Soul-fire," I said.

Taylor's face was suffused with sadness. "Do you suppose that's why Ethan stopped wearing his pentangle – because he doesn't believe in justice any more?"

"The timing makes sense," I said. "The verdict came down Monday morning and you said Ethan wasn't wearing his pentangle Monday night."

Taylor picked up her coat and bookbag and hung them on the hall tree. "What will happen to Ethan now that his mum's dead?"

"He'll probably go to his dad's."

"But his dad's new wife says Ethan doesn't fit into their family."

"I guess Ethan will have to find a way to fit in."

"It's not fair," Taylor said.

I put my arm around her shoulder. "No," I said. "It's not fair, but that's the way it is."

At five o'clock, Zack, the Family Man, came by unannounced and asked what we wanted to do about supper. No one was hungry, but as he pointed out sensibly, we had to eat. We went to Earl's, a restaurant we all liked, and the familiar ambience – the sounds of other people's laughter, the taped music, the clink of cutlery against china – was balm to our raw nerve ends. So was the litre of Shiraz Zack and I split and the virgin Caesar with extra pepper that Taylor ordered.

As she sipped, my younger daughter was still deeply concerned about Ethan's fate. Taylor was not a person who worried privately, so Ethan and his future dominated our conversation. It was a grim topic. By the time our entrees arrived, we were all in need of diversion. A large and noisy birthday party at the next table offered deliverance. Taylor's eleventh birthday was less than two weeks away, and Zack made the connection.

"Looks like they're having fun over there, Taylor," he said. "What have you got planned for your birthday?"

Taylor's brow furrowed in concentration. "No party," she said. "We just had one. Besides, with Ethan and everything, it doesn't seem right."

Zack's fork stopped in mid-air. "So November 11 will be just another day – no gifts, no cake, no nothing."

"I didn't say that," Taylor said quickly. Then realizing she was being teased, her brown eyes shone. "I love presents, and Jo always makes a cake. Maybe we could just have the family and Gracie and Isobel." She turned to me. "Would that be okay?"

"It's your champagne birthday – you're turning eleven on the eleventh day of the eleventh month. You get to do whatever you want – within reason of course."

Taylor's smile was mischievous. "And since it's my champagne birthday, I'm the one who gets to decide what's 'within reason.'"

Given the circumstances, the evening was a success. When Zack dropped us off, Taylor ran ahead so she could go inside and call Gracie and Isobel. We watched as she unlocked the door and disappeared inside. "She'll be okay," Zack said.

"I think so," I said. "She's still upset about Ethan. So am I. Every time I think about what's ahead for him, I want to cry. But to be honest, I'm grateful Taylor doesn't have to deal with him any more. His feelings for her were just too intense. He confused her, and I think he frightened her."

"Ethan frightens himself," Zack said. "But kids survive some terrible things. Let's hope Ethan's one of the lucky ones who gets to cut his own direction in life."

"Like you," I said.

"And you," he said. "One of the things I love about you is that you do what you want to do and to hell with what people think."

"Do you really see me that way?" I said.

"Sure you wear that same black dress every time we go to something fancy, and you're marrying me. I rest my case. Now come on, Ms. Kilbourn, we were having a pleasant evening, let's keep the good vibe going."

"Do you want to come in?"

Zack shook his head. "Yes, but I have to go back to the office. Glenda called while you and Taylor were in the bathroom at the restaurant. She needs to talk. I'm meeting her at eight." He glanced at his watch. "By my reckoning, that gives you and me time for a short session of romance."

I moved closer. "It's always all about you, isn't it?"

"You bet. I paid for dinner, and that chocolate mud pie you ordered didn't come cheap."

It was too early to go to bed, I was too restless to read, and there was nothing I wanted to watch on TV. Inspiration about how I could spend the evening came when I looked out my bedroom window and saw a lone figure dart into the front yard of a house two doors down from me, emerge with a pumpkin in its hands, and spike it on the pavement. The village of jack-o'-lanterns we had created in front of our house was ripe for the picking. It was time to give our pumpkins an honourable burial in the compost bin. I started to call Taylor to help, but the prospect of spending time alone in the fresh cold air, stretching my muscles in a totally mindless task was seductive, so I tiptoed past her door.

I'd made one trip to the compost pile with the wheelbarrow and was on the front lawn loading up again when a voice called to me from the darkness. "Need a hand with that?"

I turned and saw Howard Dowhanuik. I was struck by two things: no matter the weather, Howard's bald head was bare, but tonight he was wearing a toque; equally significantly, he was still sober. "Be my guest," I said. We worked silently but comfortably, and when the last jack-o'-lantern was broken and stirred into the dead leaves, I suggested we go inside for tea. Howard didn't ask for anything stronger, and I took that as a good sign.

We sat at the kitchen table. Howard made no effort to remove his toque. For the first time in a long time, he seemed at peace with himself, and the toque, scarlet with a whimsical Nordic pattern of elves at play, made him look reassuringly avuncular.

"So how did you make out with Margot?" I asked.

"Good. She's a smart broad." Howard caught himself. "Make that a smart 'woman.'"

"Duly noted," I said. I poured our tea. "Howard, what's going on?"

"I told you. I thought I needed a lawyer, and I was right. The cops were back this afternoon. They went through all the garbage cans at the condo. It seems someone dumped my garbage and Kathryn's, hosed down the cans, then put the garbage back in. My garbage was all mixed up with hers. Probably a prank."

"No doubt," I said. "The old dump-out-the-garbage/hose-down-the-cans/replace-the-garbage trick. We've all done it."

Howard had the grace to look chagrined. "I'm sorry," he said. "I shouldn't have tried to snow you, but you did ask, and my lawyer has instructed me not to tell."

"All right," I said. "I'll do the talking. I saw Charlie this afternoon. I went to his house to convey your message."

Howard grunted, but he leaned forward, eager to hear news of his son. "And . . . ?"

"And," I said. "Mieka and Peter were with him. I won't lie to you, Howard. I'm not thrilled that Charlie is involving my kids. Last night, Mieka and Pete both walked away from their own lives to be with your son, and this isn't kid stuff any more. There will be consequences – serious consequences."

My reference to the price my kids were paying for their loyalty to Charlie bounced right off Howard. His focus was narrow. "So why did Charlie want Mieka and Pete there?"

"Make an educated guess," I said.

"Charlie needs an alibi," Howard said.

"Bingo," I said. "And Mieka is prepared to say she spent the night with Charlie. In my opinion, it's a stupid decision. If she's lying, she's opening herself to a charge of perjury. If she's telling the truth, she's jeopardizing her marriage."

"That's not the point," Howard said. "The question is – can she and Charlie make this story stick?" In a gesture I knew well from the old political days, each word of his question was separated by a pause and each pause was punctuated by a chop of his hand.

I was livid. "Is that all that matters to you? You've known Mieka all her life. Don't you care about her marriage or about the fact that she's doing something unethical? Howard, Peter left his clinic today to help Charlie work out a story. You're Pete's godfather. Don't you care about him?"

"I'm sorry Mieka and Pete are involved, Jo. Really, I am. But your kids are strong enough to see this through. Through no fault of his own, Charlie isn't."

"So we pay for the fact that you were a lousy parent," I said.

"Yes," Howard said. "You do, because this is my last chance." He reached up to rub his head and his hand encountered the toque. He ripped it off angrily. "Why the hell didn't you tell me I was still wearing this?" He didn't give me a chance to respond. "Do you know who gave me this? My daughters? Remember them?"

"Of course," I said. "Both medical doctors. Marnie was very proud of them. She was proud of all her children."

"She wouldn't be proud of the way they've cut themselves off from me. I hear from them twice a year – on my birthday and at Christmas. This goddamn clown's hat was last year's gift – from both of them. That's how little they know their father."

"How could they know you," I said. "You were never there."

I regretted my words as soon as they were out of my mouth. Howard slumped. "Do you think I don't know that? But I'm trying to make amends."

"By saving Charlie," I said.

"Did you know that today is All Saints' Day?" Howard said. "Every year the good sisters who took care of Marnie send me a church calendar."

"They haven't given up on your soul," I said.

"They're the only ones," Howard said grimly. "Anyway, today is the day the faithful light a votive candle and recite a rosary for the departed. This morning while I was shaving, I started thinking about who would say the rosary for me – couldn't think of a goddamned person."

"What about me?" I said.

Howard frowned. "You're not even Catholic," he said.

"I could learn how to say a rosary," I said.

Howard stood up and pulled on his toque. "Well, get started," he said. "Because I'm going to need all the help I can get."

CHAPTER

13

There was a cab idling in front of my house when Willie and I came back from our run the next morning. It was still dark, just before seven o'clock, but the streetlight's beam was bright enough to outline the silhouettes of two figures in the taxi's front seat. Unsettling, but not so troubling as the solitary figure on my front door step. The collar of his pea-jacket was turned up and his watch cap was pulled low to obscure his face, but even from the street, I had no trouble recognizing the slender figure of Ethan Thorpe. He was carrying a box about the size of a small city's telephone book, and he seemed frozen, unsure of what to do next.

I let Willie off his leash and he bounded up the walk towards Ethan. When Ethan turned to pat him, I called hello. Ethan was a handsome boy, but the unforgiving porch light revealed eyes that were swollen from crying and a face crushed by pain.

He held up the box. "I wanted to give this to Taylor. I rang the doorbell, but nobody came."

"Taylor's the Queen of the Sound Sleepers," I said. "I can take the box if you like."

Ethan clutched it to his chest. "I wanted to give it to her personally," he said.

The cabbie honked his horn. Ethan darted a glance at the taxi. "I have to go," he said. "We're catching a plane."

"*We?*" I repeated.

"My father and me," he said.

"So you're moving to Ottawa," I said.

"No, Winnipeg – to a boarding school." Ethan swallowed hard. "It's supposed to be pretty good."

The cab driver hit the horn again. Ethan thrust the package into my hands.

"Ethan, I'm sorry about everything that's happened. I know how difficult this is for you."

His eyes met mine, and I hoped I would never again see such desolation. There had been no happy ending for Ethan. With a dead mother and an indifferent father, he was at the end of the line. I was all too familiar with the pattern. The private school at which I had been a boarder had been a fine one, but we all knew we were there because nobody else wanted us.

"Stay in touch, Ethan," I said. "I mean that. I want to know how you're doing."

His laugh was harsh. "Yeah, right," he said. "Could you tell Taylor . . ."

"Tell her what?"

The horn sounded for the third time. "Tell her I wish we could have been like Soul-fire and Chloe." He ran down the path, jumped in the back seat of the cab, and slammed the door. I watched as the car sped away.

In our family, we always left mail and messages on the kitchen table, but I took Ethan's parcel up to my room and placed it on the top shelf of my cupboard. It was going to be tough enough for Taylor to deal with the rumours and gossip at school; she didn't need to start her day with a fresh reminder of Ethan.

I sat down on the bed and dialed Zack's number. "I was just going to call you," he said. "The contractor's going to meet us at the new house in two hours."

"I'll be there," I said.

"You don't sound very enthusiastic," Zack said.

"I am enthusiastic," I said. "Ethan Thorpe just left. He wanted to say goodbye."

Zack sighed. "You didn't need that."

"Agreed. I would have felt better if Ethan and I'd had a chance to talk, but his father was in the cab waiting impatiently."

"So Dad's going to step up to the plate after all."

"No," I said. "Dad's going to drop Ethan off at boarding school in Winnipeg."

"What a champ," Zack said. "We should introduce him to Mrs. Parker. They appear to be birds of a feather. Last night, Glenda asked me if there was any legal way her mother could keep her from attending Sam's funeral."

"Beverly's trying to do that?"

"Yes. She even tried to enlist me to smooth the process."

"What did you tell her?"

"Take a guess."

I laughed. "My hero."

Zack's car was already at the house, but the contractor and I arrived at the same time. He was a balding, affable man with a very shiny green truck. He walked over to me with his hand out. "Ms. Shreve?" he said.

"Joanne Kilbourn," I said. "But Zack and I are getting married."

"Congratulations," he said. "Incidentally, my name's McCudden."

"I'm pleased to meet you."

Zack was in the living room, staring at his BlackBerry. He and Mr. McCudden introduced themselves and then we got down to business. There was a window seat in the living room, so Mr. McCudden and I sat there and Zack wheeled his chair over. I had come armed with a file folder full of clippings from magazines and printouts from the Internet. Zack had his own folder of notes. Mr. McCudden dropped both folders into his briefcase without opening them. "I'll go through these tonight," he said. "I've renovated about a dozen houses to make them accessible," he said. "But you may have an idea I haven't run into. Now, accessibility aside, tell me in one sentence what you want."

"We want a good solid family home," I said.

Mr. McCudden smiled. "Because you're a good solid family."

"That's exactly what we are," Zack said.

"In that case," Mr. McCudden said. "I have some ideas you might like."

Mr. McCudden zipped his jacket. "I'll meet you here tomorrow with some preliminary drawings. Same time?"

When he left, I turned to Zack. "He doesn't waste time, does he?"

"No, and considering that we'll be paying his crew a bundle to get the job done fast and well, that's a virtue."

"How much is this going to cost us?"

"We'll find out tomorrow, but it doesn't matter."

"If you want something, go for it," I said.

Zack raised an eyebrow. "Are you mocking me?"

"No. Just quoting. But let me know if I'm going to have to take in laundry to pay for this."

"I'll let you know," he said. "In the meantime, I have a favour to ask."

"Your wish is my command."

"You know, that doesn't sound cheesy when you say it."

"It's because I mean it."

"Good, because this is a biggie. It's about Glenda Parker."

"How did your meeting with her go last night?"

"Not great. Sam's funeral is on Friday at Beverly's place of worship in Calgary. It's one of those big, evangelical, Family Values churches, and Beverly wants to put on a real show. She's too savvy to hire goons to keep Glenda away, but she says if Glenda shows up, she'll be shunned."

"Ostracized? Wow. Beverly plays hardball, doesn't she?"

"Glenda plays hardball too," Zack said. "She's determined to be at the funeral, and she is going to attend as a woman."

"To spite Beverly?"

"No, to honour Sam. Glenda and I had a long talk last night. You know how she was during the trial – always there, but never drawing attention to herself. I figured that was just her style, but as it turns out she was afraid if she was overtly female she might jeopardize her father's case. Do you know that every morning before she went to court she bound her breasts?"

"Oh, Zack, that's terrible. I didn't realize . . ."

"That Glenda has breasts. Well, she does. Her endocrinologist has her on female hormones. Apparently, Glenda has to live as a female for two full years before the specialists will do the surgery. Sam knew how important the surgery was to Glenda. He didn't want her to lose any time, so he urged her to dress as a woman during the trial."

"But she wanted to protect him."

"Right. Anyway, now she wants to honour him by appearing in public as the person she really is."

"Good for her," I said.

Zack squeezed my hand. "I figured you'd say that. Jo, Sam's funeral is going to be a tough day for Glenda. I told her you and I would go with her."

"I'm glad you did," I said. "Is that the favour?"

"No, Glenda wants to make sure she gets 'the right look' for the funeral. She wondered if you could help her pick something out."

I groaned. "Zack, you must have noticed that fashion isn't exactly my strong suit."

"You always look great."

"And 90 per cent of the time I'm wearing jeans and a sweater. But I do know where the good shops are, and I'd be happy to take Glenda around. So what are you going to do while Glenda and I are bonding?"

"Catch up on my files. I've been letting things slip lately."

"So the Statue of Liberty has returned to her place in New York Harbour," I said.

Zack held up an admonishing finger. "I'm going to cut back. You watch."

"I plan to," I said. Then I kissed him hard.

Knowing that the city's centre wouldn't be as busy as the malls, we drove downtown where there would be fewer heads to turn and eyes to stare. Money was not an issue, so I took Glenda to the most expensive store in town. I am a reluctant shopper, and the concept of retail therapy has always eluded me, but as Glenda stood in the muted light, holding a creamy silk blouse against the gentle curves of her new breasts, the tension left her body. After a lifetime of masquerade, she was at last going to be herself.

The saleswoman who helped us was discreet and knowledgeable. She offered possibilities that flattered Glenda's lithe, athletic body, and withdrew so that Glenda could make her own choices. In the end, Glenda chose a cool and cleanly cut oyster boucle suit that concealed and revealed in all the right places. When we left the shop, we were triumphant. Our only real problem came later when we tried to find women's dress shoes that would fit Glenda's long and very narrow feet. At the third store, we succeeded and Glenda's relief was palpable. When she found a pair of runners in her size and, they were on sale, we decided to celebrate with a glass of wine at my house.

After we carried in our booty and hung up our coats, it was reward time. "So what'll it be, Glenda," I asked. "White or red?"

"Would you mind if we wait on the wine," she said. "I'd like to try my outfit here where I can really look at it. I was a little rattled when we were at the shop."

"I know the feeling," I said. "There's a full-length mirror in my room upstairs. Take your time."

It was half an hour before Glenda returned, but when she came into the kitchen I saw that she hadn't just been trying on clothes; she had been transforming herself. She had smoothed back the long bang that had partially hidden her face and for the first time since I'd met her, she was wearing makeup. Her blush and lipstick were subtly and flatteringly applied, and the startlingly blue eyes that were so like her father's were now accented by shadow, liner, and mascara. It was clear she had spent more than a few evenings practising. She'd added a delicate gold chain and thin hoop earrings to her outfit, and the effect was stunning.

She touched her necklace. "This belonged to my dad's mother. Does it work – I don't mean just the chain – the whole thing?"

"It works," I said. "You look beautiful."

Glenda's eyes filled with tears. "I've been waiting my whole life to hear someone say that."

I handed her a tissue from the box on the counter. "Here's a tip," I said. "Don't wear mascara if you're in a situation where you think you might cry."

Glenda dabbed at her eyes. "It's the hormones," she said. "But thanks – I'll skip the mascara when I go the funeral."

After she'd changed into her everyday clothes, Glenda came back downstairs. "I appreciate this, Joanne. It was good of you to give up your day."

"The day's not over."

Glenda shook her head. "No," she said. "It yawns before me. Would you mind if I listened to those old records of my dad's again?"

"Not at all," I said. "Indifferent housekeeper that I am, everything's just as we left it."

She winced. "Not quite everything," she said.

After Glenda disappeared into the family room, I Googled the website of Beverly's church and read her minister's most recent sermon. He called upon the faithful to enter the battle for our nation's soul by becoming politically involved. His version of Onward Christian Soldiers was scary stuff, but I knew this was a vein worth mining for my book, so I opened the link to past sermons and read on. I was engrossed in the complexities of his attack on the separation of church and state when Taylor came in.

She pitched her backpack on a chair, poured herself a glass of milk, and sat down opposite me. "Who's here?" she said.

"Glenda Parker," I said. "How did you know there was somebody here?"

Taylor rolled her eyes. "Sweet yellow Volks beetle in the driveway. Bunch of boxes from Hall & Rae in the living room. Music playing in the family room. So where's Glenda?"

"She's listening to those records her dad made."

Taylor nodded. "Ethan wasn't in school today."

"I know," I said. I took a breath. "Taylor, Ethan won't be back at Lakeview. He came by this morning before you were up. He's going to school in Winnipeg."

"But his father lives in Ottawa."

"It's a boarding school. Ethan says it's supposed to be pretty good."

"Did he seem okay?"

"No," I said. "But he's dealing with some heavy stuff. He needs time."

Taylor picked up her milk then put it down without drinking. "I'm glad he's gone," she said quietly. The words tumbled out. "I'm sorry about Ethan's mother, and I'm sorry that he couldn't move to Ottawa with his dad, but I'm still glad I don't have to see him every day." She looked at me gloomily. "That was an awful thing to say, wasn't it?"

"Not if it's true," I said.

"But Ethan's so alone," Taylor said.

"Maybe after a while, you can e-mail him."

"No," she said. "I don't even want to think about him."

Her vehemence shocked me. "Was it that bad, Taylor?" I said.

"Yes," she said. She pushed her chair back. "I'm going up to my room. I need to talk to Isobel and Gracie."

"I'll call you when dinner's ready," I said.

She glanced back over her shoulder. "What are we having?"

"Something cheap, fast, and irresistible," I said.

"You haven't decided, right?"

"Right."

It was close to five when Glenda came out of the family room. It was obvious she'd been crying, but she was composed and ready to talk. "The night my father died, I had a kind of breakdown – my psychiatrist called it a 'psychiatric episode.' I can't remember anything that happened from the time I left the hospital to the time I woke up in my apartment the next morning. My doctor says it's not that uncommon – that if there are too many assaults on the mind, it can just shut down – self-preservation, he says."

"That makes sense," I said. "Still, it must have been frightening."

Glenda put her fingers to her temples. "It was terrifying. But just now, when I was listening to my father sing, it was as if he was right there in the room with me. We used to joke about being able to read each other's minds. Hearing his voice again brought him close. I knew exactly what he'd say about my 'psychiatric episode.'" Glenda straightened her spine so that her posture was like her father's. "He'd say, 'Kiddo, those were the worst hours of your life, why would you want to remember them?' And he's right. I have years of wonderful memories. Those are the times that matter."

I followed Glenda into the front hall. She shrugged on her jacket, then bent to pick up her packages. "And now," she said. "Back to what I laughingly call my life."

"Glenda, why don't you take the records with you?" I said.

She smiled. "I don't have a record player."

"Then take the record player too," I said. "Zack and I are getting married soon. We'll both have to leave things behind. I'd really like you to have the Sam and Bev collection."

"In that case, I'll take it – the whole kit and caboodle – as my dad would have said. And I'll cherish them, Joanne. I promise you that."

Zack was home at six o'clock on the button. Over our martinis, I filled him in on my afternoon with Glenda. Taylor was subdued at dinner, but she perked up when Zack asked her if she had any ideas for the bare, institutional walls of the room that housed the pool at our new home. As she started to float possibilities, the light came back into her eyes, and I thought, not for the first time, how lucky she was to have her art.

At eight, Zack finished his coffee and turned his chair towards the door. "Time to go," he said.

"I thought you were going to cut back," I said.

"I am," he said. "I called McCudden this afternoon. If it's okay with you, he's going to convert that bedroom at the end of the hall into an office. That way, I'll be able to work at home."

"That doesn't move the Statue of Liberty," I said.

"Does it please you?"

"Yes," I said. "It does. Apart from teaching and office hours, I can work at home too."

"Better and better," Zack said. "Okay, now I've really got to make tracks."

"Is this a foretaste of what's to come?" I said.

"Probably," he said. "Are you all right with it?"

"Yes," I said. "Are you all right with the fact that I have a full life of my own?"

His gaze was steady. "That's another reason I love you," he said.

Taylor and I were unloading the dishwasher when Howard Dowhanuik called. I asked him to hold till I moved to another room. When I picked up, I explained that I didn't want Taylor to hear me talking about Kathryn Morrissey's death.

Howard was gruff. "I'm not going to say anything to upset the apple cart. I just wanted you to know (a) that Margot Wright is a great choice for a lawyer, (b) that the cops were back this afternoon, and (c) that they took my fucking vacuum cleaner."

"Thanks for the update," I said.

"You're welcome, but I wanted your opinion about that vacuum cleaner. Why would the cops take it?"

"I'm guessing they talked to your neighbours and discovered that in the eighteen months since you moved into your condo, you never had a fire. On Halloween night, smoke would have been billowing out of your chimney. Neighbours in condos tend to notice things like that. And the police probably took note of the fact that by the time they interviewed you early on the morning after Kathryn's death, you had already vacuumed up the ashes from your one and only fire."

"Shit," he said.

"Whatever," I said. "Tell Margot. She's paid to listen, and she can't be asked to testify against you in court. I can. And Howard, talk to Charlie. You're getting in deep and I'm not certain you have to."

"Do you know something?"

"No," I said. "But tread carefully. Martyrs have to wait hundreds of years before they're recognized as saints."

"You think I'm trying to be a martyr."

"I know you are. And lately, there've been times when I would have paid good money to see you flayed, but this isn't one of them. You're setting yourself up, my friend. Talk to Charlie."

"I'll try."

I hadn't even made it back to the kitchen when the phone rang again. It was Howard. "My son answered and when he heard my voice, he slammed the phone down in my ear. What do I do now?"

"Short of keeping your lawyer informed and your mouth shut, I don't know. I'll let you know if I come up with anything."

After Howard hung up, I stared at the phone. Charlie might not be talking to his father, but my kids were still talking to me. I dialed Peter's number. He was voluble about the emergency that had taken him back to the clinic Halloween night. There'd been a call on his answering machine around nine from a boy whose dog had been hit by a car. The dog was hanging on, and Peter had gone to the clinic to do what he could. It hadn't been enough, the dog died. He was home shortly after eleven.

"And your sister was with Charlie then."

"Mum, please . . ."

"Peter, this is important."

"They were together when I got back."

"Where were they – in the living room, the kitchen, where?"

"Mum, don't do this."

"Were they in Charlie's room when you got home?"

"Yes."

"Were they just talking or what?"

Peter's voice was exasperated. "They were in the same room," he said. "I didn't go in there to see what was going on. You've never once asked us to rat on each other. Don't start now."

"I won't. I'm sorry, Pete. I'm getting a little desperate."

"I know, Mum, but it'll be all right. Really, it will."

My daughter and I had never had any trouble keeping open the lines of communication. Most often our conversations were as inconsequential as they were deeply satisfying, but the Mieka who answered the phone that night at her home in Saskatoon was a stranger – guarded and suspicious.

As soon as she heard my voice, she established the boundaries. "I'm not going to talk about Charlie, Mum."

"You have to, Mieka. The police are finding evidence that connects Howard to the murder."

"What kind of evidence?"

I told her about the police's interest in the garbage cans that belonged to Howard and Kathryn Morrissey, and about the fact that the forensic people had taken Howard's vacuum for testing.

For the first time she sounded frightened. "Do the police think that Howard found something incriminating and burned it?"

"I don't know what the police think, Mieka, but that's what I think."

I had knocked her off base. The sureness was gone from her voice. "I'll talk to Charlie."

"You do that," I said. "And, Mieka, I know your feelings for Charlie have always been intense, but you can't let Howard take the responsibility for a crime he didn't commit."

"The police will find something that will prove Howard's innocent. Then he can just walk away."

"Mieka, this isn't a TV show. There are real consequences here."

"I have to go, Mum," she said. "The girls need me."

"That's right," I said. "They do. Don't lose sight of that, Mieka. If you know something, tell the authorities or at least talk to me. Please."

We were taking the eleven o'clock flight to Calgary for the funeral, so I had time to stop by Howard's Friday morning before we left. Nothing had changed. The silence from my daughter had been resounding, and Charlie hadn't returned Howard's calls. The police, however, had been attentive. The mills of the gods were grinding, but Howard seemed oddly tranquil. He was sober. He liked Margot. He seemed reconciled to his fate. When I left, he asked me to tell Glenda Parker that she had been fortunate to have Sam Parker as a father.

We shared our cab to the airport with Glenda. It was the first time Zack had seen her as a woman, and when he told

her she was lovely, her pleasure was poignant. On the flight
west, Glenda was quiet but controlled. As a white-knuckle
flyer, I was working on control myself. Whether it was the
diamond brilliance of the day or the fact that Zack never let
go of my hand, my pulse didn't lurch into triple digits during
the hour and fifteen minutes we were in the air. When the
mountains came into view, Zack leaned towards me. "How
would you like to come out here for our honeymoon?"

I turned to him. "I'd love it," I said. "I love the mountains
and the sky and the trees and the air and the light. When the
kids were all at home, we used to strap our ski equipment
to the luggage rack of the station wagon and drive here for
the weekend."

"I didn't know you skied."

"Well, we do. Mieka's really good," I said.

"We could get a place out here if you want," he said.

"Skiing wouldn't be much fun for you," I said.

"But it'd be fun to watch," he said.

Beverly Parker's church was on the airport side of the city.
It was a sprawling octagon surrounded by a parking lot with
enough spaces to service a mid-sized shopping mall. Our cab
dropped us off at the main entrance where a burly man with
a brushcut, a fixed smile, and eyes glazed with the joy of
being born again greeted us. He pumped Zack's hand. "I recognize you from the trial," he said. "Thank you for clearing
Sam Parker's name." The man took my hand and pumped
it. "Welcome," he said. "We're glad you're here." His eyes
slipped over Glenda and focused at a point beyond my shoulder. "More people arriving," he said. "This is going to be a
big one."

"Thank you for helping us honour my father, Mr.
Phillips," Glenda said to the man's retreating back.

"Someone you know?" Zack asked.

"My Little League coach," Glenda said. "Taught me how to throw a curve ball."

Zack picked up on the tension in Glenda's voice. "Even assholes have their uses," he said evenly. He looked around. "So what's the deal with this church – it is a church, isn't it?"

"Not just *a* church – the one *true* church. And as you can read on that tasteful sign over the main doorway, this atrium was the gift of Samuel and Beverly Parker. I'm surprised my father's name is still there. He left the church when the elders came to him and advised him to disown me."

The sign was tasteful; the lobby, less so. The Samuel and Beverly Parker Atrium had all the defining features of an overpriced shoddily built hotel: the soaring glass roof, the water fountain that spewed eternal healing streams of recirculated water, the small forest of flourishing tropical plants, the groupings of plush, welcoming couches and chairs. But there were also concessions to the day-to-day demands of running a church that apparently aimed to meet all its parishioners' needs. Signs indicated the location of gyms and meeting rooms. A wall was lined with machines that dispensed soft drinks, chips, and candy bars. A large pixelboard streamed announcements of events that would fill the calendars of the faithful from cradle to grave: Moms and Moppets, Junior Explorers, Volleyball (boys), Volleyball (girls), Teen Movie Night, Networking for Success, Family Life, Single-again Bridge, Estate Planning for Seniors.

Zack was fascinated by the range of activities. "If you belonged to this church, you'd never have to leave the building," he said.

"That's the idea," Glenda said dryly. "They want to keep you safe from the taint of secular humanism." She squared her shoulders. "I guess we'd better go into the worship space. I doubt if anyone's reserved a seat for me."

The large auditorium had a stage, a podium, and hundreds of seats banked theatre-style. The place was already packed, but there was an accessibility section in the first row that still had room. We settled in and listened as a disembodied voice on the sound system announced that television screens had been set up in the gymnasium and meeting rooms and over-flow seating was available. Finally, Beverly Parker entered and took her place, not far at all from where we were sitting. In a terrible and tasteless cosmic joke, the suit she was wearing bore an uncanny resemblance to Glenda's.

Even Zack noticed. He leaned close to Glenda and whis-pered, "It looks better on you," and the three of us exchanged furtive smiles. It was our last light moment. When Sam's casket, mahogany, dark, and gleaming, was carried in, Glenda's intake of breath was jagged. After the pallbearers had set the casket in place, Beverly stood and placed a simple spray of roses on its lid. The flowers were of the same deli-cate pink as Alberta's provincial flower, the wild rose, and I swallowed hard.

The service was simple and mercifully short. The hymns, played over the public address system, had a professional slickness that kept them from tugging at the heart; the eulogy, delivered by an old rancher friend of Sam's, was brief and affectionate. The minister delivered the prayers and read the psalms with practised ease, and when he offered the benediction, I thought we were home free. But as the pall-bearers picked up the casket and started back down the aisle, Sam's voice filled the auditorium. He sang "The Battle Hymn of the Republic" in a voice so strong, sweet, and pas-sionate that it seemed impossible it would ever be stilled. Beside me, Glenda slumped and covered her face with her hands. After the last note had died, she straightened and fixed her eyes on the space where the coffin had been. I took her hand in mine. There were no words to ease the sting of that moment.

As we made our way out of the church, I noticed an ugly and unmistakable phenomenon. Many people recognized Zack and came over to thank him for helping Sam. Picking up on my connection with Zack, people nodded and thanked me for coming. But no one acknowledged Glenda's presence. The shunning was corrosive. Glenda chewed her lip. "Apparently the mercy of our Lord and Saviour doesn't extend to me," she said.

Zack turned to his wheelchair to the door. "Let's get the rock out of Dodge," he said. "There's a bar at the airport. We could all use a drink."

"Good plan," I said. "Let me pay a quick visit to the bathroom, and I'll be right with you."

"They're a little hard to find," Glenda said. "I'll come with you."

We walked across the atrium together, and Glenda guided me down a corridor that led to the bathrooms. She pointed to the Women's. "Success," she said. "I might as well come in too."

A woman came through the door, spotted us, and stepped in front of Glenda. "That's yours over there," she said pointing to the Men's.

I glared at her. "Not any more." I opened the door to the Women's bathroom. "After you, Glenda," I said, and like heroines in an old movie, Samuel Parker's daughter and I swept in.

CHAPTER

14

The martini we had at the lounge in Calgary Airport wouldn't have made anyone's top-ten list, but it did the trick. My shoulders began to unknot and the signs of strain disappeared from Glenda's face. Zack was sanguine by nature, but Sam's funeral had hit him hard and the martini seemed to help. We were headed for the pre-boarding area when I spotted Brette Sinclair across the concourse at the ticket counter.

I touched Zack's shoulder. "Somebody I want to talk to over there," I said. "I'll catch up with you."

Brette was in line behind a man with a cat cage and a woman with three children under the age of three. She was tapping her foot and looking ticked off. She beamed when she saw me. "Boy, that was a trip, wasn't it? That church scared the be-jasus out of me. Did you check out the Topics for Discussion at the Family Life Centre? Curing Homosexuality Through Prayer, A Woman's Place, Culture-proofing your Kids. Can you believe it?"

"Well, when you're writing your article, don't blame Calgary. Blame Beverly – that church she's connected to is a little weird."

"More than a little," Brette said. "And why would I blame Calgary? I was here once for Stampede and I had me a cowboy."

"Was having a cowboy on your life list?"

"No, but he should have been."

"Anyway, why would I blame Calgary? It's a great city. You westerners are so tetchy."

"With cause," I said. "So are you headed back to Toronto?"

Brette frowned. "No such luck. I'm standing here to exchange my ticket to Toronto for one to Regina."

"What's in Regina?"

"Now who's denigrating the west?" She frowned. "I thought you would have heard. The police arrested Howard Dowhanuik. They're charging him with the murder of Kathryn Morrissey."

"Oh no," I groaned.

"Oh yes," Brette said. The man with the cat left with his ticket in one hand, his cat cage in the other, and a smile on his face. Brette watched him bounce across the concourse. "Looks like it might be my lucky day. Now if they can handle Mother Courage that quickly, I'll be set."

"Tell me what you know."

"Well, let's see. The police found a partial print from a bloody shoe in the alley and a remnant of burned rubber in the contents of Howard Dowhanuik's vacuum cleaner. They've got their man, and my old room at Hojo's is waiting for me. I can't believe NationTV hasn't been in touch with you."

"I had my cell turned off during the funeral," I said. I took the phone out of my bag and turned it on. There was a text message from Jill: "What goes on?"

"I should call in," I said.

"Be my guest," Brette said. "It's not as if I'm going any-where."

When I passed on the news of Howard's arrest, Jill was livid. She had begun her career as a press officer in Howard's government and she retained a lingering affection for him. "I don't believe this for a moment. What's the matter with those cops? Howard has had his troubles, but he's not a murderer. Jo, find out what's going on. Howard was always kind to me. Said it was about time there were more smart broads in government."

"Ever enlightened," I said. "I'm in the Calgary airport right now, but Zack knows Howard's lawyer. I'll see what I can find out."

I hung up and checked my watch. "I've got to go, Brette," I said. "I hope I'll see you on the plane."

Brette stared morosely at the woman with the three little children. "If I make it, you know who I'll be sitting beside."

When I told Zack about Howard, he immediately called Margot Wright. It was a brief call, but he picked up the essentials and relayed them to me. The police had arrested Howard at 1:00 p.m. Regina time. Howard was handling himself well – not giving anything up except his name and address. Margot had implored him to tell her the whole story. He insisted he had, but she didn't believe him.

"So where is Howard now?" I said.

"In the cells at the cop shop," Zack said. "Margot managed to get a bail hearing tomorrow, but Howard will be there overnight."

"Can I see him?"

"Nope. Just his lawyer. And, Jo, you don't want to see that place. The drunk tank is just down the hall from the cells, so the smells and sounds are pretty much what you'd expect in the seventh circle of hell."

"It might be a useful experience for Howard," I said. "Still, there must be something I can do."

"Actually, there is," Zack said. "Margot wondered if you could find out Charlie's shoe size."

Glenda had been listening impassively, but the reference to shoes caught her attention. "Why would they be interested in that?"

"Evidence," Zack said. "Somebody somewhere is trying to put the pieces together."

Glenda frowned, looked down at her own fashionable pumps, and retreated into silence.

When I got back to my house, Charlie was there. He and Taylor were watching *The Simpsons*. Charlie jumped up when he saw me.

"No need to move," I said.

"I was just sitting here wondering how you're feeling about me these days." His gaze was level. "How *are* you feeling about me these days, Jo?"

"Conflicted," I said. "But I'll work it out. Right now, your father should be the focus."

"Can I see him?"

"No," I said. "He's only allowed to see his lawyer."

"How's he doing?"

"Do you care?"

"Yes, I care. I'm not a monster, Jo. I understand what my father is doing."

I stepped closer. "What *is* he doing, Charlie?"

Charlie shrugged his thin shoulders. "Playing the hero. Taking the rap because he thinks I'm involved in what happened to Kathryn Morrissey."

"Are you?"

"I didn't kill her, Jo. My father should have more faith in me. Of course, that would involve understanding what I'm capable of, and he barely knows me."

"So are you going to step forward and tell the truth?"

Charlie's laugh was bitter. "Who do you suggest I talk to, Jo? The cops? How interested are they going to be in hearing that I didn't kill Kathryn Morrissey? My father? You tell me I'm not allowed to see him. Not that it would make any difference if I did. As always, my father has made up his mind about what needs to be done and he's doing it."

"Why do you hate him so much?" I said.

"I don't hate him. I came over today because I think this hero act of his is idiotic, and I was hoping somehow to communicate that to him. But since that appears to be impossible, I'll be off . . ."

I glanced down at Charlie's feet. He was wearing hiking boots that looked as if they'd just come out of the box. "Nice shoes," I said. "Are they new?"

"As a matter of fact they are."

"Did you get them in town?"

"On the Internet. I've got these freakish long, skinny feet. Anyway, I can give you the website if you want."

"Sure." I stepped closer to him. "Charlie, I was there when you were born. I hate the way things are with you and your father, but I haven't stopped caring about you."

Charlie nodded. "Right," he said. "I'll call my father's lawyer and see if I can get her to deliver my little message."

"Good."

He leaned forward and kissed my cheek. "Take care of yourself, Jo."

The morning newspaper was filled with news of Howard's arrest. For his trip to police headquarters, Howard chose to wear his scarlet toque with its pattern of elves at play. Margot wore leather. In the photo splashed on the front page, they made a striking couple.

Taylor and I had breakfast, then I dropped her off at school and went down to NationTV to see what I could find out.

When I arrived, Rapti was across the newsroom chatting with a colleague. I went to her cubicle and, while I waited, looked around for any new photos of Zuben.

"I haven't got our Halloween photos developed yet," Rapti said when she returned. "Zuben went as a cat."

"I wish you'd come to our place."

"Next year," Rapti said. She reached back and knotted her shining black hair into a ponytail. "So have you got something for me?"

"No. I was hoping you had something for me. Have the police found out anything more about that footprint they found in the alley?"

"Just that it was no big deal. It came from one of the shoes that poor kid – Ethan – was wearing when he found his mother's body. Apparently he tried to revive her and he got pretty bloody. He took his clothes out to the Dumpster. I guess he was in shock. Anyway, my source says the footprint is insignificant."

I stood up to leave. "Thanks," I said. "Would it be a problem if I pass this along to Howard Dowhanuik's lawyer?"

Rapti shook her head. "Be my guest. She probably already knows. And, Jo, stay in touch. Jill will want a backgrounder on Howard Dowhanuik."

"I'm around," I said.

Margot Wright wasn't on my speed dial, so I called Zack. "The footprint is a non-starter," I said. "The police say it belongs to Ethan."

"I'll tell Margot," Zack said.

"And now that it no longer matters," I said, "tell her that Charlie's feet are long and freakishly skinny. Also, Charlie's going to get in touch with her. He wants to send a message to his father."

"Hmm," Zack said. "Progress."

"I hope so."

"You sound kind of down."

"Just fresh out of optimism," I said.

"Then, let's talk about something nice. What should I get Taylor for her birthday?"

"Well, let's see, I think I covered the 'A List': a box of Kolonok Art Brushes that, Taylor tells me, are the best, a new journal, some frilly underwear, and a book about Diego Rivera. She did mention she'd like a mani-pedi at Head to Toe."

"What's a mani-pedi?"

"A manicure and a pedicure. The mani-pedi comes with an assortment of chocolate truffles – very decadent."

"If that's what Taylor wants, that's what she shall have."

"I hope it's always like this for her," I said.

"Me too," Zack said. "She's a great kid and I love that we're going to be a family. Now, gotta go. Got to do something to pay for that mani-pedi."

I spent the day working on my book. My visit to Beverly Parker's church had given me fresh insight into the new values war, and raised provocative questions about how politically combative the conservative movement in our country might become. Zack was home at six to have dinner with Taylor and me. He was gone again by eight, and I worked on my book until bedtime. Life had a pattern, and I was grateful.

On the morning of Taylor's birthday, I went in to give her a nuzzle before Willie and I took off on our run. She rolled over and smiled without opening her eyes. "Happy birthday," I said. "You smell good. What is that perfume you're wearing?"

"Gracie made it. It's a mixture of patchouli oil, lavender, and something else I can't remember."

"Gracie makes perfume?"

"There a store on 13th Avenue that has all the stuff. You just give them the person's perfume profile, and they help you pick out what you need."

"What's a perfume profile?"

Taylor propped her chin on her elbow and yawned. "Three words that describe the person. My words were 'artistic,' 'independent,' and 'loving.' Gracie and Isobel chose them."

"Gracie and Isobel were right on the money," I said. I started out of the room. Then obeying an impulse, I came back and put my arms around my daughter.

She yawned. "I had an idea for the mural in the new house."

"Want to tell me?"

"It's a secret – but I've made some little paintings – just trying things out."

"Good. Willie and I are going for our run – be back in an hour."

"Mmmm." Taylor burrowed deeper into her covers and went back to sleep.

I took her gifts downstairs, put them on her breakfast plate, then hooked Willie's leash to his collar. It was November 11, Remembrance Day, and the morning was cool, misty, and silent. Willie and I circled the lake. By the time we came to the legislature, the army trucks were bringing in the ancient cannons that would be fired at eleven o'clock, shots through history that froze the marrow.

Taylor's gifts were still wrapped and on the table when I got back. She was sleeping in, and why not when it was her birthday and a holiday to boot? After I'd showered and dressed, I came downstairs, made myself a bowl of yogurt and blueberries, picked up the newspaper, and prepared myself for the rare adventure of breakfasting alone.

It was close to eight o'clock when Zack called, asking if there were last-minute guests to add to the reservation list for dinner. Taylor had decided she wanted to go out for ribs on her birthday, and Zack needed to know if we wanted a bigger table.

I called upstairs to Taylor, and when she didn't answer, I ran up to her room. She wasn't there. I checked her bathroom. It was empty.

I picked up the extension by Taylor's bed. I had left the phone in the kitchen off the hook, and I could hear the chalk-screech dissonance of Hindemith's *Mathis der Maler* in the background. "I can't find her," I said.

"Taylor just turned eleven," Zack said. "She's probably decided it's time to see the world."

"Not funny," I said. "Also not like Taylor. She's a home-body. I don't think she'll ever leave."

"That's okay with me. I like having her around," Zack said. "Gotta go. I have a meeting downtown."

"It's Remembrance Day," I said.

"The meeting is with some money guy from Vancouver. This was the only day his calendar wasn't booked solid. Give Norine a call if we need a bigger table for dinner tonight. She'll be at the office."

"It's a stat holiday in this province, remember?"

"Holiday, shmoliday," Zack said. "There's always work. Tell Taylor I'm looking forward to watching her blow out the candles."

I stared at Taylor's empty bed. It was unmade – not a surprise, but her pyjamas weren't under her pillow, and if she'd gone out, that was unusual. Taylor was a creature of habit, and after she'd dressed, she always placed her pyjamas under her pillow. But lately, when she was working on a piece of art, she'd put on her boots, throw a jacket over her pyjamas, and work in her studio for an hour before school. It was possible our talk about the mural had ignited a spark and she was painting.

I went back downstairs, opened the door to the deck, and called her name. There was no answer and I could feel the edge of panic. I tried to cling to logic. Two hours ago, Taylor had been safe in her bed. She was still wearing her pyjamas. When she was making art, she was oblivious to everything else. If I went to her studio, I would find her content and at work.

Unless I was there by invitation, Taylor's studio was off limits, but at that moment, I was beyond respecting her privacy. The temperature had plummeted the night before, and as Willie and I walked across the lawn, the frost crunched beneath our feet.

Taylor's studio had been built when she came to live with us. She was four years old, but she was already an artist – a prodigy who had inherited her mother, Sally Love's, talent and a great deal of money. It seemed sensible to use some of that money to build Taylor a place where she could really make art. The studio was not a Sunday painter's shack. It was about the size of a modest one-car garage, but the architect had designed it with an awareness of an artist's need for light and space. The north window was large, and even from a distance, I could see that the room was empty. Hoping against hope, I knocked at the door, then opened it.

Taylor and I had long since agreed to disagree about the chaos that was her bedroom, but her workroom was always ordered: canvases, canvas stretchers, palettes, oils, acrylic paints, turpentine, brushes, rags for cleaning, rags for wiping paint into a canvas – everything had its place. The order Taylor brought to making her art was tonic, and I always felt happy in her studio. The "little painting" Taylor was working on was on her easel, and as it always did, Taylor's art took my breath away.

For much of my life, I had been around people who prided themselves on their intellect, but Taylor's gift came from a different well – one that was deep and mysterious. The painting before me had a languorous beauty. It was of our swimming pool. When Zack and I had lunch beside it on the Friday before Thanksgiving, the water had shimmered with a magic that I thought grew out of a golden afternoon and passion. But the brilliant turquoise of our forty-year-old pool had been magic for Taylor too.

As always in her paintings, Taylor herself was front and centre. A white diving board was suspended over the pool, and Taylor was sitting cross-legged on its end with her cats in the hollow of her lap. Our pool didn't have a diving board, and Bruce and Benny regarded the water as the devil's territory, but Taylor had created a place where boundaries were transcended. Despite everything, I found myself experiencing the wonder and peace of that idyllic world. Then, as quickly as it came, the spirit that flowed when I gazed at Taylor's painting contracted into the cold focus of a vanishing point. Where was the girl who had painted this picture? Where was my daughter?

I closed the door to the studio, called Willie who had been racing in circles on the lawn, and walked back to the house. When I bent to take off my runners, it hit me. If Taylor had been in her studio that morning, her footprints would be visible in the frosty grass. I went back out to check the lawn, but I saw at once that it was too late. Willie and I had obliterated whatever tracks might have been there.

I was making mistakes that I couldn't afford to make. I needed to take a deep breath and use common sense. Attached to the refrigerator door by a starfish-shaped magnet was a list of the names and phone numbers of Taylor's friends. She had written it out at my request, and the sight of the familiar names in her small neat hand brought a pang. I picked up the phone and began. It was a holiday, and my call awakened more than a few parents.

Groggy but obliging, they woke up their children. No one knew where Taylor was. Everyone was reassuring. She was a good girl, responsible, not the kind to get in trouble. When at last I reached the end of the list, I was close to tears. There was only one more call to make.

For three years I had been involved with an inspector on the Regina Police Force, and I still remembered the number for headquarters. I dialed and waited. The officer who answered was gruff. When I gave her my name and address, told her Taylor's age, and revealed that she had only been missing for three hours, the officer could barely contain her impatience.

We lived in the south end of the city, an area of geographical privilege where children were shepherded from school to lessons to play-dates by attentive parents who were only a cellphone call away. Taylor was the only child in her circle who didn't own a cell. It had been a sore spot between us, but despite her imprecations, I hadn't caved. When she argued that if she had a cell, I would always know where she was, I countered with my trump. Cellphones worked both ways, and at eleven, she should be learning to make independent decisions. I told her I trusted her, and I didn't need to be checking on her every fifteen minutes. Reluctantly, Taylor had accepted my logic.

As I stared at the unopened presents heaped at her place at the table, I knew I would give anything if Taylor had pummelled me into submission, and there was a number I could dial to hear her voice.

When my husband died, I had collapsed. We had, in theory, been all in all to each other, and it had taken me years to become a woman who didn't need another person to help her face a crisis. But that morning I needed Zack. I tried his cell, and immediately got his voice mail. If his cell was off, the meeting with the man from Vancouver must have been important. I dialed Norine MacDonald's number.

Her voice was warm. "Zack told me to expect a call," she said. "How many new best friends have been added to Taylor's guest list?"

For a beat I couldn't take in her words. Norine was a citizen of the old world of safety and certainty, and I had moved on.

"Norine, it's not about the party. I . . . I can't find Taylor."

There was silence on the other end of the line. In my mind, I could see Norine's face, impassive, intelligent, assessing the information, and deciding what to do next. "Zack's meeting is at the Delta," she said finally. "They only had a couple of hours, so they've sealed themselves off, but I can get a message to him. He'll call you."

"Thanks."

"Joanne, if there's anything I can do . . ."

"I'll let you know," I said. When I hung up, my hands were shaking. Fear and low blood sugar. I knew I should eat a piece of fruit or pour myself a glass of juice. These were sensible actions, but I couldn't move. I was frozen. When the phone rang, I leapt.

"Zack, I'm sorry to drag you out of your meeting," I said.

The man on the other end of the line cut me off. "Is this Joanne Kilbourn?"

"Yes."

"My name is Douglas Thorpe. I'm calling about my son."

When I didn't respond immediately, Douglas Thorpe felt the need to explain. "My son is Ethan Thorpe. He's a friend of your daughter Taylor." He enunciated each syllable with exaggerated slowness and clarity. A phrase my grandmother used in her old age flashed through my mind. "He spoke to me as if he were attempting to teach a cow to talk."

"Ethan's at school in Winnipeg," I said.

"But he's not *at* school. That's why I'm calling." Frustrated, Douglas Thorpe's enunciation became even more precise. "Ms. Kilbourn, the headmaster of Ethan's school just phoned me. My son is missing. The headmaster talked to Ethan's roommate. The boy found your daughter's name and telephone number in Ethan's desk. That's how I was able to call you. The roommate says Ethan wanted to be with your daughter on her birthday. Today *is* Chloe's birthday, isn't it?"

"My daughter's name is Taylor," I said, but my knees had begun to tremble.

"Then the roommate must have been in error," Douglas Thorpe said. "I'm sorry to have disturbed you."

"Don't hang up," I said. "Mr. Thorpe, Ethan drew comics. There was a character named Chloe in them. She was modelled on Taylor. Today is Taylor's birthday. She's only eleven. She's too young for this."

"I agree," he said. "Nonetheless, the headmaster believes Ethan is on his way to Regina. There are buses he could have taken or he might have hitchhiked. But the headmaster is certain he was heading for your house."

The kaleidoscope had shifted. The new images were unsettling, but not terrifying. A boy, intoxicated by the heady cocktail of hormones and loneliness, had run away from his school to see a girl who had been kind to him. As a mother of four, I was only too familiar with the wild excesses of adolescent emotion and behaviour, and I cobbled together a sequence of events that seemed plausible.

Ethan had arrived when Willie and I were off on our run. He had rung the doorbell and Taylor, half awake, clutching the joy of a day when possibilities rose like pink balloons, ran downstairs expecting a surprise. When she opened the front door, Ethan was there. She would have been taken aback, but it was her birthday. Ethan, a romantic who had somehow navigated the 550 kilometres between Winnipeg and Regina, was standing there with a gift – probably a new comic featuring the adventures of Chloe. He had suggested a walk along the creek, and that's where they were – walking.

But the fabric of this bright scenario unravelled as quickly as I wove. Taylor was frightened of Ethan's intensity. She would never have gone off alone with him.

On the other end of the line, Douglas Thorpe had raised the volume. Apparently, he thought I'd stopped listening. "Ms. Kilbourn, I asked if I could speak to your daughter."

"She's not here," I said. "Mr. Thorpe, the truth is I don't know where she is. I took our dog for a walk, and when I came back, Taylor was gone."

"Ms. Kilbourn, you should make every effort to find your daughter."

His sense of urgency was contagious. "There's something you're not telling me," I said.

"If Ethan arrives there, call me immediately." Douglas Thorpe gave me his number, and I thought our business with each other was finished. I was wrong. "One other thing," he said. "Don't leave Ethan alone with your daughter."

My heart was pounding. "Mr. Thorpe, why did you and your new wife send Ethan out here to live with his mother?"

"My wife has other children," Douglas Thorpe said.

"And so you just shipped Ethan out here because he was in the way?"

"It's more complicated than that," he said, and his tone was grudging.

"Complicated how?"

"My wife didn't want Ethan around her children."

I didn't want to hear what came next, but Douglas Thorpe had decided to share. "Ethan has problems."

"Sexual problems?"

"No. Problems with his temper. He loses control."

"So you made sure your wife's children were safe and let Ethan roam around."

"Ethan's difficulties are a great concern for my wife and me," he said primly.

The call-waiting notification beeped on my telephone. I was certain it was Zack, but I had to press ahead with Douglas Thorpe. "Call the police," I said in a voice that shocked me by its chilly authority. "Tell them what you just told me. Tell them to find Taylor and your son."

"I don't believe there's any reason to involve the authorities at this point," he said. "Just find the children and call me."

"And exactly what will you do?"

"Make certain my son gets back to school. They'll be watching him closely now."

"Because he might harm somebody."

"I think we have to face that possibility. That's why I called. Whatever you may think, I'm a responsible parent."

"Mr. Thorpe, for the record, I don't consider you a rational parent. I think you're a scumbag, and I'm not going to waste any more time talking to you. I'm going to get help."

I hung up and tried Zack's cell. He picked up on the first ring.

After the windy self-justifications of Douglas Thorpe, Zack was a relief. He heard me out and moved into gear. "I'll call the police and give them Taylor's description. Do you have any idea what she was wearing?"

"No – her pyjamas, probably her ski-jacket. It's green."

"You said you saw her what – less than three hours ago? Ethan and Taylor are kids without a car. They can't have got too far."

"If anything's happened to her . . ."

"Taylor's fine," Zack said flatly. "And so are you. I'll be there in twenty minutes."

I went back to Taylor's room and began hunting for something – anything – that would tell me where my daughter was. I had never once searched my children's rooms. When other parents talked about rummaging through drawers, reading diaries, unearthing secrets, I was appalled, but that morning I was a madwoman. When I was through I was sick at heart. My daughter's secret life was touchingly innocent – a beginner's bra hidden in her sock drawer, a boy's name written many times in many colours on a page of her journal, a paperback copy of a steamy chick-lit novel with several pages dog-eared. Blameless.

There was one last place to check. The box that Ethan had delivered the morning he left was still on the top shelf in my bedroom closet. I returned to my room, took the box from my cupboard, picked up the scissors from my desk, and slit the mailing tape. A stench – sweet and animal – assailed me. Ethan's newest comic was wrapped in heavy clear plastic. I lifted it out of the box and then I began to retch. At the bottom of the box on a piece of velvet was the pentangle. It was covered with dried and clotted blood. I ran into my bathroom and vomited. Then I splashed my face with water and went back to the horror. I picked up the comic and unwrapped the plastic. There was a note inside. Five words: *I did it for you.*

Downstairs, Willie was barking. Reflexively, I went to my window to see what had got him going. When I looked down into our backyard, I saw my daughter. She was walking towards her studio, head bowed. As I had imagined, she had put her new green ski jacket over her pyjamas. She was wearing my favourite of her winter hats: a black angora toque with little cat ears on top. Ethan was behind her, very close, with one arm draped awkwardly around her shoulder. He was wearing a winter jacket too. His was black – as were his jeans and boots.

I raced down to open the kitchen door. Willie rocketed past me. I called out to Taylor. She turned, but there was something unusual about the way she moved. My daughter was a girl who bounced through life, but that morning she was like a sleepwalker. With the grace of a long-time dance partner, Ethan turned with her. That's when I saw the sun glint off the knife he was holding at her throat.

The moment Willie spotted Taylor, he had bounded towards her. Now, tail pounding the frozen earth, he sat in front of her and Ethan, waiting for someone to acknowledge his presence.

Ethan tensed. "Get the dog away," he said. He looked as if he was going to cry, but the hand holding the knife against my daughter's throat didn't move. "Get the dog away. If he jumps up on me now, my hand could slip."

"Willie, come," I said. He cocked his head as if he was attempting to remember a word from an ancient language.

"Come," I said again. Amazingly, he loped towards me. "Good dog," I said, then I grabbed his collar.

"Put him in the house," Ethan's voice cracked with emotion. He tightened his hold on Taylor and guided her towards the studio.

With my hand still looped through Willie's collar, I took him back to the house, pushed him into the kitchen, and closed the door. His howls of indignation followed me as I ran towards the studio; Ethan and Taylor were already inside. Surprisingly, Ethan made no move to stop me when I opened the door. He was still standing behind Taylor, but he had changed the position of the knife. Now the handle was clasped in his closed fist and the shaft was vertical with its point touching the tender flesh under my daughter's chin.

Taylor was dangerously pale. "Ethan, you have to stop this," I said. "Taylor's going into shock."

"Lean against me, Taylor," he said gently. "You know – the way Chloe leans against Soul-fire. It's all in the book I left for you." Taylor's eyes were half-closed, she swayed. "You did read it, didn't you?" Ethan asked. Taylor remained silent, and Ethan exploded. "You were supposed to read the book. It explains everything." He shook his head. "I can't believe you didn't read it. You're just like all the others." The tip of the knife pierced the skin on her throat, and a drop of blood appeared.

When I saw her blood, I reacted immediately. "I didn't give her the book," I said. "It's my fault."

Ethan eyes met mine. "So she doesn't know."

I shook my head. "No, Taylor doesn't know anything."

"I can tell her," Ethan said. His voice became very soft. "It's the end of Chloe and Soul-fire – their last adventure. They're attacked by this monster dragon. She's huge and she can't be killed. Soul-fire does his best. He takes his sword and plunges it into the dragon's neck again and again. There's blood . . . blood everywhere. Finally, the head is severed, but it grows back – not just one head but two. Every time, Soul-fire cuts off a head, two grow back in its place. He tries so hard, but he knows the dragon will always be there. Soul-fire knows that the one place the dragon won't follow him is through the Gates of Death. So he takes his golden knife and he holds it to Chloe's throat and . . ."

Taylor's eyes seemed to roll back in her head; her knees buckled and she crumpled to the floor. I knelt and took her in my arms. Ethan raised the hand that held the knife.

"Don't," I said, shielding my daughter's body with my own.

"No matter how much I try to kill her, she never goes away," Ethan said. "I smashed in her head and she grows another one. She comes to me in my dreams."

My face was pressed against my daughter's body. I turned my head so that I could see Ethan. "Who comes to you in your dreams?" I asked.

"My mother," he said.

That was when I screamed.

"Stop," Ethan said. "Please just stop." But I didn't. I screamed again and again and again.

"I don't want to kill anybody else," Ethan said. Beneath me, Taylor's body was so boneless that I could feel the beating of her heart. When the studio door opened, I felt cold air, then I heard Zack's voice. "Come over here to me, Ethan," he said.

Eyes closed, I waited, still shielding Taylor from what was to come. Ethan's footsteps moved towards the door, and I thought how vulnerable Zack was in his wheelchair. "Give me the knife," Zack said. The silence that followed was interminable. Then Zack said the words that finally allowed me to exhale. "Good move," he said. "Now we can figure out what to do next."

I helped Taylor to her feet. She was still pale, but her body was no longer limp. I took in the scene. Zack's chair blocked the doorway. Ethan was facing him, his back to us.

"What's going to happen to me?" he asked.

"The police are out front," Zack said. "We weren't sure what was going on, so they let me come ahead. What will happen next is up to you."

"I killed my mother," Ethan said. "She wasn't going to let me go trick-or-treating with Taylor."

Taylor gasped, but if he was shocked, Zack didn't reveal it. His tone was matter of fact. "Then you're going to need someone who's on your side."

Ethan hung his head. "No one's on my side."

Zack's eyes met mine. I nodded.

"I'm on your side," Zack said. "I won't lie to you. You're in a lot of trouble, but you're thirteen years old, and that means the law thinks you deserve another chance. Do you think you deserve another chance?"

"I don't know," Ethan said.

"Well, you're going to have some time to consider the question." Zack reached into his pocket, pulled out a package of Spearmint LifeSavers, and offered it to Ethan. "Want one?" he asked.

"I guess," Ethan said, and he popped a LifeSaver into his mouth.

Zack waited as Ethan crunched his candy, then he turned his chair to the door. "Time to face the music, kiddo. Are you ready?"

Ethan nodded. "Could I have another LifeSaver?"

Zack handed him the packet and looked over at me. "I'll be home in a couple of hours. Are you and Taylor going to be okay till then?"

"We're going to be fine," I said. After Zack and Ethan left, I put my arm around my daughter and led her to the house. "Taylor, I think we should see a doctor."

"No," she wailed. "No. I don't want to go out. Not now. Just let me stay here with you." Her eyes were huge and frightened.

"All right. We can stay here," I said. "Let's go up to the bathroom so I can put something on that nick under your chin."

I had to close my eyes as I dabbed hydrogen peroxide on the spot where the knife had broken my daughter's skin. If the blade had gone deeper, I could have lost her. "Ethan didn't hurt you in any other way, did he?" I asked.

Taylor shook her head, and I said a silent prayer of thanks. I ran a hot bath, poured in the lavender milk bath powder, and helped my daughter sink into the water. Then I brought her a mug of sweet, milky tea and set it on the edge of the bathtub.

"Want me to stay or leave?" I asked.

"Stay," she said. I flipped down the toilet lid, and then, for the first time since she'd moved into our house, Taylor and I spent a half-hour together in utter silence. After she'd towelled off, I helped her into her pyjamas, tucked her into bed with more tea and a plate of toast, and stayed with her until she fell asleep. Then I went into my bathroom and dialed Zack's number.

"I've been trying to get you," he said.

"I turned down the ringer on the phone so Taylor could get some rest."

"How's she doing?"

"It's hard to say. She's asleep now."

"How are you doing?"

"I wish you were here."

"I will be," he said. "A few more hoops to jump through on this end."

"So what's happening?"

"Ethan told me his story. I have to get in touch with his father. The YCJA – sorry, the Youth Criminal Justice Act – says parents have to be notified, involved, and in some cases ordered to attend youth court proceedings. But Ethan's mother is dead . . ."

"Because Ethan killed her," I said.

"Can't talk about that," Zack said, "but I do need to get in touch with Ethan's father and Ethan won't tell me his name or where he lives."

I gave Zack the number Douglas Thorpe had given me. "I should warn you," I said. "This man is a total prick."

"I've always wanted to meet a total prick," Zack said. "I guess today's my lucky day. So what do you think? Is Douglas Thorpe going to tell me to take a hike, so his trusted family lawyer who hasn't been in a criminal courtroom in thirty years can take over?"

"He won't be pleased that you're involved," I said. "You're high profile, and Mr. Thorpe wants this to go away."

"Even if his son gets buried in the system until all of us are but a memory?"

"I think that would be his preference."

"Hey, guess what?" Zack said. "Mr. Thorpe's preference doesn't count. According to the YCJA, if Ethan's father's choices aren't in Ethan's best interests, Ethan has the right to be represented by a counsel independent of dear old Dad."

"You sure you want to take this on?" I said.

"You bet," Zack said. "That kid has not had what I would call a lucky life. Right now, there's a psychologist testing him to see just how damaged he is."

"Anyone who talked to Ethan for five minutes would know he has serious problems."

"The system runs on experts, Jo. The opinion an expert forms now will help down the road when it comes to sentencing."

"What's going to happen to him?"

"The charge will be murder. Because of Ethan's age, if it's first degree, the maximum sentence is ten years; if it's second degree, seven years max."

"So Ethan could be back walking among us when he's twenty."

"Do I detect a hardening of your gentle heart?"

"I'll get over it," I said. "Whatever happened to easy answers?"

Zack laughed softly. "Welcome to my world."

CHAPTER

15

Taylor was still sleeping when I went back to her room. I pulled her desk chair close to the bed and drank her in. She was beginning to look like herself again. Her cheeks were rosy with sleep, and her breathing was deep. When she awoke, she cat-stretched and furrowed her forehead. "What time is it?"

"A little after noon. You slept through the cannons."

For a moment she seemed confused. "So it really is my birthday," she said.

"Yes."

"And all that stuff with Ethan really happened."

"Yes." I moved closer, "Taylor, I think it will help if you tell me about it."

Taylor's usual speaking voice was melodic, but that morning the music was gone. As she described the time she'd spent with Ethan, her tone was lifeless. "Somebody threw something – pebbles, I guess – against my window. I thought it was Gracie and Isobel coming to surprise me, so I ran downstairs. When I opened the kitchen door, Ethan was there. Everything happened so fast. Ethan pushed past me, slammed the door, and grabbed me. He had that knife. He said a bunch of stuff about Soul-fire and Chloe. I was really scared – not just because of the knife, but because of the way he looked. He told me to get my jacket because we were going away together. I said I didn't want to go. Then he pointed the knife at my heart." Taylor touched the left side of her chest. "This is where my heart is, isn't it?"

"Yes," I said. "That's where it is."

Taylor moved her hand reflexively over the vulnerable area. "He made me go to this place under the footbridge where he used to hang out after school." She raised her eyes to me. "He kept his knife pointed at me in case I yelled if anyone went by on the bike path. Sitting still like that I got really cold, and I said I wanted to go home. Ethan said we didn't have homes any more – we just had each other. I knew I had to get away, so I told him I'd made a painting of Soul-fire and it was in my studio."

"Was there really a painting?"

She nodded. "I was going to send it to him at his new school. I wanted him to know everybody didn't hate him. We were on our way to see the painting when . . . when you came." Taylor closed her eyes, moaned, and turned away from me. I sat on her bed and stroked her back.

"It's all right," I said. "Everything's all right."

"Where is he?" she asked.

"Zack took him to police headquarters."

"And he won't be able to get out."

"Not for a long time."

"Nothing will ever be the same," she said.

She was silent again, and I could feel her drifting from me. I had not given birth to Taylor, but from the day she came to me, the connection between us could not have been closer. She was a girl whose life was filled with passions: her family, her friends, her animals, making and experiencing art, chatting, eating with gusto everything from paella to licorice whips. No matter what her mood, I had always known how to reach her, but that day I was at a loss, and so I waited.

Finally, responding to one of those inexplicable internal shifts that push us back from the abyss and into life again, Taylor sat up. "Can we go down to the creek? There might be some birds."

"Good idea," I said. Her decision didn't surprise me. Taylor was four when she became part of our family, but she had already known a lifetime of tragedy. Within a period of six months, every adult in Taylor's life had died. I adopted her because she was the daughter of the woman who had been my closest childhood friend and because there was no one else to care for her. A frightened child, she was saved by three things: her art, our family, and the creek that flowed behind our house.

For a body of water in a residential area close to the heart of the city, it was large – twenty-five metres across. In spring, the creek was swollen and tumultuous with runoff from snowy fields on the outskirts of town; in summer and fall it was tranquil, a mirror reflecting the prairie's living skies; in winter it was ice, thick enough to support skaters and tobogganers. Always, it was a place of rustling indigenous grasses and intense bird and animal life.

The first spring Taylor was with us, I bought her a sketchbook and she and I had started a bird list. At the beginning, she had drawn pictures of the birds she spotted, and I had written their names. In later years, Taylor had recorded her finds herself, but she continued to draw detailed miniatures of the birds she identified: the rare ones that swooped down for a moment in the course of their great migration, and the usual suspects that were part of our everyday lives: western grebes, cormorants, mallards, mourning doves, thrashers, warblers, blackbirds, and the faithful and ubiquitous sparrows. She began her bird record anew every year – seven books so far. The eighth, pocket-sized and bright orange, was waiting on her plate with the rest of her forgotten birthday gifts.

Taylor pulled underwear, socks, blue jeans, and a shirt out of her dresser drawers and went into the bathroom. When she came back, she was dressed and she'd run a comb through her hair.

"Ready to go?" I said.

She hesitated. I could see the uncertainty in her eyes, but she knew she couldn't stay in bed forever.

The world we walked out into was the shade of half-mourning that grieving Victorians used to affect after the blackness of the first grief was fading. Earlier, the sun had sent out a few tentative beams, but they'd been extinguished by the weight of a November sky. Underfoot, the wintry earth was leached of colour. A skim of ice covered the silent creek.

With no particular plan, Taylor and I sat on the bench we favoured and looked around us. After a while, she pointed across the creek to a tree, leafless and gaunt against the scudding clouds. "I saw a Japanese etching like that at the Mackenzie Gallery," she said. "Just earth, tree, and sky. Ink and paper. The lines were so simple, but every stroke was right. I wanted to make art like that."

"You still can," I said. "Taylor, that tree is still there."

"And it's still beautiful," she said.

"Yes," I said. "It's still beautiful."

From the outset, Taylor was determined to go back to her old life, and all the external signs indicated that she had succeeded. The phone kept on ringing, the round of birthday parties and sleepovers continued, and as always, she was diligent about the schoolwork that she saw as a necessary evil to be dealt with before she could get back to her art. But she was edgy, easily startled, with a new and worrying habit of staring into space. For the first time ever, she asked me to sit with her in her studio while she worked. I brought in a folding chair and cleared a place for my laptop at the end of the table where she stored her paint tubes and brushes. Most of the time we worked in comfortable silence, but occasionally she asked about Ethan, and I passed along what I'd heard from Zack. The news was never good, and one afternoon I asked Taylor if she'd rather I didn't tell her what was happening.

"I need to know," she said. "It's worse just imagining."

Creating a mural for the walls that enclosed our new pool was therapeutic. Working at her sketches, Taylor seemed able to transcend the anxiety that had dogged her since the terrible morning of her birthday. When, finally, it was time to start painting in earnest, she was eager. The construction crew put up scaffolding so that Taylor could reach the tops of the walls and the ceiling, and as she climbed it, I could see her old confidence returning.

Taylor had made several small paintings of our old pool and I was curious about how the pool would figure in the new mural. As it turned out, it was the vibrant colour of the tiles that had attracted her. Before she began the mural Taylor covered the walls with a gem-bright paint that had the opalescent sheen of sun bouncing off turquoise. To stand in that room with the sunlight pouring through the windows of the room's west wall was to experience a joy that was uncomplicated and unquenchable. Then Taylor began to add shadows and half-tones, and the mood changed. Some of the areas she shaded were small. Like the missing tiles in our old pool, these splashes of black made the blue around them sparkle with greater intensity. But there were larger areas of shadow too; spaces that seemed to beckon and threaten like the mouths of underwater caves. The fish Taylor painted swimming in the sunlit water were jewel-bright and playful, but the mud-coloured fish that swam through the curling plumes of weeds in the shadows were menacing. More eloquently than words, Taylor's mural conveyed the truth that the sweetness of life can be taken away in an instant.

She waited almost two weeks before she painted the human swimmers on the mural, and the figures were unlike any she'd drawn before. Faceless, strong-bodied, wearing simply cut suits in bold primary colours, their powerful limbs propelled them effortlessly through sun and shadow alike. When I watched them come to life, the relief washed over me. My daughter was recovering.

Taylor had wanted to keep the mural a surprise for Zack until it was finished. When the big day came, she made him close his eyes as he wheeled himself in.

"This isn't a joke, is it?" he said. "I'm not headed for the edge of the pool."

"No joke!" Taylor said. "And you can open your eyes now."

It was the only time in our relationship that I ever saw Zack at a loss for words. He looked around, shook his head in disbelief, and turned his chair to face Taylor.

"This is brilliant, Taylor. You must know that." He held his hand out to her. "Could we look at it together?"

She shrugged, but I could tell she was pleased.

I watched as they moved around the mural. Occasionally, Taylor would point something out or Zack would ask a question, but mostly they simply examined her work with the care and the seriousness it demanded.

When they came back, Zack slid his arm around my waist. "How lucky can we get?" he said.

Taylor was standing on the other side of Zack's chair, and when I looked into their faces, the words formed themselves. "I was just asking myself that very thing," I said.

The weeks leading up to Christmas were full. My research on the values war was coming together, and Jill asked if I'd be interested in writing a documentary on the subject for NationTV. I'd sketched out a proposal, and it was a rush to sit at my laptop and lose track of time because I was having so much fun.

Zack was busy too, but his work wasn't fun. Ethan's case was viciously depressing – in large part because Ethan didn't care what happened to him. His despair was exacerbated by guilt. Given what we had come to know about Ethan, it wasn't a surprise when he confessed that, in an attempt to prove his worth to his mother, he had planted the bomb that blew up Zack's office. Kathryn died without knowing how desperate her son had been to gain her approval. Now her son's only lifeline was the man he tried to kill, and that painful truth was driving Ethan into a vortex of self-loathing and depression. Zack had managed to get Ethan committed to a mental health facility in North Battleford, but Ethan's prognosis was a constant source of worry. And, as always with Zack, there were new files: the juiciest involved a government minister who had allegedly harassed, stalked, and then attempted to poison a colleague.

I had my own distractions: writing a mid-sabbatical report on my work, Christmas shopping, sorting through the dozens of invitations to parties Zack and I were expected to attend, deciding if my good black dress could survive what was shaping up to be a punishing social schedule.

Then there was Howard. He had pled guilty to obstruction of justice and been sentenced to a month at the detox centre

and two hundred hours of community service. He was
working off his sentence at the food bank, and I joined him
in the warehouse two afternoons a week to pack Christmas
hampers. It was a chilly job, and Howard was never without
his scarlet, merry elves toque. When the other workers
called him Old Saint Nick, he didn't seem to mind.

Every night at six o'clock, Zack came home to have
dinner with Taylor and me, and afterwards the three of us
went over to check out developments at the new house. The
renovations were proceeding at a pace that made me wonder
if our new home would always be a work-in-progress, but
McCudden was unflappable. He assured us that, contrary to
appearances, we would be able to move in on January 1, and
he spoke with such conviction that we continued to plan as
if we would.

Every Sunday, without fail, Zack came to church with
Taylor and me. When we had formally asked the dean of our
cathedral to marry us, he hadn't been quick to agree. He suggested that before we discussed the matter further, he and
Zack have a talk alone. I didn't question James's judgment. I
was a known quantity, and Zack was a very large question
mark. The two men met several times. When I asked Zack
what they'd discussed, he was circumspect. "Mostly, we
talked about the kind of person you are and the kind of
person I am. Then James asked me if I knew the difference
between a contract and a covenant."

"Did you?"

"Sure. A covenant is a contract made with the heart."

A week before Christmas, Taylor came back from a shopping expedition with Gracie and Isobel, went to her room,
and returned with a package in a gift bag. "Do you think
Zack could get this to Ethan?" she asked.

"Zack always seems to find a way," I said. "Could you tell me what's in there?"

Taylor looked away. "Drawing pens and a sketchbook."

When I gave Zack the package, he nodded approvingly. "I'm grateful to Taylor," he said. "This present takes one name off my Christmas list. And I wasn't looking forward to trying to find a gift for the kid who has nothing."

"Is Ethan making any headway?"

"Without revealing too much, my client thinks his life is over. He may be right, but he still has another sixty years to put in on this planet, so he's going to have to figure something out. Taylor's present was inspired. I'll see what else I can find to give him a reason to wake up in the morning."

My family had always been hidebound traditionalists when it came to Christmas. We always bought the same kind of tree, put it up on the same day, and decorated it with the ornaments we'd used since the kids were little. We always unwrapped one present Christmas Eve and saved stockings and the rest of the gifts until morning. Even the suggestion that we might experiment with the recipe for the Yorkshire pudding we served with the Christmas rolled prime rib was rejected out of hand.

We were a family who found comfort in settling into the old grooves, but that year, for many reasons, the old grooves were no longer a comfortable fit. Mieka and Greg were still together, but they'd come to Regina at the end of November to tell us they were going to give their girls the best Christmas possible, then separate in the New Year. I was heartsick, but I was powerless to change the situation and so I focused on getting us through holidays.

It wasn't easy. Greg had been at the centre of our festivities for thirteen years. He was the one who made the eggnog, led the carol singing, and shook the sleigh bells outside the window to tell us all that Santa was on his way. Knowing that this would be the last time he would be a part of our traditions would be painful for us all.

Taylor, too, was a concern. When I first broached the subject of moving, she was reluctant. The Regina Avenue house was the only home she could remember, but since the morning of her birthday the bad memories had crowded out the good. When she told me she no longer felt safe at the old house, I realized that Christmas there would be, at best, a mixed experience for her. Finally, there was Zack. He was, as Taylor memorably put it, my big sparkly top banana, but he had played no role in the years of Christmases we had celebrated on Regina Avenue.

It was time to start over, and so we went to the lake. Our decision was a good one. Zack's partners and their families came out for the holidays too. The weather was cold and bright, and the snow was carol-perfect: deep and crisp and even. We skied, skated, tobogganed, ate too much, and went to bed early. We bought the last tree from a lot in Fort Qu'Appelle. The tree, of uncertain parentage, was frozen solid, and when it thawed, we discovered serious flaws. We strung it with lights that we paid far too much for, turned its bad side to the wall, and decorated it with paper snowflakes and marshmallows. We all agreed it was the most beautiful tree ever.

Given the circumstances, it was a good Christmas, and there was an unexpected gift. Over the holidays, Pantera found the owner with whom he wanted to spend the rest of his life. Pete and he had tried to make a go of it, but Pantera was too gregarious to spend days cheering up ailing animals at the clinic and too rambunctious to be left alone. Pantera did, however, love Zack, tolerate Taylor and me, and get along surprisingly well with Willie. And so, Zack and I left the lake to begin our life as a family with our daughter, her two cats, and our two dogs.

After Zack and I had announced our engagement, there had been no shortage of suggestions about the kind of wedding Zack and I should have. Angus was persuasive about the delights of a destination wedding – preferably somewhere he and Leah could surf and toss around a Frisbee. The idea of getting married on a beach with the waves splashing against the shore was appealing, but travel was difficult for Zack, so Bali was out. Taylor loved the idea of a formal wedding. When we cleaned out the basement, she unearthed the picture of the wedding gown I'd drawn for *Katy Keene* comics and showed it to Zack. He was fulsome in his praise. He was particularly fond of the way the doves nestling on Katy's breasts reached towards one another to exchange a beaky kiss over her cleavage. But in the end we decided on something less elaborate.

When we told James that we wanted the quietest of weddings, he pointed out that in the Anglican Church, couples can marry during the ordinary morning service. The provision is an old one, a leftover from the days when flushed, apple-cheeked lads and lasses donned their Sunday best, stepped forth during the service to be married, and went back to picking hops or hoeing turnips the next day. The simplicity of the service appealed to us both, and so Zack and I were married during the Cathedral's 10:30 Eucharist.

Not many people attend church on New Year's Day. In addition to our family and Zack's partners and their families, there were fewer than thirty congregants. The worshippers were evenly split between smartly dressed ladies from the seniors' home next door and street people who wanted a place of warmth on a cold day. Mieka and Zack's partner, Blake Falconer, were our witnesses. I carried a spray of white orchids and Zack had a boutonniere of marigolds.

Not surprisingly, the sermon was about beginnings, and James was pensive as he discussed the fact that Zack and I had chosen this first day of the New Year to begin our marriage. He quoted a Kierkegaard scholar who wrote that human existence requires real passion as well as thought, and James said that he was certain two people as passionate and thoughtful as we were could make a fine life together. He ended his sermon by saying that in a world in which the one certain thing is that we live in absolute uncertainty, celebrating the beginning of a new marriage on the first day of a new year demanded a leap of faith. Then he looked directly at Zack and me. "Leaping into uncertainty is terrifying," he said, "but I saw your faces when you joined hands to take your vows. You two will land on solid ground. Just remember not to let go of each other."

If you enjoyed

THE ENDLESS KNOT

treat yourself to all of the
Joanne Kilbourn mysteries,
now available in stunning new
trade paperback editions
and as eBooks

McCLELLAND & STEWART

www.mcclelland.com
www.mysterybooks.ca

DEADLY APPEARANCES

When Andy Boychuk drops dead at a political picnic, the evidence points to his wife. Joanne takes her first "case" as Canada's favourite amateur sleuth as she seeks to clear Eve Boychuk, discovering along the way a Bible college that isn't all it seems . . .

"A compelling novel infused with a subtext that's both inventive and diabolical." – Montreal *Gazette*

Trade Paperback 978-0-7710-1324-9   Ebook 978-0-7710-1322-5

MURDER AT THE MENDEL

Joanne's childhood friend, Sally Love, is an artist who courts controversy. When Sally's former partner turns up dead, Joanne discovers the past they shared was much more complicated, sordid, and deadly than she ever guessed.

"Classic. . . . Enough twists to qualify as a page turner. . . . Bowen and her genteel sleuth are here to stay." – Saskatoon *StarPhoenix*

Trade Paperback 978-0-7710-1321-8   Ebook 978-0-7710-1320-1

THE WANDERING SOUL MURDERS

Joanne's peace is destroyed when her daughter finds a young woman's body near her shop. The next day, her son's girlfriend drowns, an apparent suicide. When it is discovered that the two young women had at least one thing in common, Joanne is drawn into a twilight world where money can buy anything.

"With her rare talent for plumbing emotional pain, Bowen makes you feel the shock of murder." – *Kirkus Reviews*

Trade Paperback 978-0-7710-1319-5   Ebook 978-0-7710-1318-8

A COLDER KIND OF DEATH

When the man convicted of murdering her husband six years earlier is himself shot, Joanne is forced to relive the most horrible time of her life. But it soon gets much worse: the prisoner's menacing wife, is found dead a few nights later, strangled with Joanne's own silk scarf . . .

"A terrific story with a slick twist at the end."
– *Globe and Mail*

Trade Paperback 978-0-7710-1317-1   Ebook 978-0-7710-1316-4

A KILLING SPRING

The head of the School of Journalism at Joanne's university is found in a seedy rooming house wearing only women's lingerie and an electrical cord around his neck. When other events indicate that it was not a case of accidental suicide, Joanne finds herself deep in a world of fear, deceit, and danger.

"A compelling novel as well as a gripping mystery."
– *Publishers Weekly*

Trade Paperback 978-0-7710-1315-7   Ebook 978-1-5519-9613-4

VERDICT IN BLOOD

The corpse of the respected — and feared — Judge Justine Blackwell is found in a Regina park. Joanne tries to help a good friend involved in a struggle over which of Blackwell's wills is valid, and those who stand to lose the inheritance may well be murderers willing to strike again.

"An entirely satisfying example of why Gail Bowen has become one of the best mystery writers in the country."
– *London Free Press*

Trade Paperback 978-0-7710-1311-9   Ebook 978-1-5519-9614-1

BURYING ARIEL

Ariel Warren, a young colleague at Joanne's university, is stabbed to death in the library, and two men are under suspicion. The apparently tight-knit academic community is bitterly divided, vengeance is in the air, and Joanne is desperate to keep the wrong person from being punished for Ariel's death.

"Nearly flawless plotting, characterization, and writing." – *London Free Press*

Trade Paperback 978-0-7710-1309-6   Ebook 978-1-5519-9615-8

THE GLASS COFFIN

Joanne's friend Jill is about to marry a celebrated documentary filmmaker, both of whose previous wives committed suicide – after he had made films about them. When the best man's dead body is found just hours before the ceremony, Joanne begins to truly fear for her friend's safety.

"Chilling and unexpected." – *Globe and Mail*

Trade Paperback 978-0-7710-1305-8   Ebook 978-1-5519-9616-5

THE LAST GOOD DAY

Joanne is on holiday at a cottage in an exclusive enclave owned by lawyers from the same prestigious firm. When one of them kills himself the night after a long talk with Joanne, she is pushed into an investigation that has startling – and possibly fatal – consequences.

"A classic whodunit in which everything from setting to plot to character works beautifully. . . . A treat from first page to final paragraph." – *Globe and Mail*

Trade Paperback 978-0-7710-1349-2   Ebook 978-1-5519-9617-2

THE ENDLESS KNOT

After journalist Kathryn Morrissey publishes a tell-all book on the adult children of Canadian celebrities, one of the parents angrily confronts her and as a result is charged with attempted murder. When the parent hires Zack Shreve, the new love in Joanne's life, to defend him, her own understanding the knot that binds parent and child becomes both personal and very urgent.

"A late-night page turner. . . . A rich and satisfying read." – *Edmonton Journal*

Trade Paperback 978-0-7710-1347-8   Ebook 978-1-5519-9246-4

THE BRUTAL HEART

A local call girl is dead, and her impressive client list includes the name of Joanne's new husband. Shaken that Zack saw the woman regularly before they met, Joanne throws herself into her work and is soon embroiled in a bitter and increasingly strange custody battle of a local MP, who is simultaneously trying to win an election.

"Elegant. . . . Joanne rules the narrative. [*The Brutal Heart*] slips along with grace and style."– *Toronto Star*

Trade Paperback 978-0-7710-0994-5   Ebook 978-1-5519-9233-4

THE NESTING DOLLS

Just before she is murdered, a young woman hands her baby to a perfect stranger and disappears. The stranger is the daughter of lawyer Delia Wainberg, and soon a secret from Delia's youth comes out. Not only is a killer on the loose, but the dead woman's partner is demanding custody of the child, and the battle threatens to tear apart Joanne's own family.

"The underlying human drama of love and good intentions gone very, very bad make the novel a compelling read." – *Vancouver Sun*

Trade Paperback 978-0-7710-1276-1   Ebook 978-0-7710-1277-8

Edward Willet

GAIL BOWEN's first Joanne Kilbourn mystery, *Deadly Appearances* (1990), was nominated for the W.H. Smith/ Books in Canada Best First Novel Award. It was followed by *Murder at the Mendel* (1991), *The Wandering Soul Murders* (1992), *A Colder Kind of Death* (1994) (which won an Arthur Ellis Award for best crime novel), *A Killing Spring* (1996), *Verdict in Blood* (1998), *Burying Ariel* (2000), *The Glass Coffin* (2002), *The Last Good Day* (2004), *The Endless Knot* (2006), *The Brutal Heart* (2008), and *The Nesting Dolls* (2010). In 2008 *Reader's Digest* named Bowen Canada's Best Mystery Novelist; in 2009 she received the Derrick Murdoch Award from the Crime Writers of Canada. Bowen has also written plays that have been produced across Canada and on CBC Radio. Now retired from teaching at First Nations University of Canada, Gail Bowen lives in Regina. Please visit the author at www.gailbowen.com.